PRAISE FOR THE
NOVELS OF THE HALF-LIGHT CITY

Fire Kin

"Entertaining ... Scott's dramatic story will satisfy both fans and new readers." —*Publishers Weekly*

"This is one urban fantasy series that I will continue to come back to.... Fans of authors Christina Henry of the Madeline Black series and Keri Arthur of the Dark Angels series will love the Half-Light City series."
—Seeing Night Book Reviews

Iron Kin

"The world building in this series is one of its strengths, and delving deeper into the politics of this world made it even richer.... *Iron Kin* was jam-packed with action [and] juicy politics." —All Things Urban Fantasy

"A fantastical mix of paranormal and steampunk ... the novels of the Half-Light City fall into the category of 'buy and devour immediately' for me. Strong and complex world building, emotionally layered relationships, and enough action to keep me up long past my bedtime."
—Vampire Book Club

continued ...

Blood Kin

"Not only was this book just as entertaining and immensely readable as *Shadow Kin*—it sang in harmony with it and spun its own story, all the while continuing the grander symphony that is slowly becoming the Half-Light City story.... Smart, funny, dangerous, addictive, and seductive in its languorous sexuality. I can think of no better book to recommend to anyone to read this summer. I loved every single page except the last one, and that's only because it meant the story was done. For now, at least."
—seattlepi.com

"*Blood Kin* was one of those books that I really didn't want to put down, as it hit all of my buttons for an entertaining story. It had the intrigue and danger of a spy novel, intense action scenes, and a romance that evolved organically over the course of the story.... Whether this is your first visit to Half-Light City or you're already a fan, *Blood Kin* expertly weaves the events from *Shadow Kin* throughout this sequel in a way that entices new readers without boring old ones. I am really looking forward to continuing this enthralling ride."
—All Things Urban Fantasy

"*Blood Kin* had everything I love about urban fantasies: kick-butt action, fantastic characters, romance that makes the heart beat fast, and a plot that was fast-paced all the way through. Even more so, the villains are meaner, stronger, and downright fantastic—I never knew what they were going to do next. You don't want to miss out on this series."
—Seeing Night Book Reviews

"An exciting thriller ... fast-paced and well written."
—Genre Go Round Reviews

Shadow Kin

"M. J. Scott's *Shadow Kin* is a steampunky romantic fantasy with vampires that doesn't miss its mark."
—#1 *New York Times* bestselling author Patricia Briggs

"*Shadow Kin* is an entertaining novel. Lily and Simon are sympathetic characters who feel the weight of past actions and secrets as they respond to their attraction for each other."
— *New York Times* bestselling author Anne Bishop

"M. J. Scott weaves a fantastic tale of love, betrayal, hope, and sacrifice against a world broken by darkness and light, where the only chance for survival rests within the strength of a woman made of shadow and the faith of a man made of light."
—national bestselling author Devon Monk

"Exciting and rife with political intrigue and magic, *Shadow Kin* is hard to put down right from the start. Magic, faeries, vampires, werewolves, and Templar knights all come together to create an intriguing story with a unique take on all these fantasy tropes. . . . The lore and history of Scott's world is well fleshed out, and the action scenes are exhilarating and fast."
— *RT Book Reviews*

"A fabulous tale."
—Genre Go Round Reviews

THE
SHATTERED
COURT

A NOVEL OF THE FOUR ARTS

M. J. SCOTT

A ROC BOOK

ROC
Published by the Penguin Group
Penguin Group (USA) LLC, 375 Hudson Street,
New York, New York 10014

USA | Canada | UK | Ireland | Australia | New Zealand | India | South Africa | China
penguin.com
A Penguin Random House Company

First published by Roc, an imprint of New American Library,
a division of Penguin Group (USA) LLC

First Printing, May 2015

ROC REGISTERED TRADEMARK—MARCA REGISTRADA

ISBN 978-0-451-46539-9

Printed in the United States of America
10 9 8 7 6 5 4 3 2

For the other Sophie (who is small and fluffy)
and her mad pal, Callie.

Excellent writer cats.

ACKNOWLEDGMENTS

As always, I have to thank Jessica Wade for helping me see my story better, Miriam Kriss for providing excellent advice and excellent margaritas, and the Roc art department, who truly put the *art* in cover art. Big thanks and hugs also to all my writer pals who get me through the hard bits and celebrate the good bits and the rest of my family and friends, who do likewise. And to all the lovely readers who keep reading my stories, thank you. You're all awesome!

Deep the earth
Its harvest life
Bright the blood
Sharpest in strife
Swift the air
To hide and fool
False the water
The deadly pool

CHAPTER ONE

"Milady, please pay attention."

It was precisely the last thing she wanted to do. For a second, Sophie Kendall rebelled, lingering where she was, hands pressed into the pale gray skirts of her dress, no doubt wrinkling the silk. She had a sudden wild urge to bolt through the half-open glass doors and flee. But then her good sense, or at least her sense of resignation, returned, and she forced herself to turn away and smile apologetically at her tutor.

"But they're playing so well." She looked back over her shoulder at the two teams of young men playing roundball on the Indigo Lawn outside the doors, envy biting. Oh, to be so free. Here in the palace she wouldn't be able to join in the game. Proper young ladies, let alone ladies-in-waiting, didn't play roundball at court. But she could, at least, sit and watch. Or she could if she ever had the luxury of nothing to do.

Just an hour or two to herself in the sunshine. Was that too much to ask for?

She couldn't remember the last time she'd had a spare hour or two alone. And right now she couldn't imagine when she might next do so.

Captain Turner's bushy white eyebrows drew together, but his expression was kind. "Milady, your twenty-first birthday is in two days. There will be plenty of time for frivolity then. But now you need to learn this." He gestured to the large leather book on the table in front of him. "Your Ais-Seann is not a trivial matter. Do I need to remind you that you're—"

"Thirty-second in line to the throne, about to come into my birthright if I have one," Sophie said. "I know the speech, Captain. It's just . . ." *I want to be more than Lady Sophia Kendall, valuable broodmare.* But proper young ladies didn't say such things out loud. At times, being a proper young lady was enough to make her want to scream.

"It's such a nice day," she continued, trying not to sound too impatient. Sunlight streamed through the windows, making the lesson room seem dull in comparison. The breeze coming through the outer doors was just strong enough to carry the scent of grass and the early-blooming blossoms and possibility into the room. It made her skin itch. It made her want to tell the royal family and the court and everyone else weighing her down with expectation to go to hell. Made her want to run far, far away.

But the captain's face showed no sympathy for the restlessness she'd been feeling all day, and she doubted he'd show any actual sympathy if she tried a grander rebellion like leaving the room. Most likely he'd just send a squad of the guard after her to carry her back.

The king, the crown princess, and several hundred years of Anglese tradition wanted her prepared for her Ais-Seann, so she would be prepared for her Ais-Seann. Her Age of Beginning. Beginning of adulthood. Beginning, possibly, of magic. Beginning of many things she wasn't entirely sure she wanted to begin.

If indeed she proved to have any magic, her power would be dedicated to the goddess with all the proper rites and her person married off promptly to whichever nobleman the king thought best. A royal witch was a prize for the men of the court, and the stronger she was, the higher ranked and more influential the noble to whom she would be wed would be. Not that any of the available high lords of the court struck her as men she was longing to spend her life with. Most of them were fifteen or twenty years older than her, for a start.

If she turned out *not* to have any power, she'd be married off less promptly to some more obscure lordling and might at least get to leave Kingswell and the relentless mores and rules of the court.

The lesser of two evils, just. Maybe. She wasn't entirely sure. Her hands began twining in her skirts again, and she forced them to relax.

There was nothing to be done to protest her fate or escape from it. She didn't have any control over whether she was going to manifest magic, and she'd been schooled from birth to take her place in the court and the society of Anglion. She just wasn't entirely sure why, when she'd known since she was old enough to understand what would happen when she turned twenty-one, it was becoming harder and harder to meekly accept with each passing hour. Perhaps it was just nerves.

Perhaps everything would be perfectly fine if she just kept putting one foot in front of the other and did as she was asked to do. So, like a proper young lady, she smoothed her skirts where her hands had gripped them and sat back down next to the captain.

"I know this seems tedious, child," he said. "But you need to know how to control your magic if it comes in. Royal witches are strong, and we can't predict how your gift will behave when it manifests."

"You can't predict that it will manifest at all," Sophie said, trying not to let irritation shade her words.

"Given your bloodlines, there is a high probability that you will have power, Lady Sophia."

"Much good that will do me," Sophie muttered. One

hand strayed to the silver-gray pearl hanging from the slender chain at her throat. *Salt protect me. Lady give me light.*

Her thumb rubbed the surface of the pearl again, the smoothness a comfort, though she still missed the uneven texture of the strand of five natural pearls she'd worn for as long as she could remember. But they were a creamy white, and as long as the princess was in half mourning, her ladies couldn't wear white.

The gray had been a gift from the princess herself. Its color alone made it expensive, more than Sophie's family could afford. It was not as darkly beautiful as the rope of black pearls Princess Eloisa herself wore. But then again, Eloisa's pearls could have bought Sophie's family estates many times over.

A true symbol of her family's wealth. And Eloisa's power. Both mundane and magical.

The princess was the strongest royal witch yet living. Magic hadn't ruined her life.

But Sophie was not the crown princess. Magic would bring a woman of her rank only unwelcome attention and an even more narrowly prescribed life: Performing the seasonal rituals. Keeping the water sources blessed. Tending to her husband's lands or the court's as demanded. Earth witchery was hardly exciting. Useful, in a prosaic sort of way, being able to coax crops and animals into fruitfulness and supposedly anchor the prosperity of the court and the country. But hardly exciting.

Once, royal witches had been able to do more, to call the weather and do other things only hinted at in the history books. But it had been long years since any royal witch of Anglion had been able to do such things. Eloisa was the strongest living royal witch, and she was gifted with wards and healing and, so it was said, foretelling, but she couldn't, as far as Sophie knew, move so much as a puff of air.

She'd asked her mother once, long ago, why royal witches no longer did such things. Her mother, possessed of only a little power herself, had said that no one knew. Her father, overhearing, had muttered something about inbreeding but then laughed when her mother had told him not to be an idiot.

Privately, since coming to court, Sophie had decided that maybe they just never got the chance to try to do anything exciting. Royal witches were carefully hemmed in with rules and protocol so that their powers served the Crown as the Crown wished to be served. And after that, they served the goddess and her church. It didn't leave much time for trying to tame lightning. And with the pampered court life, there was really no need to try for more.

She tried to imagine the look on Captain Turner's face if she asked him what she would need to do to call lightning. He would probably have apoplexy. And then possibly march her straight to the temple for a lecture on the proper uses of earth magic. She sighed, finger and thumb rubbing the pearl again. It was disappointing to think that actually doing earth magic, or the variety she would be allowed—if she was even able—would be even less exciting than learning the theory.

The captain cleared his throat, drawing her attention back to him. "Maybe magic will be of more use to you than you realize."

"It's not as though I'll be allowed to do anything useful with it. Witches don't fight battles or anything."

He lifted the book they had been studying. "You've been talking to the crown princess again. Earth magic keeps Anglion prosperous. Feeds our people. Fighting battles isn't everything, milady."

"I believe your fellow soldiers in the Red Guard would disagree with you, Captain. And it's difficult to avoid talking to Princess Eloisa when I'm one of her ladies." The princess, widowed just over a year, had certain views about marriage and the role that women should play in the court. Views that were not exactly conven-

tional. She had, so far, avoided being wed again. Sophie
wondered just how long past her mourning time Eloisa
would continue to get away with that. Her father doted
on her, but he also wasn't a man to waste a prize in his
possession. Not one that could be traded for strength
and loyalty. Or he hadn't been before his recent illness.
He was recovering from the sickness that had gripped him
most of the winter and spring, but there were whispers in
the court that he was weakened for life.

Captain Turner laughed beside her, a friendly deep,
rumbly laugh, at odds with his stern weather-carved face.
"Maybe so. Still, you won't need to fight battles, milady. No
one crosses a royal witch. No one sensible, at least."

That made her smile, unwilling as she was. She picked
up her notebook and tried to remember the last thing the
captain had said about grounding to a ley line. She knew
the theory off by heart. After all, she had been schooled
in the history and tenets of earth magic and the lore of
the goddess since she was fifteen. Captain Turner was
charged with ensuring that those lessons were retained.
She thought it strange that a Red Guard battle mage was
the chosen instructor for potential royal witches, but that
was what the temple had decreed. She also had regular
sessions with temple priors, but they always stuck to the
lore of the goddess and wouldn't discuss earth magic.
She'd even had one nerve-racking session with the icily
formidable Domina Skey, who was in charge of the Kingswell temple and therefore also in charge of all of Anglion when it came to matters of the goddess. But Sophie
hadn't learned anything new from her. Anything she
hadn't learned by now, well, it seemed that it was just
about too late.

Of course, amongst that learning was a large hole
about the actual rites undertaken by a royal witch—that
information being deemed unsuitable for those without
power to know of—which seemed entirely unfair. But

that was another improper thought for young ladies. Until her power manifested, all she was allowed to know was the foundational theories of magic developed by the temple. The ones that underpinned all three branches of power. And there was nothing she could do about that, either. "All right, Captain. We have another hour. The princess asked me to attend her at midday."

Just after eleven in the morning, Lieutenant Cameron Mackenzie reported for duty.

"You're late, Lieutenant," the duty captain grumbled. "The princess rang for you five minutes ago."

Cameron shrugged. "Sorry," he said, not meaning it. Wallace—the captain—was an officious toady. One who'd avoided any sort of real danger in his time in the guard. A silk soldier. Cameron might be guilty of many things, but not that. "Business with my father."

"Your father should not keep you from the Princess Royal," Wallace said with a flick of his hand toward the roster on the desk before him. But he sounded slightly mollified. Or, rather, reluctant to anger the Erl of Inglewood. Cameron wondered what the captain would think if he knew the duke had been, as usual, berating his son about why he hadn't managed to make the princess fall in love with him.

"I'm sure he didn't mean to inconvenience Her Highness," Cameron said, knowing full well that was exactly what His Grace had wanted.

In his father's convoluted mind, Eloisa would pine for Cameron if deprived of his company. Cameron himself was clear on the fact that Eloisa didn't pine for anyone— except poor dead Iain, perhaps. But the erl was convinced he could become father-in-law to the first in line to the throne if only Cameron would properly apply himself.

It didn't matter how many times Cameron pointed out that Eloisa was still in half mourning, and at any rate, was exceedingly unlikely to be given permission to marry someone as lowly as a third son who held only a minor courtesy title and a few acres of northern Scarp land buried far in the high reaches of Carnarvan. Let alone bring up that it was more than improper for a bodyguard to be involved with his charge. His father was ambitious. In fact, Lord Inglewood practically defined the word.

"Just be punctual next time," Wallace said. "Now, you should go." He made a note—probably recording Cameron's lateness—in the ledger, the black letters curving with perfect precision, and waved Cameron away.

Cameron saluted and headed down the corridor. The door guards let him into the suite, and he found Eloisa in her morning room. Alone. He stopped short at that. She was usually surrounded by a gaggle of ladies-in-waiting. He hadn't been alone with her for close to three weeks.

He bowed, the obeisance instinctive despite their solitude. "Good morning, Your Highness." He straightened and scanned the room quickly.

Definitely alone.

The room seemed larger without the usual crowd. Eloisa wore a deep green dress—not strictly a half-mourning color, but who would quibble with the Princess Royal? With her witch-red hair caught casually behind her head rather than piled up in the elaborate curls currently favored at court, she dominated the room like a flame against the pale yellow of the walls and furnishings. Cameron told himself not to jump to conclusions about what the absence of her ladies might mean and stayed where he was.

Eloisa tapped her fingernails against the arm of her daintily curved chair and arched an eyebrow at him. "Good morning? It's practically midday," she said in a mock-annoyed voice.

Cameron hid a smile. So she was in a mood, was she? Obviously his duties today would include charming a royal witch into a better temper. He pulled his watch from its pocket on the inside of his uniform jacket. "Merely a little after eleven, Highness. Midday is still a ways off. Where are your attendants? You shouldn't be left alone."

"Why not?" she asked, with another tap of one long nail against the light-colored wood. "I have such a big, strong bodyguard to protect me."

"I only just arrived," he pointed out. He crossed his arms, mock stern as he looked at her. So close, the scent of her, smoke and spice and night-heavy roses, bloomed around him like an invitation. A dangerous invitation. He'd never quite worked out if Eloisa's scent was perfume or magic or one of the incenses earth witches used, but regardless of its source, it was delicious. Designed to make men fall at her feet or howl at the moon.

"There are guards outside," she countered in a bored tone.

"There should've been your night man," Cameron said, suddenly truly serious. "Why isn't he here?"

"I let him go early," she said, flicking at the black lace edging the neckline of her dress. The movement drew attention to her cleavage, which he was sure was intentional. The witch was toying with him.

"It was that Smythe-Stuart idiot," she said with another flick. It was clear that Smythe-Stuart had been lucky to escape being hexed.

"Lieutenant Smythe-Stuart is very capable," Cameron felt compelled to say. It was the truth. No man made it into the ranks of the Red Guard, let alone the royal bodyguards, without being an elite soldier. Pity they didn't also test for personality.

"He's a bore," Eloisa retorted. "And I don't want to talk about him." She curled a lock of her hair around her finger. The deep red of it against her pale skin was a pointed reminder he was dealing with a royal witch. One who was, perhaps, feeling a little fey today. He could feel his own magic—minor as it was—curling within him. Eloisa always could rouse him.

"Where, might I inquire, are your ladies?" Cameron asked, hoping to steer the conversation back to safer waters.

"Off planning the celebrations," Eloisa said with a smile.

"Ah, Lady Sophia. The one you all have such high hopes for." Sophia Kendall was the last royal female—though in her case the royal claim was quite removed—of her birth year to turn twenty-one. And after her, there was a five-year gap until the next oldest girl with royal blood. Her upcoming Ais-Seann was the subject of much court speculation and anticipation.

Neither of the two other girls who had come into their majority this year had manifested the gift, and both of them had been unceremoniously married off to minor lordlings and had yet to reappear at court. Cameron wouldn't like to be in Lady Sophia's shoes at all. Her fate was to be a pawn either way. All that was to be determined was just how big a prize she would gain for her family. Or the king, really. Cameron had met Lady Kendall's father, Barron Leeheld, and he had struck Cam as a decent man who had little interest in court intrigues. He had spoken somewhat wistfully of his estate and the upcoming grape harvest, not of whom best to marry his only daughter to.

"Yes," Eloisa said. "I think she at least deserves some fun before you men usurp her life."

"If she manifests, she'll have some more training before she's handed over to whoever the lucky man is, won't she?"

"And if she doesn't, she'll be married before the turn of the year," Eloisa snapped. "And I'll get some new country bumpkin who doesn't know a hairpin from a hatpin to attend me."

Ah, so that was what was bothering her witchness. She didn't want to lose a friend. "You think she won't?"

Eloisa shrugged. "I don't know."

"You're sure about that?" Eloisa's gift ran strongly to psychic abilities, but she tended to keep her premonitions close to her chest when she thought it best to do so. It drove her father, the king, wild.

"Yes. I haven't seen anything about Sophie."

Well, that was good. Then he replayed the sentence in his head. Perhaps not. "Does that mean you've seen something else?"

She shook her head but didn't look at him, instead toying with the midnight-colored pearls circling her wrist. "Nothing important."

"Highness . . ?"

Silk rustled as she came out of her chair and crossed to him. The wild smoky rose scent filled his nose, making his pulse speed a little.

"All I see," she said with a wicked smile, "is a man who is wasting a perfectly good opportunity." She tilted her head back and looked up at him. "What's the matter, Cameron? Out whoring last night, were you?"

She pressed her hand against his chest, and he struggled to keep his train of thought. "You know I don't . . ."

Her hand trailed lower. "Saving yourself for me? That's sweet." Fingers slid beneath the waistband of his breeches, and his cock rose to meet her. "Why don't you show me?"

"Witch." He picked her up and carried her into her bedroom. The princess might not want to marry a minor lord, he thought as she started unbuttoning his jacket, but she surely didn't mind fucking one.

⌘

As always, it was hot and fast and wild between them. He'd never figured out what it was about Eloisa that drove him so crazy—whether she used her magic on him or whether his power just craved hers—but he felt her trigger the barrier around the room so they wouldn't be heard or interrupted, and the second her magic flowed across his skin, he was engulfed.

Green silk tore beneath his hands as he ripped at her dress, desperate to touch her. Her eager response only egged him on. His own jacket and shirt vanished somehow, and her mouth rose to meet his with a hunger that matched his own.

Spice and smoke and roses engulfed him, fogged him, caught him as his hands closed over her breasts. She moved beneath him, and the buttons on his breeches opened of their own accord as she pulled him closer. There were benefits to bedding a witch, he thought hazily as her fingers closed around his cock again, guiding him to her. Then, as he slid home and she closed around him, he didn't think anything more for a long time.

◆◆◆◆◆

When he finally opened his eyes afterward, Eloisa lay beside him, one hand idly tracing patterns on his bare chest.

"You have to get dressed," she said. "Sophia will be here at twelve."

The clock beside her bed said it was ten minutes to midday. And the princess trained her ladies to be prompt. Still, he couldn't quite force himself to rise just yet. "So eager to get rid of me?" He tugged lazily at a curl that had found its way onto his pillow.

She closed her eyes.

"Elly?" he said. "Is something wrong?"

The deep red of her hair caught the sunlight as she shook her head. "No, nothing."

Something inside him twisted. His own magic didn't run much to forewarning or truth seeking, but he didn't believe what she was saying. "Promise me you're telling the truth."

Her lids drifted upward, and her blue eyes were clear. "I am," she said firmly. "Nothing's wrong. Everything is just as it should be." She kissed him quickly. "Now get dressed. I want you to escort Lady Sophia to Portholme."

"Send one of the guards," he said, rolling out of bed. "I'm your bodyguard, not hers."

Eloisa walked naked to her dressing table and started brushing her hair, pulling it back into the same loose style she'd worn when he arrived. "Father wants to see me. I'll be perfectly safe in his chambers. You can even escort me there yourself before you go. Besides, I want some herbs, and Chloe has the best at her shop."

"Lady Sophia shouldn't be going anywhere near Portholme. Or Madame de Montesse. Even with a royal bodyguard," Cameron said, pulling on his shirt.

He could see Eloisa frowning at him in the mirror. "If she manifests, she needs to know where to get the best when she needs it," she said coolly. "I do not intend for her to be fobbed off with inferior tools. Besides, I've ordered some things for her birthday. You can collect those and pretend they're for me."

"She'll be showered with more gifts than she can possibly use for her Ais-Seann."

"Most of which will be near useless." Eloisa sniffed as she shoved a last hairpin in place, then rose and crossed to her armoire. "You know most of the court witches are weak. I'm the strongest by far, and I can't do half what my grandmother could. Most of them couldn't tell blindroot from dandelion. Sophia deserves better. And I trust you to see she gets it." She pulled a silk shift over her head, then reached for the dress they'd left lying on the floor and started working her way into it, easing the sleeves and bodice and the complex folds of the skirt into place.

He walked over to help. "I don't like leaving you whilst I'm on duty. You're my charge, not Lady Sophia."

She twisted around and kissed him again, a hard, fast press of her lips that still made his blood sing. "You don't have to like it. What's that oath you men swear? Protect and *serve*?"

He stepped back and bowed, falling back on obedience because he had run out of protests. "I am, of course, at your command."

As he straightened, she smiled at him. "Thank you. I'm lucky to have you, Cameron. My dearest friend."

Friend. A two-edged sword, that word. He'd spoken truth to his father. Eloisa wasn't going to let herself fall in love with a minor noble. Thankfully, he had avoided that trap himself. He didn't think he loved her. But sometimes he wished things could be different. And he knew if she ever—by some twist of the goddess—decided to flout her father's will and marry as she chose, not to mention got over losing her husband, that it would be very easy to fall for her.

"Always, milady."

She smiled again, all sweetness again now that he had given in. "Good. Now, how do I look?"

"Beautiful. You know you do."

"Not like I've just been . . . ?"

"No one would guess." Least of all him. Satisfaction still flowed through his body, making him wish they had more time; the scent and sight of her were still temptation. But Elly looked every inch the cool, regal princess, even though he knew she'd enjoyed herself as much as he had.

"Excellent." She waved a hand, and the shield she'd woven around the room dissolved. "Then we should go back out. Because, if I'm not mistaken, I can hear Sophia in the hall."

CHAPTER TWO

When Sophie arrived at Princess Eloisa's apartments, she was somewhat surprised to find the princess in her parlor, feet tucked up under her skirts as she sat reading a book on one of the silk-clad sofas. Alone. Well, alone apart from the silent presence of today's bodyguard standing just inside the door.

He barely glanced at her as she entered. None of the Red Guard were talkative, but this one, Lieutenant Mackenzie, had elevated silence to an art form. Sophie couldn't remember ever having heard him speak unless Eloisa or one of the other soldiers or ladies-in-waiting spoke to him directly.

"How was your lesson?" Eloisa put down her book with a smile. "I was beginning to think Captain Turner had refused to let you leave."

"My lesson was fine, Your Highness." Sophie willed herself not to blush. She had taken the long way back to Eloisa's apartments, pausing for a minute or two longer than she should have by one of the doors that led out to the Indigo Lawn to watch the roundball game before the first chimes of the hour bell had pulled her attention back to where she was supposed to be.

"By which you mean it was deathly dull," Eloisa said with another smile.

"Captain Turner isn't dull," Sophie protested.

"No, but learning magical theory when you can't use it is," Eloisa said. "I remember that feeling." She swung her feet down and patted the sofa beside her. "Come; sit down."

Sophie would have preferred to stand after spending so long seated already that day, but she moved to the sofa obediently. "Where is everybody?" she asked as she smoothed her skirts and sat.

"Here and there," Eloisa said.

By which Sophie understood that all the other ladies-in-waiting were doing something connected with her Ais-Seann celebration and that she wouldn't find out anything more from the princess. And that she was probably going to be kept by Eloisa's side all afternoon, so that she was out of the way of whatever was happening.

Across the room, she was aware of Lieutenant Mackenzie watching them. Some of Eloisa's other bodyguards managed to fade into the background when they were on duty so that you didn't notice them. But Lieutenant Mackenzie didn't fade. He loomed rather.

He was tall, dark, and, quite frankly, intimidating. Serious deep blue eyes and a slight red light to his dark hair were the only hints that he had Carnarvan heritage. Otherwise he looked like the very model of a good Anglion noble and soldier. All stoic silent muscle and devotion to the Crown.

Though today she rather thought the expression in his dark blue eyes was disapproving instead of just serious. But his mood was hardly her concern. No, her concern was whatever the princess desired it to be. "Was there something you needed me to do, Your Highness?" she asked hopefully.

"Actually, there is," Eloisa said. "I have an errand for you. Lieutenant Mackenzie is going to escort you to Portholme to fetch some supplies."

Sophie stopped her jaw from falling open with an effort of will. Portholme? All the way to the harbor? Eloisa had never requested such a thing before. "But who will stay with you, milady?" She looked from Eloisa to the lieutenant, who was definitely looking disapproving now. He didn't protest, though, so presumably Eloisa had already informed him of the plan and overruled any objections he had.

Eloisa waved her hand. "The door guards will serve me well. I have to see my father, but after that I have an urge to be completely lazy and just sit here and read for the afternoon. And it's far too pretty a day for you to be cooped up here with me just because I'm a sluggard. So no arguments. Fetch your cloak, and the two of you can be on your way."

"Stay close, milady," Lieutenant Mackenzie said as he handed Sophie down from the carriage.

"I know the rules, Lieutenant," she said with more bravado than she felt. It wasn't like she went to Portholme terribly often. And never alone, with just one guard for escort. The few times she'd been here, she'd been arriving or departing the port, her family accompanied by a squad of guardsmen to and from the palace. Once Eloisa and her ladies had ridden this way, but they'd barely reached the borders of the port before the Red Guards escorting them had turned them back to safer paths.

But she wasn't going to give the lieutenant the satisfaction of seeing that she was even the slightest bit nervous. He'd been silent, his displeasure with the situation perfectly clear, for most of the carriage ride to Portholme after an initial barrage of instructions on how she was to behave whilst they were dockside.

Definitely intimidating.

Sophie knew Cameron Mackenzie was Elly's favorite

guard, but perhaps Her Highness got to see a side of him that wasn't on display currently.

Though right now, even if he did view her as an inconvenience, his looming presence was somewhat comforting. With him beside her, so unyieldingly proper and professional—not to mention so damned large—she doubted anyone would be unwise enough to bother them.

She looked down at the cloak draped over her arm. Rule one of traversing Portholme. Don't look too rich. The cloak and her plain gray dress should help with that. But it was hot despite the port-fragranced breeze coming off the water, and she didn't really fancy even the lightest layer of wool against her skin. She was stifling enough in the three layers of petticoats under her dress.

Besides, what good did it do for her to wear a cloak when the lieutenant's deep red uniform jacket made it clear what he was? The Red Guard were named for the battle magic they wielded and the blood they shed, not the color of their uniforms, but they weren't above reinforcing the former with the latter. "I know the rules," she repeated when he didn't answer her.

"Good," he said, scanning the crowded street before them. "Make sure you follow them."

"I'm not a child," she muttered. She was sick of being ordered and bossed and curtailed. Maybe turning twenty-one wouldn't be so bad after all. Perhaps magic would give her some tiny bit of control over her life. Or marriage. Married ladies were not as tightly policed as virgins. If her husband—whoever that might turn out to be—were reasonable, she would be able to decide some small things for herself.

She straightened her shoulders, hoping the low cut of her gown—and she would be very glad when the current court craze for reviving the gowns of two centuries ago was over—would emphasize the fact that she was quite grown up, thank you very much. Not that the lieutenant would notice her that way. Everyone knew he was basically a monk.

A well-armed monk, she thought as he clasped one hand around his largely ceremonial sword and straightened his pistol in its holster. But still, not one of the ladies who'd tried throwing themselves at him—after all, he was handsome if you ignored the stony soldier facade—had succeeded, to her knowledge. And there were no rumors of his tastes running in a less conventional direction. No counterweight love amongst his brother soldiers. Which would, given he was a third son, be acceptable if his own brothers had already spawned heirs. She tried to remember what she knew of Lord Inglewood's family, but other than the fact that Cameron had two older brothers, it escaped her for the moment.

Much like the knowledge that she was female seemed to have escaped the lieutenant. His gaze remained firmly on the crowds of people swelling around them, not so much as a glance at her cleavage.

"Shall we, Lieutenant?" she said, putting a snap in her voice. The man could at least look. Yes, as a royal virgin, she was off-limits, but how was she supposed to learn how to deal with men as a woman if they all insisted on treating her like a cloistered prior of the goddess? Watching Eloisa gave her a good idea of the principles of flirtation, but being an untouchable, unwed lady-in-waiting offered little chance to practice them. Men danced with her at court because they had to. Until she was of age and of power, she was no use to a courtier, and the repercussions for a dalliance with a potential royal witch were severe enough to keep them from trying anything below board.

"Stay close," Cameron said again as he offered his arm and stepped forward.

Sophie moved with him, drinking in the novelty of being in such a place. Portholme felt like an entirely different country from the court and the parts of Kingswell that surrounded it. The smells were different—salt and fish and the sweat of too many bodies rather than the perfumes, lamp oil, and incense that cloyed the court. The salty stink wasn't exactly pleasant, yet it was refreshing somehow.

Even more refreshing was the way no one kept their voices to polite court tones. Sailors yelled at one another across the street, carters cursed their horses, and women screeched at the stallholders and the children who ran screaming as they played almost underfoot of the passing traffic.

And beneath it all were the not-so-distant lapping waves breaking against the docks and the cries of the sun gulls as they squabbled over fish scraps.

It was hard to know where to look. The cobbled streets were crowded. The buildings huddled together as well. Made of wood and brick and solid gray stone rather than the green-veined granite of the palace, they were oddly foreign. Suddenly the large presence of the lieutenant seemed comforting rather than annoying, his arm reassuringly solid beneath hers and the leather and wool smell of his uniform a touch of familiarity as he moved them smoothly through the crowd and across the street to their destination.

Madame de Montesse's store was larger than Sophie had expected, clean and airy as far as an elderly narrow Portholme building could be. As she took in the rows of jars, bottles, and pouches that lined the shelves, she realized she didn't recognize what half of them held despite all her years of lessons. Which meant they were used for things other than the earth magic she was being taught. Which could be entirely illegal.

Battle magic didn't require any supplies and the Arts of Air only a few. Of course, in Illvya, they also practiced the fourth art. Water magic. Magic strictly forbidden here in Anglion, involving as it did, demons and darker things declared forbidden by the goddess. She moved closer to the nearest shelf, intrigued. Was Madame de Montesse truly brave enough to sell such things? Or was it just that Sophie was looking at supplies used for other purposes? Medicines and such. Supplies for seed witches and midwives and the healers without magic. Or earth magic that hadn't been included in her lessons.

"Lieutenant Mackenzie, what a surprise."

"Madame de Montesse, your health."

Sophie turned quickly, just in time to see the lieutenant bow, a gesture as precisely polite as his greeting. The woman he bowed to smiled broadly, her bright green gown, cut even lower than Sophie's, rustling as she bobbed an answering curtsy.

Sophie didn't follow the lieutenant's example. No one was entirely sure of the truth of Chloe de Montesse's background. She claimed to be a widow, though Sophie had heard rumors that that was merely a fabrication, designed to sway some sympathy in Madame de Montesse's direction when she had first come to Anglion as a refugee. That seemed more like court gossip and spite than anything else to Sophie. But she was sure of one thing. As a member of the court, she outranked the woman. She wasn't bowing first.

Madame de Montesse laughed. "So formal, Lieutenant? Such a pity." Her voice was airy and amused, her Anglish underscored ever so faintly with the accent of her former country. "And who have you brought to my humble establishment?" Her dark eyes flicked briefly to Sophie and then returned to the lieutenant.

"May I present Lady Sophia Kendall?" He made another shallow bow. Sophie moved closer to them out of politeness and, she had to admit, a certain degree of curiosity.

"Ah," Madame de Montesse said, smiling again as she bobbed another curtsy. "The one we hear so much speculation about." She laughed and loosed a stream of ques-

tions in the liquid syllables of her native Illvyan at the
lieutenant.

Sophie returned the curtsy with a version of her own
that was even shallower, more interested in following the
conversation. But the speed of the exchange was too
much for her—far quicker than her Illvyan tutor had ever
spoken to her, though the lieutenant seemed to have no
difficulty. She made out only a few words. "Flower" and
"the game." The lieutenant's reply was short, causing Madame to break into another peal of laughter as she spoke
again. The word for "prize" was about all Sophie could
decipher this time.

Sophie bristled. "I am not a prize, Madame." She
didn't know exactly how old the Illvyan woman was—
her skin was smooth, but she was definitely older than
Sophie. Older than the princess, too, perhaps. Near thirty.
Maybe more. One also heard rumors of Illvyan women
being able to stay young beyond their years.

"You speak Illvyan?" Madame de Montesse asked,
looking completely unperturbed that Sophie had understood her.

"Some," Sophie replied, trying for the same air of
unconcern. All Anglion nobles learned Illvyan to some
degree. The official reason given was the maintenance of
the tightly controlled trade agreements. Privately Sophie
thought that it was more a case of knowing one's enemy.

Illvya's use of the fourth art meant that they now controlled most of their continent. But the demons the Illvyan wizards summoned couldn't cross salt water. So
Anglion, protected by the ocean that surrounded it, was
still free. But no one believed the Illvyans wouldn't try
again to add Anglion to their empire.

"Court ladies. So . . . accomplished." The nose beneath
those amused dark eyes wrinkled despite the seeming
compliment, and Sophie felt an unwilling admiration for
the woman.

Chloe de Montesse was no Anglion. Though, as an Ill-vyan refugee, she seemed to follow the rules of her adopted country. The pearls dangling from gold wires threaded through her earlobes testified to that.

But she couldn't hide the fact that she hadn't always followed Anglion ways. No, she was a free witch. Un-hampered by custom. Her hair wasn't the rich red of the royal witches, deepened by their contact with the earth. It was a color closer to flame, licked here and there with threads that were near black. Sophie wondered exactly what powers she had dallied with before coming to An-glion to achieve that color and whether she thought So-phie herself should aspire to a similar shade rather than submit tamely to the fate decreed for her by tradition.

Though to do that, she would have to leave Anglion. The keepers of the goddess's temple did not truck with anyone practicing those arts that had been forbidden on Anglese soil. And they expressed their displeasure forc-ibly. Having hair like Madame de Montesse's was a sure path to trouble unless, like Madame de Montesse, one could claim to have given up the habits of her homeland. If she was being less than truthful about that, then no one had ever proven it.

"Do Illvyan ladies not learn Anglion?" Sophie coun tered.

Madame de Montesse nodded, the gesture almost ap-proving. "Some do. Those who have . . . need."

Need? Those who did magic, perhaps? Those who would end up with hair like Madame's?

Sophie tried to shake off the thread of speculation. There was no certainty that her hair would ever be any different from how it was now. If her power didn't mani-fest at her Ais-Seann, then it would remain nondescript brown. And if she did, there was no way it would end up any shade near Madame de Montesse's. It would be the same as all the other earth witches. Earth red. Deeper if she was stronger. Just a hint—like her mother had—if she were not. She had tried and failed to imagine herself with hair the color of Eloisa's—a red so rich it drew the eye like rubies. It suited the princess's milky complexion, but skin like Eloisa's was a rarity in the court. It cropped up now and again in the royal family, a reminder that they had both ties to the north and, though it was scarcely admitted to these days, links to the paler-skinned Illvyans as well.

But Sophie's skin was the usual golden shade of most Anglions. She couldn't help feeling that red hair might just make her look like an unstruck matchstick.

The lieutenant produced a piece of paper from his jacket pocket and started reading out a list of herbs and other supplies that were at least familiar to Sophie from her studies. His words drew Madame de Montesse's attention back to him, her smile and fluttering eyelashes firmly directed at him as she started to fetch things from the shelves.

Sophie turned back to her study of the cabinets and shelves, carefully clasping her hands behind her back so she wouldn't break anything delicate or touch anything dangerous. Illvyans didn't limit themselves to the three arts of Anglion magic. And even in Anglion, some of the ingredients used in magical workings were dangerous. Safer to look and not touch.

Just as Sophie had nearly decided that the tiny skeleton in a jar just out of reach on one of the higher shelves must definitely be a conar lizard, the lieutenant called her name, making her jump and bump the shelf. Jars rattled, but luckily nothing came crashing down around her ears. She put a hand out to settle the last of them back into place, willing the blush that had sprung into her cheeks to leave before she turned. "Sir?"

"Come and see this. The princess would want your opinion before I spend her money."

On the opposite side of the counter to him, Madame de Montesse didn't look overly pleased at the insinuation she'd sell anything that wasn't worth the high prices she charged.

Sophie hid a smile—it was nice to know that the lieutenant could annoy others as well as her—and joined him. Laid out on the counter was a supple leather roll, currently unfurled. The length of rich brown hide gleamed dully under the light coming through the window. On it lay a variety of smaller leather pouches, two slender silver knives, and a length of gold chain, held in place with thongs sewn into the roll. She'd never seen anything like it before, though it was clear that it was intended for a witch.

"What do you think?" he asked.

Sophie reached out and stroked the leather, her finger slipping across the softness easily. Yet it had the sheen of waterproofing. "It's lovely."

"High quality?"

She looked up at him, trying to see whether he was joking. "You're the mage here. You tell me."

He shrugged. "This is witch magic. Warriors don't use this stuff. I barely know mandrake from marjoram."

"I'm sure you understate things. The Red Guard trains its mages well."

"Yes, the ones who have strong talent. I'm average at best. Basic defense spells. Nothing requiring herbs or silver."

Madame de Montesse arched a dark brow at this but stayed quiet.

"You're a royal bodyguard," Sophie protested.

"Princess Eloisa is stronger than I'll ever be. I serve her best with my sword, not my magic." He looked uncomfortable, perhaps because he was discussing such a subject in front of someone not of the court.

"I see." Sophie untied the thongs wrapped around one

of the knives and picked it up, trying to see if it evoked any response. It was more a dagger than a knife, really. The hilt was chased with runes and fit her hand well. It had the heavy sheen of good silver, but otherwise she sensed nothing. Likewise the chain. The pouches were a little easier. She could at least recognize the contents by sight and smell—a wide array of herbs and other ingredients for spells—but she didn't know how to judge their magical strength. She wouldn't be able to tell that until her own powers showed up. If they did.

"Milady?" The lieutenant interrupted her thoughts.

She sighed and slipped the knife back into the loop designed for it. "It looks perfectly fine to me."

"Good. If you please, Madame." He nodded at the roll, and Madame de Montesse busied herself repacking the roll, adding it to the pile of packages on the counter in front of the lieutenant. Eloisa must have sent him with quite the list.

❦

Cameron reached for his pouch for the coins Eloisa had given him. Thank the goddess that this errand running was nearly over and that he could get Lady Sophia back to the palace. Then his unplanned babysitting stint would be over, and he could get back to his duties instead. The girl was pleasant enough, but her wide-eyed air of curiosity about the port and Madame de Montesse's dubious store was proof that she didn't belong in Portholme. But as he lifted the pouch, a growling rumble boomed through the air. A second later, the building shook violently. Jars crashed off the shelves, the sound of shattering glass echoed by an outcry of cries and screams from the street.

"What was that?" Sophia said, twisting.

"Stay here, milady." He strode to the door and wrenched it open, drawing his sword. The crowd was beginning to move, screams and cries filling the street as stallholders tried to stow away their goods or run away. If he were any judge, they were minutes away from full-blown panic. He grabbed the nearest man. "What's happening?"

The man only shook his head and pointed.

Cameron followed the direction of his arm and went cold. Smoke billowed from one of the palace's wide round towers—the east tower, which sat at the intersection of the northern front wall and the east wall. As he watched, another roaring rumble was followed by a flash of fire, and a hole appeared in one of the walls of the west tower. An explosion that large was no fire or accident. They were being attacked. Instinctively, he started toward the palace but checked himself after half a step. *Lady Sophia.*

He couldn't leave her unprotected. Who knew what was happening? She was part of the royal family—however distant a part—and if they were under attack, then his duty was also to her.

Another rumble, and stones spewed into the air. Goddess. *Elly.* What was happening to her? But fear for his lover didn't change his duty to the girl in the store.

"What is that?" Sophia appeared beside him, looking terrified.

"Get back inside," he snarled. He didn't wait for her to protest or argue, just bundled her back into the shop, bolted the door, and drew the shades.

Chloe was standing by the window. "The palace?"

"Under attack," he said shortly.

"Attack?" Sophia echoed.

He spared her one glance. She had turned a sickly sort of yellow shade, fear dulling the sheen of her skin, but so far wasn't having hysterics. "As far as I can tell, milady." He turned back to Madame de Montesse. "Where's the nearest portal?" The safest thing would be to get Sophia out of the city altogether and hide her somewhere until he could get some idea of the situation.

"I have one here," Chloe admitted.

Now, that was unexpected. Portals cost money. A lot of money. Both to establish and maintain. But where Chloe de Montesse got that sort of cash was a question for another day. Now all that mattered was she had one. "Show me," he said, and took Sophia by the arm, leading her after Chloe.

They ducked into a back room, and then Chloe threw back a rug to reveal a trapdoor. It led down into a cellar and to another door. When he approached, he felt the familiar pull of a portal stone. As Chloe unlocked the door, he turned to Sophia. "Have you used a portal before?"

She nodded. "O-once."

"Did it make you ill?" Portals were uncomfortable for most. If she was going to faint or throw up, better to know now.

"A little," she said, straightening her shoulders as if to say "don't worry about me." "Where are we going?"

"Away from here. Never mind." He shot a look at Chloe. "My apologies, Madame, but if you do not know, you can't tell."

She nodded and pulled the door open. "I understand. Do you need a focus?"

"No. I have one." Stepping through the door, he lit the candle Chloe had handed him and raised it so he could read the symbols around the portal stone. Portals were linked to other portals. The more destinations, the more expensive and power-consuming to maintain. This one showed ten, and thankfully, he recognized two of them as being in the general direction he required. He took Sophie's hand. "Stay close." She obediently stepped nearer.

"You would be wise to run yourself, Madame. The city will not be safe. Not if . . ." He didn't want to speak the possibilities and scare Sophia. Or give them reality.

Chloe shrugged, a peculiarly Illvyan quality to her gesture. "I will wait and see how things lie. It is only a few moments' work to leave if needs be. Salt protect you."

She stepped back and closed the door, leaving them in darkness broken only by the ring of flickering light provided by the candle. "Ready?" he asked Sophia, drawing her against his chest.

She nodded, a movement he felt rather than saw. He pulled the dagger he carried in his boot free and slashed his thumb, using the blood to open the key to magic. He thought fast as his thumb throbbed and the power built; then he focused on the symbol of his chosen destination, blew out the candle, keyed the portal stone, and moved through the portal with three rapid strides, never loosening his grip on Sophia.

CHAPTER THREE

Sophie stumbled as the lieutenant practically dragged her through the portal.

He caught her before she fell. "Careful, we cannot lose time." He pushed forward past her and led the way out into sunlight. The sudden transition had Sophie blinking. She lifted a hand to shade her eyes and felt her stomach roll in protest as she got her bearings. She'd traveled by portal only once before. The one at the Kendall estate had fallen into disuse. Her mother had such a small power that she couldn't perform the rites to keep it primed, and her father didn't have the coin to spare to pay someone to do it for them.

When they traveled to and from Kingswell, they did it the hard way. By sea or over the bumpy network of roads in a carriage.

She sucked in a breath, held it, then released it slowly, praying that her stomach would cooperate and that she wasn't about to lose her last meal all over the lieutenant's beautifully polished boots. The scenery held no familiar landmarks, just a vista of trees and hills and fields that could be almost any part of rural Anglion. "Where are we?"

Cameron looked around the small clearing they were in, then crossed to a portal marker on the far side. His hand tracked down the symbols carved in the rock. "If I got this right, then we're outside a small village called Upper Tilbourne."

That left Sophie none the wiser. Her head began to ache, though she wasn't sure if it was from the portal or the thought of what lay behind them in the capital. She drew a steadying breath. Despite the sunshine, the air felt cooler than it had, which helped a little. As did the fact that the city smells were all gone, replaced by the cleaner scents of grass and damp earth and, somewhere in the distance, a faint hint of wood smoke. "Where is that exactly?"

Somehow it seemed important to know something about what was happening, even an insignificant fact like where she was.

"North of Kingswell."

That wasn't helpful. Most of Anglion was north of Kingswell. Only the Hellebride Peninsula lay below the capital. "How far north?"

The lieutenant looked around again, face grim. Then he seemed to come to a decision. "Not far enough."

He came back to Sophie, caught her shoulders, and peered at her. "Are you up to another transfer?"

Her stomach protested the thought. Strongly. She dug her fingernails into her palms, clenching her hands tightly, hoping the small pain would drive away the nausea. "Are you going to tell me what's happening? Back in the store —"

"Later. Come, milady. There is little time to make sure we get away."

Get away where? And who would be coming after her, anyway? She fought a rising urge to refuse to go any farther. But that would be foolish. The lieutenant was an experienced soldier, a royal bodyguard. The princess's bodyguard. She should trust him.

Or should she? After all, she had no idea what had

even happened. Or where he was taking her. "I'm not going anywhere until you tell me what's happening."

"There's no time."

Sophie took a step back. "Make time."

The lieutenant stared down at her, jaw clenched. His hand started to lift from his side and then dropped again. "I am trying to get you to safety. Someone attacked the palace. You saw that."

She had, and the memory of the flames and smoke shooting into the sky made her stomach tighten greasily. She swallowed. Hard. She'd seen the hole in the east tower. Eloisa's apartments were in the eastern wing. "I did. So we should go back. People will need help."

"I'm a royal guard," he said. "If the palace is under attack, then my duty is to secure the royal family. Right now you're the closest member of the royal family I can get to. So I'm taking you to safety."

"How do I know you're safe?"

He gave her a look that was almost approving. "Milady, if I were part of the plot, I probably would have killed you, turned you over to the attackers, or at least knocked you out so I could take you wherever I was supposed to take you by now."

"Or you could just be telling me that."

"Suspicious little thing, aren't you? Good. Thinking is good. But right now we don't have time to waste." He pulled his pistol out of its holster. "Do you know how to shoot?"

She hadn't fired a gun for a very long time, though her father had taught her. She knew the general theory of how a gun worked. "A little," she said.

His mouth twisted, but he handed the gun over anyway. "That's going to have to do for now. No time for a lesson right this minute, and we can't risk drawing attention. Take that. If I try to kill you, try to shoot me first."

It wasn't the most reassuring speech she'd ever heard

in her lifetime, but it was better than nothing. She took the gun and wrapped her fingers awkwardly around the carved wooden grip. It was shaped for a man's hands, but it would have to do. "All right. Now tell me where you're taking me."

"Right now, away from here," said the lieutenant. "I want distance between us and Kingswell until we know what is going on. And one transfer isn't enough. Someone could trace where we've gone."

Sophie bit her lip. Another reasonable explanation. And he was right. If someone was pursuing them—pursuing her, most likely, given who she was—then they could already be at Madame de Montesse's shop. It was no secret that that was where she'd been bound this afternoon. Besides Eloisa's ladies and guards, there must have been half a hundred people in the palace alone who had seen her leaving the grounds with the lieutenant.

If they found the portal at Madame's store, they could find them. There were ways to cleanse a portal of the traces of its most recently used destination, but they couldn't rely on the good Madame to have done so on her end.

Not that any of that changed the fact that she wanted to know where he was taking her. "Are you taking me home?"

"Home?" He stopped, frowning. "No. Why would I do that?"

"Because it would be sensible."

"Milady, if someone is after the royal family, then an estate belonging to members of that family isn't going to be terribly safe."

For a moment she felt as though the bottom had dropped out of the world. She hadn't thought about that. There'd been no time to think in the few rushed minutes since the lieutenant had taken charge. To realize that her family might be in danger, too. And then she remembered that they weren't at home. They were, in fact, supposed to be arriving in Kingswell that evening. A week of unseasonable storms had delayed their departure, but the latest messages had assured her that they would arrive in good time for her birthday.

Just in time to land in the middle of a battle zone. She wrenched her arm free of the lieutenant's grip, whirled, and headed back the way they had come.

He caught her after a few steps. "What do you think you're doing?"

"We have to go back," she said, jerking her arm. But he was ready for her, and his hand simply tightened. She yanked again. "We have to go back. My family is in Kingswell."

"So is mine," he said flatly. "But I can't help them. I can only help you."

"You can help me by taking me back," she said, voice rising.

"No."

"I outrank you, Lieutenant."

"Not when it comes to decisions about your safety. I'm a member of the Red Guard, and I am charged with keeping you alive."

Sophie suddenly remembered the gun. Her fingers tightened around the grip.

He must have noticed the movement. "If you shoot me, then who is going to work the portal for you?"

Dust of the goddess. She hadn't thought about that. She had no magic. She couldn't use a portal. And she was halfway across the country. By the time she made it back any other way, assuming she could make it back in one piece—it wasn't as if she'd brought much money with her or had fresh clothing or a means of transport—matters in Kingswell would likely be settled anyway. One way or another.

The lieutenant stayed very still, watching her with

those serious blue eyes. "Please, milady. You have to trust me. Or if you can't trust me, then trust the princess. She gave me her trust when she chose me as a bodyguard."

That was true. But had the princess been mistaken?

Her head throbbed a protest as she tried to think through the implications. The gun was growing rapidly heavier in her hand. If she held it up much longer, her hand would start to shake and then she might not even hit him.

She had to make a decision. And right now there seemed to be only one real choice. She lowered the gun. "All right. I'll come with you. But you have to tell me your plan."

&c&

It turned out the plan involved more portals. Too many portals. After the third transfer, Sophie was feeling regretful that she hadn't dug her heels in and insisted on being taken back to Kingswell. She'd lost what little she'd eaten earlier in the day as she'd staggered across the portal boundary after the second journey.

The lieutenant had waited politely for her to finish and then handed her his handkerchief. But that had been the extent of his sympathy. He'd taken her by the arm and headed into the wooded area behind the portal. He seemed to know where he was going. Which meant that one of them did.

"Where are we now?" she demanded, trying to keep her skirts free of the fallen branches and other obstacles littering the path. Apparently, not many of the locals took this path to the portal.

"South Westby," he said.

She'd never heard of it. "Would you care to narrow that down a little? Perhaps give me a county or a town I might have heard of?"

"Caloteen," he said. "Sort of east."

Caloteen was one of the middle counties. About half a day's ride from her father's lands. The lieutenant had made it clear they weren't going there. But at least it gave her a fixed point to cling to. At least until the next transfer, when they might end up goddess only knew where.

They walked away from the portal for several miles until they came to another small stand of woods. The lieutenant led the way into the trees and paused when they reached a clearing near a narrow stream. He scanned their surroundings for several minutes. Sophie leaned against a convenient Oran tree and tried not to think about how foul her mouth tasted.

"We'll rest here," he said eventually, and she nodded and walked toward the stream as fast as her aching legs would take her, dropping to her knees to drink and rinse out her mouth. The stream wasn't flowing full force in the heat of late summer, but the water seemed fresh enough and the lower water level meant there wasn't too much mud on her dress when she stood. The dark gray — she'd never thought she'd be thankful for gray after wearing it for most of a year — hid the worst of the stains.

The lieutenant was moving around the clearing, gathering up sticks and branches.

"Just how long is this stay to be?" she asked.

"We'll sleep here," he said. "There's a village a few miles on. I'll walk there early, see if I can find us some clothes and horses."

"Horses?"

"If we need them. There may be news that means we can make our way back, but if not, I think we should stay away from the portals for another day."

"The day after tomorrow is my birthday," she pointed out.

"I know. And I'll get you back to the palace if we have the all clear."

"And if not?"

"Then your birthday party will be delayed."

He didn't sound terribly sympathetic.

"It's hardly the party that concerns me."

"Then what is it?"

She shook her head at him. "The part where I may come into my power. It's my Ais-Seann. I'm supposed to complete the dedication to the Goddess on my birthday."

"That's just a ritual, isn't it? A day or two won't hurt."

"I suppose." She wasn't entirely sure if it was *just* a ritual. Through all her lessons, the importance of the dedication taking place on her birthday had been driven home to her, though no one had offered an explanation other than tradition and the fact that the goddess demanded it. Still, it was enough to make her uneasy. She hadn't been at court the last time a royal witch had been dedicated, so she hadn't ever seen the ritual in person. Women outside the nobility who manifested went to their local temples, but they seldom showed any real degree of power. Seed witches, able to coax plants to prosper, perhaps, but nothing more.

"I'm sure we can find a chapel if it comes to that," the lieutenant said. He laid his armful of wood down in the middle of the clearing and began separating it into smaller and larger branches.

"If you think someone is looking for us, is a fire safe?"

He looked up. "I can build it small and do a thing or two to shield the smoke. It may not get too cold tonight, so maybe we can do without, but it's easier to prepare it now than in the dark." He continued sorting the wood as he spoke, moving with an ease that spoke of having done it many times. If she had to be hiding in the woods with somebody, a soldier was at least useful. She wouldn't have had any idea how to build a fire outside, let alone light one without matches or magic.

And he was right. It was cooler here than it had been in the capital but still not cold. Perhaps she should have been thankful that they hadn't traveled farther north into Carnarvan. "We need food."

"Think you'd keep it down?"

She flushed. "It was the portal. I'll be fine in a moment."

He studied her a moment. "We'll see. If you are sure you can eat, I can go looking. There should be berries at least. Maybe some mushrooms."

"If the stream gets any deeper farther on, there might be fish," she offered.

"But no rod," he pointed out. "And no, I won't be shooting anything. The noise would draw attention."

"I have pins in my purse," Sophie said. "And thread."

"Pins?" He looked surprised. "Can you make a fish hook from a pin?"

"I used to fish with my little brothers," Sophie said. "So, yes. I have pins because you never know when you might need to pin a hem or something at court," she continued as explanation. The other things in her purse—smelling salts, packets of herbal powders for headaches and such, and tiny vials of perfume and rouge—were unlikely to be helpful. When she got back to the castle, she would start carrying matches, too, she decided. Though maybe, if her magic came, she would be able to call a candle flame as some of the royal witches could.

"All right. Make your hook whilst I finish the fire, and then I'll see where the stream leads. If you promise to stay put."

"Where would I go?" she asked, feeling suddenly very lost as the truth of those words struck home. She was dependent on him and his good graces, at least for another day. Her eyes stung suddenly, and she blinked and ducked her head as she slipped her hand through the slit in the side of her skirt to reach her purse where it hung between her skirt and the first layer of petticoats.

∞

"What are you thinking about?"

Sophie came back to herself with a start. "Yeast cakes." It was dark now, and the lieutenant had made a very small fire to cook the single fish he'd caught with her makeshift line. That, with the berries he'd also found, had been a paltry meal. Not enough when she'd lost everything she'd eaten earlier in the day.

The lieutenant chuckled, a low rumbling sound in the darkness. "Yeast cakes?"

"Yes," she said, staring down at the last few berries in her lap with distaste. She'd never been overly fond of blackberries. But she was too hungry to waste any. "The one Cook at the castle makes. With the glaze." Her stomach rumbled at the memory.

"I always preferred the spiced pear tarts," he said, dropping another small branch on the fire.

Sophie bit into another berry, chewed, then swallowed, the faint acidic sweetness lingering on her tongue. "The tarts are good, too, but yeast cakes are my favorite. Hot, just cooked. I used to go down to the kitchen sometimes to fetch some for the princess, and Cook would give me one straight from the pan." Her appetite died when she realized Cook might well be dead or captured. Shivering, she moved closer to the tiny fire. Stupid to worry about food when she didn't know if her family was alive.

"Milady? Are you cold?"

She wrapped the cloak more tightly around herself, welcoming the warmth. The lieutenant had been correct in his predictions. It wasn't a cold night, but her skin was cool. "It's nothing." It did no good to share her thoughts with him. He had friends and family in the castle, too.

And his fellow soldiers. If anyone was in the line of danger, it would be the Red Guard. Besides which, he probably wanted to be back there, doing his duty instead of hiding in the woods protecting her.

He was a battle mage. His magic was meant for fighting. He was probably feeling as frustrated as her.

Or maybe not. He at least could do useful things like make a fire. He could protect them with his magic if he had to. Whereas she was helpless. Even if she manifested power, she would still be limited.

"Why do women only get taught earth magic?" she asked, staring at the flames, hoping he wouldn't read the curiosity in her face.

"Some women learn other magics."

She knew prevarication when she heard it. The polite tone of "don't pursue this." Well, goddess curse it. She was in the woods, maybe being hunted, and she wanted to know. There was no time for polite. "Not royal witches."

"No," he agreed.

"Why not?"

He shrugged, the firelight glinting off the gold braid on the shoulder of his jacket. "I never really thought about it. Tradition?"

She snorted. "That's not an answer." Turning, she looked him in the eye.

He frowned. "Earth magic is the deepest. The closest to the goddess. Why do you need more?"

"If earth is deepest, why do men use other magics in battle?"

"It's hard to defeat someone by raining on him. That doesn't mean earth is weaker; it just has different uses."

"You could strike someone with lightning."

"Milady, no one has been strong enough to call lightning in a very long time."

"That's my point. Why not teach royal witches the other magics?"

"Royal witches are protected. The Arts of Air—illusion, concealment—what use does a lady have for those?"

"Have you never tried to negotiate a ballroom without getting your"—she broke off; ladies did not mention bottoms in polite conversation—"without getting pinched?"

The flickering firelight revealed his smile. "Ah, no. But the Arts require more . . ." He made a gesture that she couldn't quite decipher. "It's an inner thing. And it isn't for such uses."

"What? Women are not intelligent enough?"

"No. It's not that. But the Arts illusions and wards and far-seeing are used together with battle magic. And that's something different."

"Different how? Because women should wait quietly at home and let men protect them?"

He shook his head. "Maybe they think women shouldn't be put at risk of being hurt."

"Hurt?" She was beginning to feel like Eloisa's pet parrot, repeating everything he said.

"To learn battle magic—to access the power—you have to be angry. Enraged almost. In the army, the first few times, the instructor punches you. In the face. I'm guessing most women wouldn't want that."

"Anger can be raised in other ways."

"This is quicker. Blood is quicker."

She stayed silent, considering his words. "But once you know how to latch onto the power, do you still need to be angry?"

❧

Cameron poked the fire with his foot, wondering how to answer. He wasn't sure he should be discussing this at all. But it was better than her bursting into tears. So far she'd been very calm. Her stunt with the gun had been foolish, but it had been brave. Seemingly calm was not the same as actually calm, though, and it was hard to know if hysterics lurked below the facade. He'd seen good men fall apart under attack, and Lady Sophia wasn't a trained soldier. If magic distracted her, then magic they would discuss. "There's usually plenty of emotion in the thick of battle. You can use that. But there's another reason."

"And that is?"

"You use battle magic to hurt someone and it hurts you. A sword is safer. You use the magic for distraction — a cramp, a twitch. Otherwise it can hurt too much. Pain makes you vulnerable."

"What about killing? You can kill someone with battle magic, yes?"

He couldn't help the shudder that ran down his spine. Memories he tried to suppress whispered in the back of his mind. "It's not recommended. Not directly."

"Why not?"

Goddess. How many questions could she ask? "Because you feel them die. Trust me. You don't want to know what that feels like."

"Have you ever . . . ?"

"Once. When someone was trying to kill me."

"You obviously survived the experience."

Survived. There was a word. He was still alive, true. But he still dreamed about it. About that moment when he'd felt everything stop. Felt the pull of terror and oblivion. Still woke from those dreams covered in sweat, if he managed not to scream. Looking into Sophia's eyes, turned some nameless color by the firelight, he knew exactly why no one wanted women to learn battle magic. The thought of her feeling anything close to what he'd experienced was incomprehensible.

"Yes, I did. But believe me, it's not something you want to know about." He poked at the fire again. "Perhaps you should try to sleep. It's been a long day." And tomorrow would likely be longer. He'd told her that there might be good news, that they might get to return to Kingswell tomorrow, but he didn't think it was likely.

Which left him potentially shepherding a brand-new royal witch through the countryside, trying to keep her alive.

He was starting to think that the goddess didn't like him very much.

CHAPTER FOUR

Sophie woke with a start when a sugarjay screeched somewhere above her. It took a few seconds to remember where she was. Which was somewhere in the middle of nowhere in Caloteen. On the run. With Lieutenant Mackenzie. She was tempted to pinch herself to make sure she hadn't dreamed the whole thing, but the blue sky above her and the ache in her bones as she rolled over seemed evidence enough. It was real. Someone had attacked the palace. Attacked the royal family.

Illvyans? Or was one of the lords trying to take advantage of King Stefan's illness and make a play for power? There hadn't been a lords' rebellion in three generations. Not since Stefan's grandfather had seized power after the last Illvyan incursion had left half the former court dead.

She shivered, partly from the unwelcome thoughts and partly from the chill morning air. Her cloak was Kingswell weight. The border of the Hellebride Peninsula, where the capital lay, was the warmest part of Anglion. It grew colder as you headed north, and now they were halfway up the country, if Lieutenant Mackenzie was telling her the truth.

She rolled toward the fire and realized then that the lieutenant wasn't lying on the other side as he had been when she'd finally fallen asleep. She'd watched him through the low flames of the fire for an age before she'd finally slept. Too much had happened in a day for her to feel safe enough to sleep, no matter how her body, drained from the frantic portal journey, had wanted to. But she had succumbed eventually. And evidently slept too deeply to hear the lieutenant when he'd left.

Which meant, hopefully, that he had felt sorry for her and let her sleep rather than he'd taken the opportunity to desert his unwanted charge in the night. Given his reluctance to let her go yesterday, she couldn't believe it was the latter.

She pushed herself up to a sitting position, paying for the action with the shriek of muscles not used to sleeping on hard, cold ground, and gathered the cloak around her. The lieutenant had fed the fire before he'd left. There was a small log burning solidly enough to shed a little warmth, and she wriggled closer and just sat and soaked up the heat for a few minutes. Which was when she noticed the pile of berries sitting on top of the neatly folded uniform jacket he'd left by what remained of the small stack of wood he'd gathered the previous night.

More blackberries. Her stomach rumbled even as she wished for something else. If the lieutenant's trip to the village he had mentioned was successful, then perhaps he would bring back something more sustaining.

She ate the berries, then climbed to her feet and ventured down the stream to drink and wash and take care of her other pressing need. Squatting behind a bush with her skirts hiked around her shoulders was far less embarrassing when she knew nobody else was within earshot.

Still, when she returned to the fire, she wished the lieutenant had woken her when he'd left. Then she might have some idea of how long he had been gone and when he would return. Until then, there was nothing she could

do except wait. They would be leaving this place, so there
was no point looking for more wood, and she really
didn't want to pick more blackberries unless she had to.

She settled back down by the fire, poking idly at it
with a branch, watching the low flames flickering. From
the position of the sun, still relatively low in the sky, she
thought it might still be only eighth hour, maybe ninth.
The sun rose near seventh at this time of year, so assuming the lieutenant had left at first light, he might not be
much longer. He'd said the village was only a few miles
away.

Worry started to gnaw at her stomach. Something could
have gone wrong. Anything. What would she do if he
didn't return? She didn't even know which direction the
village was. She could retrace her steps to the road perhaps and then find somewhere with people. Find someone
to help her.

Had there been help for those left back at the castle?
She'd caught a glimpse of the shattered east tower before
Cameron had dragged her back inside Madame de Montesse's store and away through the portal. People would
have died in that explosion. More would have been hurt.
And goddess knew what might have happened next. If
there was an Illvyan invasion, based on history, there would
be carnage.

Worry started to flare into panic. She clenched her
hands and made herself breathe, counting back from one
hundred in one of the calming exercises Captain Turner
had drilled in to her so relentlessly. It helped a little, tamed
the fear back to a manageable lead knot in her gut. Distraction, that was what she needed. She started to recite
the proper ways to ground to a ley line in her head, over
and over again until a jingle of metal snapped her out of
her reverie.

She froze, straining. She heard a soft whicker and a
creak of leather. A horse. Or horses. The lieutenant? Or

someone else? Without thinking, she sprang to her feet and bolted toward the trees at the edge of the clearing, hiding herself behind the thickest trunk she could find.

The sounds grew louder. She peered round the trunk cautiously when she heard the snap of a branch that sounded close enough to come from the clearing itself. Relief washed over her when she recognized the lieutenant. He led two horses and wore a dark brown rough woolen jacket and brown trousers rather than the black ones of his uniform. Camouflage of a sort, she supposed. No point advertising he was a Red Guard if they were trying to go unnoticed.

"Lady Sophia?" he called softly.

She stepped out from the tree, and his expression mirrored the relief she felt. Had he thought she would make a run for it again? Try to get away from him?

"Good morning," she said when she reached him. "Your errand was successful, then?" She stretched out a hand to the smaller of the two horses, a flat-nosed dun with a pretty black mane and tail. The horse nudged her hand, then snorted, probably disappointed that it didn't hold any treats. The other horse, a big bay, flicked his ears toward the dun but stayed quiet under the lieutenant's hands.

"A piece of luck," he said. "Market day. I got these two and some supplies. You can have some breakfast, and then we'll be away from here."

"Was there any news?"

He shook his head. "Nothing definite. They'd had word of the attack, but I couldn't find out any more. The capital is apparently well locked down."

"So you don't think it's safe to return?" She couldn't quite keep the disappointment out of her voice.

"No." He pulled a bundle out of one of the saddlebags on the larger horse's back and tossed it toward her. "You should change."

"Change?"

"I got you some breeches. Too hard to find a sidesaddle in these parts."

Because farmers' wives and villagers were too sensible to try to ride in skirts just to look elegant. Her mother had insisted that Sophie be taught both ways, and she vastly preferred riding astride, not that she got the chance in Kingswell. Royal ladies rode sedately, dressed in elegant habits. Sophie sometimes wondered if they drugged the horses to stop them getting bored from slow walks around the royal parks with the odd canter if Eloisa was feeling rebellious.

"You can ride astride, I assume?" Cam said.

"Yes." She nodded. "I can." Stiff and sore as she was from the night sleeping outdoors, a long ride wasn't likely to be pleasant. "Where are we bound?"

"I'd like us to go farther north. And west. Put some distance between us and the portals we've used. Just in case someone is looking for us. Then we'll find another portal."

Ah. Yes. He'd used blood to trigger the portals. A strong battle mage with a tracking talent could follow that trail. So his plan made sense. She nodded again. "Let's get started."

⟨≈⟩

Cam pushed as hard as he dared with the horses and Lady Sophia herself. She hadn't been lying when she had said she could ride astride. She sat on the little dun very well, but she wasn't used to riding at a traveling pace for hours at a time over roads and countryside. He wanted her in one piece, not falling off her horse from exhaustion or too stiff to walk.

They stopped to eat in the middle of the day, finding a small stream with a shrine as they rode through a scrubby wood following a half-overgrown track.

"Do you think anyone's keeping up the blessing?" Sophia asked as they stared down at the water.

Cam looked at the small pile of stones and the graceful curving lines carved on them. "No moss, so maybe. Not much we can do about it if they're not." Running water was supposed to be safe even without a blessing. He shook his head. It was nonsense anyway. The blessings were to protect the water from being used to summon a demon. And no one in Anglion practiced water magic. Even if the attack in Kingswell had been set in motion by Illvya, it wasn't like there was an Illvyan wizard lurking behind the next tree, disturbed midsummoning. It was a stream in the middle of the damned country. But he didn't know how superstitious—or observant— Lady Sophia was, so he pricked his thumb, let the drop of blood fall into the water, and muttered, "Salt to bind, blood to save, goddess bless this place." It was the shortest, most perfunctory of blessings. With his level of magic and without enough blood to truly add enough salt to the water to make it poison to a demon, it wouldn't have done anything to interfere with an Illvyan summoning anyway, but hopefully it would make her feel more comfortable.

She hadn't asked about the stream the previous day. Too panicked and confused. If her question now meant that she was adjusting to her situation, then it was worth a drop of blood. He sucked his thumb to stop the bleeding. The nicks he'd made yesterday to power the portals were all healing, but the friction of the reins and his sweat had turned each one into a stinging annoyance. They had to keep moving, and he'd never had any skill for healing magic or herbcraft, so he couldn't heal the cuts. He ignored the small pains, scooped water to rinse his hands off, and then drank before topping up the water bags.

Sophia bent to drink, too, splashing the water over her

face. She'd pulled her hair back into a simple braid and, in the breeches and the too-large dark blue jacket and shirt he'd found for her, she looked very young.

She was a pretty thing, her eyes the clear brown of strong tea and her hair several shades darker. Her face was made up of angles. Eyes that tilted in the southern way, sharp cheekbones, and a face more pointed than the rounder-faced looks that most southerners had. All in all a face that suggested she might just have a stronger will than one would expect from a court lady. Some north-erner blood somewhere in the family tree to give her those bones. Or Illvyan. The hair would change, of course, if her power manifested. She'd wind up with rich red hair, as all earth witches did. He tried to picture it for a moment and failed.

Then he pulled his mind back to the job at hand. Get-ting her to safety and keeping her there to ensure that she would live to get that red hair. They had a few more hours to get to the portal he was aiming for. Then they could make the final leg of the journey once he had found somewhere to sell or leave the horses. Theoretically, you could take an animal the size of a horse through a portal but only a very, very strong one. It would be a horrendous waste of power and, if the blessings weren't strong enough, the portal could fail altogether. No one knew what happened to those caught in a failed portal. None of them had ever been seen again to explain what happened.

"We should keep moving, milady."

Sophia nodded and took one final handful of water from the stream before heading back over to the little dun. She hadn't complained about the journey so far, but she moved a little stiffly. Even though it was plain she knew how to ride astride, he doubted she'd ever had to do so for hours on end for a long time. She looked at the horse and made a face before feeding it the core of one of the apples they'd had for lunch.

Cameron hooked the water bag back onto his saddle and made sure the other saddlebags were closed before moving to check Sophia's as well. She stood stroking the dun's ears.

"I'll give you a hand to mount," he said, and came around to her side of the horse.

"I can do it," she protested.

"I'm sure you can. But you're not used to riding all day, so conserving energy is only sensible." He regarded her for a moment. She was shorter and slighter than Eloisa, her figure sleek rather than extravagant. He could probably just pick her up and put her in the saddle, but that might be skirting the bounds of what was respectable. Particularly with her in breeches, with no layers of skirts and petticoats to shield her body from his hands. There were fairly strict rules around touching unmarried women of the court other than for socially accepted reasons such as dancing or offering an arm or a hand up into a carriage. The rules only got stricter when it came to unmarried potential royal witches. Of course, out here there was no one to see if he touched her—but there was no point shocking her virgin sensibilities if he didn't have to.

He crouched and cupped his hands instead so she could use them as a substitute for a mounting block. She did so and gained the saddle with no difficulty, gathering the reins with a determined expression and no hint of discomfort.

Small but tough, he decided, and went over to mount his own horse.

❦

The best-laid plans often came to nothing though, and his plan was far from best laid. After three hours or so of riding, when they were once again in a stand of scrubby woods that covered a few square miles, his horse stumbled and then started to limp. On inspection, he discovered that it had managed to lose a shoe.

He cursed under his breath. They were going to have to keep going on foot. Well, Sophia could ride and he would lead his horse. He wasn't going to abandon the damned thing in the middle of the woods. Sophia's horse wasn't large enough to carry both of them, at least not for any length of time. If his memory served, there was a largish farm near where the road to the portal he wanted forked from one of the other main roads. They could leave the horses there and continue on.

They moved off again, but as they reached the edge of the woods, it started to rain. Heavy, soaking rain accompanied by a biting wind. Sophia started to shiver after about twenty minutes or so.

Dust of the goddess. There was no point continuing on if she was going to catch lung fever from being dragged through the rain.

So, new plan. Find shelter.

Another mile or so down the road, he spotted a stone structure in the distance. It was small and very basic. Four walls and a roof and what was revealed as they came closer to be a half-rotted wooden door. He wasn't sure if it was a shelter for humans or animals, but no one seemed to be using it currently, so it would have to do.

They halted in front of the hut. Cameron swung down from the saddle and peered through the rain. There was still no sign of any occupant, human or otherwise, so he opened the ruined door carefully. The room was empty of furniture, but there was a stone floor to go with the walls, even though it was damp in spots where the roof was letting in some of the rain.

There was a small stack of firewood tucked in one corner and a rudimentary hearth in another. Maybe it was a shepherd's shelter. The farmers in this part of the country ran both sheep and cattle. Even the odd goat. But whomever it belonged to, it didn't matter now. The hut would give them shelter and, if the wood would light, some warmth. Enough to stop them from freezing half to death in the rain.

He leaned back out the door and beckoned for Sophia to join him. Her dismount from the horse wasn't graceful, and she looked pale as she came into the hut.

He made a fire, then went back out to get their saddlebags, which held their other clothes. He told Sophie to change back into her dress, which would be dry at least, and occupy her for the time it took him to make sure the horses were secured in a good spot. When he came back in, she had done so and had wrapped her cloak around herself. She'd laid her breeches and the woolen jacket by the fire. She was still shivering but maybe not so hard.

Cam pulled off the jacket he'd bought at the market and put his uniform jacket back on. It was a bit warmer inside, but the building let the wind in somewhat. Dry clothes helped, but what they really needed was something hot to eat and drink. Whoever had left the firewood hadn't been kind enough to also leave a kettle or any cooking utensils, however, so he sliced bread and used a damp stick to toast it over the fire.

Sophia ate it in silence and looked better having done so, some of the color coming back to her face as she warmed up.

"Do you think the rain will last?" she asked.

"Hard to tell this time of year." Summers in Kingswell were mostly dry, but as the season went on, the counties in the middle and north of the country were prone to storms. Some of them bad. So far there hadn't been any thunder or lightning, but that didn't mean they weren't coming. The driving rain and wind were bad enough. "We'll stay here until it stops."

If that was much longer than another hour, they might as well spend the night. It would be starting to get dark, and by foot he wasn't sure they could reach the portal before it was full night.

Sophie pulled the cloak tighter around herself and stared at the fire. He wondered what she was thinking. Tomorrow was her birthday. If they'd been back in Kingswell, tonight she would have been having a feast with her family and then spending the night in the castle's shrine to await her fate in the morning.

"Are you warmer, milady?" The small fire was as hot as he could make it, but he couldn't risk building it up to be any larger.

"I think you should call me Sophie," she said. "Every time you say 'milady' like that, I start looking around for my mother. And we're hardly in the situation to stand on ceremony, are we?"

He smiled. "No. All right, then. Sophie. You don't like Sophia?" She was Lady Sophia at court though he had heard Eloisa's ladies calling her Sophie at times.

She shrugged. "There's nothing wrong with Sophia, but my family always called me Sophie. I'm named after my mother's mother, and she was still alive when I was little and living with us. I think they called me Sophie to make things less confusing. Lady Sophia still sounds odd to me."

Cam couldn't remember which family Sophie's mother came from, so he wasn't sure which Sophia was her grandmother. It was a common enough name amongst the court, and there had been several dowager Lady Sophias that he could think of who seemed to be about the right age. Not that it mattered. "Sophie it is, then. Which I guess means I'm Cameron."

"But 'lieutenant' sounds so dashing," Sophie said with a sudden grin. "That's what the princess's ladies call you. The dashing Lieutenant Mackenzie."

"Do they? Goddess, how appalling. All the more reason to call me Cameron."

"Better dashing than some of the names they call the other officers."

He held up a hand. "I think it's better if I don't know."

"Perhaps," she said. "But some of them are quite amusing."

"I'm sure they are. But I need to be able to look my brother officers in the eye."

"Ah, yes. Can't upset the dignity of the Red Guard," she said with another quick smile.

"We're supposed to be dignified; we're royal guards," he pointed out.

"I know," she said. "But don't you find the court a bit ... stifling at times? All that protocol and rules and having to find three servants and two page boys just to organize an impromptu afternoon tea "

"You don't like being at court?"

"Sometimes. I love the princess—she's been very kind to me—and there are so many things to do and see, but sometimes I'd just like to be home, where I can run around and do what I want and be with my family and not worry every other second whether my hem is one inch too long or if I'm going to say the wrong thing to someone."

"I can understand that," he said. "My family has spent part of the year at court all my life, so I'm more used to it, I suppose, but there are definitely moments when I'd just like to be home again." Particularly when his father had remained at court and there was no one bellowing at him and his brothers every few minutes that they weren't behaving as Mackenzies should.

Whatever that meant.

These days, however, being away from court would mean being away from Elly. Though perhaps that would be a good thing. There was no future in what they shared, so a separation would bring an ending of his folly.

Of course, right now he had no idea if there was even a court to return to. And if that were true, he really had no idea what to do next. He went to the door and peered out. Rain still streamed from the sky like someone had opened a sluice above them.

He turned back to Sophie. "I think we're here for the night."

Sophie looked up. "Tomorrow's my birthday."

"I know. We'll start early and get to the portal, and then we'll be all right."

"Are you going to tell me where we're going yet?"

There was little point keeping her in the dark. It seemed unlikely that anyone would stumble over them in this hut in the next twelve hours or so. "If all goes well, my brother's estate."

"Carnarvon?"

"Yes. Way up north. From there, if we need to, we have other options. But if we have to keep going, we need money and supplies, and Alec will give us those." Presuming that whoever had attacked the capital hadn't gone after any other members of the nobility. But Alec was second son. Liam was the eldest. He lived on the main estate. Alec's property was miles away from there, and the portal path there was a minor one. It was the safer option.

Sophie looked pensive.

"Don't worry. It may yet be good news. Now, build up that fire a little. I'm going to check on the horses."

CHAPTER FIVE

Sophie woke to the sound of Cameron stirring the fire. The air was cool—though not as bitterly cold as it had been overnight—and she curled deeper into her cloak for a moment before she forced herself to open her eyes.

How would she know if her power had manifested? She didn't think she felt any different. Should she feel different?

Cameron smiled at her. "Good morning. And happy birthday."

She thanked him and pushed to her feet, moving to the door. "Has it stopped raining?"

Gingerly, stiffness making the movement an exercise in discomfort, she pushed open the half-ruined door and peered outside. The sky was a deep, clear blue—a summery shade that belied the cold. No sign of the storm remained. Which meant they could keep moving. Maybe even get to go home to the court today. She stepped through the door. Then stopped with a jolt. Beyond the center of the little field where the hut stood, a line of sparkling light bisected the grass. It glittered: first gold, then silver, then some strange color that shimmered on the edge of sight. It was bright enough to hurt her eyes, and she lifted a hand to shield them. "What is that?" she asked.

Cameron looked over his shoulder at her. "What?"

She pointed to the line. "That."

He got up from his spot by the fire and joined her in the doorway. He frowned as he looked in the direction she pointed, and then his face cleared. "The ley line?"

"That's a ley line?" She moved her hand to take a better look, then froze again. "Great goddess, I can see the ley line."

"Happy birthday," Cameron said again. "I guess that answers one question."

"It's bright." She lifted a hand to shield her eyes against the dazzle. "No one ever said a ley line was so bright."

"Everyone sees them differently." He looked at her curiously. "What does it look like?"

"A line of light. Bright, sparkly light. What do you see?"

"Only a reddish shimmer. Not terribly bright. This isn't a major line."

Sophie squinted her eyes at the shimmering length. If this one wasn't a major line, then she wasn't sure she wanted to see a stronger one. The light was near blinding. And more than that, it called to her. She wanted to go over and roll around in the light, let it coat her skin and—

"Whoa, there," Cameron said, grabbing her arm.

Sophie started. She hadn't even noticed him move over to her. "What?" she said irritably. Then realized she was standing almost on top of the line. And had no knowledge of having moved.

"You don't know what you're doing."

"I just want to touch it."

"No."

"Why not?" She could feel the line tugging at her—warm and tempting. It felt good. What harm could it possibly do?

Cameron sighed and tugged her back a foot or so. "Try to remember your lessons. Too much power will

hurt you if you can't control it. You can't just step onto a
ley line if you don't know what you're doing."

She frowned and stretched her arm back toward the
line, feeling a tingle in her fingertips. Warmth flowed up
her arm, and she giggled, suddenly feeling like she'd had
too much summer wine. "I can do it." She didn't know
how she knew, but she was certain it was true. Stepping
onto the line wouldn't hurt her.

"Goddess save me from young witches," Cameron
muttered. He grabbed her hand and pulled her even farther away from the line, not stopping until they were
nearly back to the hut. She pulled against him, but it was
like trying to pull against one of the giant oaks in the
castle grounds.

"Stay here," he said when he stopped.

She tugged her hand free with a scowl. "I just want to
have a closer look."

"I don't think that's a good idea. We should get on our
way again. Get to the portal. If we get to Alec's and it's
good news, you could be home today. Still have a prior
oversee the first time you use your power, as it should be."

No. She wanted to know it now. Wanted to feel that
warmth around her. She stepped a little farther away
from the door and then darted toward the ley line.

Behind her, Cam shouted, and then she heard the
sound of him running, but it was too late. She reached
the line and stepped onto it.

Heat and light exploded through her. She'd never felt
anything like it before. Never imagined anything could
feel like this. It was like standing in the center of something immense and unknown, feeling it spin around her,
wanting to show her its secrets.

She stretched out her arms, tried to pull it closer. The
sensations grew stronger. Hotter. Brighter. She felt herself begin to tremble, felt the power bear down on her,
the weight of it burning.

And then Cameron's hand closed around hers, and he yanked her off the line. The sensation stopped so fast, it was almost like being blinded. She stumbled as her knees buckled.

"Goddess, what the hell did you think you were doing?" Cameron snarled in her ear. He sank to the ground, bringing her with him. His hand, still closed over hers, forced her palm flat against the damp earth. "Ground it, Sophie. Now."

"What—"

"Do what they taught you. Ground it."

She tried to remember. Something about opening. Visualizing the ley line power sinking into the earth. The world still spun around her, and she closed her eyes.

"Ground it," Cameron snarled. "Now."

She pictured the light, the color sparking behind her eyes. Then tried to grab that image and force it down into the earth. Something shivered through her and then pushed outward with the speed of a snake striking. She heard Cameron cry out, and then things went dark.

When she came back to herself, she was lying on the grass with Cameron leaning over her, looking frantic. Her head ached fiercely, and she shut her eyes again.

"Oh, no, you don't," he said. "You stay awake." He took her hand, tugged her upright so she was sitting, half propped, against him. "Do you hear me?"

Sophie shivered as his fingers closed around hers. It felt good. Tempting. Not like the ley line. Different. Something deep and powerful coiled within him, and she wanted to know more. She stared up at him. At eyes that were suddenly a fascinating shade of blue. She felt the pulse of power in him again and felt an answering curl, hot and hungry somehow, low in her belly.

She tightened her hand around his, the movement

feeling as natural as though she had touched him a thousand times before, and she thought she saw a glimmer of light pass through him, like he'd swallowed the ley line. His eyes turned a darker shade of blue, and then his mouth came down on hers, kissing her. Light exploded through her again. Burning and searing.

It washed over and through her, and she felt a click like coming home and sliding the key into the lock to open the front door. Meant to be. Natural.

She wrapped her arms around his neck and pulled him down, falling back, feeling the weight of him land on top of her with a surge of relief and desire that made her head spin. His mouth on hers was hot, and he tasted like heat and power, the combination addictive, so that she wanted to drink all of him. One of her legs curled itself up around his hip, and Cameron groaned against her mouth. His hand pushed her dress farther up, sliding up her bare leg and higher, her skin burning and aching with pleasure as though she'd stepped into the ley line again in the wake of his touch.

Everywhere his skin touched hers, the spark and heat and burn seemed to intensify. More than just the humming weight of the magic, this was darker and deeper. Sensation spiking and bursting and leaving trails of pleasure in its wake that made her feel half drugged.

Cameron made a harsh noise in his throat and pulled her closer as his fingers slipped between her legs.

Her knees fell apart without her thinking as he pressed against something that felt so good, she thought she might faint. But fainting would mean all this would stop. She didn't want it to stop.

She jerked her mouth free of his with a gasp and tugged at the neck of his shirt, wanting to touch him like he touched her.

His fingers stroked, pressed, then slid down and inside her, and she buried her face in the curve of his neck, mouth and teeth pressing against the strong line of muscle to stop from screaming. The taste of his skin, hot and male and salt sweat, different from anything she'd ever tasted before, was addictive, and she pressed her teeth harder.

Cameron swore and pulled her head back, mouth coming down on hers, demanding and drugging. Pulling her deeper and deeper into the spinning rush of sensation, further and further from any rational thought.

His fingers slid free of her, and she moaned a protest.

"Wait," he said fiercely before he kissed her again. Kissed her like he meant to brand the taste of his lips and the feel of his mouth on her forever. Somewhere far off she heard the swish of fabric as he pulled her skirt farther up and then another rustle before his hand was on her thigh, pressing her legs farther apart. Then she felt something hard and hot press against her, slide the length of her, hitting all those good places again before it nudged her entrance.

He paused a moment, and she tugged him closer, wrapping her legs around him and arching her hips by instinct so that he groaned and then pushed and slid inside her.

There was one bright burst of pain, but then it disintegrated against the sheer pleasure of the sensation of him deep inside her.

"Yes," she said. "Goddess, yes." She arched her hips again, and he began to move. Slow at first. Slow but not overly gentle. Each move strong and sure, burying himself deeper inside. And then not slow either. She caught the rhythm of it, the dance that it became. Retreat and advance and push and slide. All the time with those kisses stealing her breath and the humming pulse of the ley line burning through her, making her want more and more.

In the end it felt more like a war—or an annexation,

perhaps. A hard-fought alliance, each wild thrust a welcome attack, one she answered with her own offense until at last the thin edge of control snapped completely and she tumbled over into someplace beyond sensation. Where there was only the two of them and what they had become.

She lay back, trying to gather herself, basking in the pleasure still washing through her.

Until Cameron wrenched himself away from her with another muttered oath.

Her eyes snapped open, and she reached for him.

He lifted a hand to hold her off. "No!" He rolled to his feet and staggered back several paces, chest heaving as he fastened his breeches again with jerky movements.

He might as well have slapped her. The pain of his rejection was sharp and hot. But that didn't stop the overpowering need to go to him again. She scrambled to stand, pushing her skirts down as she did so. She stepped toward him, felt a twinge between her legs, hesitated, then moved again as the hunger for him rose again despite the other emotions twisting through her.

"No!" It was practically a shout, his face twisted with tension, and she halted. "Milady . . ." He hesitated, swallowed, softened his tone. "Sophie, please. Stay there."

"But—"

"But nothing, milady. That was wrong." He shook his head, face set.

"It didn't feel wrong." She watched him as she said the words, and the chagrin on his face made her think that he agreed with her. That he had liked it. Which was both satisfying and frustrating when he made no move to come any closer. But then he straightened his shoulders and his expression turned grim once more.

"Milady—"

"It's *Sophie*." They'd just—well, she wasn't sure what you called that. The romantic poetry the ladies favored spoke of things like the sweet delights of the marriage bed, her mother had used words like "marital relations," and there were coarser terms she wasn't supposed know. "Bedded." "Fucked." But this didn't feel like any of that. He'd been inside her. He'd been joined with her. He could at least use her name.

"I think we're safer sticking to 'milady' for now. Goddess, what we just did—"

She scowled at him. "It felt good."

"It was wrong. I should have—" He stopped, face twisting. "Milady, you just stepped straight onto a ley line without any preparation or knowing what you're doing. You might as well have just drunk a liter of Iska. Anything would feel good."

That struck her a particularly stupid thing to say. "I'm fairly certain that if I'd kissed one of the horses, it wouldn't have felt the same."

"No. It wouldn't. And this is my fault, not yours. I should have realized. Shouldn't have touched you when you were in that state."

"You didn't like it?" How could he have not liked it? She'd never felt anything better in her entire life.

"I did," he said.

"Then—"

"It was wrong of me." He looked almost . . . wretched. "The power caught us both. And I apologize. So please, milady. Can you just listen to me and trust me that I know what I'm saying? Magic takes some people this way. Particularly the first few times. It feels good. Makes you want to be reckless. Makes you think you can do anything."

"Maybe I can."

"No. You can't. You're a royal witch. And right now, for all we know, you could be the only surviving royal witch. You're supposed to be a virgin. Goddess. You cannot do—" He broke off, mouth twisting as if he didn't know what to say. "That," he continued eventually. "Have sex. With anybody. Except your husband."

His words were like cold water poured down her spine. Husband. She had power. She would be married. Soon. "It's not like anyone will ever know." Though she wasn't feeling so certain now. The haze of pleasure was retreating, and in its place a tide of confusion swarmed in. She'd had . . . sex with Cameron. It was as good a term as any, she supposed. She was no longer virgin. And an unmarried royal witch. If it was discovered, there would be hell to pay.

Cameron didn't look convinced either. "Are you sure of that? You'll excuse me for being blunt, milady, but you have power. Your value in court just went up immeasurably. You will be married. And nobles expect virgin brides."

Sophie stiffened. She knew what nobles expected. But she also knew that there was no easy way to tell if a girl was a virgin. Eloisa and her ladies talked frankly, filling in the gaps of her official teachings about marital duties. She knew that not all girls bled the first time. "My husband, whoever he may be, will be getting a royal witch for a bride. He is unlikely to make a fuss. Besides, the princess " She broke off, as Cameron's expression shut down even further at the word "princess." Something cold settled in her stomach. Why did he look like that? "Besides," she said, starting again, "it's likely the court has bigger issues than me right now. If we do not say anything, we won't be discovered."

"I hope you're right, milady," Cameron said. "And I apologize. Again. I should not have treated you that way."

She gaped at him. *Treated* her? That's what he was calling it. There was a hard, hot knot of humiliation forming in her belly. But she ignored it and the heat that wanted to flare in her cheeks. "I was hardly unwilling, Lieutenant," she said coldly.

"You were confused by the power."

"In which case, so were you, I presume, if you felt it in the same way I did. So if anyone is to blame, it is me. I'm the one who touched the ley line. I'm the one who will take any blame. I'm sorry that you found it . . . objectionable."

He swore then, or at least, she thought the rolling Carnarveine dialect syllables were curses. They sounded like curses.

"As I said, it wasn't objectionable, milady. But it was a mistake. One we can't repeat. So to be safe, you will not touch me again unless there is an immediate risk. Is that clear?"

It was perfectly clear from his tone. Clear that he had no desire to touch her again. That he wanted to be free of her. Probably couldn't wait to get her back to the capital and see her safely married before what they had shared could become a problem. He'd probably rather cut off his far-too-honorable hand than touch her again. Which sent another boiling surge of guilt and humiliation into her gut. Because she still wanted to touch him. "Yes, Lieutenant," she said. "You've made your point."

His hand curled at his side a moment, the knuckles stark white against the darker skin. "Good. Then I think we should be on our way. Go and change if your other clothes are dry. I'll get the horses ready."

❧

Cameron was careful not to touch Sophie skin to skin again as they made their way to the portal. His horse seemed to have lost the limp overnight, but he still made sure to take things a little more slowly than he would otherwise have liked. It was nearing midday when they neared the portal, and several times he'd had to block Sophie's path when she had turned toward a ley line.

She'd been flustered and apologetic each time it happened, but at the same time, he'd seen the hunger in her
eyes as he'd led her horse away from the temptation. The
same hunger he'd seen this morning when she'd looked
at him. The same hunger that had led to his utter . . . well,
he wasn't sure it was stupidity, because once that surge
of power had swept through them, it hadn't been a con-
scious decision on his part to—he shied away from the
thought of what he'd actually done. Gone and fucked a
virgin royal witch. On the ground. In the open. When
they were supposed to be running for their lives. Granted,
the mere fact that he'd laid hands on her   and more—
was the gravest part of his sin, but the way he'd let her
response to the power take him off guard was at best
carelessness.

It wasn't as though he'd been trained in how to handle
a royal witch on her twenty-first birthday. In the normal
fashion, by the time a royal witch who had manifested was
presented to the court, she had already been attended by
the temple and dedicated to the goddess. Which presumably gave her control of her power, because he'd never
been to a birthday celebration or heard of one that had
broken out into an orgy, despite the fact that several ley
lines ran through the foundations of the castle.

But he did know that the first taste of power could be
heady. He should have at least thought about the possibility that Sophie might have that sort of reaction. But
no. He'd been too busy trying to figure out what their
next moves must be to think it through properly. His old
squad commander would have had him serving night
duty in the coldest corner of the castle for months for
that sort of failure. The Red Guard were taught to think
of all the possibilities that might eventuate and then
think of some more.

He'd failed that particular charge last night. And
worse this morning.

He'd taken her. Or maybe she'd taken him. He didn't know exactly what had happened. But the outcome was the same regardless.

Still, there was nothing he could do to take back what had happened. His body tightened even remembering, and he wasn't entirely sure that he would take it back if he could. It had been . . . incredible. Overwhelming. He'd thought they might just both go up in flames, the fierceness of it and the leap of his power to answer hers even stronger than it was with Elly.

Goddess. Elly. They'd made no promises to each other about keeping chaste. She could make no promises to him, after all, besides temporary admittance to her bed, but he felt guilty all the same. Sophie—Lady Sophia, as he was trying to force himself to think of her—was one of her ladies and a protégée of a sort.

So he'd managed to royally fuck things up.

His hands tightened on the reins reflexively, and the horse tossed his head, sidling a few steps sideways toward the edge of the narrow track. Cameron loosened his grip and pressed with his leg to guide the beast back to the center of the path. The last thing he needed was for the fool creature to go lame again.

Twisting in the saddle, he checked on Lady Sophia, following behind him. She looked down when their eyes met, mouth flat, and Cameron bit down a curse as he turned back. Now she couldn't even look at him. Royally fucked up didn't begin to describe the situation. And if he felt this way, he could hardly imagine how she must have felt. After all, she was the one who'd been, um, deflowered in a fairly unusual fashion. He'd never actually slept with a virgin before, but he imagined there were better ways to introduce women to lovemaking than the frantic coupling they'd shared. She was giving no sign of discomfort—at least no more than she had previously—and she'd claimed, when he'd inquired, that he hadn't hurt her, but he couldn't imagine that was true. And now he was making her ride miles and miles on a horse.

No wonder she couldn't look at him. She probably thought him the biggest bastard in the kingdom right about now. But if that were true, then he was just going to have to live with it. Her safety—and his—took precedence over a few physical aches and pains. She could at least bathe when they got to Alec's holdings and, if luck decided to be in their favor for once, Alec might be able to summon a temple prior or devout to perform whatever could be performed in the way of Ais-Seann rites for her. Even if it wasn't the full panoply of whatever ceremonies royal witches underwent, there must be something that could be done to at least help her manage her power—for it was evident that she had plenty of that—a little more easily.

His horse snorted and tossed his head again, and Cameron realized that they'd come to the fork in the path he'd been looking for. If his mental map of the area—memory for such things a gift of his blood magic—was right, there was a small clearing a few hundred feet up the right-hand path. There was a stream there, and they could leave the horses and then come back and take the other fork. The one to the portal. Either someone would come across the horses, or, perhaps, Alec would be able to spare someone to come back and collect them and take them to the nearest small town to be sold.

He turned back to Sophie and pointed to the right-hand path. She nodded and then fixed her gaze where he'd pointed, deliberately not meeting his eyes again. Cameron sighed and turned back to the job at hand.

❧

Two hours later, they emerged from the portal on Alec's land, having taken another two quick stops on the way to help confuse any followers. Sophie was slightly green in the face again, her expression set as she followed him out of the portal and onto the road that led up to the house.

"Do you need water?" he asked.

She shook her head. "How far is it?"

"Not far. Maybe fifteen minutes' walk." At least she hadn't thrown up at each portal this time. Maybe her magic was shielding her a little from the effects of the transfer.

She nodded and hitched the saddlebag that held her gown and cloak higher on her shoulder.

Cameron took that to mean that he should get on with things. He gestured toward the road and started walking, still keeping a safe distance between them now that he didn't have to touch her for the portal transit. Each time he touched her, it became harder to move away again, his senses drawn to her in the same way she was drawn to the ley lines they passed. At least the only ley line here at Alec's was a minor one, and it looped around the other side of the portal and in a different direction to the road, so he wouldn't need to shepherd Sophie away from temptation. No, all he had to do was shepherd himself. Even now he wanted to turn and look at her. Not to make sure that she was following—he could hear well enough the crunch of her footsteps on the gravel road—but just to watch her.

He didn't like it, this growing urge to be near her. He hoped it was just some strange effect of her newborn power spilling out onto him rather than something more tangled than that born of their ill-advised activities of the morning.

It wasn't as though she had suddenly become beautiful overnight. Magic didn't work that way. Royal witches could work small spells to make themselves more attractive, but true glamour and illusion was more the province of practitioners of the Arts of Air, and there was no reason why Sophie would have had any training in those.

So anything he saw in her now had been there, still the

same brown eyes and dark hair and slim build. So why the pull?

Because he had no explanation, he was determined to ignore it. So he kept walking, the weight of the saddle-bags he carried with the remains of the food he'd bought and his uniform pulling at his shoulder. They weren't particularly heavy, but he was growing tired after two days' travel and portal hopping and sleeping out in the open. He was reaching the limits of how far the power of fear and worry could drive him without more sleep and a few meals containing food more substantial than half-burned fish, day-old cheap bread, and cheese and ham. Lucy, Alec's wife, was a good cook, so unless the house was in an uproar due to the problems in the capital, that problem should be solved sooner rather than later. Sleep would have to wait until he knew what was happening and what their next steps would be.

They reached the bend in the road that brought them into view of the house, and his heart eased a little at the sight of the sturdy structure, the green veins of the local granite that formed its walls—the same prized granite that had been carted the length of the country to build the palace at Kingswell two centuries ago—shining in the sun. Before his father's father had died, when Cameron had been just short of five years old, they had lived here at the northern holdings for a year or so when the main house at Loch Kenzie had undergone some much-needed renovations. It had been the freest time in Cameron's life, and he and his brothers had been left to run much wilder than they had been before.

In a way, he envied Alec for getting to live here now, with all those pleasant memories and tucked away from his father's immediate line of sight. "Almost there, mi-lady," he said, turning back to Sophie. From the direction of the house, a storm of barking started up. Alec's hounds had noticed them even if no one else had yet.

The dogs came bounding down the road as they came closer to the house, their warning barks changing to something more friendly as Ludo, the largest of the pack, recognized Cameron and loped over to try to lick him to death. Cameron told him to get down with a stern "Off." Ludo complied but only as far as to stop licking and sit at his feet, leaning his not inconsiderable weight against Cam's leg.

To his right, Sophie was ringed by the other five dogs, two more banehounds like Ludo, large and shaggy beasts of red-and-black fur, who came up past her waist and were butting their heads against her for pats whilst the other three—two quicksilver white-and-gray herders and Lucy's aging small brown curly dog, Bit, whose parentage had never been fully distinguished, darted around her legs. She was smiling and patting and talking softly to all of them, seemingly not bothered by so many dogs at once. But, then, she'd grown up on a small estate, too. She would be used to animals.

She looked beautiful with the smile lighting her face and chasing away the tension. Like she had earlier when he —

No. He wasn't going to think that. Wasn't going to watch her. It only made his hands tingle with an oddly strong urge to touch her.

Ludo barked then, a soft greeting *whuff* of welcome that Cameron recognized. He turned his gaze from Sophie and saw Alec had emerged from the house and was walking toward them. His brother was dressed in head-to-toe black.

CHAPTER SIX

❧

Sophie saw the smile on Cameron's face die and turned to see what he was looking at. A man dressed all in black was walking toward them. From the height and the dark hair and the clearly Mackenzie angles of jaw and cheeks, Sophie gathered this was Cameron's brother Alec.

Dressed in mourning clothes.

For whom, exactly?

The pleasure she'd felt in the wagging tails and soft fur of the dogs surrounding her drained away in an instant, replaced by the return of the sick gray worry that had become so familiar in the last two days.

"Who?" Cameron demanded as Alec reached them.

Alec put his hand on Cameron's arm. "Come inside, little brother."

"Who?" Cameron repeated.

Alec shook his head and then slanted his gaze at Sophie. "You'll be Lady Sophia, then, milady?"

She nodded, not trusting herself to be able to answer without also asking who.

Relief flashed over Alec's face, and he gestured back at the house. "There was word from the capital that you would likely be with my brother, milady. Please come inside."

Sophie was worried that Cameron was going to come to blows with his brother by the time they were seated inside in what would have been a comfortably cozy parlor if it were not for the tension filling the air. She suspected the only thing stopping Cam was the presence of Alec's wife, Lucy, a tiny woman who had come armed with a baby strategically placed on her hip.

"Who is—" Cameron demanded again, and Lucy shook her head.

"Not yet," Lucy said decisively. "You need something to eat and drink. There won't be much—" She cut off the words, shook her head. "You can wait a few more minutes."

Won't be much what? Time? Sophie didn't like the sound of that. She felt the urge to go to Cameron, to touch him for reassurance, but that would hardly be wise. He had been clear that there wasn't to be a repeat of the morning.

She bit her lip, tried not to watch the muscles clenching and unclenching in Cameron's jaw and neck as he tried to stay silent.

Food and tea appeared as Lucy busied herself making sure Sophie was comfortable. Sophie sipped the hot tea gratefully, but she wasn't sure that her stomach would deal with food just now. Not until she had heard the news.

"Enough," Cameron said abruptly. Lucy gave him a sidelong glance, but she didn't say anything.

Cameron turned to Alec. "Tell us. What's happened? Who is the black for? What's happening in Kingswell?"

Alec's face was bleak. "I assume, because you're both here, that you know about the attack."

"We were in Kingswell when it started," Cameron said. "But out of the palace. So we left." His shoulders squared a little, as though he was bracing himself for criticism, but Alec just nodded.

"Well, that was wise. There was a lot of damage."

"We saw the explosion," Cameron said. "We know there's damage. I don't care about the palace. What about the people?"

"Long live the queen-to-be," Alec said.

Sophie heard the words, but it took a moment for them to make any sense. When her brain finally assigned them a meaning, the breath left her body in a rush, like she'd fallen and winded herself.

"The king is dead?" Cameron asked. "Eloisa is queen?"

"She will be, once she can be crowned," Alec said. "The queen-to-be was hurt, but she is recovering."

"Hurt how?" Cameron demanded, a little too fiercely. Something twisted in Sophie's stomach. Cameron was one of Elly's bodyguards, but there was something in his tone that sounded . . . more.

"There were no details in the message that came. Just that the Red Guard has control of the palace once more and to send you and Lady Sophia back if you should turn up."

"And Margaretta?" Sophie asked.

"She is alive," Alec said. "The message said that much."

Well, that was a relief. It meant that Eloisa had an heir for now. Which would buy Eloisa some time to marry and beget some more direct heirs.

Cameron took a breath. "What else did the message say? Do they know who is behind the attack?"

"No. Nothing on that yet. But—" Alec looked down, his hands braced on his knees a moment, shoulders sagging forward. Sophie's throat went tight and hot as he looked back, pain clear on his face.

"I regret to tell you, Cameron," he said, "that our father is dead."

❦

When they emerged in the portal outside the gates of the palace, Cameron let go of Sophie's arm so fast that she nearly stumbled. She caught herself on the wall of the small room, her fingers pressing against the smooth plaster for a moment, as she fought down the ridiculous feeling of rejection that mingled with the faint nauseous sensation of the portal transfer.

For a minute or so—the length of their journey back from the portal in Alec's house—Cameron had actually been close to her again, and she had felt something other than the fear and grief that had swept down over her with each name Alec had recited on the list of the dead.

Her parents hadn't been amongst the names, which made her feel first glad and then guilty as it became clear that Cameron's father was only the first of what seemed like the names of half the court.

Cameron had gone stone-faced and silent ever since Alec had given them the news of Lord Inglewood's death. He had listened to the rest of the list impassively and merely nodded when Alec had told them that they were ordered back to the palace.

Lucy had hustled Sophie off to wash and restore some order to her appearance. She'd found a black silk shawl for Sophie to wear over her sober gray dress, and that would have to do until proper mourning clothes could be found.

Presumably a court in disarray would have better things to do than worry about the finer points of etiquette. Sophie didn't really know what to say to Lucy, who had just lost her father-in-law and was presumably dealing with a grieving husband and family on top of other losses. Sophie didn't even know who Lucy's family was. Alec was Lord Inglewood's second son, so it was almost certain that Lucy was from the noble families.

But Alec was five years older than Cameron and Lucy was also older than Sophie. She didn't recall ever having seen the pair of them at court in the year she'd been attending the princess.

So she'd merely thanked Lucy for her care and then followed Alec and Cam obediently back to the portal gate. She was surprised that an out-of-the-way portal had a direct link back to the capital, but she was glad that it did.

She wanted to be back in Kingswell. To be at Eloisa's side. To find out where her parents were and confirm that they were safe.

So when Cameron had taken her hand and tucked her in close to his side, she'd been startled by the rush of longing that had swept through her. Not just to touch him but to stay here with him. Suspended in the moment before they had to actually begin to deal with this dangerous new reality.

There were two Red Guards outside the Kingswell portal—which was not normal but made sense, she supposed.

When she and Cameron first emerged, the guards had drawn their weapons but relaxed as they recognized Cameron. And then her, it seemed.

Because the sight of her made them both come to attention and then bow in her direction.

"Lady Sophia," the taller of the two, a dark-haired man with deep shadows under his eyes, said. "We have orders to take you to the palace." He turned to Cameron. "You should report to the commander, Lieutenant."

Cameron shook his head. "I will. But the prin—the queen-to-be charged me with Lady Sophia's care. Until the queen-to-be tells me otherwise, Lady Sophia remains with me. I'll escort her to the palace."

The guard looked annoyed, but he didn't argue. Red Guards couldn't countermand an order from the royal family.

"Report as quickly as you can," the guard said. "We need all the men we can gather."

Cameron nodded. "I will. Come along, milady."

He didn't look back at Sophie, and she felt another pang, but she followed him to the palace, trying not to wander off toward the shining ley line that ran alongside the neatly paved path they took. She still felt the pull of the power—the ley line here was so bright she could hardly look at it—but it was strangely diluted now by the pull toward Cameron.

"Did Alec tell you anything more about what's been happening?" she asked. She assumed Cameron had grilled Alec for further information when she'd been with Lucy. There might have been things in the message that were for Cameron only. She'd asked Lucy, but Lucy had claimed not to know anything more. Sophie hadn't wanted to press her further, not knowing who amongst the list of casualties might be Lucy's family. "Anything more about who did this?"

Cameron turned his head to her, slowed his pace a little. But kept walking. "Nothing more than it being unclear. Illvyans. Or those who act for them, presumably. There have been no other sources of unrest lately."

Illvyans.

She'd assumed as much, but still, it was unsettling to hear the words spoken. There hadn't been a serious attempt on Anglion by Illvya for close to ten years. The seas that surrounded Anglion meant the Illvyan wizards couldn't bring their demons across the salt water. The last attempt had been an attack on a trade delegation in an effort to substitute a wizard into their ranks. But to set off an explosion in the palace itself? That was unthinkable. How had they breached the—

They came around the bend in the path that brought the palace into view. Or what remained of it. The ley line ended in a pile of rubble where part of the outer wall had once stood.

In the bright sunlight she could see only three towers. Three, not five. And those that remained were the smaller rear towers. The narrow spikes of the Salt Spire and the Sea Roost flanked the larger south tower. The east and west towers that guarded the front of the palace at either end of the northern wall were jagged wrecks instead of the massive gray columns they had been. She stopped, hand on her mouth, as her stomach churned. So much damage—how many must have died?

Pale silver light flickered over the stones and filled the gaps in the walls. Wards, she realized. She could see the wards now. The shock of that didn't make her feel any better. The eastern wall seemed mostly intact, and from their current position they couldn't see the western wall, though the west tower itself was nothing but rubble. The east tower was a wreck, too, but more of it still stood.

Cameron halted a few paces in front of her. He stared in the same direction as she was, his shoulders set. Then he turned back. "It will be all right, milady. Come along."

The words didn't ring any truer than his denial of her had.

⬦⬦⬦

Cameron wasn't sure where exactly he was taking Sophie. With so much damage to the palace, he had no idea where Elly—no, where the *queen-to-be*—might be found. His mind kept shying away from looking at the ruined west tower where his father had been with King Stefan at the time of the attack.

The Salt Hall, used for audiences with the monarch, was in the western wing of the palace. So it could be in ruins like the tower. Eloisa's personal apartments, which she had moved into when she returned from her late

husband's estates after his death, were in the east wing.
A break with tradition for her not to be with the royal
family, but her father had given in to her at the time.
Luckily, they weren't near the east tower or she might be
dead, too. The question was whether Eloisa had stayed
in her own apartments or moved into the rooms—if they
were undamaged—usually occupied by the king or queen.
There was no way to know. But they would find out when
they reached the palace.

He was aware of Sophie walking behind him, her silent presence like a tingle of awareness on his back. And
he didn't think the fact that he knew where she was when
he couldn't see her was entirely due to his guilty con-
science. He didn't know what it was due to, though, and
the sooner he could hand her back to the court and the
temple to go through her birthday rites, which should see
her safely back on whatever path had been decided for
her, the better.

Oh, really? The voice in his head was scornful.

He tried to ignore it. They reached the northern gates
of the palace. The huge gate looked odd standing as it
did in an undamaged section of wall. The wards shimmering around the broken towers themselves made it
perfectly clear that the gate could do little to keep out
anyone who found a way to break the wards. He knew
from his training that the palace had been built so that
the walls themselves could stand without the towers, but
he'd never thought he'd see that fact demonstrated in
real life. The guards let them through with little bluster
after their initial challenge. They recognized Cameron
and Sophie. In fact, the sergeant in charge of the squad
sent for one of the house pages to escort them immediately to the queen-to-be.

The girl appeared within two minutes. Dark circles
under her eyes and the wrinkled state of her livery at-
tested to the current state of disarray of the palace.

But she bobbed a quick curtsy and led them back through the corridors toward Eloisa's personal chambers. The corridors were eerily silent as they moved. No sounds of the usual music or laughing voices. The few people they passed were grim-faced and silent, only one or two sparing them a curious glance. Lord Sylvain stopped to express his sympathy on the erl's death with a few gruff words and an invitation for Cameron to dine with him if he needed a meal. Cameron nodded politely in response, but he expected to barely have time to sleep over the coming days, let alone take leisurely meals. If indeed he got to sleep at all in the next few days. More likely he'd be drinking the vile redwort tisane that the Red Guard got from the temple to use in times when they needed to go without sleep.

The stuff tasted like drinking death itself, but it worked, even if it left you wishing you were dead when it finally wore off.

A full half squad of six guards stood outside the doors to the queen-to-be's apartments.

Too little, too late, Cameron thought, and waited to be admitted. He'd braced himself for a repeat of the challenge at the gates—for him to be ordered away—but instead the guards gave way and opened the doors.

The outer chamber—the one he'd last been in when Elly had ordered him to take Sophie to Portsholme only, what . . . ? three days ago . . . was occupied by several of Eloisa's ladies-in-waiting. Black silk and velvet covered them from neck to toes, layers and frills of unrelenting darkness presenting a picture even more somber than the dull colors they had previously confined themselves to in deference to Eloisa's unfinished mourning year. Several of them had very red eyes even under the layers of cosmetics smoothing their faces into some semblance of normality. He was not the only one to have suffered a loss.

His mind shied away from the thought and the complicated brew of grief and guilt and relief that was tightening his throat and burning his stomach. He had no time for such things. Not yet. Time enough for grief when he had Iska and his brothers and no pull of duty binding him to put his own concerns aside.

That wasn't likely to be for quite some time, either.

The ladies started exclaiming when they saw Sophie behind Cameron, giving something of the impression of a flock of crows come to life, but he ignored them.

"We need to see the queen-to-be," he said bluntly.

Lady Beata, the most senior of Eloisa's band of ladies, stepped forward and frowned. "The Domina is with her now."

"I'm sure the Domina will be pleased to see Lady Sophia returned to Kingswell. After all, today is her Ais-Seann."

Lady Beata's mouth flew open; then her bejeweled hand flew up to cover it. The jet and pearl and onyx rings glittered darkly in the lamplight. "I had forgotten." Her eyes—an unusual dark brown nearly as black as the rings that had won her many admirers in the court—narrowed at Sophie. "Sophie, did you develop—"

"That is a matter for the Domina and the queen-to-be," Cameron said. "Will you let us pass?"

❧

The queen-to-be's bedchamber was darker than Sophie was used to, the velvet curtains drawn, the light coming from flickering candles and small oil lamps. Normally there would be earth-light globes brightening the dimness to supplement the candles, but with so many injured, presumably none of the temple priors and devouts, nor the royal witches, were wasting power on such things.

The lighting was brightest around the bed itself,

though there were too many people surrounding the bed
for Sophie to be able to see Eloisa herself. She could
make out the figure of Domina Skey, purely because she
was dressed in deep earth-brown temple robes, red hair
coiled around her head as she bent over the bed. Everyone else in the room wore black.

Cameron approached the bed, and the Domina looked
up. And then right past him, directly at Sophie.

"Lady Sophia," she said, surprise lighting her face as
she straightened. Then her golden brown eyes widened.
"You manifested, I see."

There was little to say to that. Sophie could see a glow
around the Domina and a fainter version of that same
light surrounding those of Eloisa's ladies who had some
power. She assumed the Domina could see the same coming from her, even if she hadn't noticed anything herself.
Maybe you couldn't see your own power. She nodded politely. "Yes, Lady Domina."

"Then we don't have time to lose," the Domina said.
She passed the glass bottle she held to the nearest lady-
in-waiting.

"Sophie?" A weak voice came from behind the Domina. Weak but unmistakably Eloisa's. Sophie pushed
forward so that she could see the princess. She reached
the edge of the bed in a rush, almost shouldering the last
of the ladies-in-waiting who stood in her way aside to
reach the inner circle nearest the bed.

"I'm here, Your Highness," Sophie said, then bit her
lip, realizing she'd gotten the title wrong. But right now
her brain refused to provide the correct title for a queen
who hadn't been crowned. She was too busy trying not
to stare at Eloisa herself.

Half the princess's head was swathed in bandages, and
any skin that remained uncovered was bruised and swollen, livid purples and angry reds marring the pale flesh.
Eloisa's arms, which were the only part of her on view

below her neck, due to the sheets covering her, were also bandaged down to the fingertips.

What had happened to her? The injuries were obviously severe if she still looked so bad after being attended by the Domina. Domina Skey held her position by way of being the strongest of the temple witches. She was also the most skilled healer in the country. And yet the princess looked like she had been freshly beaten.

"Sophie," the princess said again, and one side of her mouth lifted slightly, or Sophie thought it did. It was hard to tell with the swelling distorting Eloisa's lips.

"Lady Sophia needs to come with me to the temple," Domina Skey said firmly. "And you need to rest, milady."

"Lady Sophia is in my charge," Cameron interjected.

The Domina looked at him as though she'd only just noticed he was there. And wasn't well pleased to discover his presence. "And you have fulfilled your charge, Lieutenant. The lady will be safe with me."

Cameron's face twisted as though he wanted to argue.

"Let her go," Eloisa said. Cameron turned to the bed, and Sophie saw his face drop into its stony mask as he studied Eloisa. From which Sophie inferred that he was as horrified as she had been by Eloisa's injuries. He seemed to have forgotten anyone else was in the room as he stared down at her.

The Domina took advantage of his inattention and beckoned to Sophie. "Come. There are things to be done."

CHAPTER SEVEN

The Domina whisked Sophie through the palace halls
out to one of the stable yards. On the way, they'd
collected a squad of Red Guard, who'd jumped to do the
Domina's bidding when she barked a command to accompany them. The speed at which they did so made Sophie wonder just who was in charge of the palace with
Eloisa recuperating.

Time enough to worry about that. Right now she had
bigger things on her plate. Like the forthcoming Ais-
Seann rites. She turned back to the palace, looking the
way they'd come just before the Domina hustled her into
the waiting carriage. As the door closed behind her, Sophie realized that she'd been hoping to see Cameron
coming after her.

But no. Apparently that had been foolish. Cameron
was staying with his queen-to-be. She'd tried to tell herself that it was his duty to do so, but she couldn't help
feeling somewhat bereft. She'd grown used to his presence these last few days, and then there was the inconve-
nient thing that had sparked to life between them with
the ley line and the . . . No, she wasn't going to think that
particular thing when she was rattling slowly over Kingswell's cobbled roads in a carriage whose only other occupant was the Domina of all of Anglion.

Temple witches, like royal witches, served the goddess and used earth magic. Traditionally, the royal witches were said to have more power and more obvious influence, but there were always rumors that the temple witches kept a few tricks up their sleeves.

So no. No thinking about the sex she shouldn't have had and the man she shouldn't have had it with. She was going to sit here like a good royal virgin and try to remember all those things that Captain Turner and the temple devout who'd taught her had said.

"Nervous, milady?" the Domina said. Her voice was deep for a woman, and rich. It seemed overloud in the small carriage, maybe because the Domina was used to speaking in the vast space of the Grand Temple.

Sophie jumped and then tried to pretend she hadn't just reacted like a guilty child. "A little," she admitted. "The last few days have been so . . . so unusual, I confess that I hadn't time to think about the rites."

"When did you know you'd manifested?"

"As soon as I woke up," Sophie said. "I went outside and then I saw the ley line—so bright—and Cam—the lieutenant—told me what it was."

The Domina cocked her head, and a glint of light through the window caught her hair turning the color to a deep bloodred. "And how did the ley line look to you?"

"Like a river of light," Sophie said in a rush. "So beautiful—" She stopped as the Domina's brows drew together slightly. "Is that wrong?"

"No." A head shake produced more glints of red. "Each sees the power of the goddess in her own way."

Sophie took a breath and tamped down her enthusiasm. Reminded herself that the city was in turmoil right now and that she had no idea whom she could trust. An hour ago she would have said Cameron, but he had abandoned her without a backward glance. And now the Domina was commanding Red Guards and taking Sophie out of the palace again. She snuck a glance out the window. They were on the right road to the temple. In fact, she could see the faded blue-green of the massive bronze dome that topped its roof from where she sat.

Stop being paranoid.

"Anyway, that's what I saw. And Lieutenant Mackenzie brought me back here as soon as he could, once we knew."

"Let us hope it was soon enough," the Domina said.

What did that mean? Sophie's stomach turned a little, a greasy roll and slide that made her wish she wasn't in the swaying carriage. Fortunately, the Domina didn't ask her any more questions in the short time it took them to reach the temple.

⟨∞⟩

The Red Guard escorted them to the temple door but stopped there. The Ais-Seann rites of a royal witch were not for men, even though other rites of the goddess and the weekly worship were.

Sophie blinked as the door clicked shut behind her. The temple was dim after the bright sunshine outside, and she couldn't see immediately. But as she breathed in the familiar scent of sage and salt grass and spices in the temple incense and the unique smell of the temple fires, she felt herself relax. This was familiar. This was routine and ritual and safety.

Less familiar was the humming beneath her feet, the sudden rush of the same enticing sensation she'd felt in the ley line. She couldn't see the ley lines there—they ran beneath the temple—but she could feel them, rivers of possibility running through the earth below. The temple sat where the three major ley lines that passed through Kingswell converged. But no one had ever explained to her exactly what a convergence of ley lines felt like.

She wondered how any royal witch ever sat still

through a temple service. The power made her skin itch and tingle, and she suddenly wanted to run or dance. Simply move for the satisfaction of muscle and bone moving and blood pumping and air flowing through her lungs.

And she felt a sudden piercing throb of longing for Cameron.

She clamped down on all of it. She could only imagine the Domina's face if she suddenly ran down the aisle toward the altar. And she trembled to imagine what the same face would look like if she had any inkling of what Sophie felt toward Cameron Mackenzie. Or what she'd done with him.

Her eyes began to clear, and she followed the Domina down the central aisle to the altar, where the earth fire burned eternal—the flames from the saltwater-soaked logs flickering orange and green and blue.

This much was familiar, and she pricked her finger on the blade that the Domina offered and squeezed a drop of blood onto one of the small bundles of salt grass piled in the offering basket. Sophie tossed the offering into the fire as she recited the prayer for protection she'd been saying since she was old enough to speak. The flame flared brighter, and the grass disintegrated into flaring ash. She bowed to the fire and dipped her finger in the salt water in the silver dish at the base of the altar, for once not minding the tiny sting of salt in the knife prick.

When she straightened, the Domina's expression was almost approving, and the sick feeling in Sophie's stomach eased. Sometimes the salt grass didn't catch immediately or was sucked up out of the flames and out of the temple via the vent in the roof immediately above the altar. The latter was counted as an omen of ill luck and the former only slightly less so. So it seemed, at least for now, the goddess hadn't turned her back on Sophie.

They left the main temple, the Domina's fast walk

looking like a glide, her brown skirts skimming along the marble floor. She led Sophie out past the second altar with the statue of the goddess and through a carved wooden door that Sophie hadn't even been aware existed.

She put a hand up to her hair, nervous. Wondering if it looked any redder yet. It was too early, of course, but she couldn't help the thought.

"This way," the Domina said, and led her through another door and a cool, sunlit hall ending in another door. The Domina produced a key, and the door creaked open. A cloud of steam wafted through the opening, the scent of it salty and green, like standing by the ocean in a field of herbs.

"The salt baths," the Domina said, ushering Sophie in. "Undress. I'll find a devout to attend you."

She turned and pulled the door shut as she left, leaving Sophie alone.

The room wasn't as hot as the steam suggested. The bath, a massive, sunken square pool lined with green marble, shimmered darkly in the light from the lamps hanging above. No windows in this room. No chance for anyone to spy on the witches bathing here. Earth-lights glowed dimly at each of its four corners. Steam rose in wisps above the water, and the marble shone wetly.

Sophie untied her boots and eased off her stockings awkwardly. A shock ran through her when her bare feet touched the marble, the humming power from the ley lines even stronger still. She curled her hands into a ball, fought the urge to strip all her clothes off and lie on the marble, to get closer to that power.

She was reaching for the button at the neck of her gray dress when the door creaked open behind her again. Turning, she saw a temple devout wearing green-and-white robes, red hair loose over her shoulders. The shade was still more auburn than true red like the Domina's and Eloisa's. A newer witch then. The devout had something white draped over her arm, and she nodded politely at Sophie. "Milady."

Sophie curtsied.

The devout helped Sophie out of her clothes, unbound her hair, and sent her into the pool.

Sophie had been schooled in this part of the ritual. She submerged herself fully, letting the hot, salty water wash over her. It felt so sinfully good against muscles still aching from the travel of the last three days that she was tempted to lie back and float and let the heat soak the weariness from her bones entirely.

But doubtless the efficient devout would just wade in and drag her out if she took too long, so she surfaced, sluiced the water from her face, and then moved through the chest-deep water to repeat the process at each of the four corners of the pool. In each place, she silently recited a plea to the goddess to preserve her power and her life.

The whole thing took barely a few minutes, and then she was climbing up the slick marble stairs to exit the pool. Normally, there would have been several devouts attending her and, Sophie presumed, the whole thing might have been a little more leisurely.

But if there was no power to spare for the earth-lights in the palace due to the need to tend to the injured, then, doubtless, there were few devouts to attend to the ritual of a minor royal witch.

Sophie was glad of it, actually. She wanted to get back to the palace. Back to Eloisa.

Back to Cameron?

No. There was no "back to Cameron." He had delivered her home and washed his hands of her. She was a royal witch. She would be married to whomever the king—no, whomever *Eloisa*—decided she should be married to.

All thoughts of Cameron needed to be ignored. Forgotten. Burned and sent to dissolve to ash and float away like the bundle of salt grass in the temple.

Oblivious to these thoughts, the devout patted Sophie dry with a linen towel and then rubbed her down briskly with scented oil. The smell of cedar and salt grass mingled with something headier. Sophie breathed it in, trying to bring her mind back to the ritual.

A comb was coaxed through her hair, leaving it still dripping but at least pulled back from her face, the wet length of it falling halfway down her back. More oil was smoothed through it, the smell even stronger, making Sophie vaguely sleepy as the scent curled around her, filling her nose and her senses. The devout retrieved the robe from the hook and helped Sophie into it.

The robe, little more than a long cotton shift, stuck in places to her oiled skin, outlining her breasts and legs in a way that would be considered indecent back at the palace. But there was no one in the temple other than women to see her, so she made no effort to twitch the fabric away as she followed the devout out of the room and through another series of turns and corridors until they came to the small chapel of the goddess at the far end of the complex.

Rectangular in shape, the chapel's walls were pure white and the floor was marble so dark a green as to be nearly black. Inside, the Domina stood waiting before an altar where another small fire burned. Sophie's feet tingled even more strongly as she approached, the sensation making her catch her breath. Two devouts stood on either side of the Domina, each holding a silver platter covered with white linen. Both of them watched Sophie, eyes curious despite their grave expressions.

Waiting to see if she was truly a royal witch?

Heat suddenly swept over her skin, chasing the chill caused by walking in damp clothing through stone halls away. Sophie made herself focus on the Domina, made herself keep walking though the tingling and the heat and the odd smell of the oil were combining to make her head spin a little.

The Domina held a small globe of pale green stone in her hands. An unlit earth-light. The ritual of dedication was fairly simple. Sophie had to approach the Domina, use her power to light the earth-light to prove that she had manifested—though why that part was necessary when the Domina had been able to tell just by looking at her was unclear—and then the Domina would perform the actual dedication. Which was the part that no one spoke of.

But it couldn't be too terrible. After all, all the royal witches before her had survived it. Still, nerves bloomed anew in her stomach as she took one last step and halted in front of the Domina. The anxiety, combined with the faint dizziness, made Sophie feel ill. She swallowed and waited, head bowed as she had been taught.

"Sophia Elizabeth Constance Kendall. You are a child of the royal line. Do you come here today to be anointed to the goddess? To pledge your power to serve her and the kingdom for all your days?"

For the briefest of moments, as the dizzying sensation in her head increased, she wondered if anybody had ever answered no to that question. Then sanity prevailed and she said, "Yes."

"Then show your power to the goddess."

Sophie placed her right hand on the earth-light, every lesson Captain Turner had ever given her tumbling through her head and slipping away. Then she remembered. She felt the humming beneath her feet. That was the ley line. She was supposed to draw power from around her, send it into the globe, then send the excess back to the earth. The way she had with Cameron. Though she had no idea how she'd drawn the power then. Still, all she could do was try.

Focusing on the buzzing on her skin, she closed her eyes,

tried to draw the sensation deeper within her. One breath, then another as the feelings intensified until she thought the humming might shake her apart. Then she opened her eyes and let go.

The earth-light flared into white brilliance, dazzling her, and then cracked into pieces with a noise like a hammer blow.

The Domina's eyebrows flew upward, but she merely nodded as Sophie stared at the two halves of the globe now lying in the Domina's hands, biting her lip, wondering what exactly she'd done. Earth-lights did break sometimes. Perhaps it was not that unusual.

The Domina passed the broken globe to the devout standing behind Sophie. The devout stationed to the Domina's right stepped forward, holding the silver platter higher so the Domina could remove the cloth.

"Kneel," the Domina said.

Sophie sank to the floor obediently. The marble was hard and cold against her knees, the sensation chasing away the dizziness for a moment before it surged again even stronger. She presented her hands, palms up as she had been taught.

A sharp sting as the Domina pricked her finger again, this time the blood falling into a small vial of black liquid. Sophie held still, not knowing what was coming next. She tried to count the heartbeats as they pulsed in her ears, tried to slow her breath with each beat as the Domina shook the vial and then replaced it on the tray. The second devout came forward. Her platter, it was revealed, held a silver bowl full of water. The Domina tipped half of it over Sophie's hands.

A droplet splashed upward, landed on her lip. Her tongue darted out. Salt. As expected. The water dripped off her hands and pooled in front of her, some of it dampening her knees and the cotton robe even more.

Soft linen brushed her hands, patting them dry as the

Domina recited a string of words in the elder-tongue used for the most solemn temple rituals. Sophie knew a little of it, but she was too focused on staying still, on not letting the dizziness and the power pulsing through her send her swooning beneath the Domina's feet to pay too close attention.

She caught "Seagh-acha" a time or two, which was the name of the goddess and "*brau-na-li*" which was something like "blood's truth." Or an oath. Or maybe both.

The Domina retrieved the vial of liquid, holding a quill made from a brilliant white feather in her right hand. With swift strokes, she dipped the quill and traced the sigil of the goddess, the four swift lines of the bisected triangle, on each of Sophie's palms. The liquid stung a little but wasn't truly painful. More like a distillation of the humming sensation, so that each of the lines seemed to vibrate hotly against her skin.

The black lines seemed very dark against her skin, the faint acidic smell of the liquid mingling oddly with the smell of the oil on her body and the salt smoke of the goddess fire.

The quill and vial went back on the silver tray. To Sophie's surprise, the devouts left the chapel, leaving her alone with the Domina. Sophie waited, trying to ignore the sensations rippling through her and stay still. The seconds seemed to stretch into forever as she waited. Then, finally, the Domina placed her hands over Sophie's, palm to palm, skin cool for a moment before it warmed.

Another string of liquid elder-tongue about blood and the goddess and oaths, ending in Sophie's name in a questioning tone and a pause that Sophie took to be for her. "Yes," she repeated, and the Domina looked satisfied.

The older woman closed her eyes, and there was a rushing flare of power that made Sophie cry out as it burned through her. Her eyes closed against the feeling of heat and light and *other* that tolled through her like a bell ringing lightning. But almost as swiftly as it had risen, the feeling died. Sophie's eyes flew open.

The Domina took a deep gasping breath and opened hers, too. She looked down at Sophie and then raised her hands, starting to speak as she lifted them, "Blessed, are—" She stopped midsentence, face frozen as she stared down at Sophie's palms. The two sigils were still there, black and strong against her skin.

Sophie's gut went cold as the Domina's face turned thunderous. She didn't know what was wrong, but it was clear something was.

The Domina gripped Sophie's wrists as she stared down. "Milady Sophia," she said in a voice like ice. "What did you do?"

CHAPTER EIGHT

"D-do?" Sophie stammered. "What do you mean?"
The Domina tapped her right hand, the movement almost a slap. "The sigils are still there. If the goddess accepts you, they vanish."

Accepts you? Sophie didn't even know what that meant. She'd assumed the ritual was just that. Ritual. A recognition of her status after she'd proved her power. But apparently there was something deeper at work. She stared at the marks on her palms. "I haven't done anything."

"Lying isn't going to help," the Domina snapped. Then she stepped back. "Get up. We need to return to the palace."

The Domina practically dragged Sophie back through the palace to Eloisa's apartments. Sophie had the distinct impression that she would have liked to literally drag her. But either she had a little too much decorum for that, or she had no desire for Sophie's failing to become public knowledge, so she merely marched through the halls after ordering Sophie to follow her in a voice that brooked no argument.

Sophie did so, having little desire for getting any deeper

into trouble. And, fortunately, it seemed the disarray at the palace in the wake of the attack was enough to limit the time that anybody they passed had to be curious about the Domina's rapid pace. At one of the many corridor junctions, she caught a glimpse of a broad back and a dark head in a brilliant red coat. Cameron. Or so she thought. But there was no time to be sure before the Domina moved on, and there was nothing he could do to help her. Indeed, involving him at this point was the one thing she could think of that was near certain to make the situation worse.

"Leave us," the Domina snapped as they walked into the queen-to-be's bedchamber. "All of you," she added as startled glances from both the devouts and the ladies-in-waiting questioned who she was talking to.

Black- and brown-clad women scurried from the room obediently. No one, it seemed, was willing to take on the Domina to demand to be left with Eloisa. Further proof that the Domina was holding the power currently. Which was a state of affairs that Sophie would have worried about if the sense of dread about what exactly was going to happen to her hadn't been too strong to let worries about anything else in.

Eloisa, whose swollen face had also registered surprise at their abrupt return, tried to sit up straighter against the pile of pillows at her back, her movements tentative. Sophie wasn't sure if her expression was a wince or a frown. She wanted to help Eloisa but didn't want to risk the Domina's wrath.

"What happened?" Eloisa said. "Did something disrupt the ritual?"

The Domina shook her head. "No. No disruption." She beckoned at Sophie. "Come here, girl."

Her heart pounded so hard she thought her bones must be vibrating, but she obeyed and joined the Domina bedside.

"Show her," the Domina said, voice like a whip crack. "Show your hands."

Sophie fought the urge to wipe her palms, suddenly damp, down her skirts. It wasn't likely to remove the offending marks.

She was a royal witch—probably. She would damn well act like one.

She offered her hands to Eloisa, palms up.

Eloisa's one visible brow lifted, the movement followed by what was definitely a wince. Her green eye focused on Sophie and then on the Domina. "Are you telling me that she didn't manifest?"

"No." The Domina shook her head. "No. She has power aplenty. Cracked the earth-light into pieces. No. She has magic. But the binding didn't work."

"Binding?" Sophie blurted. She dropped her hands to her sides, curling her hands shut to hide the offending sigils.

"Quiet," the Domina snapped. "I am speaking with the queen-to-be."

"About me," Sophie said, suddenly furious. If she was going to be in trouble—and it was clear that she was—she might as well have all the facts. "What binding? What are you talking about? What was the ritual meant to do?"

"Dedicate you to the goddess," the Domina said.

"You said 'bind,' not 'dedicate,'" Sophie objected.

"You are in no position to question me," the Domina said, "and as the goddess rejected you, in no position to be trusted with temple secrets."

Eloisa looked as though the conversation was giving her a headache. Or a worse one. Whatever injuries were hidden beneath the bandages had to hurt like the very depths of hell. "If she has power, then the binding should have worked, shouldn't it? She was taught by the same tutors and in the same way as we all were."

The Domina scowled. "Given where she's been for the

last few days, I think that's a question best asked of the Mackenzie lad."

"You think—" Eloisa's gaze narrowed, her eye suddenly focused precisely on Sophie. She reached out and rang the bell on the carved table beside her bed.

Lady Beata came through the door with a speed that suggested she had been hovering not far outside. "Your Highness?" she said. Her eyes swept over Sophie, clearly dying to know what was happening. Sophie pretended not to notice. She kept her gaze on Eloisa.

"Have one of the guards fetch Lieutenant Mackenzie. Immediately."

"I think he went to the barracks," Lady Beata said in a nervous voice.

"I don't care," Eloisa said flatly. "Tell the guard. He is to come to me immediately, no matter what other duty he has been assigned."

Lady Beata cast a sidelong glance at Sophie but didn't offer any further comment. She simply bobbed a curtsy and retreated from the room.

The silence deepened. Sophie suddenly wished desperately that she did know something about the Arts of Air. Then perhaps she could throw a cloak of illusion over herself and make a getaway. But concealment wasn't a talent that came with earth magic.

So all she could do was stand and await her fate.

Apparently, the Domina and the queen-to-be had come to some mutual unspoken agreement that there would be no further discussion of the situation until Cameron appeared.

Instead, the Domina busied herself with mixing something from the array of herbs and powders lined up in bottles and jars on the long table arrayed on the far wall and then brewing a tea, which she coaxed Eloisa to drink.

It must have contained something to help deal with the pain, because a little color returned to Eloisa's face as she drank, and she relaxed back against the pillows, her posture less strained.

Sophie watched the hands on the tiny gilded clock that hung on the wall move around. Each circuit seemed to take far longer than the minute it was supposedly marking. By the time ten had passed, she felt like she had been standing there for an age. With each passing second, the fear bit harder. Her palms were definitely damp now, and sweat pooled against her back, making her dress stick to her from more than the remnants of the temple oil. The room was overly warm, presumably to keep Eloisa comfortable, but that wasn't the only reason Sophie was sweating. As even more time dragged by, Sophie wasn't entirely sure she wasn't going to faint. The roar of her pulse in her ears grew louder and her breaths grew shallower due to the nerves turning her muscles to stone.

When a knock came at the door, she started as violently as if the sound had been a gunshot.

She knotted her fingers into her skirts, determined to stay still, but her head turned of its own volition toward the door as it opened and Cameron stepped through.

He'd shaved and his uniform jacket was fresh scarlet. Bright as blood. She made herself look away, not wanting to see if he looked for her.

Cameron bowed as he halted at the foot of the bed. "Your Highness, you asked for me."

"I did." Eloisa looked past him to Lady Beata, who had shown him in. "That will be all, Beata. We are not to be disturbed."

After the doors had closed again, Eloisa waved a hand, and Sophie felt a sudden pulse of power.

"Princess!" the Domina protested. "You shouldn't be exerting yourself."

"If I'm at risk from a little warding, then you are slipping, Domina Skey," Eloisa said tartly. "Right now I think it is more important that no one hears what happens in this room than I tire myself a little."

The Domina shook her head, but she didn't argue.

"Lieutenant Mackenzie," Eloisa said. "We appear to have a dilemma."

Sophie saw the tightening of the broad shoulders.

"I am, as ever, at your service, Your Highness," Cameron said.

Sophie knew that flat tone. She'd heard that voice many times during their journey. That was his professional, give-no-clues, locked-down voice. She wondered how well Eloisa knew her bodyguard's moods.

"The dilemma is something that we would not commonly discuss with a man. So I need your word that you won't reveal this information to anyone."

"You have my word," he said. The voice was a little sharper now. As though he thought Eloisa should know better than to question his loyalty. If only Sophie could see his face. But then, if she saw his, her own might give her away.

"Lady Sophia went to the temple to complete her Ais-Seann rites," Eloisa said. "Normally, as you know, these would have taken place as soon as she woke on her birthday."

"Yes, Your Highness." Flat again. Flatter than before, if possible. Which meant, Sophie thought, that he was starting to see where this conversation might lead. Just as she could.

Her hand stole up to the pearl hanging at her neck. *Salt, protect me. Goddess, forgive me.*

"Normally there are certain indications that the goddess is . . . pleased with the outcome of the ritual," Eloisa continued. Her voice was cool rather than flat. Sophie knew that tone, too. The queen-to-be was unhappy with the situation. With her. With them.

She repeated her plea to the goddess under her breath, frozen in place as she waited for Eloisa's next words.

Cameron stayed silent, too.

"These indications did not occur in Lady Sophia's case," Eloisa said.

"But she manifested. She saw the ley line," Cameron said. There was no question in his voice, only certainty.

"So we understand. And it doesn't seem to be a question of power. Only of . . . allegiance."

"I'm not sure I understand," Cameron said.

Neither did Sophie.

Eloisa looked at the Domina. The Domina gave a short nod, lips pressed together.

"During the ritual, a portion of the witch's power is . . . dedicated . . . to the goddess. A binding of a kind, you might say, so that part of the power serves the temple and the land," Eloisa said. "There are very few men who know this," she added. "Some amongst the Illusioners. My father, before he died."

Cameron was almost completely still. Only the expansion and contraction of his back as he breathed gave any indication that he was flesh rather than stone. He didn't speak. Sophie had to remind herself to take a breath, head spinning. Part of her power bound? To the temple? How did that work? And what did it mean?

"In Lady Sophia's case, it seems that the binding did not take."

"Does that happen often?" Cameron asked.

The Domina shook her head. "No. Very seldom. Sometimes if the witch has a very small power. But I am unaware of an instance of the ritual not being completed where a royal witch is concerned."

Another wave of dizziness overtook Sophie. Truly, if this didn't end soon, she was going to either faint or throw up.

"Never?" Cameron asked, turning his head to the Domina.

"Never," the Domina repeated flatly. She gestured at Eloisa. Cameron looked back at the queen-to-be. He still hadn't looked at Sophie.

"The second ritual a royal witch undertakes is on her wedding day," Eloisa continued.

"I know there are temple rites for weddings, yes," Cameron said.

Sophie knew that, too. But she hadn't known that they were anything more than tradition.

"That ritual also cedes a small part of a witch's power. To her husband."

"It does?" Sophie said at almost exactly the same moment as Cameron. His voice was startled, the first hint of emotion it had revealed since he had entered.

"Yes," Eloisa said.

"Men can't use earth magic," Cameron said.

"The lords who marry royal witches cannot wield the power directly," Eloisa said. "But it helps them in other ways. Keeps them healthy, helps them heal."

It was true that nobles tended to live long lives. But Sophie had never heard even a hint that it was due to anything more than better food and easier lives and more money to buy temple healings when necessary.

"Lady Sophia isn't married," Cameron said. "I'm not sure I understand."

"Royal witches are virgins when they undertake their dedication rites," the Domina interjected. "And when the final part of the wedding rite occurs. There are reasons why this is so."

"Am I allowed to know what those are?" Cameron asked.

"To avoid exactly this situation," the Domina said. "To avoid her power becoming tangled with another's before it can be bound."

Tangled? What in the name of the goddess did that mean? Sophie bit her lip. Hard. Hard enough to keep the

river of questions in her head from spilling out and making things worse.

"Which forces us to an unpleasant conclusion," Eloisa
said. "That perhaps Lady Sophia is not a virgin. That
would explain why the ritual didn't work." She straightened a little on her pillows and looked squarely at Cameron. "So tell me, Lieutenant Mackenzie, did you by any
chance bed Lady Sophia in the last few days?"

∾

Eloisa might as well have slapped him. The bite of her
question hit Cameron with the same force as a blow. Behind him, he heard Sophie gasp, but he forced himself
not to turn. Not to go to her as his instincts urged.

No. Instead, better to watch the royal witch in front of
him. His queen-to-be. His sometimes lover. Who was, if
he was any judge at all of her temper, supremely displeased with him.

"Well?" Eloisa snapped when he didn't immediately
answer. "Did you bed the girl or not, Cameron?"

That was a slip, he realized. The queen-to-be should
call her bodyguards by their ranks, not their names. He
hoped Sophie wouldn't notice. He was near certain, however, that the Domina would. Domina Skey was fiercely
intelligent to go along with the power she wielded. She
was the one woman, besides Eloisa herself, he'd ever seen
get the upper hand with King Stefan in an argument.

But that was beside the point right now. Right now he
had to answer the question. Lying would be useless. Easy
enough to have one of the healers confirm that Sophie
was no longer a virgin. And he was the obvious candidate, being the only man to have spent time alone with
Sophie since she had manifested her power. She didn't
strike him as the type to try to coax anybody else into
dalliance before she had turned twenty-one, and the
penalties for harming a royal witch—or a potential one—

were severe enough to keep any sane man from being tempted. "I—"

"It was my fault," Sophie said firmly. There was a faint rustle of skirts as she moved to stand next to him.

"You seduced him?" Eloisa asked. "Truly, Sophie, you expect me to believe that?" She sounded almost scornful, and out of the corner of his eye, he saw Sophie flush.

But she didn't flinch or look away. If anything, she drew herself straighter, moving fractionally closer to the bed. "It was the ley line," she said.

Eloisa's expression of icy immobility—somewhat of a feat to achieve such a look when her face was so damaged—didn't alter as she studied Sophie. Her eyes had turned a dangerous green, like the heart of a hunting cat's gaze. A warning that danger—if not death—stalked nearby. "I fail to understand what a ley line has to do with Lieutenant Mackenzie relieving an unmarried royal witch of her virginity."

"I stepped into it. This morning. I woke, and we were near a ley line—we were using the portals—and I couldn't stop myself," Sophie said. "And it—it . . ."

"The power overwhelmed her," Cameron said. "I pulled her away, and then, well, we—"

"You fucked her," Eloisa said flatly.

"It wasn't intentional," he said. "I'm well aware that that sounds ridiculous and I'm willing to take my punishment, but it was never my intention to . . . dishonor Lady Sophia."

"You didn't," Sophie said beside him. Her cheeks burned red, but her chin lifted and her back was ramrod straight. "I did. Any punishment should fall to me."

He heard the Domina murmur something that sounded like agreement.

"No," he said. "It's not Sophie's fault."

"Traditionally, the punishment for harming a royal

witch is death," Eloisa said. She might as well have been making a comment about the weather.

Sweat began to form under the tight collar of his jacket. He had fucked up. Literally. He had known that the minute his head had cleared after Sophie had come screaming beneath him. But he hadn't truly thought through the consequences. He hadn't expected that they would be discovered. Hadn't known about the buggering ash-blown rituals. How could he?

Yet he had done what he was accused of. And now both he and Sophie were in danger. He was a battle mage, used to peril, and he recognized the scent and tingle of potential disaster and violence in the air.

Well. He had been charged with keeping Lady Sophia safe. And he'd be damned if he would forswear that oath even if he'd blighted his honor. He would make sure she was safe. He would shoulder the blame and any punishment merited.

But to do so he had to tread very carefully. Elly was sick and injured, and he could feel the echoes of her power—angry even though it felt oddly distorted—in the air.

The silence that followed her words seemed to ripple with it.

It was Sophie who risked breaking that silence. "I am not harmed."

Her voice didn't tremble. He was impressed. Then again, she had served Eloisa for quite some time now. Perhaps Sophie knew as well as he did how to read her moods. Though now she had the added complication of trying to judge the queen-to-be's magic as well. She wouldn't have been able to do that before.

He wondered what it felt like to her. He was male and a battle mage. The currents of earth magic were shrouded to him, so that all he could sense were whispers—like catching a snatch of conversation borne on a breeze. Maybe Sophie could hear every word. She had certainly channeled the power from a ley line without damaging herself or him, other than inciting them to stupidity. She was obviously strong.

Hopefully strong enough for what was to come.

"You could be with child," the Domina said.

"Perhaps. Though I don't see a child as harm either," Sophie said. He thought he detected a faint quaver in her voice. Perhaps. Maybe he was listening for what wasn't there.

"You would disgrace your family," the Domina started. "Rejected by the goddess, a child out of wedlock."

Sophie's chin lifted higher. "My family loves me. They'd be happy to have me come home."

"Are you sure of that?" the Domina said.

"Yes—"

"I think we have strayed from the point," Eloisa interjected.

"And what is the point exactly?" Cameron asked, trying to stay calm. "Sophie is still a royal witch. Does it really matter so much if she doesn't have this . . . binding to the goddess?"

The small shudder that ran over Eloisa's face as she frowned made him feel ill. He wanted to hurt those who had done this to her. Who had done this to all of them. Taken his father. Taken their king. Hurt Eloisa.

Hurt Sophie in a roundabout way. If there had been no attack, then he wouldn't be standing there. He never would have been stranded with Sophie. Never been alone with her.

An image of her face awash with pleasure flashed through his mind, and he felt the ghost touch of her body on his again. He should regret it.

But he found he could not, despite the wrongness of it. Found, if he was honest with himself, that there was a small part of him that hungered to touch her again despite all his better judgment.

But that wasn't the point. The point was to free her of this mess. At whatever cost. He took a breath, nodded at Eloisa. "After all, she has served you loyally for what . . . a year now? She is a member of the court and a subject of the Crown. Your subject. What has changed?"

"Royal witches are expected to serve the court through their marriages," Domina Skey said. "No lord will want her now. Not if the marriage ritual won't work. They would want to know why."

Eloisa tilted her head, the movement slow and careful this time, though it was still echoed by a shiver of pain that made Cameron flatten his palms to his sides against the urge to soothe that hurt. That would be one way to make this situation even worse.

"It is true that Sophie has served me well," Eloisa said. "And perhaps it is truly no fault of either of you what happened." She sounded less convinced of this part, but the words gave Cameron a little hope. "So maybe there is a simpler solution in front of us."

"Which is?" the Domina asked before Cameron could.

"She can marry Cameron," Eloisa said. She met Cam's eyes as she spoke, as though waiting to see his reaction. Only force of will kept him still through the shock, the words hitting deeper this time. Beside him Sophie made a shocked sound as rapidly stifled as his own reaction.

Marriage. He had not contemplated ever doing such a thing as long as he was in the Red Guard. A third son was of little interest to the matchmaking mothers of the court, particularly with Alec already producing children to put even more distance between him and any chance of the title. There was little incentive for him to marry, and with Eloisa willing to allow him into her bed, he hadn't had eyes for any other ladies.

Until Sophie had touched him.

Guilt twisted his gut again. "I—" he began, but the Domina held up a hand, cutting him off.

"She should be married to a powerful lord," the Domina said. "Her power should seal the loyalty of someone other than a lieutenant in the Red Guard."

"Cameron is now the brother of the Erl of Inglewood. Not just a third son. If I remember correctly, Liam is yet to have any children. And we are somewhat short of eligible lords, if the casualty reports I've been given are truthful. No one will blink if Liam chooses to gift his brother with one of his minor titles and increase his landholdings now that he himself is the erl. That will increase his eligibility." For a moment her expression softened. "Our condolences on the loss of your father, Lieutenant Mackenzie. He was a good and faithful servant of the court."

Not a good man, Cameron noted. Just a good servant. A good tool to be deployed as the court and the Crown wished. As, or so it appeared, was he. He gritted his teeth but bowed and murmured, "Thank you."

"Your father would have had someone in mind for the girl. Someone other than a minor lordling." the Domina protested. "She's strong. You can use that to your advantage."

He noticed she didn't look at Sophie when she said this. And that the sting of angry power in the air wasn't Eloisa's alone. The Domina was not pleased by this situation. What that might mean in the future, he did not know. But the Domina had to bow to the will of the monarch when it came to the marriages of royal witches. He knew that much. So it was Eloisa he needed to be most concerned about right now. He could avoid the Domina easily enough. He went to temple on eighth day as part of the Red Guard, but as a battle mage, he had rites and obeisances of a different nature to honor the source of his magic.

Sophie wouldn't be so lucky. But once she was married—married as directed by Eloisa—then surely the Domina would have to move on.

Eloisa's mouth thinned. "If my father had a husband in mind for Sophie, then he didn't choose to share that choice with me. And he is no longer in a position to make that decision. I am." The last two words cracked into the silence.

A reminder that she was no longer a princess but a queen-to-be. Eloisa and her father had not always seen eye to eye, but he had raised her as his heir. He had not been a teacher who would accept less than excellence in his pupils. Eloisa had been prepared to wield Anglion's power. It seemed she intended to do so, no matter what the wishes of the temple might be.

"You are forgetting that the two of them are most likely bound. Which means she cannot be bound to another. Even if we try to pass her power off as a lesser one, it would be difficult to explain to her potential husband why his marriage rites can't be completed. And if Sophie ever slipped up and revealed the extent of her power, then we would have a problem. So we need a solution that will prevent any scandal. The court cannot afford any further disruption right now. We need a husband for Sophie who doesn't need marriage rites and whose interests are best served if the truth of the situation stays a secret. If Cameron marries her, then the problem is solved. People will assume that Sophie is not strong in magic because we are marrying her to a lesser lord. He will keep quiet because if the court finds out he deflowered a royal witch, he could lose everything."

"That doesn't solve the problem of her being unbound to the goddess," the Domina said.

"No," Eloisa agreed. "But you will school her to manage her power so she doesn't get into any more trouble and so that we know what power she has should we need to call on her. As Cameron has said, Sophie is loyal to me. And has given us no reason to think otherwise."

Cameron looked at Sophie again. Her skin was very

pale, her chest rising and falling rapidly, as though she were running rather than standing still. He wondered if the same desire to try to awaken from a dream that was not a dream that filled him filled her.

But she had not voiced a rejection of Eloisa's proposed solution. So perhaps she was as loyal as Eloisa thought and would do precisely as she was bidden.

Still, he would rather know that she was not unwilling. He had always known that perhaps he would marry for duty. But that did not mean he wanted a bride who hated the very thought of marrying him. He turned to her, once again schooling himself against the urge to touch her to take her hand so that she might know she had an ally in this disaster. "Lady Sophia? Do you have something to say about this?"

The Domina bristled. "I think she forfeited her right to complain about her wedding when she—"

"I was speaking to my wife-to-be. I would know her mind on this matter," Cameron said shortly. Normally he wouldn't cut the Domina off, but there was nothing normal about this situation, and it was already clear that he was in disgrace. It didn't seem like determining whether Sophie hated him or not was likely to worsen the situation.

Sophie's head turned slowly toward him. Her eyes were very dark and very wide. "I have a question. No, two questions."

He nodded. "That seems fair."

Sophie turned back to Eloisa. He saw her hands gripping her skirts so tightly her knuckles were stark white in the golden skin. "Your Highness," she said, voice quavering ever so slightly. "I wish to know if my parents are alive."

Goddess wept, had no one told her that yet? He almost reached for her hand but stopped himself.

"They were coming here for my birthday celebration,"

Sophie continued. "They were supposed to arrive the day of the attack."

Eloisa was frowning again. "I remember. They were coming by sea, were they not?"

"Yes, my lady. On the *Salt Blessed*."

"I am told the port was closed as soon the attack occurred," Eloisa said. "It has not been reopened. At least, I have given no such orders. Lieutenant, were you brought up to speed on the current situation when you returned to the barracks?"

"Yes, Your Highness. The port remains closed. There is a defensive blockade. Some ships that were making for Kingswell put to anchor beyond the heads; others would have gone to Skydown or Aislight Rock, I suppose." Those were the nearest ports to Kingswell.

Eloisa nodded. "Very well. We will get the Illusioners to send messages to the port masters and locate your family, Sophie."

"Thank you, my lady." She bobbed a curtsy.

"You said you had two questions," Cameron said gently.

Sophie looked at him, seemingly startled. Then she nodded. "My second question is easier. When are we to be wed?"

CHAPTER NINE

It seemed, however, that the question of exactly when her wedding was to take place was not so simple. When Cameron suggested three days hence, the Domina, somewhat to Sophie's surprise, put her foot down.

"It cannot be too hasty," she said. "That will draw attention."

"Not to mention," Eloisa interjected, "there is the small matter of my father's funeral and a coronation to be held first. After all, the law requires a royal proclamation for a royal witch to marry. There cannot be a royal proclamation with no monarch."

That statement had diverted the Domina's attention from any thought of weddings. She and Eloisa proceeded to argue about when the queen-to-be would be well enough for such things.

Under tradition, King Stefan should be buried within a week, his body safely stored in salt until he could be laid to rest in the royal vault. The Domina was in favor of giving Eloisa more time to recover before the funeral took place. Eloisa was not.

Sophie and Cameron stood like statues as the two of them argued, learning in the process that the question of the preservation of the king's body was somewhat moot as he had been killed by the fire from the explosion. Charred bones didn't spoil.

Sophie thought she might finally throw up when she heard that little tidbit come out of the Domina's mouth. She bit down, clenching her jaw tightly and swallowing. Cameron must have noticed something because he stepped closer. "Are you quite well, milady?" he asked in a tone just above a whisper.

Milady. They were to be married and he was sticking to that? The irritation pushed back the queasiness in her stomach, and she managed a nod.

But the movement caught Eloisa's attention as well.

"Lady Sophia, you are dismissed. Attend me in the morning. Lieutenant, you may also leave. Please do not speak of this to anyone yet."

"I must inform my brother, the erl, Your Highness," Cameron objected.

Eloisa considered. "Very well. But charge him to keep his counsel until the betrothal is announced. The Erl of Inglewood does not need to start his tenure with our disfavor."

That was a blunt enough warning. Sophie dropped into a curtsy and then made for the door, Cameron at her heels. They stepped out into a semicircle of curious ladies-in-waiting, faces expectant above the black dresses they wore, for all the world like a row of crows waiting for carrion to feed upon.

"Lady Sophia," Lady Beata said. "We assume felicitations are due upon the happy day of your Ais-Seann?"

Sophie suddenly remembered the sigils on her palms. None of Eloisa's ladies were witches, so presumably they would not know the significance of the symbols, but still she curled her palms in to her dress as she bobbed a much shallower curtsy to Beata. "Yes. Thank you for your care. The queen-to-be has asked that I attend her in the morning. I think I will retire. It has been a difficult few days. As it has been for all of you, I would imagine."

Behind Beata, Lady Aria's face looked stricken. She was the lady-in-waiting closest to Sophie's age. And the most friendly. She stepped forward and whispered something in Beata's ear.

Beata nodded, a flash of weariness revealed for a moment under her careful court expression. "Sophie, the ladies' quarters were damaged. Those of us not with the queen-to-be have been staying with family or other connections, as can be arranged. I'm afraid the rooms assigned to your family for your birthday were also damaged. Do you have somewhere to stay?"

Her family, unlike Cameron's, didn't have a permanent apartment in the palace. Until she knew her parents' whereabouts, she couldn't join them in whatever lodgings they had managed to secure. If, indeed, they had secured somewhere.

"I was told that the Lord of Inglewood's suite is intact," Cameron said. "I'm sure my brother will have room for Lady Sophia."

That raised almost every pair of eyebrows in the room. But Sophie couldn't bring herself to protest to Cameron. If she denied his offer and had to beg to share a bed or sleep on a cot in a room with one of the other ladies, there was no way she would avoid being relentlessly interrogated about her time away from the palace or hide the sigils on her hands. Which would not please the queen-to-be.

She turned to Cameron and curtsied again. "Your kindness does you credit, Lieutenant. I would be most grateful for your family's hospitality."

Relief flashed in his eyes. Apparently his thoughts had been traveling similar paths to hers.

He extended an arm. "In that case, milady, let us depart. I have to return to the barracks as soon as possible."

❦

Sophie kept her hands pressed against the sides of her skirts as they walked, wishing she had gloves to hide her hands or that women's clothes had useful things like pockets, as men's did. The route they took was, of necessity, a little convoluted.

The Erl of Inglewood's apartments were a large set of rooms that lay between the Salt Spire—the oldest of the rearward palace towers—and the western wing of the palace on the third floor. As much of the western wing was blocked off due to the damage to the west tower, which had extended to part of the wing itself, they had to cut through the middle of the palace. Working their way through the center of the palace, a maze of rooms and passageways designed to confuse anyone who wasn't familiar with the routes, took time.

King Stefan's great-grandfather had built most of the central palace after he'd come to power in the wake of the last true Illvyan incursion. He'd been deadly serious about wanting a palace that was strongly defended. He was the one who'd added the moat—fed by a labyrinthine system of aqueducts and pumps with seawater from the harbor—that circled the palace itself with nearly fifteen feet of salt water and sent a narrower tendril through the stone channels outside the walls of the grounds as well.

As he'd won his way to power after defeating an Illvyan wizard and his demon sanctii leading an army bent on conquest, a bit of well-placed paranoia could be forgiven.

If it was the Illvyans who had attacked the palace, then presumably blowing up the east and west towers had been partly an attempt to form a bridge of rubble over the moat. One that a demon could have crossed. But no demons had been detected that she knew of. Or had they? Surely the palace would be deserted if a sanctii had gotten inside. Besides which, it seemed unlikely that Eloisa or Margaretta would still be alive if a demon had been present. Wiping out the royal family would have to be a primary goal of any Illvyan plot.

She could ask Cameron, of course, but something stayed her questions. She had already caused enough trouble for him. A lifetime's worth. He was being forced to marry her, for goddess' sake. An outcome he couldn't have possibly wanted. Yet he was being nothing but courteous in return. Taking her to stay with his family.

Had he even seen his brother—the new erl—since they had returned to Kingswell? Or had a moment to mourn his father? Did he mourn his father?

She shivered. She knew so little about him. She had grown to trust him during their time together. But she had known him only a few scant days. Days where he had kept her safe, true, but that had been only his duty. She had no idea if he even liked her. And yet they were going to be married. Married. For life.

True, there were far less appealing options for a husband in the court than Cameron Mackenzie, but still, the reality of marrying a stranger was more daunting than she had expected.

She shivered again.

"Milady? Are you cold?" Cameron asked.

What was he going to do? Take off his jacket and give it to her here in the middle of the palace? Unlikely. The Red Guard uniform was a badge of honor. She pulled the black shawl more tightly around her shoulders and shook her head. "No, not cold." Kingswell was hot in the summer, though the inner rooms of the palace stayed cool. "Just tired, I think. It's been a long day." She offered an awkward smile. "I'm sorry—"

"We can talk once we reach the suite." Cameron glanced around. The gallery they were walking through was deserted—the court was lacking its usual bustling

throngs, which only added to the oddness of the day—
but sound carried oddly in the palace, and anyone could
be approaching around a corner or standing near one of
the half-shattered windows on the other side of the outer
wall.

Sophie ducked her head and nodded her agreement.
Another shiver skimmed through her, and she began to
realize she hadn't been lying. She was exhausted and
both hungry and queasy at the same time. She would be
equally happy to eat, sleep, or burst into tears, and right
now she had no idea which of the three was more likely
to happen. Fortunately, they were almost at their destination.

⌘

Two guards stood outside the door to the Inglewood
suite. Black armbands ringed the gray, blue and silver
dress uniforms they wore. They stepped forward as Sophie and Cameron came around the turn in the corridor.
The sharp expressions on their faces eased as they recognized Cameron, and they stepped back into place on
either side of the door after quick bows.

Inside the suite, the first servant who caught sight of
them looked briefly horrified before she bobbed a curtsy,
wheeled around, and headed for the nearest doorway,
the covered tray she was carrying seemingly forgotten.

She was probably going to fetch whoever the house
servitor was. From the opposite direction, through another open door, there was a sound of low voices and
clinking china.

Cameron took her arm, though she noticed he was
careful not to touch her bare hand.

"This way," he said, and headed for the doorway the
sounds were coming through.

Apparently, they weren't waiting for the servitor.
Which made sense. A son of the household didn't need

to be announced, and he could bring whomever he chose with him.

At least, that's how it would work in Sophie's family.

But the Mackenzies, though not of the line direct like the Kendalls, were far grander than Sophie's family. The Kendall line had a few bends in it. Her father's mother—the Sophia she was named for—had been one of King Leo's—Stefan's father's—four sisters, the youngest of them, to boot, and one of the two who had not manifested, which had eliminated her chances of ever succeeding her brother. Or rather, of holding the throne if she did. Anglion had had queens, but all of them had been witches.

Because of her lack of power, she'd been married to Anthony Kendall, a favorite of her father's due to his skill with a sword, though a man of little enough fortune for a noble.

Sophia and Anthony had brought the estate a little more prosperity and three sons. Sophie's father was the only one who'd survived past six years of age. Without brothers to go out and further the family fortunes, her father had merely solidified the work of his parents, marrying her mother, who was from a similarly low-level noble family. Which left Sophie with a pedigree that had some distinction at surface level but no fortune or hope of actual succession to lend her any true desirability to a court lord.

Until she had come into her power. That changed things a little.

A royal witch should be prize enough for the Mackenzies, who had always been part of first King Leo's and then King Stefan's inner circle of councilors.

If the former Lord Inglewood had still been alive, he probably would have been pleased with the match, power trumping pedigree, after all. He had been, the few times she'd had any close contact with him, hard and autocratic and clearly ambitious. No time for fools.

And he had raised Cameron.

What kind of man had he wrought?

One whose arm was strong and warm under her hand. One who kissed like one of Illvya's fabled courtesans might teach a man to kiss.

Who had stood by her and offered himself up as culprit for the trouble she had caused.

She would hold to that.

The conversation died as they walked into the receiving room, heads turning to see who was interrupting. There were nine—no, ten—adults in the room and several young children, though they were mostly gathered around a small table, playing with a set of salt sticks.

The tallest of the men, who looked remarkably like Cameron, came to his feet abruptly.

Sophie had met Liam Mackenzie once, she thought. The first time she'd come to court, when she was nearly sixteen. Before he had married. Lord Inglewood had introduced his heir out of courtesy to Sophie's heritage, but he'd married Liam off to Jeanne Listfold the next year to strengthen Inglewood's alliances with the Erl of Airlight, her father.

"Cameron," Liam said, sounding relieved. He wore head-to-toe black, only the blue of the Inglewood sapphire in his ring and the gray glimmer of the pearls adorning his jacket breaking the darkness. His eyes were blue like Cameron's, though bracketed by deeper lines. But the shadows beneath them and the stoic expression they held were identical to his brother's.

Cameron let go of Sophie, and the brothers embraced. She looked away, not wanting to intrude. Only to realize that everybody else in the room was staring at her. Jeanne Mackenzie recovered herself first and rose from the spindle-legged chair she occupied to stand beside her husband.

She nodded at Sophie. "It's Lady Sophia, isn't it?"

"Yes, Your Grace," Sophie said. Jeanne's eyes were curious, but she didn't have time for more questions before the men broke apart and Cameron said, "We need to talk, brother."

Behind him, the expressions of interest on the other adults deepened. Sophie only recognized a few of them. Which meant, she assumed, that the others had come from Inglewood with Liam. The ladies-in-waiting were schooled relentlessly on all the members of the court, and she had a good head for faces and names. She didn't think she'd seen any of the people she didn't recognize before. None of them had any power that she could sense, either.

There was very little magic detectable in the room. Nothing like the roiling power that had filled Eloisa's chambers. Maybe something from Liam. She didn't think he'd ever been in the Red Guard, but that didn't mean he wouldn't have been trained in battle magic. Still, the lack of the immediate pressing presence of magic was a relief of a sort after her hours in the temple and with the Domina and the queen-to-be today. Like she had been able to step out of a stuffy room into fresh air for a space of time. But she still made sure her hands were covered by the folds of her shawl, just in case one of the women might know the significance of the sigils.

"Indeed," Liam said. "There is much to discuss about the estate. And Father." His voice grew a little rough. "But won't you eat first?"

Cameron declined with a headshake. "Now, if it pleases Your Grace."

Liam's eyebrows lifted at the formality. "If you insist. Jeanne, will you take care of Cameron's . . . guest?"

"She needs to come with us," Cameron said.

Liam's expression turned shuttered. "I see. Well, then. We can go to the study. It's a mess, but we will have privacy there." He exchanged a look with his wife that clearly meant "keep things under control here" and then led the way out of the room, through another smaller receiving room, and across a narrow hall into a well-sized book-lined study dominated by a carved blackwood desk. Two narrow cots had been set up near the fire on the farthest side of the room. Obviously, the family was already housing more guests than the suite was intended for.

And now she was about to impose. Her face went hot. Neither of the men seemed to notice.

Cameron held one of the chairs near the desk for her, and she sat, knowing that neither of them would until she did so. The more she could do to speed this interview, the better.

"What's this about, Cam?" Liam asked, settling himself behind the desk, looking a little uncomfortable about doing so.

"You know that I wasn't in the city for the attack," Cameron said.

"Commander Peters told me as much when we first arrived," Liam agreed. "Said you were with one of the ladies-in-waiting. The one with the imminent birthday."

"Lady Sophia Kendall," Sophie interrupted. "Pleased to meet you, Your Grace. My condolences on your loss."

Cameron was looking at her oddly. "You hadn't introduced us," she pointed out.

"Lady Sophia," Liam said, one side of his mouth lifting in an expression very like Cameron's half smile, though lacking the dimple and the transformation that Cameron's smile wrought on his face. "I thank you for your sympathy. I see that my brother has brought you home again."

"Yes, Your Grace. Cam—Lieutenant Mackenzie has been very kind."

"I see," Liam said. He folded his hands in front of him on the table. The sapphire signet ring, slightly loose on his finger, shifted and caught the light, flaring deep blue. "Cameron. You were saying?"

"Lady Sophia and I were in Portholme when the attack happened. As it happened, near a portal. I deemed it safer to take her away from the city until we could find out what was happening. She is of the line direct, after all."

Liam nodded, made a little "go on" gesture before clasping his hands again.

"It's a somewhat long story," Cameron said, "and I know you must have more than enough to do right now. So the short version is that the queen-to-be, on our return here, has decided that I am to marry Sophie."

Liam's mouth dropped open. "You?" He frowned at Sophie. "Did you not manifest, milady?"

"She did," Cameron said.

"Then I would have thought that the queen-to-be would be looking for a bigger prize than you, little brother," Liam said. "If she's got a royal witch to go fishing with, she should want to bind one of her lords close again."

"I rather suspect she thinks she's binding you," Cameron said. "A new Erl of Inglewood. An unknown quantity."

"Eloisa and I spent several summers in court before she was wed. I think she has my measure," Liam said with a sound close to a snort. "I doubt she's as concerned about me as she would have been about Father." He tilted his head, a gleam in the blue eyes—several shades darker again than Cameron's—that suggested Eloisa might be foolish to discount him. "Which brings me back to why she's giving you a prize. Did you save her life or something when I wasn't looking?"

Cameron's face was set. "No."

Liam leaned back. "Then perhaps I need the longer version of this story after all."

"Why? It won't change anything. She doesn't need your permission, given I'm not your heir," Cameron said.

"The queen-to-be rarely changes her mind once she's set her course."

"Is that so? You seem to know her well."

"I've been one of her bodyguards for nearly a year. I know her well enough," Cameron said somewhat stiffly.

Sophie was starting to wish rather desperately that a hole would open up before her feet and swallow her. She really didn't want Cameron to have to tell his brother that they had ... transgressed. Not when she was present, at least.

Liam turned his gaze to her. "And you, Lady Sophia. Are you amenable to marrying my little brother?"

She forced a smile. "I am happy to serve my queen-to-be as she bids, Your Grace. Lieutenant Mackenzie has always been kind to me. I'm sure we will be very happy together." She looked down, hoping she looked demure and maidenly, like a well-bred young court flower rather than shifty.

"I see," Liam said. He took a breath. Blew it out. "Well. I imagine that Father might have had many things to say on this subject, but he is no longer here to speak them."

Cameron shifted in his seat. She rather thought he was thinking that his father's passing, when it came to this particular matter, was somewhat of a blessing. She could only agree with him.

"And," Liam continued, "it is a good match for you, Cameron. Better than the queen-to-be has considered, perhaps."

Sophie turned her attention back to him, wondering how he had reached that conclusion.

"How so?" Cameron said, echoing her thoughts.

Liam shrugged. "Did the commander have time to go through the casualty lists with you?"

Cameron shook his head.

Sophie's stomach grew tight. Casualty lists. What did they have to do with her?

"The west and east towers took a lot of people with them when they fell," Liam said, voice somber. "More than just Father. So many people here for the birthday celebrations."

Sophie felt a cry of protest rise in her throat, choked it back. It wasn't her fault. It was the court that wanted the birthday celebrations, not her. It wasn't her fault. This wasn't her fault.

"Who?" Cameron asked, sounding wary.

"Well, the Erl of Farkeep's entire family, for a start," Liam said.

Sophie froze, distracted from the guilt by a chill spearing through her. A previous Erl of Farkeep had married her grandmother's elder sister. A royal witch. A whole branch of the line direct gone. The line closest to the throne after Stefan's, in fact.

She counted frantically in her head, trying to think.

"Who else?" Cameron demanded.

"The lists are long," Liam said. "And falling stone and fire pay no heed to noble birth. But before you try to figure the situation, I am guessing that your lady wife-to-be is now fifth or sixth in line to the throne. Depending on how Princess Margaretta figures in all of this. We've never had a queen who wasn't a strong witch, and her power is small. Those above Sophie are all women save Barron Nester— the new Barron Nester, who is yet to be of age. And I have no idea if he's shown any aptitude as a blood mage. And, besides Eloisa, Sophie is the only other royal witch in that number."

Which meant, Sophie realized, that her true position— if the court wouldn't accept Margaretta due to her lack of power—was more like second or third. She looked at Liam in horror.

"Welcome to the family, milady," he said with a smile that was in no way reassuring.

❧

By the time Sophie returned to the palace the next afternoon, she was nearly exhausted. The Domina had carted her off to the temple for "instruction" at the first opportunity after Sophie had presented herself at the queen-to-be's apartments that morning.

Instruction meant using magic. A lot of magic. She felt as though she'd been in a battle, muscles aching from the unfamiliar effort, even though her mind buzzed with the aftershock of using her power.

Combined with a night spent lying mostly awake in what was apparently Cameron's room, trying to distract her madly spinning brain from contemplating the possible consequences of Liam's news about her place in the succession by toying with the trio of earth-lights sitting on the mantel above the fireplace, she wanted sleep quite badly.

Then she pictured the large empty bed in that room back in the Inglewood apartments and how alone she'd felt lying there. She'd spent her sleepless hours lighting the earth-lights one by one and then extinguishing them again, drawing on the ley lines she could feel skimming through the earth so many feet below her. She'd been very careful with the power she expended, not wanting to explain shattered earth-lights to the erl or his wife in the morning. Or to Cameron, for that matter.

Cameron, whom she hadn't seen since he'd left with Liam and Jeanne the previous day. Jeanne, at least, had been sympathetic and had been happy to provide food for Sophie in Cameron's room, so she hadn't had to face meeting the strangers downstairs. She'd crept out just after dawn, leaving a note for Jeanne with one of the door guards, explaining she was required to attend on Eloisa.

She wasn't looking forward to returning to the Mackenzies without Cameron.

Not that she had much choice. It was either the Mackenzies or beg a bed from one of the other ladies-in-waiting. At least at the Mackenzies, she had a semblance of privacy.

So far the only bright spot in the day had been the Domina removing the sigils—the proof of her rejection—from her hands with a foul-smelling liquid that had stung like fire. But pain was better than every woman in the palace who'd ever been through the ritual knowing what the sigils meant.

The ley line that ran north-south through the palace shimmered beside the path to the main gate. She had no desire to step into it now. Enough magic for one day. But the dancing light was a pleasant distraction, and she let her tired eyes focus on it and trace the patterns in the sparkling glimmers rather than keep thinking.

"Lady Sophia?"

The voice jerked her back to reality. She turned in the direction of the sound to discover Madame de Montesse was standing a little behind her on the path. The Illvyan woman was carrying a stack of neatly wrapped parcels, and a younger woman stood with her, carrying even more boxes and bags. Unlike Sophie, who was feeling distinctly rumpled by the day's activities, Madame de Montesse looked immaculate, from the tips of the polished black boots just visible beneath her skirts to the neat straw hat hiding her extraordinary hair.

"Madame de Montesse," Sophie said, a little warily. "Good afternoon."

Madame de Montesse smiled at her. "I am glad to see you safely returned to Kingswell, milady." Her dark eyes narrowed a little. "And felicitations on your birthday, I see."

"Thank you," Sophie said. Madame de Montesse could

clearly tell that Sophie's power had manifested. "What
brings you to court?" An Illvyan, even one who had lived
in Kingswell for as many years as Madame de Montesse
had, couldn't be the most welcome of sights in the palace
now.

"I am bringing some supplies to the healers." A particularly Illvyan shrug flowed through her shoulders.
"Doing my part. And you? I would have thought they'd
be making sure you stayed safely in the palace."

They both looked toward the main gate flanked by the
broken wall and the piles of rubble where the towers had
stood. Workmen were moving stones but it would take
time for any repairs to be completed. Hardly a haven of
safety.

"I've been to the temple," Sophie said, averting her
gaze from the broken towers.

"Ah, yes. Lessons." Madame de Montesse averted her
nose. "So tiresome."

"But necessary."

Another shrug. Which reminded Sophie that Madame
de Montesse was a free witch. Not sworn to the temple.
At least not here in Anglion. Perhaps she might know
something that would help Sophie with her problem.
Perhaps Illvyans knew of other ways to funnel power to
the goddess. Or how to manage if she couldn't. The Domina hadn't brought up the question of her failed rites
again, and Sophie wasn't going to be the first to raise the
subject with her. Nor was she comfortable asking the
Domina any questions about magic beyond the lessons
she was being given. She didn't want to give Domina
Skey any reason to think she was seeking more power.

Which she wasn't. But she did want to understand
what had happened to her. She needed someone she
could talk to. Someone who had knowledge of magic beyond that of Anglion's traditions. Someone like Madame
de Montesse. She should try to speak with her privately.

Soon. If only to poke around the edges of the subject to learn if the Illvyan could be trusted. She seemed not to have told anyone where Sophie and Cameron had gone on the day of the attack, but that didn't mean she was an ally.

"Madame—" Sophie began to say.

"Lady Sophia." Another voice calling her. Cameron's voice. She turned toward the sound, trying to squelch the small light of happiness that sparked in her at the sight of him.

"Lady Sophia," he said again as he reached them. He nodded quickly to Madame de Montesse. "You need to come with me, milady. The Illusioners have word of your parents."

CHAPTER TEN

Cameron wished he could shake the odd clear-detached-diamond-sharp edges that the dose of red-wort tisane he'd taken gave everything. The commander had assigned him the midnight-to-sunrise shift in Eloisa's guard and then asked him to come back again for an afternoon duty, given the Red Guard was spread thin. He'd stolen about four hours' sleep, but it wasn't nearly enough. Hence the redwort to keep him on his feet.

It kept him awake and alert, but he'd never liked the sensation of it. Or the punishing collapse that came when it wore off. He could push the doses another night or two, but he would pay for it. Besides which, being artificially stimulated and still trying to adjust to the fact that he was going to be married was hardly the state he would have selected for his first meeting with his wife-to-be's parents.

He'd wanted to cry off, let someone else escort Sophie down to the house in the city where her parents were staying. But Sophie had asked him to come so that he could meet her mother and father. Difficult to come up with an excuse to avoid doing that when they were to be married. And maybe that was just as well. He had no idea if another man could react to Sophie's power in the way he had—goddess, he hoped not, because that wasn't a recipe for a good marriage—but best not to take the risk of finding out. Or letting anyone else discover just how much power she had whilst they were trying to keep that silent.

He looked down at Sophie, sitting beside him in the rocking carriage, her face alight as she took in the sights of the city through the window.

If he'd had his own way, they would have walked, but Eloisa had insisted on the carriage and a second Red Guard to accompany them. Apparently, she was taking no risks with her newest royal witch, binding or no binding.

The streets were oddly quiet, suggesting that the citizens of Kingswell shared Eloisa's apprehension about the likely safety of the capital. Some would have left altogether, he supposed, fleeing in the wake of the attack. Some might not return.

But that was Eloisa's problem. He frowned to himself, thinking of Elly and her injuries. She'd looked slightly better today when he'd been summoned to her chambers so she could give her orders to send him after Sophie, but goddess, the bandages and bruises marring her face still made him feel ill.

And enraged. Logically, he knew that, even if he'd been there, he couldn't have prevented her being hurt by fire and falling stones, but he couldn't help the irrational wish that he could have done just that.

He was one of her bodyguards. It was his duty to protect her. And instead he'd failed. Both to keep her from harm and to guard the one she had tasked him to watch.

His future wife. Whose parents were waiting for them just a few streets farther on. He forced himself to try to relax and turned his attention back to Sophie. She had tried to tamp down her happiness at finding out her parents were unharmed—out of deference for his own loss and others he imagined—but she hadn't been entirely successful. A smile flickered at the corners of her mouth as she looked out the window, and she was creeping farther forward on the carriage seat with every foot they traveled toward their destination.

It was hard not to feel the envy that slunk through his brain when he'd brought her the news. His father had been difficult and demanding, but his death had punched a hole in Cameron's world. One more thing to deepen the sensation that the world had tilted and that all was off-balance. Battle mages were taught to center themselves in times of stress or danger, to stay calm and unleash their emotions only when they needed to channel them for their magic. But right now, whenever he reached for that place of calm within himself that he had taken for granted up until now, it shifted and bent, throwing him out of kilter once more.

"Thank you for coming with me," Sophie said, turning back from the window. She smiled at him. It was a genuine smile, free of the strain that had been shadowing her expressions since they'd first fled Kingswell.

"You don't need to thank me," he said. "Your family will be my family, too, soon."

She nodded. "Did El—I mean the queen-to-be—did she say anything more about when we might marry? She didn't really speak to me this morning." Her smile vanished like someone had blown out a candle. Her lips flattened, hands twisting in her lap. "I think she's very angry with me."

"With both of us," Cameron offered. He leaned across and patted her arm. A buzz of awareness hit his skin, warmed, flowed through his body, rousing it. He pulled back, trying not to look too obvious about it. But Sophie's pupils had flared suddenly dark. It was clear she'd felt it, too.

"The queen-to-be will forget this soon enough," he said. Once they were safely married. Though, with no

chance to speak to her privately, he had no way to judge
how she felt about handing her sometime lover over to
Sophie. "She had plenty of other problems to deal with
besides us."

"I just wish I could do something to fix it. Or at least
to help her. She needs to get well. If she recovers, the city
will, too. *Anglion* will, too."

"Domina Skey is taking good care of her," Cameron
said. "It's been only a few days. She will be well soon
enough."

Sophie bit her lip, and he remembered again what
would happen when Eloïsa rose from her sickbed. A funeral. A coronation. And then a wedding. "Perhaps you
could ask Domina Skey if there is anything you can do
to help."

That earned him a perhaps well-deserved look of skep-
ticism. "I don't think the Domina likes me very much."

"Perhaps not, but she would be foolish to turn down
any assistance she can get at this point." Domina Skey
hadn't achieved her position by being stupid or slow to
use any resources offered to her. The temple had to be
stretched as thin as the Red Guard, tending to the in
jured. Though it wouldn't hurt Sophie to seem eager to
please. Which reminded him of something else.

"It might be wiser not to be seen with Madame de
Montesse."

Sophie's brows lifted. "Madame de Montesse helped
us escape. Am I supposed to ignore her if our paths cross?
Because that's what happened. I met her by chance. I
didn't seek her out." She sounded defensive.

"I didn't think you had. But the mood in the city will
be dangerous for any refugee for some time to come. We
haven't discovered who was behind the attacks, but the
prevailing theory is that it was Illvya."

"If it was an Illvyan magician, it seems odd that there
has been no following attacks, does it not?"

He shrugged. "Perhaps. Perhaps they miscalculated and got caught in their own destruction. Or perhaps they were working through agents. Which is why it would be wisest to avoid Illvyans right now."

"She helped us," Sophie protested. "She got us away from the attack. She didn't have to tell us she had a portal. Besides, she's been here for years. And she swore the oaths of loyalty to the Crown. Otherwise she wouldn't be allowed to own a store selling the things she does."

"Oaths can be broken," Cameron said. "And I don't think you and I need any more attention just now. It's not like you were going to seek her out anyway, is it? So just try not to have any dealings with her until things are calmer." He thought it was irritation that flashed in her brown eyes. But then she looked away, out the window again as the carriage reached its destination and came to a halt.

❧

Sophie had barely stepped out of the carriage before the door of the small house they had stopped in front of flew open and a man and a woman he had to assume were her parents rushed toward her, enveloping her in tight embraces when they reached their daughter. Three identical expressions of delight shone from their faces, and he swallowed against a sudden stab of grief as he stepped onto the cobbles paving the small front yard.

Sophie's father let go of her and looked past Sophie to Cameron. "And who is this, my dear?" he asked. He was a man of only middle height, his eyes the same clear brown as Sophie's, dark hair graying. But his smile was warm, and the hand he extended to Cameron clasped his firmly.

"This is Lieutenant Mackenzie," Sophie said hesitantly. "He—he kept me safe during the attack."

"Then you have my thanks, sir," Sophie's father said. "Mackenzie? One of Inglewood's boys?"

"Yes, sir," Cameron replied. Sophie's father was a marque, the lowest of the three noble ranks, if he was remembering correctly, which made him just Sir Kendall, not a lord like an erl or a barron. "I'm Cameron, the youngest."

Sir Kendall's expression turned sober. "I saw the casualty list. I'm very sorry for your loss, Lieutenant. Your father was a good man. A great loss to the court."

"Thank you, sir." There wasn't much else to be said.

"This is my wife, Emma," Sir Kendall continued, reaching out a hand to draw his wife away from Sophie. Cameron bowed politely.

"It was good of you to escort Sophie," Lady Kendall said with a brilliant smile. She shared the same coloring as her daughter and husband, though her hair shone with a reddish tint in the sunlight that made him think she must have some small earth magic. Not enough for the true red of a strong earth witch but enough to be noted.

"The queen-to-be thought it best," Cameron said. "The streets are still—nervous."

"We know," Sir Kendall said dryly. "Else we would have been here the day of the attack. It's taken until now for us to be allowed to come any closer to the city." He smiled at his daughter. "Which I assume is your doing, my dear. The Illusioners who found us mentioned that your power had manifested. That is a happy thing in the midst of all this sadness." He bent and kissed Sophie's cheek, and she looked so purely delighted for a moment that Cameron's heart turned over. She hadn't looked like that since the moment they'd—well, perhaps better not to think of such things in front of her parents.

He looked away and saw Lady Kendall watching him with a curious expression.

"Perhaps it would be better if we went inside," she said. "We have tea and managed to procure a cake. It's not exactly the birthday celebration we were planning, but it will have to do until things return to normal."

She proceeded to move them into the house with the efficiency of one of Alec's best herders, and Cameron founded himself seated in a small parlor, tastefully decorated in pale green and blue, seated on a sofa opposite Sophie and her mother. Tea appeared, and he drank gratefully, hoping it might offer an antidote to some of the redwort's effects.

Sophie cut the cake, and he ate, wondering if she felt as uncomfortable as he did, knowing what they had to tell her parents. He took a second slice, redwort making him unusually hungry, as always, but refused a third politely.

Sir Kendall—Cameron's brain offered up Grant as his first name, and he hoped that was correct—leaned forward a little in his chair.

"Now that we've eaten, perhaps wc can talk a little," he said. "The way the two of you are avoiding looking at each other, am I to assume there is something you haven't yet told us?"

He looked from Cameron to his daughter. Sophie put down her teacup, the china rattling slightly in her grip. "Lieutenant Mackenzie isn't just my escort," she said in a rush. "The queen-to-be has decided that we are to marry."

Blunt dark brows flew upward on her father's face. "So soon?" He looked at Cameron. "A royal witch would normally have her celebrations before any betrothal."

Cameron didn't try to avoid the slightly accusing gaze. "It's not exactly normal circumstances, sir. The queen-to-be thinks it best if Sophie is married quickly. Partly to show that things are business as usual, I think."

"Hmmmph. Well, she could at least have waited to speak to me. The marriage of royal witches is the Crown's prerogative, but it is a courtesy to involve the parents. It seems I need to go to court and speak to young Eloisa."

"The queen-to-be was injured in the attack, Father," Sophie said quickly. "She's not holding audiences right now. She needs to rest and recover."

"Be that as it may," Sir Kendall said firmly. "If she's healthy enough to decide on your husband, she's healthy enough to tell me so face-to-face."

Sophie looked somewhat mortified. "I am happy to marry Lieutenant Mackenzie," she said. "You don't need to worry."

"And you?" Sir Kendall asked, directing his gaze back to Cameron. "Are you happy with the match, Lieutenant? And your brother, the erl?"

"I am more than happy. As any man would be who was granted your daughter's hand," Cameron said, smiling quickly at Sophie. "Liam will not object to the match. He is a servant of the court, as am I. Not that his objection would change the queen-to-be's mind. You must know that about her."

"She always was headstrong," Sir Kendall agreed. "But that doesn't mean she doesn't have to observe protocol. Perhaps I'll return to court with you now." He made as if to rise from his seat, and Sophie made a small noise of protest in her throat.

"It is nearly the end of the day," Cameron said. "The queen-to-be will be tired. I am on shift tonight—I am one of her personal guard—" He saw Sir Kendall's brows lift again. "I'm sure I can arrange an audience for tomorrow." He wasn't sure, but he saw Sophie's expression relax and decided that providing a delay was the right decision. Give Sir Kendall the night to think about things and calm down a little before he spoke to Eloisa. A good night's sleep might reconcile him to the situation.

"That sounds like a perfect solution," Lady Kendall said before her husband could speak again. "Lieutenant Mackenzie can send word when things are arranged, and we can proceed from there." She looked at Sophie. "The queen-to-be hasn't decided on a date for the wedding, has she?"

Sophie shook her head. "No. There are other things that must happen first. King Stefan's funeral. And the coronation."

Lady Kendall looked relieved. "Well, that's good. It will give us longer to get to know the lieutenant. And to make some arrangements."

Goddess, he'd seen that gleam in women's eyes before. Mostly his mother's when she'd been involved in arranging weddings for his brothers. No good came from such things. But his mother had died shortly after Alec's wedding. So she wouldn't be able to try to turn his wedding into a court spectacle. He and Sophie needed a quick and quiet wedding, much as he hated the thought that neither of his parents would be present.

But perhaps now wasn't the best time to voice that opinion. Not with her father still likely to go off half-cocked if he thought his daughter was being slighted. He got the impression that Sophie had gotten that stubborn streak she'd demonstrated from him, along with the temper she mostly tried to hide.

From outside he heard the chimes of an hour bell somewhere nearby start to ring. Six. It would be growing dark. He was under strict orders to have Sophie back in the palace before nightfall. Which was another thing her parents weren't going to like. But best to get it over with.

"We should be going," he said. "It will be night soon."

Lady Kendall looked stricken. "So soon? I thought you would be staying with us, Sophie."

"The queen-to-be thinks Sophie will be safest in the palace."

"The palace has bloody holes in its walls," Sir Kendall objected.

"It's also full of battle mages, Illusioners, and temple

devouts," Cameron said. "Given her powers, she is best protected by those for now. Goddess forbid there should be another attack, but if there is, Sophie will be of interest now that she's manifested."

"All the more reason to hide her away somewhere unexpected," Sir Kendall grumbled, but he waved a hand. "Fine, then. Take her away. But I expect word of an audience time first thing in the morning. And, Sophie, you are to come see us again tomorrow."

"I have to go to the temple," Sophie said. "I'm having . . . instruction. And I need to attend the queen-to-be as well."

"I'm sure you will still have a spare hour or two," Sir Kendall said firmly. "Come here and let us fuss over you a bit. We're not going to let the palace steal all of you from us. Not just yet." He shot Cameron a look that brooked no argument. So Cameron didn't offer one, just made his good-byes, gathered up his wife-to-be, and fled back to the palace.

The carriage shuddered and jolted over the cobblestones, and Sophie tried not to wish that she were staying behind with her parents, where things could be uncomplicated for a few hours, whether her father was angry or not. She didn't think he would actually object to the wedding and, quite frankly, it wouldn't matter if he did. Royal witches were the court's to command.

She wasn't sure she liked that thought now that it was real. Of course, the court could degree any noble marriage, but in reality that seldom happened where magic wasn't involved.

A sigh escaped her, and Cameron looked back from the carriage window.

"Are you all right, milady?"

"Yes." She sighed again, irritated at his insistence on

formality. "Can't you call me Sophie again? After all, we're going to be married."

His lips pressed together briefly; then he nodded. "As you wish. Sophie. When we're in private."

"Then you won't have to remember it very often until after we're married. Not if things continue as they have for the last day."

"This is hardly a normal situation."

"I know. It's just . . ." She hesitated. "It's just that we haven't had a chance to talk. About this—" She waved a hand between them. "And I haven't had a chance to . . . to apologize. I brought this on you."

He shook his head. "It took two of us, Sophie."

"I stepped into the ley line."

"And I should have thought to warn you not to. Not to mention known better than to touch you once you did." He shook his head again, looked rueful.

"You knew?"

"Knew what?"

"That a ley line might do . . . that." She didn't know how much the Red Guard standing outside on the back of the carriage where a groom would usually ride might be able to hear, so she kept her voice low.

Blue eyes widened for a second. "That it would make us power-crazed?" Cameron opened his mouth, then paused. "I had . . . heard," he said eventually, and she knew he wasn't about to tell her the whole truth, "that if two people with magic do such things, the power can make it more . . . intense."

The words weren't meant to hurt her, but they did. Because they meant that he could have been with any royal witch and he would have reacted the same way.

She looked away. "I see."

"Forgive me," he said. "I didn't mean to offend you."

"I'm not offended. You were honest." She leaned forward, touched his hand quickly, then drew back as the heat flared between them again. "I would like to think that we can give each other that, at least. Maybe we didn't choose this marriage, but we can choose how to behave. Give each other respect, and maybe other things can come."

He nodded. "That seems fair to me. All right, honesty, milady. I will give you that. If you will do the same for me."

"Then can I ask you a question?"

Wariness. But then he nodded. "Of course."

"Is there someone else? Someone you were hoping to wed?"

He straightened on the seat, large and solid in the small space. "No," he said firmly. "No one I was hoping to wed."

Which didn't answer all of her question. The part about there being someone else. That made her think there was. Someone he wasn't going to wed. Someone already married, perhaps.

"I wasn't a virgin," he added. "I have had other women in my bed."

That brought an unexpectedly sharp pang of jealousy.

"But I will not again. I intend to be faithful. Unless you wish otherwise?" He cocked his head. "Is there someone you were thinking of?"

She shook her head quickly. "Oh no. I've always known I wouldn't get to choose, so it seemed silly to even think about it. And it's not like young men in the court go out of their way to flirt with potential royal witches," she said. "The rules are strict, after all. As we have discovered."

"I would have thought perhaps that some of the older ones, the ones with actual chances of being granted a witch for a wife, might do some courting."

"They try. Indirectly." She wrinkled her nose. "But in truth, I tried to avoid such things. There was no one amongst the older lords who caught my attention. Some of them were kind to me, but nothing more. Believe me, I am happy with the queen-to-be's choice. You're not twenty years older than me, for a start." She paused, realizing she actually had no idea how old he was.

"I'm seven and twenty," he said. "If you were wondering."

"I was going to look you up in the court records when I got a chance," she said with a smile. "I know a little about your family but not enough. Ladies-in-waiting are taught court history, of course, but there's so much of it."

"I'm sure the Illusioners' library will be full of tales of Inglewood scandals you can read about," Cameron said. In addition to wielding their art to glamour and to hide and to seek secrets, the Illusioners were scholars and archivists.

"Are you scandalous?" she said.

"Any old family has scandals," Cameron said. "My family stood with King Leo, but we were part of the court well before Leo's reign. Long enough to cause some problems over the years."

"So you're continuing the family tradition?" she asked.

"My father's view of the family tradition would be that it was get what you want by any means possible," he said. "So accidentally acquiring a wife is not quite what he would approve of. If I'd planned it all out, he would have approved." He smiled, the expression somewhat rueful again. "Though I'm sure he would have approved of you regardless of my part in the process."

"Because I'm a witch?"

He nodded. "Honestly, yes. He arranged Liam's marriage to his satisfaction, but I'm not sure Lucy was quite to his taste."

"And you, did he have plans for you?" she asked, amused.

"I'm sure he did," Cameron said, voice going flat.

Idiot, she thought. Making jests about his not-yet-dead-a-week father. "I'm sorry. I can't imagine losing my parents. I wish I could make it easier for you."

"You do." He smiled then, and she was, once again, startled by just how much it changed his face when he smiled and meant it. With how handsome her husband-to-be was. And how much she wished he would touch her again. Make everything go away again. If only for a little while. Impulsively, she leaned forward, laid her hand on his. Left it there.

Watched him as they touched. Saw his pupils flare dark in the blue eyes, just as she was sure hers did. Just two hands touching, and yet it made her want him badly. She barely knew how sex should be between two people. She only knew how it had been between them. But she didn't know if this hunger was usual. How much of it was power and how much of it was them? It was difficult to care when just a simple touch could feel so good.

Cameron sucked in a breath and then lifted her hand away. "I think it's best if we avoid that. Until we're married, I mean."

"Why?" she said, not ready to let the feeling go. "We're already going to be married. We can't make things any worse, can we?"

"Perhaps not. But the queen-to-be wants this to be quiet. Simple. Hard to avoid a scandal if someone catches us doing . . ."

Did that mean he wanted to? Right now? As much as she did? It was a pleasing thought. Maybe he had been sharing a bed with someone else before. But she intended to keep him in hers now. Maybe she had been power-crazed, but having him inside her in the open with no bed and no time had felt so good that she was more than willing to try again. What might it be like to share a bed with him with nights and nights—a lifetime, really—to explore each other?

The ladies-in-waiting talked about men, of course. More frankly than those men might be happy to hear. But they were still somewhat circumspect in front of those who, like Sophie, were unmarried. She had over-heard Beata talking about books once, though. Books meant to instruct married couples. If such things existed, then the Illusioners' library, which was meant to hold a copy of every book in Anglion, seemed a likely place to find them. They sought knowledge. Knowledge was power, after all.

And she was becoming tired of feeling as though everyone around her thought they could control her. To distract herself from thoughts of Cameron and marriage, she made herself return to the other topic that was consuming her. Magic. The Domina was teaching her how to use hers, but Sophie was certain there were many things she wasn't being told.

"Can I ask you something else?" she said.

"Of course."

"The Domina said something about my power being tangled with yours. Do you know what she meant?"

He shook his head. "No. I'm sorry. I know about battle magic but never had need to study the other arts. I showed no aptitude for illusions." He paused, looking thoughtful.

Damn. She had hoped he understood better than she. She was starting to think earth magic involved entirely too much secrecy. If she'd known more about the realities of her power, then neither of them would be in this position, after all.

"The Domina would know the answer," Cameron said.

She shook her head. "I don't think the Domina wants me asking questions. Not right now. And I doubt any of the ladies-in-waiting would know. Only a few of them have any power and none of those are strong." Her mother's power wasn't strong enough for her to know such things, either. Madame de Montesse's face suddenly sprang to mind. A free witch. Schooled in Illvya. She would know. But that path was risky whilst she was in disgrace with Eloisa and the Domina. The last thing she needed was them thinking she was curious about Illvya.

"The Illusioners have books on the arts," Cameron said suddenly. "Now that you have manifested, you're entitled to see them."

She could have kissed him. And that thought brought the desire to do exactly that. She fought it back, focusing instead on the solution he offered.

So, find out more. That was the most sensible course of action. Most of the Illusioners' library was open to the court, though generally the ladies went there only for novels and poetry, as far as she knew. But, as Cameron had said, now that she had power, she could access those books that were off-limits to those without. Or the ones about earth magic, at least. She could see if there was anything that would help her understand what had happened. Knowledge, after all, was power.

CHAPTER ELEVEN

"Sophie?" Lady Beata said as Sophie stepped into the queen-to-be's antechamber. "I thought you were dismissed for the day."

Sophie nodded, smiling at Beata and the ladies grouped on the chairs around the fireplace. "I thought I was, too, but there was a note waiting when I got back to the erl's apartments. It requested that I return."

"I didn't send a note," Beata said.

"No. It came from the Domina."

"I see." Beata glanced down at Sophie's hand as if expecting to see something there.

A betrothal ring, perhaps? After last night's events, the ladies had to be curious about why the queen-to-be had wanted Cameron and what had happened behind the closed doors to Eloisa's chambers. All the more reason to obey the Domina's summons and get past the ladies as soon as possible.

Besides which, once she had finished doing whatever it was the Domina wanted of her, she could finally get the sleep she was starting to desperately need. "I must attend the queen-to-be," she said firmly, and walked past Beata. She didn't miss the speculative glances directed at her, though the look Beata gave her was more frustrated than curious.

Lady Beata was used to being the one in charge of the ladies-in-waiting and one of Eloisa's closest confidantes. She wasn't taking being kept out of the flow of information very well. But Sophie wasn't here to make Beata feel better, so she ignored her and the other ladies and knocked on the door to the bedchamber.

Inside the room, the scene was much the same as it had been earlier in the day. Eloisa in the bed, face still bandaged, the Domina and a temple devout standing nearby. As Sophie closed the door behind her, Eloisa lifted her head.

"Sophie?"

She went to the bed, curtsied. "Yes, I'm here, Your Highness."

"Your parents are well?"

"Yes, milady. They hadn't reached the capital before the—well, they are unhurt."

"Did you tell them of your betrothal?" Eloisa asked. Her voice sounded weaker. Softer and less certain than it had been earlier in the day.

Sophie glanced at the Domina, who made a little "go on" gesture. "Yes, my lady. We did. My father wishes to speak to you, but I do not think he is displeased."

"Your father should be grateful to the queen-to-be for saving your skin," the Domina said.

Sophie bit the inside of her lip, determined not to rise to the bait. The Domina had been needling at her all day, but Sophie wasn't going to give her even more ammunition to vent her anger.

"Tell the duty captain when you leave," Eloisa said. "He will be able to make an appointment for your father to see me."

"You shouldn't be seeing anyone yet," the Domina protested. "You need to heal."

"There are things to be done," Eloisa said, pushing up on her pillows. "The kingdom needs to know that some-

one is in charge again. That we are unbroken. That we—"
She broke off with a gasp, clutching at her head.

"My lady?" Sophie said, but the Domina was there,
pushing her out of the way.

"Where does it hurt?" Domina Skey demanded.

"H-head," Eloisa gasped, then cried out, one hand
clutching at her skull.

The Domina laid a hand over Eloisa's. Sophie saw a
shimmering pulse of power—faint silver rather than the
brighter shade that the Domina's magic had been earlier
in the day. Apparently, she wasn't the only tired one.

Sophie held her breath, but Eloisa's expression didn't
alter.

"Give me your hand," the Domina demanded, and
Sophie held it out obediently.

The Domina's fingers clasped hard around hers, biting
like a vise. There was a curious sensation like the room
doubling in front of her eyes and then a roar in her ears
as a rush of power moved through her like a burning
tide. Too much. Too fast.

Sophie gasped, but the Domina's fingers merely tightened to the point where the bones in her hand began to
throb a protest. The sensation was secondary to the searing pulse of the power.

Too much.

Her head started to spin, and she closed her eyes,
swallowing against the dizziness. It didn't help. She felt
herself stagger, and then she fell, the room fading around
her.

When Sophie opened her eyes again, she was lying on
the floor, one cheek pressed to the expensive silk carpet.
It took a few seconds to remember where she was, what
she had been doing. The queen-to-be. She rolled and
pushed up, ignoring the dizziness that rose with the
movement of looking toward the bed. The Domina stood
there, looking down at Eloisa, who seemed to be sleeping.

The Domina turned at the movement. Her face as she studied Sophie was cool. "Interesting," she said.

"The queen-to-be?" Sophie asked. She didn't know what the Domina found interesting about this situation. She wanted to know if Eloisa was all right.

"She's sleeping. She is all right. For now."

Sophie tried to stand but had to stop when the room spun around her.

The Domina's face was unsympathetic. "You are dismissed. I suggest you find a ley line before you sleep. The queen-to-be expects her ladies to be healthy."

⤜⤛⤚

When Sophie woke in the morning in the Mackenzies' apartments, she wasn't entirely clear how she had gotten back there.

The journey back from the queen-to-be's room was foggy, though she had a fleeting memory of descending down to the ground floor of the palace, glimpsing the moon shining through the warded broken wall as she sat next to a ley line and tried to draw power back into herself.

But she had no memory of actually reaching the Mackenzies' rooms or of getting into bed. Her stomach rumbled suddenly. There was definitely no memory of eating.

The high-pitched toll of the hour bell in the Salt Spire suddenly began to ring out, and she counted the chimes off. Six. Still early. With Eloisa unwell, there were none of the usual morning rituals of dressing for breakfast with the court or preparing for the king holding audience or even the weekly dawn temple services on seventh day. She frowned at that, trying to work out what day it even was. It had been seventh day, she thought, the day of the attack.

Which meant today was . . . sixth day? The events of the week were running together in her mind, the way night had.

She would check at breakfast. Lady Mackenzie had one of the artificer's day clocks, which showed the hour and the day. They cost a fortune, which was why they weren't common, but in this case, she was thankful such things existed so she wouldn't have to make a fool of herself by actually asking.

She swung her legs over the edge of the bed and then froze as she caught sight of her reflection in the looking glass hanging on the wall. Her hair, caught in the morning light streaming through the window, looked distinctly red.

But that couldn't be right. It took months, sometimes years, for an earth witch's hair to change color, from prolonged exposure to the earth magic she wielded. Peering closer at the mirror, she studied her hair. It was hardly the deep red of Eloisa's hair, but there was definitely a reddish tinge to the boring brown that hadn't been there before.

Goddess. How much power had the Domina pulled through her night?

Her stomach growled again. More urgent than knowing what day it was or why her hair was changing too fast was food, it seemed. She felt better than she had the previous day. Tired but not exhausted. She would take the Domina's advice again and go to the ley line before she went back to the queen-to-be's chambers.

The thought made her stomach twist in a different way. Worry for Eloisa and whether she had recovered from whatever had happened last night, but also worry about what the Domina had done and the expression on her face as she'd looked down at Sophie on the floor, like she was studying a cow or a pig, trying to determine if it suited her. Something to be used or discarded.

Foolish, Sophie thought. *You're just being foolish.*

The Domina had been worried about Eloisa, as So-

phie was. And the queen-to-be's health was more important than anything else right now.

❧

When she reached the breakfast table, having bathed
and dressed in yet another black dress, it was still early.
The silk of the dress was stiff and confining. She had no
shortage of black dresses. The princess had been in full
mourning for Prince Iain for the first six months Sophie
had been at court, and her ladies-in-waiting had donned
it with her. They'd looked like a flock of crows moving
through the court. The court had followed Eloisa's fashion lead to a degree. King Stefan had not chosen to wear
black for his son-in-law, though, so the court had merely
favored a more subdued palette. The whole court had
felt gloomy and bleak, a sea of darker colors, broken
only by the pale gleam of pearls.

Eloisa had worn only her black pearls during that period, looped around her throat, gleaming like dark-
sheened rainbows against her skin. Other jewels had quite
fallen out of favor, the customary ritual pearls becoming
crowded on necks and hands with any other pieces of
pearl jewelry the courtiers could lay their hands on.

And now, just as they were reaching the end of the
mourning period for Eloisa's husband, when colors other
than gray and dark blue and green might have been acceptable, they would be donning black again for the king.
Though Sophie wasn't sure exactly how long that might
be required. Kings were different. They died, but that was
immediately followed by the installation of a new monarch, which was meant to be a time of celebration. No
one wore black to coronations. That would be ill luck.
Eloisa would set the style for the court again after her
coronation. If she chose to go into mourning again, then
the court would follow.

The breakfast table was already stocked with rolls and meats and cheese and platters of berries and nuts. A servant appeared and silently poured tea. Sophie sipped and squinted across the room to where the clock sat on the mantel. Sixth day.

Good.

She reached for a roll, then froze as Cameron appeared in the doorway of the dining room.

He started, too, when he saw her; then he smiled and bowed. "Good morning, milady," he said. "You're up early."

Was she imagining things, or had he looked at her hair a second time? She fought the urge to smooth it down further. She'd braided and pinned it so tightly to her head that she was sure to have a headache by the end of the day. "I have to attend Eloisa. I thought you had the late duty."

"I do. But Liam wanted to see me this morning and the barracks are chaos, so I thought I might try to catch a few hours' sleep here. Might be quieter."

Sophie had her doubts about that. The Inglewood apartments were stuffed nearly to the rafters with guests. "Is there any news?"

"News?" He took a seat opposite her, which was only proper when no one in the household staff knew that they were betrothed. But she wished he would sit next to her. Maybe he would ease her nerves.

"Of who was behind the attack?"

He shook his head. "No, but I believe they've cleared most of the rubble from the Salt Hall. Commander Peters has had most of the battle mages moving stones for days. Now the Illusioners can come in. See if they can find anything."

"So the attack was magical?"

"Most likely. To do so much damage . . . Well, perhaps gunpowder and other things could achieve it, but you'd need an awful lot of it. Magic seems more likely."

"Illvyan?"

He shrugged, reaching for a roll. "That remains to be seen."

She bit into her roll, chewed, swallowed. Reached for more tea. "What do you think will happen if they find out?"

Cameron shook his head. "That is entirely up to the queen-to-be."

<hr>

When Sophie reached Eloisa's chambers, she wasn't greeted by the flock of ladies-in-waiting in the antechamber. Instead, the door to the bedroom stood open and the sound of excited voices turned the air into the familiar high-pitched chatter she was used to when the ladies were in full flight.

A glance through the doorway confirmed that the bedroom was full. Over the heads of the four ladies closest to the door, she thought she saw Eloisa's bright red head leaning against the embroidered headboard. But that made no sense. Her head had still been bandaged last night. She pushed her way past the ladies without thinking.

"Milady, are you recovered?"

The chatter in the room died as all eyes focused on her. She ignored the sudden scrutiny, focusing instead on Eloisa, who was indeed free of bandages. On her face at least. Bruises still marked her skin—though more green-yellow than vivid purple now. Her hair was shorter than it had been, cut off to nearly shoulder length. To hide the damage from burns perhaps? But it was clean, and Lady Beata stood close to the bed with a hairbrush.

Eloisa looked at Sophie, and for a moment there was warmth in her green eyes. But then her expression turned shuttered and controlled. "A little," she said.

"She is doing much better," Lady Beata chirped, dark eyes also focused on Sophie.

Sophie wondered why everyone was staring at her, then realized that they were wondering if she had anything to do with the rapid improvement in Eloisa's health. And therefore wondering exactly what powers she had manifested.

Most of the temple witches had healing skills to a degree, but usually the magic was used to increase the effectiveness of the herbs and other medicines they used. There were stories of the early days of Anglion. Of saints of the goddess who could heal just by touch, but those were legends. No one had shown such powers in centuries. Much like no royal witch had been able to call the weather.

"She is," Domina Skey said, moving into view from behind another of the ladies. Sophie started. She hadn't noticed the Domina. She controlled the movement with a force of will, ignoring the sudden urge to move farther away from the woman who rose in the wake of the initial surprise. The Domina was no one to be scared of. She was intimidating, yes, but she was a servant of the goddess. Dedicated to the good of Anglion and its people.

Still, the calculating look in the Domina's brown eyes made her want to run away as she heard the words from last night again in her head. The casual dismissal. The lack of concern that whatever she had done had left Sophie unconscious on the floor.

"Ladies," Domina Skey said with a wave of her hand. "The queen-to-be had matters to discuss with Lady Sophia. Leave us, please."

Sophie was somewhat dismayed to see how readily they followed the Domina's instructions, filing from the room without waiting for confirmation of the order from Eloisa. Eloisa, who was queen-to-be. Who was the one in charge.

The Domina's influence had grown quickly in the days since the attack, it seemed. Or perhaps the ladies were just grateful to have someone take charge in uncertain times. But regardless of why, they shouldn't just be blindly following the Domina's orders. She had done that last night and ended up on the floor. She needed to be more cautious. The Domina was the servant of the goddess, yes, but they all needed to remember that she was merely human as well, subject to human desires, perhaps. Like ambition. Ambition to seize influence over a young, inexperienced, and injured queen? King Stefan had been respectful to the temple, and the Domina had been consulted where appropriate, but his closest coun-cilors came from the men of the court. Erls and barrons. Nobles and warriors like himself. But Eloisa wasn't a warrior. She was a royal witch. Dedicated to the country and the goddess. So the Domina bore watching. If Eloisa didn't realize that now because of her injuries, well, then Sophie would have to watch for her. Wait for a chance to speak if she decided it was necessary.

She watched Beata, last to leave as usual, close the door, her expression wildly curious. Sophie didn't think she would be able to escape being interrogated by the ladies-in-waiting much longer. But she would keep her mouth firmly closed until the queen-to-be gave her leave to discuss her betrothal.

"Come here," the Domina said after they had heard the *thunk* of the latch falling into place on the other side of the door. Sophie moved closer, trying not to reveal her caution. The Domina waved at the door, and a ward shimmered into life over it. Keeping them in or shielding them from listening ears? A shiver ran down her spine. The Domina could do anything she wanted, really. The queen-to-be was too ill to stop her, and Sophie had no-where near enough control of her powers yet.

The Domina bent over the queen-to-be. "I need to remove the bandages on your arm. See how the burn is healing."

Eloisa winced a little but nodded. Sophie held her breath. Burns were hard to treat. She'd assisted her mother tending to women on the estate who'd burned themselves with hearth fires or kitchen accidents. The pain of the injuries had been hard to watch. Her mother had tended to err on the side of dosing them liberally with the strongest pain tonics they could brew, which could be a risky strategy.

The other complication with burns was that the wounds grew infected easily. Even if infection was escaped, there was inevitably scarring. There were liniments and salves that could prevent the worst of it, but Sophie had never seen anyone walk away from a serious burn fully recovered. Would Eloisa carry the scars of the attack her whole life?

Before she could worry too much, the Domina told her to fetch a basin and bandages from the table on the far side of the room, which was littered with bottles of tonics and potions, small jars of powders, and piles of dressings. Sophie watched, trying not to wince as the Domina eased the bandage free from Eloisa's arm. The burn revealed was raw-looking but not as bad as Sophie had expected. She leaned a little closer, watching carefully as the Domina gently cleaned the damaged skin. If Sophie hadn't known better, she would have guessed the wound had been healing for several weeks.

"Has the pain improved?" the Domina asked.

Eloisa glanced at Sophie. "Yes. It's far less today." She looked back at the Domina. "Is this because of what we discussed earlier?"

Sophie kept her eyes fixed on the basin she held. Had they been talking about her? About what the Domina had done—not that Sophie was entirely clear what that might have been. The Domina dropped the cotton she had been using back into the basin.

"I think so. But it warrants another experiment."

Sophie's stomach curled uneasily. She didn't like the sound of that. Or of the speculative expression on the Domina's face when she risked looking up.

"Return the basin and then come back here," the Domina ordered.

Her heartbeat doubled as she made the journey to the table and back. She couldn't walk slowly, couldn't appear reluctant, though her nerves shrieked at her to do exactly that. She had to trust the queen-to-be. Sophie was sworn to serve her. She would honor her vow. She was too aware of her chest rising and falling fast against the restrictive dress and corset as she returned to the Domina's side.

"Give me your hand."

It was worse the second time. The searing surge of power came faster and stronger, setting her nerves alight with the feeling of fire. There was no hesitation in the Domina's demand on her power or her connection to the earth magic or whatever it was she was using. She just dragged the power up through Sophie like she was calling a lightning bolt up from the earth beneath Sophie's feet. Sophie fought to breathe, to remember who she was. To remember why she was trying to stand there and take this. The pain ricocheted and echoed, seeming to double with each hard-won breath, until she dissolved into nothing but the pain and light, a flare of hard, gold sensation that licked at her and bit until, once again, she lost the fight.

This time when she woke, it was to the sound of voices. The Domina's and Eloisa's. Somehow, through the memory of pain and the exhaustion that made her want nothing more than to surrender back to the darkness, she managed to tell herself to stay very still.

If you are awake, they'll stop talking, a voice from somewhere deep in her mind said. *You'll learn nothing. Do not move.*

It seemed as sensible a plan as any other. She lay quietly, keeping her breaths slow and shallow, drawing on the skills she'd used to fool her little brothers when they'd wanted to wake her up early. Her mother had forbidden them from waking her if she was sleeping, so the ability to feign sleep came in useful on the mornings when she couldn't face a near-dawn excursion to chase frogs or whatever crazed plan occupied their boyish brains for the day. She let her brain focus on the voices above her.

"—have an explanation for this?" Eloisa said. Her voice was clear. Strong. As it had always sounded. Was she healed? Sophie almost lifted her head but stopped herself.

"I have a theory," the Domina said. "But not an explanation. I would have to search the archives to see if there are precedents."

"That sounds time-consuming. Tell me your theory for now. We'll start from there."

"I think it's because she's unbound." The voice was blunt. "Normally, the binding locks a certain portion of power to the goddess. For the temple to call upon. But she—" There was a pause, and Sophie tried to look as asleep as possible, wondering if the Domina was looking at her. And if she was ever going to call her something other than "she" in a tone of disgust.

"She is unbound. So there is no limit to the power I can access through her."

"Wouldn't it be limited by her power?"

"She seems to be strong. But using her as a channel is different from drawing on her power directly. That takes blood or . . ." She trailed off.

"Water magic," Eloisa said.

Sophie clenched her teeth, determined not to react. No one ever mentioned the fourth art in public. It was forbidden here. Water magic was the magic of the Illvyan mages and their demon sanctii. Dangerous. Uncontrollable. Wild. Anathema to the goddess, by the law of the temple and the land.

"Exactly," agreed the Domina, as if they were discussing nothing more important than the weather. "Though she is so open, there is no need to try a different approach."

"It doesn't seem to be so good for her," Eloisa observed. "I don't want to hurt her."

"She is sworn to you. Yours to command. Given that she cannot be bound, I think you need to keep her on a tight leash, milady. Make her understand who is in control. Before she becomes a threat."

"A threat? Sophie? She's sweet. Hardly a threat."

"That was before. Now she is unbound. And much higher in the succession. If others discover her power, then she could become a useful tool for them. A focus. The court is unsettled, and you need to take control. And keep it. Which means it would be foolish not to master any . . . advantage offered to you."

"Still," Eloisa said. "Wouldn't it be better to bind her? It's always safer to remove a wild card. If she's married to the Mackenzie boy, then her children will be further down the line. The Mackenzies lack the blood direct."

"I agree with the marriage. That keeps the illusion intact. But I have not found another way to bind her yet."

"Keep looking," Eloisa said.

"I will," the Domina said. "But until then, I recommend you treat her with the caution she warrants."

CHAPTER TWELVE

Cameron gave up on sleep after a few hours of fitful tossing and turning. Apparently, the redwort was still in his system. He had hours before he had to report for duty, but if he stayed where he was, he had no doubt Liam would be grilling him more about his unexpected betrothal. Or worse, about estate matters, now that their father was dead.

Cameron was in no mood to discuss his father yet. Or what his death might mean for Cameron himself. He was near certain that Liam would raise the possibility, or rather the command couched as a possibility, of his leaving the Red Guard and taking over one of the family properties. Either that or stay and play courtier with his royal witch wife. Better, perhaps, to go outside, try to get some exercise, and see if he could wear the last of the 'wort from his system before he wound up having to take another dose.

He slipped out of Liam's apartment and headed toward the westward rose garden. In the tail end of summer, the flowers were past their best and the heat pooled in the stone walls, making it less popular with the court, so he might be undisturbed there to walk and think.

He would prefer to ride, of course, but he needed his horse rested in case he was assigned to something more active than guarding the still convalescent queen-to-be.

And there was something else better not thought about.

In truth, he hadn't really thought about Eloisa today. Sophie had been on his mind, though. He'd thought her hair redder at breakfast, a reminder of what she had become.

A royal witch. Soon to be his wife. Sharing his bed.

Despite the lingering guilt over Eloisa, he found himself increasingly thinking of his wedding night. Of another taste of Sophie.

Who was standing smack-dab in the middle of the rose garden, right beside the place where one of the ley lines cut the garden in half.

He made himself stay a safe distance away. Eager or not, they couldn't afford a repeat of what had happened in Caloteen. Particularly not here in the middle of the palace grounds, where they were guaranteed to be seen.

The queen-to-be would not thank him for breaching her trust, and he rather suspected that Domina Skey would try to skin him alive.

"Milady, it might be best if you stayed a little farther away from the ley line for now," he called.

Sophie jumped and turned. Her face seemed alarmingly pale in the sunlight, the red tinge in her hair even more obvious against the faded gold tone of her skin. She swayed as he turned, and he stopped thinking and moved to catch her before she fell.

She protested as he reached her, lifted her, and carried her over to the nearest bench. It was a wrench to let her go, but he made himself do it. Too risky to keep her in his arms. Instead he crouched by her legs, keeping hold of her hands, which were icy despite the heat of the day.

"Sophie, what's wrong?" he said.

She shook her head. Tried to tug her hands free. "Nothing."

"I don't believe you." In fact, he fancied he could feel

the lie in the pulse of her power moving through him. "You're freezing, and it's roasting out here. What happened? Did you touch the ley line again?"

"N-no," she said, teeth half chattering. "I tried, but I couldn't reach it."

"Couldn't?" That didn't sound good. He tugged off his jacket, which was too damned hot anyway, despite its being court wear made of linen rather than the wool of his uniform, and settled it around her shoulders. "What do you mean?"

"The Domina, she said I needed to. After. And I tried, but I couldn't."

"The Domina told you to touch the ley line?" He tried not to let the surprise show in his voice. Battle mages had their contact with ley lines strictly controlled until they could demonstrate that they had control of their magic. To avoid the sort of thing that had happened to him and Sophie or other more deadly accidents. A newly minted royal witch, especially one who hadn't been bound to the goddess—whatever that meant—was even more likely to come to grief if she were exposed to too much power. "Sophie? Is that right?"

Sophie nodded, shivering again.

"Why? What did she do?" The only reason to tap a ley line directly, unless you were going to attempt something that required a hell of a lot of power, the sort of thing someone with Sophie's lack of experience should not be attempting, was to replenish your energy when it had been drained by magic.

"She was helping the princess," Sophie said, voice still shaky.

The "princess," not the "queen-to-be," Cameron noted. Whatever had happened, it was clear that Sophie was indeed near exhaustion. So she needed the ley line but couldn't access it?

"All right," he said. He wanted to ask more questions,

but that could wait until she didn't look as though she was about to faint. "We can try together. Has the Domina taught you about how to share power safely?" They had done it before, after all. But that had been wild and uncontrolled. He hoped that the Domina had taught her some modicum of control in the lessons she'd had since then.

Sophie nodded, but her eyes were unfocused.

He glanced over at the ley line. Fuck. There were no good alternatives. He could try to fetch a temple devout or another of the court ladies who had small powers, but by then Sophie would probably have passed out. He picked her up again and carried her back over to the ley line. Put her down on the grass and sat between her and it. He took her hand in his left and, gingerly, reached his hand into the faint red light.

The power tingled like standing in the middle of a storm.

He let it run through him, didn't touch it with the part of him that used magic, sent it toward Sophie. "Can you feel that?"

She nodded.

"Then take it," he said.

There was a buzz and then the ghost of a faint snap in the palm of his right hand where her fingers lay. Then he felt the power start to flow into her. Slowly. Too slowly, he thought as another bout of shivers shook her body. More contact. She needed more contact. Skin on skin was easiest, and the more skin the better, but he could hardly strip her here in the garden. So instead he did the next best thing he could think of and, after tapping a small thread of power to throw up a ward that might obscure them from vision if he was lucky, leaned forward and kissed her.

Sophie gasped but didn't pull away. He kept the pressure gentle, more resting his mouth on hers than truly kissing her, keeping the movements small and soft, nip-

ping at her softly to get her to take what he was offering.

For a moment or so, she didn't respond, but then she
took a deep breath and leaned in to him, and he felt the
slow roll of power become a surge as she took the power
in, drinking him down.

He felt himself tumble into heat and the taste of her
as their mouths grew fierce, as she opened to him and
invited him in.

It was a fight to keep his head, to remember where
they were and what he was doing and that there was no
way in hell that he could afford to do anything more than
kiss her. His hand tightened around hers, and he kept his
right resolutely in the ley line despite the urge to move
it to her waist and pull her tighter against him. He
counted heartbeats desperately in his head, knowing his
was pounding too fast to let him keep any accurate pace.
When he reached one hundred, he pulled his hand free
of the ley line and his mouth free of hers, the former far
easier than the latter.

Then he pushed her away gently and studied her face.
Her cheeks were no longer pale, and her eyes were clear.
Clear and fathoms deep, flaring pupils darkening them
to a shade of pure temptation despite the sunshine.

"Better?" he asked.

She took a shuddering breath, then nodded. "Yes. I
think so." She nodded again, more certainly. "Yes." She
smiled then, the expression rueful. "At least, I have exchanged one problem for another more pleasant."

He arched an eyebrow at her. "And I think we're back
to the point where we need to move away from the ley
line. The queen-to-be won't be pleased if we reveal our-
selves before she is ready."

At the mention of Eloisa, her smile died. It was time to
find out exactly what had happened. He climbed to his feet
and extended a hand to help her up. She shook her head.

"I think you are correct. Best if we not touch just now," she murmured as she stood as well. She tugged his jacket from her shoulders and held it out to him. "Thank you. I am quite warm again."

He took the jacket, looked at it with disfavor. But he really shouldn't be in shirtsleeves in public with a lady, so he pulled it back on and then nodded toward the bench. "Do you want to walk or sit whilst you tell me what's going on?"

She studied the bench. "I told you it was nothing."

"That was not nothing. And I think, unless you were told not to, it would be better if I knew what was going on. I'm going to be your husband, Sophie. It's my job to protect you."

"Your job is to serve the queen-to-be," she said.

"I made vows to her, yes. But I'll be making vows to you, too. I don't break my vows."

Her eyes widened at that, and she nodded. "All right. Let's walk. This damned dress isn't comfortable to sit in for long."

"It's a very pretty dress," he said.

She glanced up at him. "Black is not my best color."

"Perhaps not. Regardless, it is a pretty dress." It was a simple cut, close to her body in the top half in a way that he appreciated right now. The skirts widened out, hiding her legs and the rest of her shape, but somehow seemed to hint that such things existed beneath the fabric.

Besides which, he suspected that right now he'd like any dress she wore. The only thing he'd like more would be to take her out of one, but that would have to wait. He hoped the damned Domina was doing her job well and would have Eloisa back on her feet as quickly as possible. He was starting to think a prolonged engagement was a very bad idea.

"Let's walk," he said before his thoughts could continue much further in that direction. He should offer her his arm, but that didn't seem exactly wise just now.

He set off along one of the paths that would lead them out of the rose garden and into one of the orchards. It would be cooler there, at least. And, hopefully, still secluded. Most people in the palace had better things to do than promenade through the gardens right now, and it wasn't apple season.

"So what happened?" he prompted when they reached the outer wall of the rose garden. Sophie was walking smoothly, and her color was still good. She had obviously recovered for now. Though what she might have done if he hadn't been there, he didn't really want to think about.

She frowned at his question. "You can't tell anyone about this. Promise me."

"You have my word," he said. He wasn't keen to cause any more trouble for the pair of them. "This is just you and me."

"Last night the queen-to-be, she had ... well, I'm not sure. Some sort of relapse perhaps? A sudden pain in her head. The Domina ... well, she did something like what we just did. Only she just took my hand and pulled power through me. I didn't know what was happening. And in the end, I fainted."

"She let you faint?" His gut tightened as anger flared.

"She was trying to help Eloisa," Sophie said hastily. "I doubt she was thinking about me. I'm a problem. I'm not entirely sure she wouldn't be happier if something happened to take care of me." He frowned, and she shot him an apologetic smile. "I'm sorry. I shouldn't say that. I didn't mean it. Not really."

Not really. Which meant there was a thread of truth in there somewhere.

"And just now? Am I to assume that she repeated the process today?"

Sophie nodded. "Eloisa was much better this morning. The Domina made me help with a dressing, and her burns ... well, they looked a month old. So the Domina did it again." She shivered.

"Are you feeling faint again?"

"No. No, I'm all right. It just ... It wasn't ... pleasant."

"You fainted again?"

"Yes. And this time when I came to, I heard them talking. The Domina said she thought she could channel more power through me because the binding to the goddess didn't work." She shook her head suddenly, looking frustrated. "I don't understand it. I need to know more about the bindings. About true earth magic. The Domina said something about the temple archives, but I hardly think she'll let me loose in those. I'm half tempted to talk to Madame de—"

"That wouldn't be wise," Cameron said quickly.

Sophie's expression turned mutinous. "Maybe she could help me. Help us."

He couldn't fault her logic. Just the timing. He had to admit to a growing degree of curiosity about what had happened between them, but there had to be safer ways. "I'm not saying never," he continued. "But there are other sources of information to try first. You haven't been to the Illusioners' library yet, have you?"

"No. There hasn't been time," Sophie said.

"You should go. This is the perfect time. Most of the Illusioners will be busy combing over the Salt Hall and the other wreckage. No one will be paying too close attention to what books you choose to look at."

"Unless the Domina has told them not to let me in."

"Perhaps. Though I'm not sure what reason she could give without revealing what happened. As far as the court knows, you're a royal witch. You should go now."

A smile curved across her lips again. "You're right. I

don't have to be back with the queen-to-be until past luncheon. The Domina sent me out here to recover. So I have time."

"I'll walk with you," Cameron said. It had been years since he'd set foot in the Illusioners' Hall or had need to investigate the library. Back then he'd been a too-keen, wet-behind-the-ears recruit. This time perhaps he could learn something more useful than where they kept the standard manuals on battle magic and tactical philosophy.

⌘

Sophie's lips were still tingling as they reached the Illusioners' Hall. Cameron had stayed mostly silent on the short walk from the palace — apparently not wanting to discuss what they had been talking about in a more public place. He had defaulted back to the calm quiet she had grown accustomed to during their time away from the palace. Not a big one for small talk, her husband-to-be. Well, she would just have to learn how to coax him into conversation. There was an interesting man behind the soldierly stoicism. Maybe she could bribe him with kisses to talk to her more.

Though, perhaps that wouldn't be the most sensible approach, at least not immediately. Maybe after they had been married for a time; then things wouldn't flare so hot between them when they touched. Until then, and part of her suddenly hoped that it would be a very faraway then, kisses were likely to lead to activities other than talking.

Activities that made the faintest of shivers ghost over her skin when she thought about them. A shiver chased by a blush. She pulled her thoughts back. As far as anyone who saw them knew, they were merely a court lady and her escort. Nothing more.

The Illusioners' Hall was, or at least, today it appeared

to be, made of solid black marble. She was well aware
that underneath the illusion was more ordinary stone,
but she still felt a small thrill every time she saw it appear as something other than it was. Today in particular
it seemed a proclamation of normality, of nothing to see
here and undefeated defiance that they would spare the
power to keep up their glamour.

They passed up the flight of stairs and instead of going
left to the area Sophie had been before, to the library
open to all, they turned right and walked to the entrance
hall to the library proper. The one where the magical
texts were held. A young-looking man in a pale gray nov-
ice robe, arms banded with mourning black, opened the
door to them. His expression was distinctly unwelcoming.

"This is Lady Sophia Kendall," Cameron said, and the
boy's face quickly smoothed to something more welcoming.

Still, that didn't stop him from saying, "And you are?"
in a snooty voice.

"Lieutenant Cameron Mackenzie of the Red Guard,"
Cameron said dryly. "The queen-to-be sent me to escort
her lady-in-waiting to use the library. So how about you
let us in?"

The boy's face flushed. "Yes, sir," he muttered. "Milady, if you could place your hand here." He indicated a
circle of silver on the inner door. Sophie glanced at Cameron, who nodded, then did as asked. The silver chimed
and then flashed white. The door swung inward.

Sophie stepped through into the library. She had heard
much about the Hall of Three, to give it its proper title,
but nothing had prepared her for the size of the room she
entered. It was three-sided, as the name suggested, floor
blinding white and walls chased with gold and silver. The
walls seemed to rise toward the ceiling forever, far higher
than the height of the building suggested was possible.

She squinted upward, trying to see if she could spot

the edges of the illusion. She thought maybe there was a faint shimmer about one-third up the expanse, but she couldn't be certain. Something else to ask Madame de Montesse about, perhaps. She wouldn't be taught other magics here in Anglion, but it would be a handy thing, in court, to be able to spot an illusion.

Despite Cameron's warning, she fully intended to speak to the Illvyan woman. She could be careful about it. She would invite her to meet at her parents' house. That would be out of sight of the court, and if anyone asked, her mother could claim to be stocking the house with suitable supplies for their stay. Madame de Montesse would know about illusions. Women weren't limited to earth magic in Illvya. Or at least, that was what she had been told.

What she had been told was less and less satisfying with each passing hour. Which was exactly why she was standing here in the library. Best not to waste time. She could worry about Madame de Montesse later. Right now she needed to see what knowledge there was to be gained from the Illusioners.

She studied the triangular room carefully. The only thing that broke the expanse of each towering wall was a ten-foot-tall door. One brown, one red, one Illusioner white. Earth, blood, and air. The three arts.

Perhaps in Illvyan such places would be square. And there would be a blue door to step through. But she was hardly likely to ever find out if that were true, so she recalled her mind to the task at hand and walked toward the earth door. Cameron had said that he would look in the blood mage section and see if they would let him into the Illusioners' shelves. Technically, men were allowed to know the basics of both arts. Cameron could claim he wanted to brush up on his skills of glamour and petty illusions to entertain the court, perhaps.

Whereas she, well, she was going to have to content

herself with what she could find in the section she was allowed to access. The thought rankled a little. Now that she was a royal witch, the thought of being ignorant about the other arts didn't sit any better with her than it had when she had been studying. But wishing for things beyond reach for now wasn't going to assist her with her search, and she was going to run out of time today if she didn't begin.

The only good thing about being restricted in access to just the earth room meant that the boy didn't try to follow her in. Which meant he wasn't a full-fledged archivist. Only the archivists amongst the Illusioners were allowed access to the earth-magic books. As she understood it, they swore vows to the temple in addition to their Illusioner brotherhood. Damned temple wanted a little part of everyone, it seemed.

The earth room maintained the illusion of being many stories high, but even though there were rows and rows of shelves filled with books, it wasn't an impossible number of texts to contemplate searching.

She walked to the nearest shelf and bent to study some of the books. The first one she recognized was the fat tome that had graced Captain Turner's desk during her lessons. Did that mean that perhaps this shelf held beginning texts? She picked up another of the books, leafed through it carefully. Its contents seemed similar enough to the book she knew that she replaced it quickly and moved a few shelves deeper into the rows.

The next shelf she tried was full of books on healing and common rituals. A glance at some of those revealed that they were full of water blessings and crop lore and the like. Not exactly what she was looking for. No, she needed something older. She moved deeper still, stopping to pull volumes out as they caught her eye. More of the same.

She had nearly reached the last set of the shelves when

a slim green book caught her eye. It was thinner and less elaborately covered than the others—the binding looked to be plain green leather without the embossing or gilding that seemed to be the usual for magical texts. Perhaps the lack of ornamentation was what had caught her eye.

She stood on tiptoe to reach for the book, tugging it free of its neighbors with her fingertips. The cover was plain, no title apparent in the aged and somewhat brittle-looking leather, so she opened it gingerly, not wanting to do any damage.

The title page read simply "On Bindings," and Sophie felt a tingle in her spine. She carried the book over to one of the desks supplied for those who wished to study the texts and started to read.

All too soon she heard the hour bell sounding in the tower that stood behind the building. An hour past noon. She would have to be back in the palace soon. She flipped pages in the book a little faster, feeling frustrated. So far it had confirmed what the Domina had told her, that bindings were a way of sharing power between witches or with the temple or to lend a small amount of power to a man through a blood rite, either on a permanent or temporary basis. She hadn't, so far, managed to determine how any of these was achieved. The somewhat archaic handwriting was like spider scribblings, each word taking time to decipher. She flipped pages again, going deeper into the book.

The next chapter heading read simply "Amplification." Amplification? What did that mean? She squinted at the writing, trying to will it to come clear. The inked words were paler and scrawling, making the task even more impossible. Something about two magics? And was that "bound"? Or "found"? The next sentence down started with a phrase that might have been "joining of power," but the ink was faded to near nothing. The other side of the page was no better. It was going to take forever to puzzle out what it read. She could make out only snippets. Something she thought might be "Unclaimed witch" and "Deliberate or accidental, when joined in this . . . The two are bound . . . The power grows. Greater than the parts . . ." Accidental? Could power be bound accidentally? Is that what the Domina meant by tangled? That she and Cameron were bound somehow?

She stared down at the page, wishing that sheer concentration would make the words come clear. Unclaimed witch? Did that mean a virgin or one not bound to the goddess? The quarter bell tolled above her, and she swore under her breath. She would have to leave now to get back to the palace in time. Just when she was getting somewhere. There was no way she could take the book out of the library. The Illusioners' Hall had wards upon wards to protect the knowledge it stored. She was just going to have to find a way to return. Soon.

She pushed the chair back from the desk and walked to the shelves. Acting on an impulse she didn't quite understand, she pushed it back onto a different shelf from the one she'd found it, sliding it in between two much larger books. The dust coating the tops of their pages told her both that perhaps the archivists weren't all that interested in cleaning the shelves and that none of them had been moved to seek out treatises on the uses of earth magic in the treatment of sheep lately. The little green book was hardly visible between the two larger volumes. She stroked its spine, wishing she had more time. Then, hoping she had hidden her treasure as safely as possible for now, she turned and went to find Cameron.

CHAPTER THIRTEEN

Sophie practically skidded through the door to Eloisa's suite as the hour bell tolled two over her head, having made her way through the palace at a pace that was as fast as she could manage without actually breaking into a run. Which wouldn't do. For one thing, given the current atmosphere in the court, the sight of one of the queen-to-be's ladies running through the palace might just make people panic. Plus there was always a chance that in her current gown and corset, trying to run could cause her to faint all over again. Or that she might, her head still full of what she had read in the library and what it might mean, run someone down.

She caught herself on the doorjamb and tried to act composed as she stepped into her place at the rear of the group of ladies waiting to be readmitted to Eloisa's bedchamber. Beata wasn't there—she had to sleep sometime—so Lady Naiomi was the most senior lady present and in charge of the group. Naiomi turned at the sound of Sophie's arrival and glared her disapproval.

Sophie bobbed a quick curtsy of apology, and Naiomi pursed her lips but nodded. Lady Honoria, who was with Sophie in the last row of ladies, sent a semicurious but sympathetic smile in Sophie's direction. As Naiomi turned back to face the bedroom door, Lady Honoria leaned over

and whispered, "Where were you? And what happened
earlier? The Domina hasn't let any of us back in yet. Just
some priors. Beata was fuming when she left."

Sophie shook her head. "It's a long way from the erl's
apartments," she said, prevaricating. "I misjudged the
time." She stared at the bedroom door, willing it to open
before all the ladies decided this might be a perfect time
to start finding out exactly what had been happening to
Sophie since her Ais-Seann.

"You're still staying with Inglewood?" Honoria asked,
her curious expression deepening. "I thought your parents had returned to Kingswell."

"They have," Sophie said. "But they've taken a house
in town, and the queen-to-be asked that I stay in the
palace." Honoria's parents weren't any wealthier than
Sophie's and, what's more, didn't have the advantage of
a link to the line direct. "Are you offering to share your
room?" She fervently hoped not. She hated sharing a
room. In the somewhat confined world of the ladies-in-
waiting, privacy was at a premium.

"No, but why— " Honoria started to say, but then the
door opened, revealing the Domina.

"The queen-to-be will see you now," she announced.

Sophie kept her face smooth but once again felt an
inward frown. It should be one of the ladies who had
stayed with Eloisa and who told the rest of them when
Eloisa was ready for company or wanted distraction. Not
the Domina. If the healing they had done this morning
had been successful, then surely there was less need for
Domina Skey to dance attendance on Eloisa every minute of the day. She must have other duties.

As the group of ladies moved forward, Sophie heard
light footsteps behind her. Turning her head, she saw Princess Margaretta walking into the antechamber. The princess wore head-to-toe black like the rest of them. The
choker of black pearls at her neck was almost as fine as her

sister's, and there were more dark pearls at her ears and wrists. But despite her somber attire, a smile lit her face.

Automatically, Sophie curtsied and stepped back to let the princess precede her into the bedroom.

Sophie waited until the princess and the lady-in-waiting who accompanied her — a girl a year or so older than Sophie who had recently joined the court — were through the door and then followed.

Just in time to hear Margaretta exclaim, "But how is this possible?"

Sophie's view was blocked by the crowd of people. She stepped forward, wriggling her way into place between Honoria and Aria, who both gave her annoyed looks but moved apart so she could see. The queen-to-be wasn't in bed. She was, instead, sitting in a chair, having her hair dressed. Fully clothed. No bandages. No bruising on her face. Margaretta's face wasn't the only one showing astonishment.

Eloisa smiled and extended her hand to her sister.

Margaretta clasped it and dropped a kiss on it. "You're well again. But how?"

The queen-to-be's gaze skimmed over the assembled ladies, lingering for a moment on Sophie before moving on. "We owe thanks to the skills of Domina Skey, who has worked a miracle for me. For Anglion. So that we can answer this insult done to our country and avenge our beloved father."

There was clear, cold anger in the words. Sophie was familiar with Eloisa's temper, but she didn't think she'd seen her this way before. Not even after the worst of the clashes with her father after she had first returned to court following her husband's death.

Well, she had a right to her anger. Her father had been killed. Her palace was half in ruins. Anger might serve her well. And, as wary as she was of the Domina, Sophie was perfectly happy for the credit for Eloisa's recovery to be laid at the Domina's feet rather than her own. Half the ladies would suspect that Sophie had been involved. They knew that she had been alone with Eloisa and the Domina. However, if the queen-to-be publicly proclaimed it was the Domina's achievement, then it seemed unlikely any would contradict her.

There might be whispers and rumors. This was, after all, a court, and courts, in Sophie's limited experience of them, ran on intrigue and gossip and the trading of information. But they would remain whispers and rumors unless Sophie did something foolish and exposed her secret. She had no intention of doing so. All she wanted was to be safely married to Cameron and out of the queen-to-be's sights.

Margaretta's eyes, brown rather than the brilliant green of her sister's, had filled with tears at the mention of King Stefan. She smiled down at Eloisa, though. "Are you sure you are well?"

"Yes. There's no need to worry," Eloisa said. "No time to worry, in fact. We have much to do. And most of it requires an audience hall. I am told the Salt Hall is unusable?"

This brought nods of affirmation from everyone assembled. King Stefan's grand hall—which he had refurbished lavishly during his reign until it was a testament to the art of woodcarvers and tilers and the metalsmiths who worked with inlay and half the other artisans of the capital—was in ruins.

Eloisa frowned. "Then we need an alternative." She looked at Naiomi. "I need to speak to the commander. He should have an accounting of how many people remain at court. That will tell us how many we need to accommodate."

Sophie hadn't heard any final casualty numbers. She made a note to ask Cameron when she got the chance. If she didn't find out today.

"There's always the ballroom, milady," ventured Naiomi. "That would do."

Eloisa looked thoughtful. "The ballroom will be required for other things."

Naiomi shrugged one of her elegant shoulders. "I'm sure the servants can handle any necessary changes to make it fit whatever purposes you desire, Your Highness."

That would be true if there were still a full complement of servants in the palace. But Sophie wondered if Naiomi was overestimating what could be achieved with everything in its current disarray. There were plenty of servants amongst the dead and injured as well.

But if that were true, it didn't seem to be a concern to Eloisa, who smiled at Naiomi. "I will consider it," she said. "Meanwhile, I need a list of other options. Perhaps Master Egan can attend me as well. With whoever is assisting him in assessing the damage." The queen-to-be paused a moment as the maid slid a long pin tipped with pearls into the coil of braids she'd fashioned at the back of Eloisa's head.

Master Egan was one of the senior Illusioners. He, along with others, tended the wards and the glamours that manipulated the interiors as needed. He always reminded Sophie of Captain Turner. Kind but determined. And unfailingly thorough. Not at all the typical image of a gadfly Illusioner. If he had been put in charge of the repairs of the palace, then things would be done properly.

"Yes, Your Highness," Naiomi said.

The queen-to-be nodded. "Good. Send word to all the members of my father's council. I will meet with them later today. We will hold the late king's funeral on first day, I will hold audience on third day, and the coronation will be sixth day."

There was a round of hastily stifled gasps at this last pronouncement. No doubt all the ladies were thinking of how much work it was going to be to procure a suitable dress for Eloisa in less than one week. Not to mention outfits for the rest of her retinue.

"And last," Eloisa continued, "we will then turn our attention to Lady Sophia. Whose Ais-Seann celebrations were so rudely interrupted. We need to do something special to mark the arrival of our latest royal witch."

Sophie held her breath, wondering if Eloisa were going to say anything more. Like announce her betrothal. Instead, she nodded at the maid to dismiss her and then stood, which sent the ladies all fluttering toward the ground in a wave of curtsies.

Maybe she didn't trust the ladies-in-waiting not to spread the word before the first audience was held. That was where such announcements would usually be made.

"I will see Master Egan and the commander in an hour," Eloisa said as she walked out of the bedroom. "Bring them here to my parlor. That will suffice until we work out better arrangements."

King Stefan had had several audience chambers of varying size, from his small private study to the eight-man council chamber to a room that could seat ten times that and the Salt Hall itself. But other than the study, which adjoined his apartments in the far end of the western wing, the others were located near the Salt Hall and presumably no longer fit for use.

Sophie could understand why Eloisa didn't want to go to her father's study. It was one thing to know that he was dead. Another to face the reality of belongings and places no longer required. She remembered helping her mother clear out her grandmother's rooms after the older Sophia had passed away and the unexpected tears that had risen over the smallest things. Eloisa seemed in no mood for tears. Nor would she want to appear weak as she took over the court.

As Eloisa left the room, Naiomi started assigning

tasks with rapid-fire orders. Sophie was assigned to writing notes to the council members and to others who
would be needed to put arrangements in place. Honoria
scored the same task. It was hardly exciting but needed
to be done, and Sophie was glad to have something to do
that would put her out of the Domina's reach.

She and Honoria fetched notepaper printed with the
princess's seal and retired to the workroom the ladies-in-
waiting shared to begin writing. As her pen dipped into
ink and touched paper, each stroke formed carefully so
as to be clear and elegant enough to pass Lady Beata's
standards, her thoughts began to wander. Back to the
library and the small green book. Amplification. She had
never heard the term before. She remembered that she
needed to invite Chloe de Montesse to take tea. Which
first meant getting her mother to agree to hosting such a
guest. She added "see my parents" to her growing list of
things to do. She could speak to her mother at the services for seventh day. And perhaps Madame de Montesse would be available on second day.

She wrote three notes and then a fourth. That one was
addressed to Liam Mackenzie, who had technically in-
herited his father's seat on the council. Eloisa was free to
change her council members, of course, so Liam's tenure
might be short-lived. But the Inglewood holdings and
the extent of their influence at court made Sophie think
it unlikely. True, Liam might have to work to retain the
power that his father had established, but from what
she'd seen of him over the last few days, she had no
doubts that he was capable of doing so.

She took extra pains with his note. He was, after all,
her future brother-in-law. But as she was reaching for a
fifth sheet of paper, Lady Naiomi bustled into the workroom and told Sophie that the queen-to-be wanted to
speak to her. She could see Honoria practically biting
her tongue to stop herself from asking what was going

on. Thankful that Eloisa's command gave her a chance to escape any questions, she put the notes aside.

She walked back to Eloisa's apartments more slowly than might have been strictly prudent. She didn't want to see the Domina again so soon after what had happened earlier. Eloisa seemed well, but Sophie didn't trust Domina Skey to want to experiment further with what exactly she could accomplish with Sophie's power.

But perhaps the Domina would have returned to the temple. With a king's funeral rites to hold and then a coronation to perform, not to mention the backlog of burials that must be waiting, surely the temple had enough pressing issues to hold Domina Skey's attention now that Eloisa was healed and presumably out of danger. On the other hand, retreating back to her temple would mean seeing less of the queen-to-be. Somehow Sophie doubted that the Domina was going to give up the influence she seemed to have gained since the attack.

Eloisa was in her parlor. And, Sophie noted thankfully, there was no sign of the Domina. Just a steady stream of servants and ladies-in-waiting ducking in and out with messages and papers and notes. Eloisa shooed Beata, apparently returned from her nap, out of the room.

"Close the door, Sophie."

Sophie did so, wondering what was about to happen. Trying not to feel nervous. This was Eloisa, not the Domina.

"You should know that I intend to announce your betrothal at my first audience," Eloisa said, taking a seat in one of the armchairs. "The court doesn't need the eligible lords being distracted from the work we need to do. Best to make it clear that you are not available as soon as possible." She paused a moment, leaving Sophie wondering if she was supposed to offer an opinion. As she had no wish to become the center of a court power wrangle, she stayed quiet.

"You and Cameron are a good match," Eloisa continued. "The court will accept my decision."

That wasn't strictly true, but Sophie wasn't going to argue. Cameron was far preferable to any of the other likely candidates. For one thing, she knew that he was a good lover. And more important, she knew that she liked him and that he seemed to like her—though the court wouldn't care about that. They would care only that Eloisa had made a choice and how strong she was in enforcing her will on the court. "Yes, milady."

"You should wear something suitable. I will not keep mourning for my father. Margaretta may, but I will not decree it for the court. We need to show strength, not weakness."

"Yes, milady," Sophie repeated. "My mother was bringing a dress for my Ais-Seann celebrations. I'm sure it will be suitable for the audience, if you want me to wear it. Do you intend for the betrothal ceremony to be held at court?" Sometimes such things were. But generally only when the husband-to-be was someone higher ranking than Cameron.

Eloisa shook her head. "No. Given the situation, we will keep the betrothal private. Your parents. Cameron's brothers, if he wishes. The Domina will perform the ceremony, and I will witness."

Sophie nodded. "Whatever you wish." She was happy not to put on a show. She had seen betrothal ceremonies, though never one for a royal witch. She hadn't been at court for the last witch's wedding. She probably should study up on it. If there were actual magical elements to the ceremony, then she wanted to know what to expect. Then maybe she could prevent anything going wrong. Another thing to add to her list.

Eloisa tilted her head, which made the black pearls studded through her hair glint dark shades of green and purple. "We have much to do. But we have not forgotten your father's request for an audience. We will find the time. Perhaps tomorrow, after the services. I will speak to him in the temple. I assume your parents will be attending?"

"Yes, milady. My family goes to the temple every week." Her mother had only a very little power, but she didn't waver in her devotion to the goddess. And she insisted that all her family attend with her.

"Good. Then I will wait after the rituals. In the private chapel. You can bring him to me there."

The thought of venturing back into the depths of the temple didn't appeal, but it wasn't like she could avoid it. If she stopped going to services, she was just going to appear guilty of something. No point giving the Domina more ammunition against her. She bobbed a curtsy, acquiescing. "Yes, milady. Was there anything else?" A wedding date, perhaps? Eloisa and the Domina had spoken of the need for haste. Or maybe even a thank-you for helping the Domina to heal her.

But Eloisa just shook her head and waved a hand toward the door. "No. You can go back to whatever it is you were doing. I will see you tomorrow at the temple."

After escorting Sophie back to the palace, Cameron tried once again to sleep. To avoid his brother, he had gone back to the barracks, but it was just as chaotic as it had been earlier. The noise and bustle, usually familiar enough for him to drown out, kept jolting him awake.

After an hour or two of fitful dozing, he gave up and went down to the barracks to see where he could be useful. To his surprise, he was sent back to the palace, to the work going on at the Salt Hall. Not to help move any remaining rubble or assist the Illusioners in their work, but to stand witness. The Red Guard, as personal guard to the king, were considered to be honest to a fault and

were sometimes used to observe events or proceedings
in order to be able to give evidence about what had occurred, should it be required.

The Salt Hall lay open to the sky, half its outer wall
and roof crumbled. The stone that remained was charred
black in many places, the paint and wood and metal that
had covered them burned away, testament to how fierce
the fire had been.

How quickly it would have killed those who'd been
trapped here.

He hadn't stopped to think about it when they'd given
him the duty, but the thought slowed his step as he
walked across to the group of Illusioners examining a
section of wall.

This was where his father had died.

The erl had been at home here, in the spectacle of the
court in full assembly. Wheeling and dealing and trying
to find the advantage in any situation. Cameron had
heard him arguing his point in this very room, presenting
a claim to the court or trying to convince the king about
the wisdom of a course of action too many times for the
Salt Hall not to be inextricably linked with his father in
his mind.

For the briefest of moments, he thought he heard it
again. That and the buzz of the court filling the room, the
noise echoing around the hall as it always had. But then
the sensation vanished, and he shook himself and pushed
the fancy away. Maybe it was a remnant of Illusioners'
art. Catching a wisp of conversation and playing it back.
He didn't want to know. His father was gone, and there
was nothing to be done about it.

He reached the group of Illusioners and saw, to his
surprise, that Lord Sylvain stood amongst them. Perhaps
he was the member of the king's council who'd been sent
to observe. Lord Sylvain, short, stout, and white-haired,
was gesturing at the wall with the blackwood stick he

carried and saying something to Master Egan, who shook his head in response.

As Cameron approached, both men turned.

"Young Mackenzie," Lord Sylvain said, his wrinkled face rearranging itself into a pleased smile. "What are you doing here?"

"I've been assigned to relieve Gregson here," he said, nodding at the Red Guard standing a few feet away from the group.

"But you're part of the queen-to-be's guard, aren't you? Shouldn't you be with her? It seems she's made a remarkable recovery."

"I'm on duty later," Cameron said, sidestepping the issue of Eloisa's recovery. That was a subject he definitely couldn't discuss. "And wanted to make myself useful until then."

"Good man," Sylvain said. "How about you come over here and we can talk whilst you watch? There isn't much to observe, to tell the truth."

Master Egan grunted something protesting at this, and Sylvain flicked his stick impatiently. "Not a criticism. It's astounding that there's anything left with the fire so hot. You Illusioners are doing what you can. If anything is here, I'm certain you'll find it."

That eased the look of annoyance on the Illusioner's face. He turned back to the wall, and Lord Sylvain led Cameron over to a group of large stone blocks sitting in the middle of the room. "They've already inspected these. So we can't hurt anything. Stand if you want, lad, but these old bones will sit." He eased himself down carefully and then sighed. "Sad to see the palace so. Seems wrong, somehow."

"It is wrong," Cameron said. He hesitated but then sat beside the old man. "This shouldn't have happened."

"True. So many dead," Sylvain said. "And lucky to find anything left of most of them. The king's personal wards spared him a little. Enough that there were bones left to bury when Eloisa decides it's time. A few others who had wards. Like your father." He reached out and patted Cameron's knee. "Bad business. I've buried a daughter and two wives. No pain like losing family."

"Two wives, Your Grace?" Cameron hadn't known that Lord Sylvain had been married twice. And quite frankly, he'd rather hear about Lord Sylvain's losses than think about his own.

"Yes. Two. My first wife, Louisa, died young. Too young. Before you were even a twinkle in your father's eye. Before he was old enough to have a twinkle, come to think of it. She was a pretty thing. A witch. Red hair and big brown eyes."

"What happened to her? If you don't mind me asking?" Cameron asked. He watched the Illusioners brushing ash and soot from the wall, but they didn't seem excited about what they were doing, so he presumed he didn't need to be, either.

"Came off her horse," Lord Sylvain said. "Never knew how it happened. She rode like the wind, and horses loved her. Never saw a horse misbehave when she was on its back. She was strong, that one. Others wanted her, but Stefan's father decided she should go to me. Always wondered if someone in the court had decided that if he couldn't have her, then I wouldn't either. Or if she was simply too strong. A risk."

"Isn't a strong witch a good thing?" Cameron said, his attention now firmly back on the old man. "We need royal witches with strength."

"So they say. Yet we tie them up to temple and man at the first sign of power. Stefan's father had just put down a rebellion of some of the northern counties, and the court was full of suspicion. Not a good time to stand out, to be a potential threat to the Crown." Lord Sylvain sighed again, tapping his fingers on the handle of his stick, his hand looking dark against the worn mother-of-pearl that covered the handle. "My second wife, Gwynne, she was a good lass, too. But I never felt about her the way I felt about Louisa." He turned dark eyes in Cameron's direction. "I guess they'll all be sniffing around the Kendall chit now. She came into her power when she was with you, didn't she?"

Cameron nodded, schooling his face to blankness. If Lord Sylvain had been married to a witch—a strong witch—then no doubt he understood perfectly the temptation they represented. "Yes, sir."

"Thought so. Then I'll tell you this, lad. If you came to know her during that time, if you care for her at all, then you keep an eye on her until she's safely married. I'd say now isn't a good time to be a threat in the court, either. I may be old, but I can count. The lass has moved a fair way up the line of succession with what happened to Farkeep and his family. If her power is anything worth talking about, if it's enough to attract interest, then she's standing in the open with very little cover. Not a safe place to be in times like these."

Cameron felt a chill start in his neck and run down his spine. Would someone really try to hurt a royal witch? Stupid question. Someone had just tried to take out the entire royal family. Though Sylvain was talking about an attack on Sophie—or a plot that sought to use her—from within the court rather than something mounted by external forces.

Lord Sylvain nodded. "Aye. Not a pleasant thought. But it seems it's not a pleasant world we're living in right now. So keep an eye out for her. I couldn't save Louisa. The Kendall chit has something of the look of her. Come to think of it, I think her grandmother and Louisa were cousins, maybe." He waved a hand. "Doesn't matter. But remember what I said."

CHAPTER FOURTEEN

After the temple services, Sophie took her father to meet with the queen-to-be. Then she took advantage of the spare minutes to drag her mother out to the gardens behind the temple to ask her to invite Chloe de Montesse to visit.

"Madame de Montesse," Emma Kendall said, looking puzzled. "The one who runs that . . . store in Portholme."

"Yes," Sophie said.

"She's Illvyan."

"Yes. I know," Sophie agreed. "But she was very kind to Cam—Lieutenant Mackenzie and me when the attack occurred. She helped us. I would like to thank her."

"You can't send a note?"

"That hardly seems sufficient. And this isn't the best time to invite an Illvyan to the palace."

"Yet it makes sense to invite her to our house? Really, Sophie, are you sure you didn't suffer a blow to the head when you were off in the wilderness with your lieutenant?"

"I'm sure. I just want to thank her. You can ask her to bring some supplies for you. No one will question that. I'm sure she knows how to be discreet." Sophie's hand stole to the pearl at her throat as she silently willed her mother to agree.

"If she was discreet, she'd dye that hair of hers a decent color," her mother said.

"She can't help being born Illvyan," Sophie said. "Obviously she didn't like it very much, or she wouldn't have risked her life to come here."

"She may have liked it perfectly well," her mother pointed out. "She may have been forced to flee by something else."

"Well, I know a little about that now," Sophie said. "About being scared and not knowing who your friends are. I would like to thank her. Please, Mother. It wouldn't take long. And I don't feel right leaving it until later. You always tell me not to put things off."

Her mother pursed her lips. "I hate it when you children quote me to me," she said, eyes twinkling.

Sophie knew that meant she had made up her mind. She leaned over and kissed her mother's cheek. "Then you shouldn't have taught us so well."

Her mother laughed. "I should have locked you up in a tower when I had the chance." Her smile died. "Are you truly happy about this marriage, darling?"

Sophie nodded. "I think he's a good man. Honestly, I would prefer a little more time to get to know him better, but in the current circumstances, that seems unlikely. The queen-to-be is keen to get everything settled again. But you don't need to worry. I'm not putting on a good face. I think Lieutenant Mackenzie and I will suit each other. Which is probably more than some royal witches can say."

"My little girl, a royal witch." Her mother shook her head. "It seems so odd. It was barely yesterday you were toddling around the garden and making mischief. Still, if you say you are happy, then I am satisfied. And I will invite your Madame de Montesse to the house. Did you have a day in mind?"

"The queen-to-be said she was going to announce my

betrothal at the audience on third day. I told her you had a dress made for my birthday that would be suitable for court, so I'm sure I'll be able to get away to see you second day. Tomorrow will be too full with the funeral and everything that comes with it. Funerals," she amended softly. "Lord Inglewood is to be buried tomorrow as well. After the king. And Lord Farkeep. And others." She swallowed against the sudden tightness in her throat and the prickle in her spine. So many dead. She kept forgetting, being caught up in everything that was happening to her. Which somehow made it worse when she did remember.

"A hard day," her mother agreed, her pretty face full of sadness. She sighed, then straightened her shoulders. "But only a day. Funerals are an ending and a beginning. Remember that. We have to let go and move on. Easier said than done, perhaps, but no less true for that."

Her sad expression brightened suddenly. "And look, here comes your father. Head still safely attached to his shoulders, so it seems he neither exploded nor provoked the queen-to-be too badly. That's a relief."

⸙

First day was as grim as Sophie had feared. She sat in the temple behind Eloisa with the other ladies-in-waiting as the rites for King Stefan were held. Eloisa sat like a statue, head held high, during the entire ceremony. In contrast, Margaretta had wept against her husband's shoulder for the entire length of the rites. Toward the end of the ritual, Sophie found herself wishing someone would slap the princess. She could at least try to maintain her composure when her sister was not in the position to be able to share her display of grief. It seemed selfish somehow. But that was Margaretta. It was just as well for Anglion that she was the younger sister.

After the rites, the ladies accompanied Eloisa and

Margaretta and the invited members of the court to see King Stefan interred in the Fairley vault in the catacombs beneath the temple, which was a singularly unpleasant experience. Sophie had never been into the catacombs before, and she fervently wished she would never have to do so again. Not that that wish was likely to come true.

The tunnels, lit with earth-lights, were too dim and too narrow. And despite the bowls of scented oils and hanging bunches of herbs everywhere, the stink of death was unmistakable. Decay and old rot. A dry, sour smell that made Sophie want to retch. But she bit her cheek and tried to breathe shallowly, determined not to make a spectacle of herself as Margaretta had.

When they emerged back aboveground, she almost gave in to the urge to cry in relief. Instead she took refuge in one of the bathrooms, to splash her face with water and try to wash some of the stink she was sure lingered on her skin away before the ritual meal of salted bread and wine. Both of which stuck in her throat, though the wine at least offered some relief, just strong enough to put a warm glow of distance between her and the rest of the afternoon, when they all sat through several more sets of rites. Lord Inglewood's, Lord Farkeep's, and then the rest of the Farkeep family.

Sophie tried not to watch Cameron during his father's rites, afraid that her face might give away how much she wished she could sit beside him, hold his hand. Do something to ease the pain she had seen in his blue eyes when he'd passed her as he and his brothers had escorted their father's coffin into the temple.

He didn't look at her, either. Which made it both better and worse. She gulped the wine a little more eagerly at the completion of those rites. And was spared another trip down to the catacombs—the Mackenzies having chosen to have only family present, as was their right.

By the time she reached her room much later that night, the wine she had drunk and the sheer exhaustion of the strain of the day sent her down into the deepest sleep she'd had for days.

∞

Sophie woke on second day feeling better than she had any right to. Sleep, it seemed, could cure an untold number of ills, including too much funeral wine. Plus, today was the day she was going to talk to Madame de Montesse.

Her cheerful mood lasted until she reached Eloisa's chambers. The atmosphere there was still distinctly somber, and everyone was on edge and fractious as they tried to do all the tasks that needed to be done before tomorrow's audience. In the midst of it, Eloisa was very cool and calm, but that didn't ease Sophie's mind any. Surely it would be more normal if Eloisa lost her temper, just for an instant.

So much had happened to her. Some human display of emotion would be reassuring.

All in all Sophie was glad to escape from the palace and take a carriage to her parents' house. She had assumed that Eloisa would insist on a Red Guard accompanying her again and had told her mother to ensure that Madame de Montesse was safely inside well before Sophie was due to arrive. The Red Guard—a Lieutenant Wilson, whom she had met several times before but had never spoken more than a few words to—would remain outside the house. After all, he was there to stop anyone snatching her or whatever it was that Eloisa feared might happen. To do that, he needed to stop the potential assailant from entering the house in the first place.

To her relief, Lieutenant Wilson did indeed insist on remaining in the front yard by the gate. Which meant that Sophie was able to sneak Madame de Montesse out from the tiny parlor where her mother was making stiff small talk and into the small walled garden at the rear of the house. It was a pretty place. Neat beds of late-summer flowers lined either side of a lawn bisected by a stone path. An elaborately carved house shrine sat against the far wall. Sophie didn't think the lieutenant was likely to come out to the garden if he thought she was safely inside.

Chloe de Montesse seemed to bear this in good spirits, not asking any questions until they were both settled on the small stone bench in front of the shrine.

"I believe," she said then, in her accented Anglion, "that the invitation was for tea, not intrigue."

"Hardly intrigue," Sophie protested.

"Hardly tea, either. You pulled me away from your mother's excellent hospitality. I was enjoying that tea."

"It comes from an estate near ours," Sophie said, not above bribery if it would improve Madame's mood. "I'm sure my mother would be happy to give you some."

"That would be most kind," Chloe said. She flashed a tight smile, sitting a little taller on the bench. "So are you going to tell me why you wanted me to come here? I'm fairly certain your mother could have lived without bindweed and nettle root for another day or two."

"I wanted to thank you," Sophie said. "We were interrupted the other day. But you were kind to Lieutenant Mackenzie and me."

Chloe flipped a hand. "No more than anyone would have been."

"Not true. You're a refugee. You have a reason to want to keep your head down."

That earned her a very aristocratic-sounding snort of disdain. "That sounds boring. I was never one for boredom."

"Still, it was kind. And I thank you."

"You are welcome. You and your lieutenant of the

broad shoulders and very blue eyes. A fine one, that man, do you not think?"

Sophie couldn't stop the blush that rose over her face. "He is very nice."

"Nice? Are you Anglion girls blind? In Illvya, someone would have snatched him up and into her bed well before now." Chloe stopped, her expression turning sympathetic. "Ah, but perhaps you are not allowing yourself to appreciate him. A royal witch does not choose in such matters."

"No," Sophie said, hoping this explanation would throw Chloe off this particular topic of conversation.

"So frustrating for you." A slim hand reached out and patted Sophie's arm sympathetically. "Once you are married and have had a son or two, I'm sure your lord will not object to the odd dalliance. Perhaps he will still be available. You are young. You will have babies quickly."

"Goddess," Sophie choked.

Chloe laughed. "Truly Anglion, though. All so proper all the time."

Not all the time. But that was hardly a subject to discuss with Madame de Montesse.

"And are you enjoying being a royal witch?" Chloe asked, expression growing more serious. She regarded Sophie for a moment, and something that wasn't too far away from doubt crossed her face.

"Everything has been so disrupted since my birthday," Sophie said. "I've hardly had time to think about it."

"But now things will return to how they were, no? With the queen-to-be recovered and the coronation so soon, surely she will turn her attention to your marriage. That's what happens to royal witches, is it not?" Chloe was studying her again.

"What is it?" Sophie asked. "Do I have a smudge on my cheek or something?

"No. No smudge."

"Then what?"

"It's just . . ." Madame de Montesse hesitated. "Forgive me if this is the wrong thing to say, but you do not look the same as the other royal witches to me. Your power is very . . . bright."

"Bright?"

"Strong? I'm not sure what the correct word might be. But royal witches always appear more tame to me."

"Maybe that's just because you're Illvyan."

"Perhaps. Or perhaps you are different." She tilted her head. "What exactly was it that you wished to say to me again?"

Sophie took a deep breath. She couldn't tell Madame de Montesse the truth. Not all of it. She wasn't sure how far she could trust her. So best to ease into the subject. "It's just, well, with everything that's happened, I feel like it would be easier if I knew more. And no one has time to teach me anything."

"You want lessons? From me? I think not. That would definitely not be a good idea. Not unless you want both of us to be thrown into the ocean with many heavy rocks tied to our necks."

"You teach some things. I've heard women talk about it."

"Small things. Herbs and such. To women with small power. Seed witches at best. Not royal witches. I'm not permitted such things. It's part of the oath I swore when I was allowed to stay here."

"Is it just an oath?" Sophie asked curiously. "Or something more?"

"More? A ritual? A binding?" Chloe shook her head. "No. No, I do not think your goddess would be able to bind a free witch. Not one who has touched more than one type of magic. It doesn't work. Once you know more than one art, you can't limit yourself back to just one."

"Women use more than earth magic there? In Illvya. I mean, I've heard the stories. Of the—"

"Demons? Water magic, yes. Though truly, more men than women choose that path. Sanctii can be troublesome. And dangerous. Too much trouble, in truth. But yes, women can do more. Is that what you wanted to ask me? It is not such a secret."

Not a secret, no. But taught to be an abomination. Abhorred by the goddess. Which Sophie had never fully understood. If magic came from the goddess, as the temple taught, how could part of it be forbidden?

And Chloe said that a binding wouldn't work if you had used more than one kind of magic. Which couldn't be the explanation in her case. She hadn't used anything but earth magic, as far as she knew. She wished she had been able to return to the library and the small green book. But perhaps she had just as useful a resource here with her now. "Madame, do you know what amplification means?"

Chloe wrinkled her nose. "Amplification?" She paused, considering. "Do you mean an *augmentier*, perhaps?"

Sophie wasn't familiar with the Illvyan word. "What is that?"

"When two people join their different magics. And the whole becomes more than the sum of the parts, as you say. Both are strengthened."

More than the sum of the parts. Greater than the whole. The book had said something like that. "How does that happen?"

Another shrug. "Ritual. Blood. Sex. It depends. But I think we are straying into those things that I am not allowed to teach to royal witches."

"Is it a permanent thing?"

"Sometimes. Between married couples, perhaps. Or very close friends. It can be dangerous."

"How?"

Chloe shook her head. "I think perhaps you should ask your temple to explain. If you are brave enough. I do not think such things are liked here."

Sophie couldn't disagree with that. And she didn't think she was brave enough to raise any such thing with the temple. But perhaps the green book would shed some more light when she could return to the Hall of Three. If this was the thing that the Domina thought had happened to her and Cameron. "Could an *augmentier* happen accidentally?"

Chloe frowned. "Accidentally? I do not—" She stopped, sat still for a moment. "I do not know. Perhaps. If there was enough power and those involved lacked control. Such a thing would be very unusual in Illvya. But not impossible, maybe. Difficult to undo, I would think, if you did not know how it was done in the first place." Her eyes narrowed. "Why do you ask?"

Sophie shook her head. She couldn't tell Madame the truth. No one was supposed to know that she was betrothed to Cameron yet, let alone that the proposal was brought about by what they'd done. She pasted on her best innocent smile. "It was just something I came across in a book. I didn't know what it meant."

The dark eyebrows arched upward. "I would not expect to find such a thing in an Anglion book on magic."

"It was just a book on bindings."

"You Anglions are overly fond of bindings. It is foolish to give up part of your power to another to control." Madame de Montesse glanced back at the house. "But again, perhaps this topic is not what I should discuss with a royal witch."

"I'm sorry," Sophie said. "I was just curious." Perhaps a change of subject was called for before Chloe grew too uncomfortable and decided they should go back inside. "What's it like? Illvya?"

Madame de Montesse looked startled. "Do you truly want to know?"

Sophie nodded. "Yes. I mean, they teach us very little. How big it is, what the capital is, what countries it claims.

But the rest is so vague. Other than it is cursed for using water magic, of course."

"Of course." Chloe smiled then. "If they were sensible, they would teach that we are very dull. So dull no one would be curious. And no one would ever try to come farther than the trade points."

Sophie didn't want to hear about trade points. Trade with Illvya was strictly limited and controlled. Exchanges of essential goods only, and that conducted under such a weight of treaties and protocols that she had nearly fallen asleep anytime anybody had tried to explain it to her.

"Is that why you left? It was too dull for you?"

"No." For a moment, Chloe looked wistful. Almost sad. "No. Never dull. Quite the opposite. It is very different, Illvya. Wilder than here, yet more civilized in some ways. Also more dangerous. Freedom brings risks, after all."

"Why did you leave?" Sophie asked before she could stop herself. When she realized what she had asked, she clapped a hand over her mouth in horror. "I'm sorry. That was terribly rude. You don't have to tell me."

"I do not mind. It is as the tales they tell of me say. My husband died. The circumstances were not good. I did not think I would be long behind him if I stayed, though the error was his and not mine. So I took the chance and ran. For me, it worked."

"I'm sorry," Sophie said. "I can't imagine." Leaving Kingswell with Cameron had been scary enough. She couldn't imagine leaving her whole life behind for good. Her hand strayed to the pearl at her throat. *Salt protect me.* If the goddess was kind, she would never have to do anything more than try to imagine such a thing.

"It was long ago. Time heals such things." Chloe straightened on the bench as the quarter bell chimed. "Now, milady, I think you have asked enough for one day.

If you linger much longer, you will not have the chance to try on that very pretty dress your mother showed me. The one she says is for your Ais-Seann celebration when it finally happens. Either that or your Red Guard friend will grow impatient. Go inside. I will wait out here until you return to the palace. No one will see me."

"Thank you," Sophie said. "I wish we could talk more."

"You know where to find me. Perhaps when things are more settled." She shook her head. "Or, perhaps, if things do not settle. Remember that."

Sophie smiled. "Thank you. I will. And yes, once things are settled, I will come to your shop. After all, the queen-to-be always says you have the best supplies, and I'm a royal witch now. My husband—whoever he turns out to be—will just have to get used to paying your bills."

"That, I would be happy to accommodate," Madame de Montesse said. She nodded toward the house. "Go now. You have a dress to try on. These things are important at court."

CHAPTER FIFTEEN

"Are you ready for this, brother?" Alec asked. He put his hand on Cameron's shoulder, peering into his face. "You look nervous."

"I'm not nervous," Cam retorted. "You're drunk."

"Not really," Alec said. "Not so you'd notice."

The Iska had flowed freely at the Mackenzie apartments since they'd returned from the rites for their father. Well, at least it had for Liam and Alec. Cameron, having to report for duty, had kept his intake low. Being on night duty had given him an excuse to escape the second round of drinking the previous night. It also meant he was desperately tired, but the anticipation of what was about to happen was generating enough nervous energy to keep him on his feet. Eloisa was holding her first audience at midday. But that didn't seem to have stopped his brothers having another few glasses of Iska already today.

Alec, at least, didn't have anything important to do at court today, so it wouldn't matter if he was a little under the weather. But Liam. Liam had a role to play. Not to mention this was his first audience since he had become erl. Maybe Cameron wasn't the only nervous one in the room. To be fair, though, Liam always could drink the rest

of them under the table. A glass or two of Iska wasn't
going to affect him much.

Hopefully. Today Eloisa would announce Cameron's
betrothal to Sophie.

Which was likely to turn the court into a three-ring
circus. Liam would need his wits about him. They all
would.

Cameron had been keeping his ears to the ground for
rumors involving Sophie, and even in the short time
since Eloisa had declared herself well again, the barracks
gossip had been full of speculation about which lord
might be granted the new royal witch. His name hadn't
come up in any serious fashion. No. So far the favored
contender was the distant Farkeep relative that the archivists had determined was the heir to the late erl, with
so many of the family killed in the attack. The man lived
halfway across the country in some obscure town. He
hadn't even reached court yet.

When he did, he would no doubt send all the mothers
of eligible daughters into matchmaking mode. But Sophie's mother wouldn't be one of them. No, because her
daughter would already be betrothed to Cameron.

He'd seen Sophie for only brief moments here and
there. The ladies-in-waiting seemed to be everywhere in
the palace, moving in small black-clad groups as they
ordered and scolded and coaxed and ensured that the
queen-to-be's wishes were being carried out exactly.

He managed a minute or two with her before breakfast this morning and had asked if she'd heard any rumors
about them. She said she hadn't, though she admitted
she thought the ladies-in-waiting suspected something.
But if they had their suspicions, they apparently weren't
sharing them with the rest of the court. The fact that Sophie was staying with his brother hadn't seemed to have
triggered anything. Half the court was displaced, and al-

most every family was hosting extra guests and providing beds and food where they could.

And with everyone focused on the queen-to-be, the
court simply lacked the time for the full-blown level of
speculation—and lobbying—there would normally be
around a royal witch. And whilst there were some puzzled whispers about how the Domina had healed the
queen-to-be so quickly, once again, Sophie's name wasn't
being mentioned. Which was good. He didn't know
whether what Lord Sylvain had told him had any truth
to it—if someone had killed the erl's first wife—but he
wasn't going to take any chances with Sophie.

They wanted him to marry her. So he would marry
her. And then he would protect her as his honor demanded.

No one would harm her as long as he had any say in
the matter.

He shook off the dark thought.

Most likely Lord Sylvain had just been seeing shadows where there were none in the wake of losing a beloved wife.

Sophie was safe. Their biggest problem was going to
be dealing with the inevitable indignation when she was
handed to someone as low in the court as himself.

Likely there'd be an outcry. Not that anyone other
than Eloisa had any say in the matter.

"Are you sure you don't want another drink, Liam?"
Alec asked, rising to refill his glass.

"Some of us have to be mostly sober," Liam said lazily
from across the room. He was reading something his
manservant had just handed him, sitting half propped on
the great blackwood desk their father had used. He
looked every inch the erl, decked out in black velvet and
linen. The Inglewood ring glittered on his left hand, and
the waistcoat beneath the long jacket was sewn with gray

pearls and jet. Jeanne had even managed to tie his hair back with a black ribbon.

"You're just getting old," Alec said, grinning at Liam. Alec's sartorial splendor was only slightly less than his brother's. He tilted the glass in his hand, watching the liquid swirl around with an assessing expression, and then turned his focus on Cameron. "Sure you don't want a soothing sip or two, little brother? Calm the nerves. Getting betrothed can be a nervous business."

"I'm not nervous," Cam repeated. He straightened the collar of his dress uniform. The bright red was familiar, but amid all the black in the room, he felt overly conspicuous. Or maybe that was just because he was about to be the center of attention. He could have worn civilian garb like his brothers but had chosen the uniform. He knew his brothers' finery was both a display of the strength of Inglewood and a display of support for him—a reminder that Cameron was a Mackenzie, brother to an erl. But it couldn't hurt to remind anyone who might object to his marriage that he was a soldier. An elite one. A trained battle mage.

He wasn't sure exactly how he felt. Looking forward to seeing Sophie. Worried about her. Wondering what came next. He hadn't had any time at all with the queen to-be. No chance to speak to her alone. To try to apologize personally. Lady Beata had discussed the betrothal arrangements with them.

Well, maybe that was best. He couldn't change what had happened, and Eloisa would have had to end it with him eventually. Even as brother to an erl, he was not fit to be consort to a queen.

"You can say you're not nervous as often as you like, but that doesn't make it true," Liam said, putting the paper down as the quarter bell rang. He glanced toward the door, where, as if on cue, Jeanne appeared.

Cam tugged at his collar one last time. Time to go to court.

Eloisa's temporary audience hall had been thoroughly transformed. It didn't look like a ballroom. It did, however, lack a throne. King Stefan's throne was presumably ash and splinters, like the rest of the furnishings in the Salt Hall. Someone had placed a large gilded chair with deep-blue velvet upholstery on the platform that had been erected at the southern end of the room. It was impressive but lacked the imposing bulk of the black-wood and nacre Salt Throne.

Cameron followed Liam down the aisle toward the front of the rows of chairs. The chairs—also gilt and velvet—looked more comfortable than the blackwood benches that the court had previously had to put up with, but they were, like the throne, harbingers of change.

Protocol demanded that Eloisa not sit on the Salt Throne before she was crowned anyway, but she should have been seated before it. The space where the throne would have been was a stark reminder of exactly what had happened. Eloisa was going to have to work harder to bring her court to heel without the weight of history the throne represented to lend her any gravitas.

Maybe she already had teams of furniture makers working on a new throne somewhere in the depths of the palace. But even an exact replica wouldn't have the same significance.

Cameron took his seat next to Alec and tried not to let anything show on his face as they waited for the court to assemble. Curiosity apparently fueled the eagerness of the courtiers today. Whether the speed was driven by the desire to see how the queen-to-be would handle the situation or whether they wanted to see for themselves who had survived and who had fallen and what that

meant for court alliances and feuds, the courtiers took
their places far more rapidly than usual. Often it took a
good half an hour past the appointed audience time for
everyone to arrive and be seated. Today Cameron didn't
think there was one empty place—other than the gaps
left by those injured or dead and the grander rows of
chairs nearest the platform left for Eloisa's retinue—by
the time the hour bell started to toll.

A hush settled over the crowded hall as swiftly as the
sun slipping below the horizon in midwinter. One minute chatter and laughter had made the air fairly vibrate;
then, the next, there was silence, bar the echoing chimes
of the great bronze bell in the Sea Rook.

When the last toll faded away, the master of court
didn't even need to bang his staff to bring the court to
order. To a person, they rose and turned to await the
entrance of the queen-to-be, row after row of silk and
satin and velvet in all the colors of the rainbow.

Eloisa had sent an edict stating that those who wished
to mourn personal losses would be permitted the choice
but that the court was not to don mourning for King
Stefan. So there was a fair sprinkling of black amongst
the brighter shades. Pearls and jewels glittered as skirts
swayed and jackets and shirts were smoothed. The room
seemed to hold its collective breath as two young pages
in Fairley blue and gold pulled back the doors and Eloisa
stood framed in the light.

Her dress was blue and gold, too. Deep blue like a
falling twilight, embroidered heavily with gold thread.
Fantastical flowers and leaves and branches twined up
her sleeves and down over her skirt. Around her neck a
triple strand of thumb-sized cream pearls circled her
throat and fell down her chest. Heavy gold beads and
sapphires broke the creamy white here and there.

Her mother had worn that particular necklace, Cameron realized. One of the first days he'd attended court

had been the day that Eloisa's betrothal had been announced, and he remembered the queen by King Stefan's side, pearls at her throat, standing very straight as
her daughter had been bound to her husband-to-be.

The jewels were spectacular, matched by a tiara set in
Eloisa's bright hair. Since she hadn't worn anything
other than black pearls and dark colors since she'd returned to court following Iain's death, the change in her
appearance was startling.

Startling enough to send a buzz of whispers running
through the crowd. Eloisa stood, waiting, until silence
descended again. Only then did she begin to walk toward the makeshift throne. Behind her, Margaretta
walked with her husband, similarly clad in blue and gold,
though her dress was not as elaborate. Then came the
Domina, wearing temple brown, simply cut. Simple but
not inexpensive—the velvet overrobe and the silver-
and-pearl circlet holding back her hair proclaimed her
status as the chief servant of the goddess.

After the Domina, the ladies-in-waiting walked sedately in pairs. They were all dressed in shades of blue
from nearly as dark as Eloisa's to something as pale as
heat-faded summer skies.

Cameron looked for Sophie and found her in the last
pair. Her hair had been caught up and braided into a pile
at the back of her head. Her gown shimmered like pea-
cock feathers, an unexpected shade of blue that made her
skin glow. It made her hair appear redder, too. A clear
sign of her change in status. Simple white pearls hung
from her ears and around her neck in a single row. Her
expression was composed, but as his eyes caught hers, she
smiled briefly, and he felt his heart stutter a little.

"Easy," Alec whispered in his ear, elbowing his ribs
lightly.

He ignored his brother, watching Sophie. When she
finally came level with their row, she didn't turn to look

at him, but he somehow knew that she wanted to. He took her in, uninterested in anything else until she had passed and Alec's elbow in his ribs told him that he'd missed something. He hastily bent in a bow as Eloisa took her seat.

It took another minute for Margaretta and the ladies to arrange themselves. Sophie wound up on the opposite side of the aisle to the Inglewood party, whether by accident or design, which gave Cameron only a partial view of the back of her head and her slim, straight back.

Frustration burned in his gut.

Alec nudged him again, and he turned his attention back to Eloisa.

He half expected the Domina to address the court first, to make some blessing or something, but, instead, Eloisa rose and began to speak.

The speech was eloquent; he had to grant her that. She spoke of sorrow and loss, of challenges. Of the need for Anglion to stand strong together. Her words were clear and passionate, and her voice carried across the room clearly. He wondered idly if one of the Illusioners was assisting with that, but then decided it didn't matter. All that mattered was that she said what she had to say and then the rest of the audience could start. He wanted to get to the betrothal whilst he still had hold of his nerves.

He risked another sideways glance toward Sophie, only to meet the curious gaze of Lord Sylvain, seated on the opposite side of the room. The older man raised a bushy white eyebrow, and Cameron nodded politely and turned back to watch Eloisa. He tried to pay attention to her words, but in all honesty, he didn't think he'd be able to repeat anything Eloisa was saying if someone held a pistol to his head.

Eloisa finally came to an end of her speech, finishing with the announcement of the date of her coronation. The court, as one, bowed again as she took her seat.

Then, to Cameron's dismay, the Domina did step up to bless the court.

Thankfully, that part of the proceedings was cut short. After that Eloisa began to speak less formally. Announcing that she was making no changes to the councilors—though Cameron thought he heard a definite "at least for now" hanging unspoken on the end of that particular sentence—speaking of arrangements for the running of the court whilst the palace was under repair, of the repairs themselves, and of the investigation into the attack.

With nothing to report on that front, a flash of frustration that perhaps only those who knew her well would recognize, appeared on Eloisa's face. But she pulled her expression back into serene composure within a second or so and continued dealing with court business.

When she had finished with logistics, she held up a hand.

"We will deal with the questions of the court in a moment. However, before then we must deal with some happier business."

There was a rustling murmur at this. The hand made a curt gesture that silenced the noise almost instantly.

"As you know," Eloisa continued, "prior to this untenable attack, we were to celebrate the Ais-Seann of our devoted lady-in-waiting, Lady Sophia Kendall, whom the goddess has seen fit to bless with the gift of power."

This raised another chattering hum, though Cameron thought that the fact that Sophie had power could hardly be news to most of those present. The palace gossip might be slowed by the aftermath of the attack, but it hadn't died completely.

"Therefore, we rejoice at the coming of another royal witch to our court. Her strength and power shall serve Anglion, as we all do." Eloisa paused and looked at Sophie directly. "And to assist her in her service, we have determined that she should wed an equally devoted servant of the court. A man who has served Anglion with blood and body and whose family has always been stalwart supporters of the throne. Lady Sophia, will you come forward?"

Sophie rose to take her place in front of the queen-to-be. She looked paler than she had earlier, but she was smiling as she dropped into a curtsy. When she straightened and turned to face the court, the court was so quiet that if a pin had fallen from her hair, it would have rung through the room like a thunderbolt. The tension in the air was fierce as several hundred nobles held their breaths to hear the name of the man who had won the prize.

Eloisa turned toward Cameron and his family, her gaze resting on Liam. "Lord Inglewood, I request the service of your brother Cameron in this matter."

Liam bowed. "Inglewood is always at your service, Your Highness. We thank you for the favor you have bestowed," he said as he straightened. Which was Cameron's cue to rise and walk over to stand beside Sophie. He bowed to Eloisa, searching her face one last time for any clue that she had any regret about this at all before he turned to take Sophie's hand, schooling himself to calm, to not react to the flare of pleasure he was growing to expect whenever they touched.

"It is our will that Cameron Mackenzie and Sophia Kendall shall wed," Eloisa said. "And our will is law. In light of the present circumstances, we wish that this wedding be sanctified to show our appreciation to the goddess for her gifts of magic as soon as possible. Therefore the wedding will take place on first day next week."

Sophie's hand tightened in his. He had been expecting haste, but two days after the coronation itself was giving new meaning to the word. Judging by the tension he could feel in her grip, Sophie hadn't known about Eloisa's timetable either. Still, he couldn't bring himself to be annoyed by the speed. Not when just the joining of their hands made him as hungry for her as a man starved for years. So, as the court began to chatter in earnest around them, he merely smiled at Sophie and escorted her back to sit beside him for the rest of the audience.

CHAPTER SIXTEEN

For Sophie the next few days flew by so quickly she wasn't quite convinced that someone wasn't winding forward the hands of all the palace clocks whenever her back was turned.

The preparations for the coronation were relentless. Hour after hour of carrying notes or writing notes or attending the queen-to-be in endless meetings and meals and gatherings. Helping Eloisa change clothes, helping her get ready for bed, helping her rise in the morning. Waiting on her every whim. And then there were the fittings. Eloisa's coronation dress was to be even more elaborate than the one she'd worn for her first audience. Pure golden silk, the Fairley blue coming from sapphires and embroidery curling in delicate waves around the hem of the skirt and sleeves. An entire fleet of seamstresses were working around the clock to finish it.

That didn't leave them much time for the dresses for the ladies-in-waiting, which were to be made of pale gold silk, embroidered with the same curling sea waves and the quartered circle of the goddess.

The seamstresses spared to that task were no less relentless than those making Eloisa's dress. Sophie and each of the ladies-in-waiting kept being called away for fitting upon fitting.

On top of which, Sophie had a wedding gown being made as well. Her mother, always prepared, had brought her own wedding dress with her from their estate. The seamstresses she had hired had exclaimed over the heavy satin fabric, not quite white, not ivory, but a shade that glowed somewhere in between. The dress was trimmed with pearl-studded lace, but the seamstresses declared that the style was too old-fashioned and that the gown needed to be remade, just not refitted. Sophie, other than requesting something not too frilly, decided to let her mother deal with design choices. She simply didn't have the time. And, truly, she didn't care what the dress looked like.

The wedding was a few hours of her life. The marriage was a lifetime.

In the whirlwind of coronation preparations, she had barely seen Cameron for more than a minute or two as they passed in corridors or outside Eloisa's rooms. They had shared one too-short formal lunch in the Inglewood apartments when Liam and Jeanne had invited her parents to dine with them. She and Cameron had been seated at opposite ends of the table, she next to Liam and Cameron next to her mother. She had made polite conversation with Liam—whom she was coming to like even though she wasn't entirely certain of him or the depths of his ambition yet—and kept an eye on her parents. Liam, who seemed to be taking on the mantle of erl easily, had spoken to her of the Inglewood estates, and she had nodded and smiled and tried not to let her eyes stray too often to Cameron. She should pay attention to what Liam was telling her. After all, she was joining the Inglewood family. She should understand their holdings. One day Cameron would be expected to take control of one of them.

She wondered which Liam had in mind. He had formerly been living at the Loch Kenzie estate, the seat of the Inglewoods, running things for his father who stayed at court most of the year. Did he intend to return or stay in Kingswell and take on his father's political role? And if he stayed, would Alec and Lucy move to Loch Kenzie? Or did Liam think Cameron would leave the Red Guard and step into that role?

She had no idea if Cameron wanted to leave the guard. With the attack so fresh, it didn't seem likely the commander would want to relinquish any of his men, though he would if the queen-to-be ordered him to, Sophie supposed. As for herself, well, she would be happy to leave Kingswell, to settle back into estate life, albeit it on a grander scale than at her parents' home. But she had no idea whether Eloisa would allow her to go, either.

The whole situation seemed complicated and somehow academic. Like the wedding itself. With things whirling around her so quickly, it was hard to shake the sensation that perhaps she was merely dreaming the whole thing and would at any moment find one of the maids waking her for her birthday.

The only thing that made her believe that she actually was betrothed, a witch, and about to be married—apart from the continuing daily lessons in earth magic at the temple—was the constant unfamiliar weight of the betrothal ring that Cameron had placed on her hand during the ceremony at the temple. The stone was a huge sapphire in a shade so dark it appeared nearly black in some lights, set in an old-fashioned gold setting that clasped the stone in a stark gold outline and unadorned band. Sophie loved it, despite the fact it was heavy. Something about the simple stark shape and the deep-blue stone reminded her of Cameron.

It was what it was. Honest. Solid.

Hopefully she wasn't wrong in her conviction that Cameron was the same.

The ring accompanied her through the long hours of

the coronation ceremony at the temple. Sophie tried to pay attention. After all, Eloisa wasn't too many years older than she was. The Fairleys tended to be long-lived. So barring accidents or illness or other ill fortune, this might be the only coronation she ever got to attend. It would definitely be the only one where she was part of the queen-to-be's retinue. By the time Eloisa's successor was crowned, Sophie would hopefully be a contented old lady surrounded by broods of her own children and grandchildren. With people serving her, not the other way around.

The ceremony itself was a glittering spectacle, the ritual raised to a true art form, with the temple priors chanting and the Domina directing everything as smoothly as a general and the queen nearly glowing in the golden dress. It was near painful to look at Eloisa in her state of perfected beauty sitting so still on the very recently completed new Salt Throne as the Domina placed the crown on her head. Sophie knew no glamour was involved. No Illusioners had come anywhere near the queen whilst she was dressing. It was all Eloisa. Which was somewhat depressing. Sophie knew that she, too, looked as beautiful as she was ever likely to, having been fussed over by the same people who had attended the queen. Yet with Eloisa in the room, no man would take a second look at any other woman.

Still, Cameron had smiled at her and bowed slightly as she had walked through the temple ahead of the queen-to-be. She hadn't been able to see his face as Eloisa entered, so she could pretend that he, at least, found his wife-to-be as beautiful as the queen.

And she would be able to dance with her husband-to-be at the coronation ball in the evening, and then, in just two more days, she would be married to him. Then, perhaps, life would return to some semblance of normality.

❧

Cameron, it seemed, danced as well as he did everything else. Sophie tried not to smile too widely as he held her and swept her around the room in a circle dance. She also tried to disguise the heat that swept through her at the close contact, hoping the flush on her face would be taken to be the fault of the overheated ballroom— temporarily converted back from audience hall for the night—and not the fact that she was trying not to think about what it felt like to be even closer to Cameron. After all, they were supposed to barely know each other.

She wasn't entirely sure the charade was working, particularly not when Cameron leaned a little closer and whispered, "We really need to get better at this," in her ear, making her stomach curl and her nipples harden under her corset. She'd rarely been thankful for the confining structure of a court dress before, but she was glad for the protection it offered from the scrutiny of the court now.

"At dancing?" she replied, pretending to misunderstand.

Cameron smiled wickedly, the expression so unfamiliar that Sophie almost stumbled midstep. "That is exactly what I meant."

"I think you dance very well, Lieutenant. You shouldn't disparage yourself." She made her tone teasing, unwilling to let this new flirtatious Cameron slip away too quickly.

"I do many things well," he said, turning her expertly.

Sophie felt her skin flush deeper. Thankfully, the music ended then, and she let Cameron lead her out of the worst of the crush and then away from the ballroom altogether, through one of the side doors that stood open to the gardens to help cool the room. The gardens were heavily guarded and warded, of course. No one was going to leave the palace exposed. But Cameron still managed to find a dark, secluded place for them to stand. She fanned herself, enjoying the feel of the night air on her heated skin, trying to regain both her composure and some control over the need to touch him.

"Does that help?" Cameron asked, and she looked up to find him watching her. "Oh, to hell with it," he muttered suddenly and yanked her close and kissed her.

Just for a moment or two. Just long enough for it to heat her all over again and wake the hunger she was trying to keep banked all the more as his tongue moved against hers. Then he pulled away, cursing softly.

"Only a few more days," she said, her voice slightly shaky.

"Too many," he said shortly, and then led her back into the ballroom before she could try to get him to kiss her again.

As they stepped back onto the dance floor, she knew she was smiling foolishly and tried to school her expression back into something more seemly. She thought she might have succeeded but then caught sight of Eloisa, seated at the high table at the end of the room, eyes narrowed as she watched Cameron put his hands on Sophie again for the next dance.

❧

"Leave us now," Eloisa said after Beata finished brushing her hair. Above them the hour bell started to chime two. In the morning. Which was not that late as court parties went, but the ladies-in-waiting had all been awake before dawn to prepare for the coronation. It had been a very long day, and Sophie hadn't known that her feet could ache quite so much.

She took the hairbrush from Beata so Beata could help the queen—the queen in truth now, not just queen-to-be—into a heavy silk robe.

"Thank you, Beata," Eloisa said with a smile. "Now go to bed. Sophie, you stay. I want to talk to you."

Sophie almost dropped the hairbrush but just managed to keep a grip.

"Now, don't look so annoyed, Bea," Eloisa said as Beata frowned. "Sophie is going to be married in two days. Time for a little girl talk. After all, Lieutenant Mackenzie is one of those wild northerners. We can't send Sophie into battle unarmed."

Beata's face cleared, annoyance changing to something akin to conspiracy. "True, Your Majesty. She keeps running away when we try to tell her things."

"I don't run away," Sophie protested. "You keep trying to talk to me when I have things to do." That wasn't entirely true. She was still avoiding speaking too closely to the ladies-in-waiting. They would try to pry the story of why the queen had chosen Cameron as her husband from her if she gave them a chance. But the fact that they kept using "you'll be married soon" as their reason for wanting to talk to her gave her the perfect excuse to stay with Eloisa now.

"Always so conscientious," Eloisa said with a laugh. "Go on, Beata. Sophie has to listen to me, even if she is shy about her wedding night."

Sophie carefully didn't react to this. The queen knew very well that Sophie had no reason to be nervous about her wedding night. It was in her interests to keep up the charade that she was a good royal virgin, but Sophie was suddenly uncertain exactly what game Eloisa was playing. There was a fey look in the green eyes that she didn't know how to read.

Eloisa hadn't tried to speak to her in any intimate fashion since the Domina had worked her last healing. So why now? So late. When they were both tired. After all, there were still a few days until the wedding, so this was hardly the only opportunity Eloisa would have to provide advice.

Sophie put the silver-chased hairbrush back in its place

on Eloisa's dressing table. When Beata left the room, she turned back to the queen, waiting to see what Eloisa would say next.

Eloisa stood and stretched. "Goddess, it's good to be out of that dress."

Sophie, whose own dress was starting to feel more uncomfortable with each passing second, her ribs beginning to feel as bruised as her feet from the hours and hours of a very tightly laced corset, understood her relief but couldn't bring herself to feel terribly sympathetic.

"You looked very beautiful, Your Majesty," Sophie said. "You should bring that head seamstress into the palace staff."

"I intend to," Eloisa said. She lowered her arms and then walked over to the taller dresser on the other side of the room, where she kept gloves and scarves and pieces of jewelry that weren't valuable enough to be locked up in the vault when not in use. Her walk was graceful and feline, the movements making the robe billow around her in a way that was unmistakably female.

Sophie wondered how exactly Eloisa had learned to be so . . . well, alluring. That was the word. She drew men's eyes to her. Women's, too. Maybe it was part of her training as a crown princess, but Sophie doubted it. Part of it had to be innate, as natural to Eloisa as breathing. Sophie walking across a bedroom in a robe would probably just look like a woman in a robe.

Whereas Eloisa was unmistakably a queen. Something to be desired. Feted. Envied. She didn't need the dress and the jewels and paint.

Sophie watched, still not sure what Eloisa wanted, as the queen skimmed one hand over the polished wood of the dresser. It came to rest on the long triple strand of black pearls that Eloisa had worn for months on end, which should have been returned to the vault with her coronation jewels.

"I suppose I will have to stop wearing these," Eloisa said, lifting the pearls and running them through her fingers. "It's a pity. I've always liked black pearls best. The colors in them are so vivid. But they're hardly an auspicious color for the start of my reign."

She placed the necklace back down and then opened one of the drawers. From it she lifted a silk-wrapped bundle. She turned, offering it to Sophie.

"Here. I wanted you to have these for your wedding."

Sophie unwrapped the silk carefully, revealing a pile of creamy—almost golden—pearls the size of small marbles. When she lifted one of them, they revealed themselves to be a long string that could be doubled or maybe tripled. Not the massive length of Eloisa's blacks but still extravagant.

"Your mother mentioned your dress was cream rather than white," Eloisa said.

"They're beautiful," Sophie said. The pearls slid smoothly across her fingers as she examined them, the sheen of them beautiful in the lamplight. "But too much, Your Majesty. Truly."

"Nonsense. What's the point of being queen if I can't indulge my friends? You are my friend, aren't you, Sophie?" The question was almost a purr. A purr voiced by a cat with razor-sharp claws, perhaps. Not an entirely friendly sound.

"Of course," Sophie said, hands suddenly clammy under the pearls as the back of her neck prickled. She started to wrap them up in the silk again, trying to pretend she hadn't noticed anything amiss in Eloisa's voice. "I will always be your loyal subject and friend, Your Majesty."

"Good," Eloisa said, green eyes cool. "Then, as your friend, I offer some advice."

Sophie looked up from the pearls. "Your Majesty?"

"You would be wise, I think, to be wary of showing your . . . affection for Lieutenant Mackenzie too openly.

Wise, actually, not to indulge it at all." She turned and walked toward the bed. "After all, it's not real, what lies between you."

Sophie's hands tightened around the bundle of pearls. "I'm not sure I understand, Your Majesty."

Eloisa sat on the end of the bed and shrugged fluidly. "I mean, it's not you that he is reacting to. It's the magic. For some men, particularly those with power, a woman's magic is, well, let's say it elevates the pleasure shared. Not all men. My husband didn't find it so, but some men do. They like to touch fire perhaps. Any fire."

"Excuse me?"

"Sorry. Was that too polite? I will be more direct. I am saying that Cameron is such a man and that any witch would rouse him. Can rouse him. So don't give him your heart. As I said, northerners are wild. They like their passions. But, in my experience, they also have limited attention spans. And, Sophie, I do speak from experience."

Sophie felt as though she'd been slapped. Had Eloisa . . . with Cameron? Suddenly the room seemed severely lacking in air.

"Oh, don't look so stricken," Eloisa said, still in that cool voice. "If I wanted him back, I would have taken him back by now. No, the next man I take to my bed will be my consort, and Cameron doesn't qualify for that role. I just wanted you to know the truth of it. After all, dear, this is a world arranged to benefit men. So it doesn't do to give them extra advantages by being foolish. Royal marriages are alliances, not affairs of the heart. You should keep that in mind." She smiled then, though there was little warmth in it. "After all, you have proven useful so far. So I would rather have you undistracted by heartbreak when he grows tired of you." She stretched again and yawned. "Now, off to bed with you. You should rest whilst you can these next days. After all, it doesn't do for a bride to look exhausted on her wedding day."

He really should have accepted Liam's offer of Iska for breakfast. Cameron couldn't remember the last time he'd felt this nervous but suspected it had probably been before his very first battle. That time he'd ended up emptying the contents of his stomach behind a handy bush.

Couldn't do that this time.

A vomiting bridegroom wasn't exactly dignified. Or desirable. Liam and Alec would never let him live it down. Nor would his fellow guards. Plus, it was entirely possible that Domina Skey would gut him if he puked in the temple.

Should've had the Iska. Iska calmed the nerves nicely. Or at least made you not care that you were nervous.

Nothing to be nervous about, he told himself firmly. It was almost noon, and that meant that very soon Sophie would come into the temple and her father would place her hand in his and they would be married. And this entire ordeal would be over and everyone would leave them alone.

At least he hoped.

He couldn't quite shake Lord Sylvain's warnings from his mind. The erl had sought him out again at the coronation hall. He'd offered him a hearty—and Cameron thought heartfelt—congratulatory speech. And then he'd reminded Cameron not to forget Louisa before he'd vanished back into the whirling dancing court and been lost to sight.

Cameron hadn't seen him in the day that had passed since. The commander had taken pity on him and, in a rare show of empathy, swapped his duty to daytime so he wouldn't have to stand watch the night before his wedding. He'd also been given a week's leave, generous under the circumstances to—as the commander had put it—become more acquainted with his new wife after the wedding. But even with day duty, assigned again to stand witness for the Illusioners in the Salt Hall, Cameron hadn't seen Lord Sylvain.

He'd barely seen Sophie, either. He'd hoped that, with the coronation over, the queen might have fewer demands on her ladies' time, but apparently not.

It was hardly proper to attempt to visit her late at night—it would no doubt lead only to something they might regret—and it was unfair to deprive her of what little sleep she was able to get.

This wedding business was harder on women after all. He'd had to get his dress uniform cleaned—Liam had pushed for Inglewood colors, but Cameron had killed that idea—and pick out a wedding gift for his wife along with a wedding band. Both the gifts were taken care of with a single visit to the court jeweler, who'd been more than eager to please the future husband of the newest royal witch. And Jeanne had taken his uniform in hand.

Whereas Sophie, no doubt, had a lot more on her plate. They weren't having a grand ball or anything after the wedding, just a smaller dinner with family and some friends—Cameron's closest from the Red Guards and Sophie's from the ladies-in-waiting and a few other girls near her age who'd come up from her parents' estate. But that was one more thing she had to be involved in arranging. Then there was the matter of the wedding dress.

He really wanted to see her in a wedding dress. She'd looked beautiful at the coronation, polished perfection but almost too perfect. Without so much pressure on the occasion as a coronation, perhaps she wouldn't be primped to within quite such an inch of her life. She'd still be beautiful, but she would look more like Sophie.

And she'd be his.

He was looking forward to that part most of all, even though the thought of it, of peeling her out of her wedding gown and taking her to bed, made his mouth dry and his stomach clench all over again. He would have time to do things properly. To go slowly. To show her how it could be between a man and a woman. The thought made his cock harden, and he was glad of the disguising length of his uniform jacket.

He took a deep breath, and Liam, standing beside him, gave him a sympathetic look.

"Not much longer, little brother. This is the worst part."

Cameron squared his shoulders. Both his brothers had survived getting married. He would, too. Of course, neither of them had married a royal witch.

A royal witch who had failed the goddess's rituals.

They were to undergo the binding of husband and wife after the marriage ceremony. The Domina had informed them, mouth flattened in disapproval, that it must be attempted, even though she had no idea if it would be successful. She seemed to think that if Cameron wasn't going to benefit from his witchly wife as other men did, it was his own fault for giving in to lust and ruining Sophie.

He wasn't overly concerned about it. He had magic of his own, and he and Sophie had already channeled power together in a small way in the garden. If he ever needed her help, no doubt she would give it if she could. He'd rather a gift freely given than one forced from the giver anyway.

He took another deep breath, willing the hour bell to ring as he flattened his palms against his thighs, trying to remove the damp feeling from them.

But before he could give in to his nerves completely, there was a sudden commotion at the far end of the temple, which had everyone turning in their seats. Above him the bell finally boomed into sonorous life, and Sophie began to walk down the long aisle toward him.

The dress she wore was creamy white. It clung to her in all the right places and belled out to the floor in a sweep of gleaming fabric and lace that made it look as though she glided rather than walked. Pearls circled her throat and dotted the hair swept up on her head.

Beautiful.

But he really didn't care about the dress. He wanted the woman in it. Sophie. Her back was very straight as she walked behind Honoria, her wedding maid, her hand resting lightly on her father's arm. In her other hand she carried a small posy of fiery red summerbells. She was smiling, but it wasn't the blinding smile he'd been looking forward to. No. No, it looked, to him at least, somewhat strained.

Which was fine. She was entitled to be as nervous as he was, after all.

He smiled at her, trying to put her at ease, but her expression didn't ease. Her eyes caught his, but then she looked past him to the queen, seated in the royal family's enclosure to the side of the altar, and then on to the Domina.

"You're on," Liam whispered, and stepped back to let Cameron move forward as Sophie reached the quartered circle of silver set in the marble in front of the altar. He waited for her to curtsy to the queen, his heart thudding in his ears loud as cannon-shot. He hoped he'd be able to hear what the Domina was saying when she began to speak.

Beside his daughter, Sir Kendall nodded at Cameron and then lifted Sophie's hand from his arm and held it out to Cameron.

He wrapped his fingers around hers, nerves easing now that they were finally touching. Her fingers were cool, but they curled around his. Together they waited whilst the Domina poured a small cup of salt water over their joined hands and then bound their wrists with dampened salt grass.

She began to recite the blessing of the goddess that was so familiar to Cameron after so many years of attending temple that he barely heard it even as he spoke the words in unison with everyone else. Instead, he watched Sophie, wishing she would stop watching the Domina and look at him.

Would see him.

See that they were in this particular mad venture together now.

But instead, she stared at the Domina, seemingly as fascinated as a bird who had spotted a cat nearby.

Cameron resigned himself to impatience as the Domina moved on from the blessing to addressing the assembled party. Apparently, she didn't believe in missing any opportunity to preach to her congregation. The speech was a little lacking in the joy of marriage and a little heavy on the sacred duty of royal witches and of Anglions to protect the land of the goddess for his taste, but finally she came to a halt and asked him if he had a ring.

He produced it, and she took it from him, dousing it and the heavy band Sophie offered in more salt water and passing the rings briefly over the altar flame before she turned back to Cameron and Sophie.

He knew this part. Had been reciting the vows in his head or out loud whenever possible so there was no chance that he would get them wrong even with the Domina there to prompt him if needed. He wanted the words to be right. For his vows to be clear.

Reaching for Sophie's unbound hand, he slipped the ring onto her finger and began to speak. The vows weren't long, but he didn't plan on saying them again in his lifetime.

"I offer my vow," he said steadily. "I am yours, body and blood. Your shield and your shelter. I will share with you what is mine and take from you your hurts and sorrows. Until we return to the blessings of the goddess and rest in earth once more."

Sophie's eyes were very large and dark in her face as

she took the band back from the Domina and put it on his finger.

"I offer my vow," she said clearly, and he smiled be-fore he could help it. "I am yours, body and blood, your solace and your shelter. I will share with you what is mine and take from you your hurts and sorrows. Until we return to the blessings of the goddess and rest in the earth once more."

"As the goddess has witnessed, as you all have witnessed, these two are married," the Domina said as she reached to slash the salt grass with a silver blade. "May their union be strong and blessed."

Above them the temple bells began to ring out, and Cameron grinned down at his wife.

⌘

If Cameron didn't stop smiling at her, Sophie thought, as she tugged another pin from her hair, she rather thought she might stab him with something. He'd been smiling all day. Smiling at her as though he hadn't forgotten to mention the small matter that the queen had once been his lover.

Ever since Eloisa had dropped that particular tidbit of information into Sophie's lap, she had been burning with fury. Did he think she was an idiot?

That she wouldn't find out?

She knew what Eloisa had been doing in telling her. Asserting her power. Reminding Sophie of her place. Very well. She might have to accept that from the queen, but she wasn't going to put up with a husband who treated her like a good little girl who could be kept in the dark and would do whatever he asked of her.

She pulled the last of the pins out and dragged her fingers into the curls, pulling the pile of hair back down around her shoulders. The ladies-in-waiting had brought her into the bedchamber in the small apartment the queen had granted to them, and they'd giggled and fussed around her, helping her off with her jewelry—she'd been tempted to fling Eloisa's pearls across the room and never pick them up again, but that would be difficult to explain—and shoes and touching up the color staining her lips and cheeks. Honoria had dabbed perfume over her, including between her breasts, and then they'd finally—*finally*—left her alone to wait for Cameron.

Alone for the first time all day, she'd finally been able to scowl as she wanted to and had reached for a cloth and water to rub the cosmetics off her face before she'd started pulling down her hair. If she could have gotten out of the wedding gown on her own, she would have. But that would require arms that bent in ways not humanly possible, thanks to the row of tiny buttons that began at the back of her neck and finished past her waist. Not to mention the corset that laced at the back rather than the front like the ones she wore day to day so she could dress herself. Truly women's clothes were stupid. If she and Cameron ever did live on an estate, she was going to stake a claim for eccentricity and wear the most comfortable clothes she could design, propriety be damned. Hopefully no one would want to upset a royal witch by telling her she couldn't.

No one but her husband perhaps. She scowled at her reflection again, wishing there was something else she could do to express her displeasure. Cameron might be expecting a pretty, painted, perfect bride waiting placidly for him, but he wasn't going to get one. She picked up the cloth again and scrubbed at her wrist where the spicy, heady scent Honoria had chosen was strongest. But apparently it had already sunk into her skin, because the smell didn't budge.

She dropped the cloth back onto the dressing table and looked around the room. There was wine on a small table near the fire. And glasses. She had refrained from drinking any more than was strictly necessary to acknowledge the toasts at the dinner following the wedding, not wanting to risk giving in to her temper in public if the wine loosened her tongue. But she didn't have to worry about that anymore. The ruby-colored wine looked pretty in the glass and tasted sweet on her tongue as she drained the first glass. She poured a second and was lifting it again when the door opened and Cameron stepped through.

He looked somewhat surprised to see the wine in her hand but then smiled—that damned stupid smile that was so attractive on his damned stupid face, even though she hated him—and held up the bottle in his own hand. "I see we had a similar thought, milady wife," he said. "I didn't know the servants had already left some."

Given the amount of Iska his brothers had pushed on him throughout dinner, it was surprising he could stomach the thought of wine at all. But that wasn't her problem. "Perhaps we'll need two bottles," she said.

Cameron locked the door and turned back to her, a sympathetic expression on his face. "Are you that nervous? There's no need—I mean, if you wish—"

"I'm not nervous," she snapped. "What do I have to be nervous about? After all, we've already done what we're here to do tonight."

"That's true," he said in a suddenly careful tone. Apparently, it might have been beginning to sink through his Iska-soaked head that she was less than happy. He crossed the room and put the bottle he held down on the table beside the open one. He didn't pour himself a glass, though. Instead, he moved closer to the fire, shrugged out of his jacket, and draped it over the nearest chair, leaving him dressed in a blindingly white shirt, black breeches, and tall boots that outlined every inch of his body in annoying detail.

Men's fashion was stupid, too, she decided, and took another mouthful of wine.

"If you're not nervous," he said after a long moment of silence, "perhaps you could do me the courtesy of explaining to me what is driving you to drink on our wedding night?"

"There's nothing wrong with drinking," she said. She drained the glass defiantly and reached for the bottle. His hand snatched it away before she touched it.

"No, there's nothing wrong with drinking," he said. "But you're not the biggest creature the goddess put on the earth, and you'll regret it in the morning. Hellebride red has kick to it like an angry mule despite the sweet face it shows your tongue."

"I've drunk Hellebride red before," she said.

"Then you know what I'm talking about. So, again, I'll ask you, what has you bristling like one of Lucy's barn cats?" He kept a firm hold on the bottle.

"Did you just call me a barn cat?" she demanded.

"I—"

"Though I suppose," she continued, "it makes sense that that would be your choice of insults, given that you have the morals of a wild tomcat yourself."

He went very still. She couldn't quite see clearly in the flickering firelight, but she thought his knuckles had turned white where he gripped the bottle. "I beg your pardon?"

"You heard me."

"What exactly are you accusing me of, Sophie?" His voice was controlled rather than calm. And somewhat lower than usual.

Against the warmth of the red in her stomach, she felt the faintest chill. She lifted her chin, not caring. "Not accusing. Just stating facts. A man with morals, after all, with honor, would have told his future wife that he had bedded the fucking queen of the country. Particularly when said future wife is one of her ladies-in-waiting. One of her friends." Rage spilled over now, and she hurled the glass toward the fire, where it shattered against the wall, shards glittering as they fell to the carpet.

Cameron didn't so much as flinch. Nor did his eyes move from her face. "Eloisa told you," he said flatly.

"Yes. She did."

"When?"

"After the coronation ball. She thought it only fair to warn me that royal witches were to your taste. Fore-warned is forearmed, after all."

"And you waited until now to speak to me about it?"

She made an exasperated gesture. "It didn't seem to matter when we had this conversation. It's not like they would let us call off the wedding."

"So you stood there and made vows to me this morn-ing, thinking I was marrying you only so I could bed an-other witch? Put another notch in some tally board? Despite everything else that has happened?"

"You were the queen's lover," she spat.

"Yes," he retorted. "I was. Before you and I had any inkling that any of this would happen. Before I had spent any time with you at all that didn't involve guard duty, to be blunt. I'm not a monk, Sophie. I won't apologize be-cause it's unfair that men get to do things before marriage that women cannot. And I won't apologize for having a lover before you had any claim on me whatsoever."

"You should have told me," she said, hearing her voice go shrill. She couldn't entirely dispute his point, but that didn't change the fact that he hadn't told her the truth. That he'd kept her in the dark. She was growing very tired of being kept ignorant.

He scrubbed a hand over his face, where stubble was beginning to darken his jaw. "Perhaps. Honestly, I thought it was better if you never knew, given that you are one of her ladies and her friend. I never dreamed that she would tell you herself."

"She's the queen. She wanted me to be clear on that

fact. On my position in this situation. On the fact that she had you first and that she could have you back anytime she chooses to crook her finger at you. After all, a royal witch and a queen has to be even more exciting than just a witch, doesn't it?"

"She might think that," Cameron said. "That doesn't make it true."

"She's the queen."

"So she is. And she's beautiful. And she's a witch. But she's not my wife. She's not the one I'm standing here with. She's not the one I made vows to in the temple today. She's not you," he growled. "And I'll thank you, wife, to have more respect for my honor than you appear to."

"You expect me to believe that you'd rather have me in your bed than her?" She swept her hand down, gesturing at her body, which had nothing like Eloisa's curves or grace.

This time it was Cameron who threw something at the fire. The bottle shattered rather more loudly, and red splashed against the wall and ran in streams over the mantel, hissing into the fire and making it flare wildly as the alcohol burned. "Yes," he ground out.

"Why?"

"Because of this," he growled. And he yanked her hard against him and kissed her. Kissed her hard. Savagely almost. It should have hurt, but instead, delight roared through her, sparking as wildly as the fire. She buried her hands in his hair, pulling him closer. His hands tightened at her waist, and he picked her up and carried her over to the bed.

Yes. Every fiber of her being shrieked it.

But then reason reared its ugly head. This was the power again. Magic. Not her.

"Wait," she said, breaking their kiss with a gasp. "This isn't real."

He looked confused. "What are you talking about?"

"This. This is what she said. That it's just the magic. Making us want each other. Admit it. You never would have touched me that first time if I hadn't stepped into the ley line."

He shook his head. "That may be true. But that doesn't explain every other time we touched. And doesn't explain why I can't stop thinking about you."

"Did you think about her?"

"Did no one ever tell you it's impolite to bring up such things on your wedding night?" he said, sounding half exasperated. "Yes. Sometimes I thought about Eloisa. But not the way it is with you." He looked at her a moment, then set her down on her feet again, though he didn't let go of her. His hands rested at her waist, heavy and warm. He stared down at her. "I'm not sure there's anything I can say to convince you, is there?"

She shrugged, feeling a sudden sting of tears. Eloisa had been right. This was never going to work.

"All right, then," he said, and this time he did step back. "Tell me to go and I'll go. And I won't come back into your bed until you ask me to. I can't unmarry you, but I'm not going to force myself on you. So, wife, if you can stand there and honestly tell me you don't want me, then I'll go."

She stared up at him, wondering if he really would go. Just like that? Just because she asked?

"Say it," he said, reaching out to touch her cheek. "Say 'Go away, Cameron.' Say 'I don't want you, Cameron.'"

Part of her wanted to. Wanted to keep her heart safe, as Eloisa had warned her. But a larger part knew that it was already too late for that. And that, magic or not, she didn't want to let go of him. She shook her head. "I won't lie to you."

He breathed out a very relieved-sounding sigh. "Good. That's one thing settled." He moved closer again. "Now we'll deal with the other part of the problem."

"I don't see how," she said.

His hand settled on her hip. "Eloisa put nonsense in your head. Whatever her reasons—and believe me, if she weren't queen, I would be informing her of the error of her tactics—she convinced you that this is just magic. Just fucking, driven by fire and fury and fever. All flash and speed until it burns out. Like it was by the ley line. That is what she told you, isn't it?"

She nodded, mouth drying as she remembered, with unrelenting clarity, with him so close, with him touching her, how it had felt when he had slid into her. She swallowed. "Something like that."

"Well, then, I believe I can prove her wrong." He smiled at her, and this time the smile was intoxicating rather than infuriating.

"How?"

"By showing you there's more than fire and fury here." His other hand lifted, and he ran a thumb over her lower lip.

"How?" she repeated as her knees went distinctly wobbly at the touch.

"Well, firstly, I intend to take you out of that dress," he said, voice rough again. "And then I'll take you out of whatever you're wearing under it. Then I'll take you to bed and show you what it's like when we go slowly." He pushed her hair back, pressed a kiss to the side of her neck. Drew back with a smile when she shuddered.

"So slowly you'll think you're going to die. But you won't."

"I won't?" She felt as though she were floating. Or melting. Perhaps both. Lost in the heat his words were rousing.

"No, my little wildcat," he said. "You won't die. You'll just come, screaming my name."

Heat flared through her even brighter, and she swayed. "Merciful goddess."

"Too late for mercy," he said. "Now turn around. Put your hands around the bedpost."

She managed to do as he asked. The wood was cool beneath her fingers, and she leaned forward to rest her forehead on it as well, helpless to fight the longing pulsing through her, the heat of it and the throb between her legs.

"Good girl," he said softly. He pushed her hair forward so the length of it fell forward over her shoulders. "I was looking forward to taking this down," he said. "To seeing it all around you. But I guess we'll save that for next time." His lips pressed against the nape of her neck, and he blew softly, the warm air brushing her neck, lighting her skin.

"Look at all these buttons," he said, and she felt his fingers move to the first one. "I think this is going to take a *very* long time."

CHAPTER SEVENTEEN

It did take a very long time.

He started with the sleeves, which had their own rows of tiny buttons. Between each button, Cam ran his fingers over her wrists, wherever the skin was bare, and followed the touch with kisses that became a slow kind of divine torture as each nerve his lips passed over flared to life. Then he straightened and reached for the next button whilst he whispered in her ear exactly what he wanted to do to her. Delicious, wicked-sounding things. Things she wasn't even sure were truly things that men and women did together.

With each button the process grew slower because there was more skin to cover, more for his lips to worship. It took an eternity for him to finish each sleeve, and she was panting softly by the time he moved his fingers back to the button at the top of the scoop of fabric that cut across her back. She was suddenly devoutly thankful that the seamstress had insisted on converting the high-collared neckline her mother had worn to this more daring one front and back. That had to have cut out at least ten or fifteen buttons. But fewer buttons didn't stop her from having to bite her lip to keep from begging him to just take her already by the time he'd worked his way down the length of her back. She'd never imagined that a man's hands on her back could make her ache so. By the time he finally slid the dress off her shoulders and down onto the floor, she was trembling with need.

She managed—with a supreme effort and a death grip on the bedpost—to stay upright when she lifted each foot at his bidding so he could pull the dress free. She was fairly certain her knees would have given out on her without the bedpost to hold on to. She was almost sure they *would* give out on her if he took much longer.

She wore only a chemise and corset under the dress. The chemise was a mere whisper of lace and silk, scandalous in its transparency. Another reason to bless the seamstress. Cameron skimmed a hand down her side, and the silk might as well have not been there, the heat of his skin searing her. She thought she heard him swear softly as she moaned, but then he reached for her laces and began teasing her all over again.

"Please," she said. She didn't even know what she was asking for.

Cameron paused. He hadn't even loosened the first lace. "Please, what?"

She turned her head. "I need—"

"So impatient." He shook his head at her. Then his dimple flashed as he smiled. "Well, as to that, I guess there's no reason why you can't scream my name more than once. Turn around, then."

She managed to obey. His eyes were dark and hungry in the firelight, the blue obscured to a nameless shade that seemed made of wanting.

"Now, there's a pretty sight," he said softly as he studied her. She glanced down. The chemise hid very little, and she was bare to his gaze except where the satin and bone corset still covered her, pushing her breasts up into a semblance of curves. "Very pretty," he said, and ran his finger along the upper edge of the corset, tracing the skin across her breasts, slowing even more when his fingers touched the very edge of the skin surrounding her nipples. If she could have lifted her arms, she would have ripped the corset off with her bare hands so he could touch her bare flesh, but she couldn't. Instead she just gasped and arched her back.

"I want you to know that this is hurting me more than it's hurting you," he said fervently, and then he dropped to his knees, pushed her legs apart, and buried his head in the thatch of hair between her legs. His tongue slid against her, two fingers slipped inside her, and she convulsed around him, gasping his name as he licked and stroked through the shudders until they quieted.

Then he climbed to his feet. "That's once. Now turn around and we'll do this damned corset."

"I hate corsets," she said, not sure she could move.

"I'd rather look at one than have to wear one," he agreed cheerfully. "They do look very nice though. Especially pretty ones like this. Like a present all wrapped up to be undone. So turn around and let me open my present."

Sophie leaned back against the bedpost. "If I move, I might just fall down."

"I'll catch you," he said, and bent to kiss her. She could taste herself on his mouth, beneath the taste of Cameron and the faint woody smoke of the Iska he'd drunk. It was strangely intoxicating. Then he lifted her, turned her, and put her hands back around the bedpost.

"Now, where were we?" he asked as he started all over again.

The corset didn't take as long as the dress, and he must have been starting to feel impatient, too, because the chemise vanished with one long stroke of a knife—she had no idea where the knife had come from—after the corset fell from her body. Then his arms came around her and lifted her onto the bed. She was burning with need again as he settled beside her, the mattress dipping under his weight.

He still wore his shirt and breeches. The boots were gone. She hadn't noticed that part of the process, which, given how long it took a man to remove tall boots, only told her how lost she was in the haze of longing he was creating.

"I want to see you," she said.

Cameron shook his head. "Not just yet. After all, there are whole parts of you I haven't even touched yet." To demonstrate his point, he brushed one finger across one of her puckered nipples and she arched up off the bed with another moan.

"Goddess," he said fervently. "I do like the noises you make." Then he set himself to exploring her breast with the same excruciating leisurely pace. First with fingers, then with tongue and teeth until she was writhing beneath him and begging again, legs falling open. This time his fingers found her and stroked just right until she came a second time, even harder than the first time, the room dissolving in a wave of pleasure.

It took a few minutes for her to open her eyes. To remember exactly who she was. And who the man next to her was. Her husband. Who was looking very pleased with himself.

"That's two," he said.

She rolled onto her side and fisted her hand around the front of his shirt. "Cameron Aled Mackenzie, if you do not exert your husbandly rights very soon, I might just have to kill you."

"Wildcat." He grinned widely as he said the word. "But who am I to deny a lady?"

"You seem to be doing pretty well denying me," she said.

"Nonsense. You're the one who's already screamed my name twice. I'm the one being denied."

"No denial here," she said. She lay back on the pillows. "Take off your clothes." She let a hand drift down to her breast, wondering idly if it felt the same if she did to herself what he had been doing to her. Not exactly, she decided. But it was still pleasant. She sighed, and this time it was Cameron who groaned. He pulled his shirt over his head with remarkable speed. The breeches took a little longer, but they soon joined the shirt on the floor.

He came back to her then. Naked. His cock was hard, straining, jutting toward her. She'd never seen a grown man fully naked before. Never thought a man would be beautiful. But he was. Lined with muscle and furred here and there with dark hair but still beautiful. Her hand reached for his cock, curiosity overriding need for a moment.

He let her wrap her hand around it, let her fingers explore, but only for a few seconds. Then his hand closed over hers.

"If you keep that up, then you'll spoil the next part of the process for both of us."

"You got to touch me," she protested.

"And I promise you can touch me all you want after this," he said, rolling on top of her. She went still. His cock has hard and warm against her, where she was wet and soft and aching. Cameron moved slightly, settling his position, and the slide of him against her made her see stars. Still, he felt much larger than she remembered, and for an instant she froze.

"Just me," he whispered in her ear. "Just us. From now on. You and me, Sophie. And this." He lifted his head, kissed her. Kissed her in a way that was somehow both soft and fierce. Kissed her until she widened her legs of her own will, as the fire rose again and all she could think of was the need to be closer. To have him inside her.

Cameron groaned as he slid inside her, stopped, pressed his forehead to hers. A shiver ran through him, and she wondered if his extraordinary control was finally close to a breaking point.

"Merciful goddess," he muttered, and began to move.

But even now, with both of them trembling, he didn't give in. Each thrust was long and slow and deep. Giving her time to adjust to the slide and length of him, to the pure sensation of hard flesh sliding across sensitive tissues. He urged her to put her legs around his waist, and he held her hands over her head. He kept up that slow, sure rhythm, letting her arch to meet him but not letting her go any faster than he wanted to go. Until all she could do was give in to him. Give in to the kisses and his determination to show her he was hers and to the sensations melting her into him. Until all there was was his face over hers and his eyes drinking her in and the pleasure building deeper and wider and hotter with each stroke.

Until at the very last, she gave in completely and called his name one last time as she exploded. Then his pace changed; then he drove harder and faster, lifting her hips and taking her hungrily as she shuddered around him, boneless and drowning in it.

He feasted on her, took her over completely. But it was her name on his lips as he finally lost control and shuddered into her with a shout. And the sound of it made her wonder if perhaps they'd both won something precious here in the darkness.

❧

"You have to get out of bed sooner or later, little wildcat." Amusement filled Cameron's voice.

Sophie rolled over, still half asleep, and opened one eye. "Why? We just got married. People expect us to want to stay in bed."

Cameron laughed, then bent to kiss her bare shoulder. "If we do that so soon after last night, you'll be a very young widow."

She sniffed. "I thought I was getting a wild northerner husband. One who could ravish me for days." She stud-

ied him. He was, for what had to be the first time since
they'd returned to the palace, not wearing his uniform,
dress or otherwise. Instead he wore a dark-blue jacket
and dark-gray breeches with a white shirt. Each of the
items was unornamented but beautifully cut. He wore no
jewelry other than his wedding band. She realized she'd
never seen him wear any. Most men wore a signet ring or
a cravat pin or, amongst the younger set, an earring.
Cameron did not. He looked delectable all the same.
Smug satisfaction that it was her ring around his finger
made her smile.

"Stop thinking what you're thinking. Even wild northerners have limits. Besides . . ." He paused and tilted his
head at her. "You're the one with the more . . . delicate . . .
parts. I don't want to hurt you."

"I feel absolutely fine." She stretched her arms over
her head. Muscles in unexpected places twinged and a
wince crossed her face. Maybe not absolutely fine.

Cameron grinned. "I think you just proved my point.
Come, milady. I've run you a bath. Once you're ready,
we'll go out."

"Out where?" Normally newlyweds would have headed
away from Kingswell altogether, to a family estate or a
guesting house at one of the popular seaside towns. Cameron and Sophie, however, had been told they would be
spending their marriage week in the palace.

"We can walk in the gardens. Or visit your parents,
maybe?"

She shook her head at that. "No. Not my parents. Not
today." Not whilst what she and Cameron had done in
this thoroughly rumpled bed was painted so fresh in her
memory. She didn't want to sit across the table from her
parents and have them *know*. "I could always just tap the
ley line. Give us both a boost. Then we can start all over
again." In truth, despite the small aches in her body, she
felt energized now that she was fully awake.

Cameron shook his head. "No. No, best not. You're still having lessons. Perhaps you should focus on those before you start playing with such things alone."

"Spoilsport." She was doing much better with her control. She hadn't shattered an earth-light in the last week. And the temple devout had taught her a useful lesson the day before the wedding. "Look," she said, and focused on one of the candles set along the mantelpiece. It flared to life with a *whoosh*, the flame shooting several inches high before it settled back down.

"Very impressive," Cameron said. "But I'd prefer not to be set alight just now."

"I wouldn't set you on fire," she said. Then she grinned. "Well, not unless you really upset me."

His brows lifted. "I'll try not to do that," he said. "But being a human matchstick, although useful, isn't going to get you dressed." He pulled back the covers, looked down at her naked body, and grinned suddenly. "Though I have a sudden urge to let you stay here."

"I like that urge."

He stepped back. "No. Not going to work. We need to be good newlyweds and go out and let people giggle at us. Eloisa wanted us married so quickly to show that the court is continuing as usual. So we have to be seen."

She tried not to frown when he spoke the queen's name. He had driven away the doubts Eloisa had planted in her mind during the long night they'd shared, but that didn't mean Sophie had forgiven her yet.

She needed to work on that. Or, if it was too soon to forgive, then on not letting her rancor show. She would be returning to the queen's ladies-in-waiting once the week was over. That could prove difficult if she was angry at the queen and unable to hide it.

Maybe Cameron was right. Better to just get on with things. Start this new life of theirs. She held out a hand

and let him help her out of bed. "How about a compromise? Come scrub my back in that gigantic bathtub, and then we'll go out."

"I like the way you think, wife," he said. Then he reached into his jacket pocket and pulled out a small wooden box. "Here. I meant to give you these last night, but the right moment didn't quite eventuate."

She took the box, feeling guilty. He'd obviously meant to give her this on their wedding night, before he'd reached their rooms to be confronted by her in a hideous temper. "I'm sorry," she said, "about last night."

He shook his head. "Nothing to apologize for. The matter is dealt with. Perhaps not in the fashion we might have liked, but"—he flashed her that grin—"I think the outcome was satisfactory in the end." He nodded at the box. "Open it."

She lifted the lid. Nestled on a pad of velvet inside was a pair of pearl earrings. Perfect spheres in an unusual bronze-green shade that she hadn't seen before, dangling from simple gold settings that echoed her betrothal ring. A tiny sapphire flanked by two topazes decorated the small bead that linked each pearl to the gold. "They're beautiful," she breathed, lifting one to the light.

"You like them?" Cameron looked nervous suddenly. "The court jeweler suggested cream—I think he knew about the necklace that the queen gave you—but this color reminded me of you."

Sophie doubted she'd be happy wearing cream pearls ever again, even though she would have to wear the queen's necklace at court often enough to be polite. The bronze, however, was gorgeous. They must have cost Cameron a pretty penny, but it wasn't their value that pleased her. It was the fact he'd chosen them for her. "They're perfect," she said, and slipped the first into her ear, then reached for the second. "There. How do they look?"

"Very good," he said, reaching to brush her hair back from her ears. Then he stilled, studying her. "They make your hair look redder. Or maybe it is redder."

She didn't want to think about that. "We were discussing pearls, not hair." She came to her knees and reached up to kiss him. "Thank you for my gift."

                           ∽∾

More than an hour later, they finally left the apartment and began to wander through the palace. Sophie occupied herself idly with trying to see the wards they passed. She fancied that she could see the layers of them now. Faint variations in color and the way they felt in her mind that told her which might be earth magic versus those laid by battle mages or the Illusioners.

"Perhaps we could go back to the Illusioners' library tomorrow," she said. "I'd like to keep up my . . . studies."

Cameron paused. They were walking along one of the portrait halls, filled with paintings of generations of Fairleys and other favored nobles of the court. "That might not be so wise. Not this week. Not whilst people are paying such attention to us."

He was right. She hadn't considered that. She was doing nothing wrong, seeking out the library, but it might be wisest to wait until Eloisa and the Domina seemed more certain of her loyalty and had forgiven her for her mishap with Cameron before she sought out the library and the book on bindings again.

The Domina had performed the binding ritual between Sophie and Cameron after the wedding yesterday, but the sigils, instead of vanishing at the completion of the ritual, had shimmered on their bound hands with a golden glow for a second or two. When the glow vanished, the sigils faded but were still visible. Eloisa, standing witness as the strongest royal witch and given the need to keep Sophie's status secret, had frowned at the Domina.

"What does that signify?"

The Domina had thrown up her hands. "Your guess is as good as mine. I'd say there is a connection of some kind, if not a full binding." She'd scrubbed their hands clean with the same burning liquid she'd used to clean Sophie's the week before. "It seems to have taken a little. Maybe she'll be able to help him if he gets a sniffle."

Sophie had stayed silent, still too angry at the queen and Cameron at that point to want to add to the conversation. But now she wanted to understand what had happened. Were they bound as an Anglion husband and wife might usually be? Or was there something more because of what they'd done? An "*augmentier*," as Madame de Montesse had named it. It was important that they knew exactly what they shared, if only to know how best to hide it if necessary. But Cameron was right. They were under scrutiny this week. Best not to put a foot wrong.

She let Cameron lead her onward through the endless corridors. The day was hot for so late in summer, and the damaged palace wasn't as cool as she remembered from previous summers.

The wards mending the shattered walls might have been keeping the rain and worse out, but apparently wards weren't as good at soaking up heat as good Carnarvon granite. The temperature varied markedly, depending on how close they were to one of the damaged sections of the palace, the heat and closeness, making even the pale green, light cotton dress she wore seem too hot.

She remembered another thing the devout had taught her and tried to sink some of the heat down through the stone at her feet. She must have sunk a little too much, because she suddenly felt icy, a shiver running through her.

"Sophie?" Cameron said, stopping their walk.

"It's nothing. Ghost walking past my grave, perhaps." It was something her grandmother had used to say.

"Don't say that."

"Ah, superstitious northerner." She smiled at him and started to walk again, the sensation of cold fading as she did. "Ghosts aren't—" She paused. Stopped what she had been about to say. Northern superstitions ranked ghosts right along with demons and other things associated with the forbidden fourth art. Which was another thing she probably shouldn't even joke about here in the palace. Even if she hadn't been out of favor with the queen already, she would rapidly find herself so if she was heard talking about anything connected with Illvya. "Never mind."

❧

Eventually their meandering path through the palace led them toward the ruined Salt Hall.

"We don't have to go this way," Cameron said as they reached the junction of the corridor.

Sophie could see the holes in the outer walls from where they stood. "No. I want to. I haven't seen it yet. I'll have to sooner or later."

"If you wish." Cameron tucked her hand through his arm, and they set off again.

When they walked into the Salt Hall, the guards on the space where the doors should have been let them past without argument. Sophie blinked a few times, startled by the bright sunlight filling the space. As her eyes adjusted, she saw that it wasn't just sunlight but the light shining from the wards that made the room so bright.

The wards shifted and shimmered, the layers and levels of color, which she could sense only faintly elsewhere in the palace, as clear as watching rainbow light in a crystal here. Perhaps because they were so freshly laid? She wasn't sure, but she just stared at them, entranced by the dancing patterns until Cameron nudged her and she looked up to find Lord Sylvain standing before them.

"Barron Scardale, Lady Scardale," Lord Sylvain said with a broad smile. "Felicitations on your wedding."

Sophie had dipped into a curtsy automatically, but halfway through rising, she suddenly remembered that Lady Scardale was her. The queen's gift to Cameron had been a title to go along with Liam's gift of extra holdings of land. A barron was a more suitable husband for a royal witch than a mere lieutenant. She suspected Liam and Eloisa had colluded in the matter. Liam had held the barronetcy that belonged to the Inglewood title whilst his father had been alive, and now it would be Alec's until Liam had a son to succeed him.

There wasn't another major title attached to the family that Liam could bestow on Cameron. So without Eloisa granting Cameron a new title, Liam couldn't have improved his brother's rank. Only his wealth by granting him more land.

Cameron had definitely been startled when Eloisa had made the announcement at the wedding dinner, but Sophie hadn't been in any mood to felicitate her husband on his elevation just then. Up until now she had forgotten it entirely, Cameron having so thoroughly distracted her.

So she was now Sophia Mackenzie, Lady Scardale. It would take some getting used to.

"Thank you, Your Grace," Cameron said. "How are you today?"

"Well enough, lad, well enough."

"And the investigations?" Cameron looked past Lord Sylvain to the group of Illusioners examining a section of outer wall.

"Much the same. Nothing to disturb your week with your lovely wife." He smiled at Sophie again, and she smiled back. Of all the erls, Lord Sylvain was her favorite. Maybe because he was now too old to be—or need to be—overly bothered with indulging in the posturing and status-proving that all the others seemed to find so fascinating. He was always amusing when he attended anything the queen invited him to and had been kind when he'd spoken to Sophie elsewhere. Old enough, too, not to worry so much about setting a foot wrong with a potential royal witch. Too old to be chosen as her husband and therefore able to treat her just as he would any other young lady he liked.

"What are they looking for exactly?" Sophie asked. "If you can tell me that," she added hastily.

"Traces of whatever was used to set off the explosions, magical or otherwise."

Sophie looked over at the Illusioners. But as she didn't understand how their magic worked, she couldn't hope to understand what it was they were actually doing. "The court seems convinced it was magical."

Lord Sylvain nodded, leaning on his cane. "It is nearly certain. The fire was too hot to be purely natural."

"But nothing has been found?"

"Not yet." Lord Sylvain swept his hand across the vast room, at the rocks and rubble piled in heaps taller than Sophie herself. "As you can see, there is much to go through."

He offered his arm to Sophie. "Let me steal you from your new husband a moment and I'll show you what they are doing." He pointed his cane at Cameron. "You can tag along if you keep quiet."

"He's very obedient," Sophie said with a laugh. "He'll keep quiet."

Cameron pulled a face at her.

Lord Sylvain laughed. "I see your marriage is off to a good start, lad. You've learned your place already." He patted Sophie's hand, and they made their way over to one of the nearest piles of broken stone.

"Each pile is sorted and studied individually," Lord Sylvain said.

Sophie tipped her head back, trying to judge how tall it was. It rose past Cameron's height. How many stones did it contain? Hundreds? And there were how many piles to go through? The Illusioners would be here for weeks. Or months.

"How do you know which has been dealt with? There are so many of them," Sophie asked.

"The archivists are keeping track. They have some sort of grid system. That part—Lord Sylvain grinned again—"is not my problem, thank the goddess. The memory isn't always what it used to be."

"Nonsense. You'll outlive us all," Sophie said.

"Not unless the Domina extends her newfound healing skills to men like me," Lord Sylvain said. He tilted his head at her, his dark eyes suddenly far more serious.

"Are you ill, Your Grace?" Sophie asked, the thought making her feel suddenly sad.

"No more than any man my age, my dear." He patted her arm again. "Don't worry about me." He tapped at the pile of rubble with his cane, and one of the smaller chunks, barely three inches across, came loose, sliding down the pile and rolling to a halt half a foot from the edge of Sophie's skirts. A chill swept over her, and she shivered.

"What is it?" Cameron said, stepping forward.

"Stay where you are," Lord Sylvain said, his voice cracking with authority. "Lady Scardale, don't move. But tell me what you feel."

"It's just a chill," she said. "Probably a draft." But the icy feeling wasn't receding as a draft would.

"I'm not so sure about that," Lord Sylvain said. He scowled. "Move back, my dear." He gestured at the stone with his cane. "I think the Illusioners should look at that."

Sophie stared down at the stone. "Is it dangerous?"

"That is for them to decide. It made you feel odd. That should be enough to interest them."

"It was just a chill," Sophie protested.

"A chill in a room that's stifling hot," Lord Scardale said. "Some earth witches can sense Illvyan magics. Perhaps you're one of them." He herded them a little way away from the pile.

"Best you continue on with your walk for now. Someone will come to fetch you if the Illusioners need to hear more about what you felt." Lord Sylvain peered at her a moment, then turned to Cameron. "Lord Scardale, I think you should bring your lady wife to take tea with me soon. Not today. I don't think there will be any time today. But soon. Tomorrow if you can."

"But what—" Cameron started to ask, but Lord Sylvain shook his head.

"Just bring her," he said, and then he shouted across the hall for Master Egan.

CHAPTER EIGHTEEN

It seemed that Lord Sylvain's prediction that there would be no time to take tea with him that day was correct. A few hours after dinner, Cameron and Sophie were summoned to Eloisa's council, the message requesting their presence delivered by no less a person than Lord Sylvain himself.

"We have made a little progress," Master Egan said once the council had seated themselves and the queen had requested that he explain why they were there. Not that any of them truly needed an explanation. Everyone knew that Master Egan was in charge of the investigation into the attack. "Earlier today, we had cause to examine one of the pieces of rubble more closely, thanks to Lady Scardale. She had a reaction to the stone, and Lord Sylvain drew our attention to it. I can confirm there's part of an Illvyan scriptii on the stone that Lady Scardale reacted to."

The assembled councilors looked grim at the Illusioner's announcement, but none of them looked overly surprised. Cameron watched Eloisa, more concerned with her reaction than any others. After all, the queen was the one who could drag the country to war if she chose.

Beside him, Sophie was silent, sitting upright in her chair as though poised to flee. He moved his knee under the table slightly to touch hers. It wouldn't be politic to take her hand, but he still wanted to give her what comfort he could.

"You're one hundred percent certain?" Liam asked when no one else spoke.

Master Egan nodded impatiently. "I could show you if you wish. But we have the stone under ward now. It would take time to fetch it."

"That isn't necessary," Eloisa said. "Your word on the matter is enough, Master Egan."

"We must act," Domina Skey said abruptly. "An Illvyan scriptii on the stone proves that Illvyan magic was involved. That Illvyan agents are at work."

"What exactly do you think it is we should do?" Lord Sylvain asked. He wasn't an active member of the council, though he had served King Stefan as councilor early in the king's reign. But he had accompanied Sophie and Cameron to the meeting when Master Egan insisted that they be there to explain what had happened. It seemed no one wanted to eject him. "We have proof of Illvyan magic, yes. But we have no idea of who placed the scriptii there. Or whom they were working with. That's hardly solid basis for starting a war."

The Domina gave him a poisonous look. "Illvyan magic is abomination. The perpetrators must be found and punished. And we must show Illvya that we will not stand idly and let them attack us."

"I don't disagree with you on that point," Lord Sylvain said. "I just disagree that we need to punish everybody. The goddess advocates mercy; does she not?"

"Not to mention that the trade delegation is not due to start home for several more days. If you make warlike noises right now, you'll sacrifice all of them. And the goods they bring," Lord Airlight said.

That brought another babble of people talking over one another. Cameron rubbed his neck where the mus-

cles were pulling tight. Sophie had been right. They
should have just stayed in bed. He could be making love
to his wife right now instead of them both being em-
broiled smack-dab in the middle of the investigation into
the attack, bringing even more attention upon themselves.

At the opposite end of the long council table, Commander Peters looked thoroughly exasperated. Cameron
began to count in his head, and before he reached five,
the commander bellowed, "Silence!"

The room went quiet, only the slightly plaintive voice
of the new Erl of Farkeep, who'd finally arrived in Kingswell the day after the coronation, saying, "I still don't
understand how she knew it was Illvyan . . ." breaking
the silence.

Cameron fought the urge to roll his eyes. The new erl
was about a year older than Sophie and apparently had
been to the capital exactly once in his life. Hopefully, the
lad would find himself a mentor in the ways of the court
sooner rather than later. He needed to start learning fast
or he would be the first one banished from Eloisa's
council, and the Farkeep family's fall would be rapid after that.

"My Lord Farkeep," Eloisa said, breaking her silence.
"Lady Scardale is a royal witch. Chosen of the goddess.
Illvyan magic—scriptii, at least—is anathema to the god-
dess. Her magic sensed the disturbance from that."

It was a pat enough explanation. Lord Farkeep wasn't
a battle mage, so he didn't understand how magic
worked. He was a third cousin of the old erl, and he'd
been living quietly on a very tiny estate with his family
somewhere in Caloteen sheep country. The explanation
would suffice for now, if the erl had the sense to ask no
more questions on the subject, having had it explained
twice now. Across the table, Lord Sylvain caught Cameron's eye, and Cameron remembered what he had prom-

ised. That he would bring Sophie to see the old man. Obviously, there was something more he had to tell them. Cameron was going to make damned sure they got the chance to hear what he had to say.

If they ever got out of the council hall. It was already past nine. It had taken time to assemble the council after Master Egan had sent the news to the queen and then more time for the Illusioners to perform whatever tests it was they had to confirm the small dark line carved into the stone was indeed an Illvyan scriptii and not some line left by one of the destroyed ornamental metalwork that had decorated the hall or something similar.

And the meeting showed no signs of ending anytime soon.

"But how the magic was discovered is a secondary consideration," the queen continued. "What matters now is that we have discovered it. And I am forced to agree with Lord Sylvain. It is too early for retaliation."

"Your Majesty, you should seize the advantage—" the Domina started to say, but Eloisa cut her off with a sharp gesture.

"We will not fight. Not yet."

"Then what do you want us to do?" Lord Airlight asked. After Lord Sylvain, he was the oldest man in the room, though he was only five and fifty or so, rather than into his seventies as Sylvain was. He was the senior surviving member of the council, having served King Stefan as councilor for more than a decade.

Eloisa pursed her lips. "We need to show them we are not intimidated by anything that has occurred. They are trying to scare us, trying to keep us off-balance. What we need is a show of strength. They need to see that life in Anglion continues as ever it did."

Lord Sylvain nodded agreement. Cameron glanced at the Domina. It was just as well for the council members that it wasn't possible for an earth witch to set a man alight. Otherwise, judging by the Domina's furious expression, the council might have been several members short.

"What did you have in mind?" Liam asked.

His brother, at least, was doing far better than Lord Farkeep. But then, Liam had been raised to take his place as erl one day. Cameron had just never quite realized how good his brother would be at it. He always thought Liam had chafed under their father's rule as much as he had done. But maybe he had only ever been biding his time until it was his turn.

"I think we should have a birthday party. For our new royal witch," Eloisa said.

"Excuse me?" Sophie said at the same time as the Domina. It was the first time Sophie had said anything when not directly asked since the meeting had begun, but she flinched back in her chair when she heard the Domina's voice with hers.

"It's perfect," Eloisa said. "We need normality. Reassurance for the populace. And a reminder that Anglion is strong in its own magic. Lady Scardale never got her Ais-Seann celebration. We should have one now. It's a little unorthodox, but it will work." She nodded decisively. "Yes. A ball for our newest witch. The Domina can teach Sophie something splashy to do at the party, and that will send the right message to everyone."

Sophie had gone completely still beside him. Cameron curled his hand into a fist at his side so he wouldn't reach for her.

Commander Peters had listened quietly to the queen, but now he nodded. "I think you are right, Your Majesty. It is just the sort of thing the city needs. It will calm everyone and distract attention from the investigation. Give whoever might be watching something to focus on whilst Master Egan and his men keep working quietly to find us more information."

"Thank you, Commander," the queen said. "Then that's settled. A party for our dear Lady Scardale. Soon I think. Sixth day, perhaps?"

∞

"Now, then, my dear," Lord Sylvain said as he settled himself back into a comfortably stuffed armchair in his front parlor, which was messy and masculine and also shimmering with more wards than Sophie had seen on any personal room in the palace. Including the queen's. "Why don't you take a pastry to go with that tea? I sent my man out specially to fetch them. He'll be heartbroken if we don't eat them."

Sophie smiled obediently and took a tiny fruit-laden tart. She wasn't terribly hungry; her appetite had fled the previous afternoon when she had accidentally discovered the stone with the scriptii. Cameron had tried to get her to eat when they'd finally been allowed to go back to their apartment after the council meeting. She'd managed a bite or two of bread and cheese to please him. Then he'd changed tactics and poured her a glass of Iska—which she wasn't sure she was ever going to grow to love—made her drink it, and took her to bed.

The combination of sex and alcohol had let her sleep at least, but the nerves fluttering in her stomach still left her with no desire for food.

She sipped the tea, which was strong and hot and sweet. That much she could stomach.

"You have to eat, Lady Scardale," Lord Sylvain said. "Royal witches use a lot of energy in what they do."

"I haven't done any magic today."

"Maybe not, but if the Domina is going to teach you some party piece for your birthday extravaganza, then you'll need your strength. My first wife was a royal witch. I know what I'm talking about."

"She was?" Sophie said, diverted from her nerves

about the party. The last thing she wanted was to be the center of attention all over again.

"Yes. Second, too, for that matter, but she was never strong, not like my Louisa."

"I never knew that," Sophie said. Which was interesting. She had been drilled in the lineage of every person in the court. She knew Lord Sylvain had been married twice, that his first wife had died young, killed in a riding accident, but she couldn't remember any mention of the fact that she'd been a witch. Why had that been left out of the court records?

"Well, she's ancient history now," Lord Sylvain said.

Sophie saw an echo of sadness in his face. She didn't think the memory of his wife was ancient history to him. "I'm very sorry for your loss."

Lord Sylvain waved a hand at her. "Eat your tart, child. It was a long time ago."

Sophie picked up the tart and glanced at Cameron. They'd agreed to let Lord Sylvain tell them whatever it was he wanted to tell them in his own time, but she was starting to think that perhaps they needed to hurry him along. She was supposed to go to the temple later to learn whatever it was the Domina came up with for her to do at her Ais-Seann ball.

Cameron put down his empty cup. "My lord, you said you wanted to talk to us."

"Mostly to your wife," Sylvain said. "Still, what I have to say concerns her well-being, which I assume is of interest to you, as well." He focused on Sophie. "So, milady, how about you tell me exactly what is going on with your powers."

Sophie almost dropped her teacup. "Your Grace?"

"There's something afoot," Lord Sylvain said. "You noticed that stone when none of the Illusioners did. Never mind that nonsense Eloisa was spouting about the goddess. And Domina Skey keeps watching you as though you might explode. Not to mention that Eloisa used to treat you like a favorite pet, and now she's giving you the cold shoulder. Now, part of that might be due to young Mackenzie here—"

Beside her, Cameron choked on the pastry he was eating and started to cough.

"Oh, don't be coy, lad," Lord Sylvain said. "You did a good job of keeping it quiet, but I wasn't born yesterday. I've known Eloisa since she was an infant, and I know what she's like with men. I was starting to wonder if she was going to try to convince Stefan that you would be a possible match, but it appears not. The fact that she tossed you to your wife here and doesn't seem so happy with the situation tells me something else is behind all of this."

"I'm not sure this is something we can talk about," Cameron said when he got his breath back.

"This room is well warded," Lord Sylvain said. "I've spent a long time studying magic, lad. I don't think even the Domina could get past my wards. Well, not unless she had some help." He looked at Sophie again as he spoke. "Now, I was married to two royal witches, and I can make an educated guess about what might have gone on, but this will be easier if you tell me."

"Sophie is just strong," Cameron said. "I think Domina Skey hasn't quite figured out how to use that talent."

"Oh, I think she has. Otherwise our queen would still be lying injured in bed," Lord Sylvain countered. "Your wife is strong, I'll give you that, but unless I have indeed finally lost my marbles, I'd say that she's also unbound."

Sophie flinched. So much for keeping their secret. "What do you know about bindings?"

"I told you, I've spent a lot of time studying magic. And not just blood and air. As I said, I was married to two earth witches. I wanted to understand them. So you tell me if I'm right and then maybe I can help you."

"Help me?"

"Survive," he said bluntly. "If you're unbound, then you're in danger here. More than you know, perhaps. Maybe if the attack hadn't happened and Stefan were still king, you would be fine. Then again, if the attack hadn't happened, you'd be safely bound and probably sharing your bed with someone other than Mackenzie. Here and now, with the Domina pushing for war—which I do not like one bit—and Eloisa listening to her a little too much, I'm not sure I like your chances if you don't know how to guard yourself."

He looked at Cameron then. "Have you made sure she knows how to fire a gun, at least? She should carry one if she can."

"I can shoot," Sophie said. "My father taught me."

Lord Sylvain nodded approval. "I always did like your father. Good. Then Cameron will get you a gun, and that will be a start. So tell me, what happened? Did the two of you fall into bed or something? All the excitement of being on the run get to you?"

Sophie felt her cheeks go hot.

"This isn't exactly a topic I wish to discuss," Cameron said.

"No time to be squeamish. And I'm too old to be shocked by anything much when it comes to people and sex. Sex has made people stupid as long as I've been alive, and I'm sure it will continue to do so long after I've returned to the earth. So, you did sleep with the lass?"

"It wasn't Cameron's fault," Sophie said, deciding to throw caution to the wind. Lord Sylvain was the first person other than Cameron who seemed to be on her side. He could be playing some sort of game, but it would have to be very deep. She couldn't see what advantage he would gain from exposing her. "It was me. The morning of my birthday. I touched the ley line, and when Cameron pulled me out, well, things happened. If you were married to a royal witch, perhaps you understand that."

The old man's expression turned faintly nostalgic. "Perhaps I do. All right. So you jumped the gun. And then the Domina couldn't bind you to the goddess. Did she explain why?"

"Not exactly. She said it was because I was no longer virgin."

Lord Sylvain shook his head. "Not such a good sign. And the marriage binding?"

"The Domina said she didn't know if it worked or not. The sigils faded but didn't disappear," Sophie admitted.

"That's too bad. I was never sick a day in my life when my wives were alive. Though perhaps that won't be an issue for you, either, Mackenzie."

"Do you know why the ritual didn't work, sir?" Cameron asked.

Lord Sylvain levered himself out of his chair and stomped over to the very crowded bookcase that took up an entire wall of the room. He put his hand on one of the books, and Sophie saw a ward flare and dissolve. Then he pulled out a slim book bound in green leather, put the ward back in place, and came back to the chair.

"Did you take that from the Illusioners' Hall?" Sophie asked.

His bushy eyebrows flew up. "They have a copy of this book there?"

"If that one is called *On Bindings*, then yes, they do. Though the writing within has faded terribly. I could hardly read any of it."

"I'd imagine it's faded deliberately," Sylvain said. "And I'm surprised it's there at all. It was written by an Illvyan."

"It was?"

"How did you get a copy?" Cameron asked.

"Ways and means, lad. Ways and means. It's not altogether impossible to get things out of Illvya besides trade goods—as the refugees prove. Not that I'd try now to obtain something like this book. Now it might be a good way of getting dead. But forty years ago, things were less well regulated."

"Does the book say why the binding didn't work?" Sophie said.

"Magic's a funny thing," Lord Sylvain said. "A slippery beast, easily put off course." He opened the book and turned the pages carefully. "Ah, yes. Here it is. This is what I suspected happened to you." He passed Sophie the book, and she saw it was open to the page titled "Amplification." She started to read. This copy wasn't faded and illegible. No, the words were clear as day. And what they described sounded a lot like what Madame de Montesse had talked about. Two magics being bound together. Both parties growing stronger as a result. The book described rituals using blood or sex. Well, they had shared both of those, she supposed, even if it had been accidental. "You think we're bound to each other in this manner?" Sophie asked. She passed the book to Cameron.

"Seems the most likely explanation. Have you tried any blood magic, lad? Since the two of you first . . . ?"

Cameron shook his head, eyes fixed on the book. He studied the open page, then turned it quickly and continued reading.

"Well, I advise trying it out somewhere deserted the first time you do. You may be stronger than you expect. And you, milady, you might be able to do things that aren't strictly earth magic. If you can, you can never let the Domina find out. She might be wary of you now, but she'll do her best to get rid of you if you break that big a taboo here. The temple has spent centuries convincing Anglion women that they need only earth magic and that they should give the temple part of their power. You don't want to be the one who threatens that."

Sophie could only agree. "I wouldn't know where to begin to even try another art," she said.

"Good." Lord Sylvain nodded firmly. "I suggest you keep it that way."

CHAPTER NINETEEN

"What are you giving Sophie for her birthday?"
Liam asked the next day as they walked down to
the palace stables. Sophie was at the temple, being
schooled for her big moment at the party tomorrow, and
wasn't likely to reappear until evening. So Cameron had
gone to lunch with his brothers, and then Liam had invited him down to the stables to look at a pair of carriage
horses he was considering.

"I have no idea," Cameron said. He had been considering the matter of a suitable Ais-Seann gift for his wife
since Eloisa had announced the ball. "She liked the earrings I gave her for a wedding gift, but the jeweler says
he doesn't have any more pearls to match, so I can't
make her a set." Even if he could afford to. "I'd take her
away somewhere, but it's doubtful the queen would let
her leave Kingswell whilst things are still unsettled."

"Probably not," Liam agreed. "Though longer term,
do you think you'll want to stay in the capital?"

"I don't know. We haven't even had a chance to discuss such things." He wouldn't have considered the possibility of leaving the Red Guard two weeks ago, but
now he was more worried about keeping Sophie safe
than his career, such as it was. And keeping Sophie safe
seemed to require getting her out of the capital as soon

as he could. "Our estate is a long way from where she's used to living."

"But she did grow up on an estate," Liam said. "She hasn't been in Kingswell all her life. She might prefer it."

"It's a moot point if the queen won't grant her leave to go," Cameron said. "And it doesn't help me solve the puzzle of her birthday present."

"Does she ride?" Liam asked.

Cameron nodded. "Quite well."

"Well, Jeanne's favorite mare—that very pretty gray— is pregnant. Goddess knows we don't need any more horses here in town. Perhaps Sophie would like a foal? It will have good bloodlines and, one hopes, its mother's looks. Both of you are welcome to use any of our horses, of course, if you need to."

"Thank you," Cameron said. He had a gelding he rode when required for guard business, but since he'd been assigned to Eloisa's men, he hadn't often had occasion to ride. One of the sergeants kept the horse exercised, but Cameron had been feeling guilty about him. He wasn't the most attractive beast in the world. Most of the court would have turned up their noses at his plain dun coat and broad face, but he was as reliable as sunrise, and that was more important than looks in an officer's horse. "I'm sure Sophie would like to ride. When she can."

"This is hardly the marriage week you were expecting, I imagine," Liam said. "Let us hope things quiet down after the party."

"Quite," Cameron agreed. "But I think that's going to depend on what else the Illusioners uncover. And how firmly the Domina is able to keep her claws in the queen."

Liam frowned. "Yes. That situation is not ideal. But Eloisa was always independent. I think she'll strike out on her own path soon enough, once she's had time to adjust to being queen."

Cameron wasn't so convinced. If Eloisa could turn on one of her own ladies-in-waiting, she could do just about anything. He had a sudden inspiration about a present for Sophie. Or one he could give to her privately, at least.

"I think you have to give her jewels," Liam said. "If the party is going to be the spectacle they're trying to make it, then the present has to be extravagant. I'll give her the foal. You give her something pretty." He paused as they reached the stable building. "There's that set of emerald bracelets Mother wore. The ones with the gems set in the gold band? Jeanne doesn't like them. She wouldn't mind if you gave them to Sophie, I'm sure."

Cameron nodded agreement but decided there was something else he needed to buy for his wife: a gun.

❧

Cameron found Sophie seated at her dressing table looking somewhat frustrated as she held one of his earrings up to her ears.

"Problem?" he asked, bending to kiss the curve where her neck met her shoulders. She smelled delicious, something spicy and warm rising from her skin. The dress she'd chosen for the ball was a rich green, like holly leaves, the neckline and hem edged with gold embroidery.

"I want to wear these," she said. "But I have to wear the queen's necklace, and they don't really match."

"Wear the necklace," he said. "I don't mind."

"I mind. I want to wear something of yours." She put the earrings down with a sigh and picked up the necklace, looping it around her neck twice. The warm color of the pearls looked good against her skin and the dress, and he let himself admire her for a moment, thinking of the part of the party he was most looking forward to . . . the moment it was over and he could bring her back up here and take the dress off again. Then he remembered why he'd come to find her earlier than he'd promised.

"As to that, I may have an answer to your dilemma." He took the case Liam had given him out from his jacket pocket and put it down in front of her. "I'm supposed to give these to you at the ball, but I'd like you to see them now. Happy birthday."

"You didn't have to get me a present. It's not even really my birthday."

"I'll spoil my wife when I choose, thank you very much," he said with a grin.

She smiled back up at him, the strain that had been shadowing her face for the last few days—despite his best efforts to distract her when he could—clearing. She opened the case, and the smile widened. "Oh. Oh, they're beautiful."

"They were my mother's," he said. He leaned past her shoulder and picked up the topmost bracelet. "Here. Let's see how they look." He undid the clasp and slipped the emeralds onto her wrist. Then he repeated the process twice more.

Sophie held her arm up, admiring the sparkle of light on the jewels. Liam had been right. They did suit her. Not wanting to spoil her happy mood, he decided he'd give her the gun later. Tomorrow even.

"Thank you," she said. She undid the bracelets after running her fingers over them a final time, put them back in the case, and handed it back to him. "Here. Take these before I change my mind and put them back on." She smiled, a little ruefully. "I promise I'll look surprised when you give these to me later."

"You're most welcome," he said. "Now you have to finish getting dressed. We have a party to attend."

Sophie entered the ballroom on Cameron's arm, reminding herself to smile. After all, this ball was for her. Theoretically. In reality, it was about almost everybody else but her. And especially the queen.

Just one night.

She could make it through just one night. After this, she could do her best to just blend in and fade out of the queen's and the Domina's immediate attention. Having spent six hours at the temple yesterday, learning how to do what the Domina had deemed was a suitable party trick, she was heartily tired of feeling like a performing monkey to be trotted out for a show. Though the Domina probably would have been more patient with a monkey than she was with Sophie.

But Sophie had gritted her teeth and done as she was asked with as big a show of goodwill and demure obedience as she could muster.

The Domina had revealed a little of her true ambitions at the council meeting, and Sophie had no desire to be dragged into the dangerous game she was playing. She wasn't going to assist any attempt to embroil the country in a war. A war that would cost the country dearly even if they won. Far better to continue as they were. Two countries with opposing ideals that left each other alone wherever possible. As long as Anglion was surrounded by oceans, there was no simple way for the wizards to overrun the place with their demon sanctii and take over. Anglion should be content with that. With freedom.

Not the sort of things she wanted to be thinking of tonight. She made herself look at the room and the crowd instead. Eloisa had spared no effort, and the ballroom had been once again put back to its intended use. The chandeliers glowed with earth-lights and candles. The dancing light reflected in the crystal glasses and silver-edged china set on the tables that lined the long edges of the room. More candles flickered on the tables, rising from arrangements of white roses that filled the air with their scent. The white decorations served as the perfect backdrop for the court, decked out once more in all the colors of the rainbow for the occasion.

They worked their way through the guests, moving toward the far end of the room to pay their respects to Eloisa, who was sitting at the high table with Lord Air-light and Margaretta and her husband. Sophie, as guest of honor, was supposed to take her place at the table as well, though she'd have preferred to sit with her parents. She and Cameron stopped in front of the table, and she curtsied as he bowed. As they rose, the room behind them fell silent. Eloisa rose.

"We welcome our devoted servant, Sophia Mackenzie, and wish her every happiness on the occasion of her birth-day and felicitations on her Ais-Seann." The court broke into applause, and Sophie curtsied again. When she straight-ened, Eloisa was holding a long blackwood box about the length of two loaves of bread, though not nearly as high as a loaf might be. It was inlaid with silver, and small pearls and nacre formed a rolling wave across the lid.

"Happy birthday, Sophia. May salt protect you and the goddess bless you," Eloisa said with a smile that seemed, for a brief moment, like the old Eloisa.

Sophie smiled back and took the box, then realized she'd have to give it to Cameron so she could open it. He took it happily, and she undid the latch and drew out a long supple roll of dark-brown leather. Memory jolted her, and she glanced up at Cameron. Unless she was mis-taken, this was the roll of magical supplies that she had seen at Madame de Montesse's shop the day of the at-tack. Had it been meant for her all along? That had to have been the height of irony.

She withdrew the roll and untied it, opening it as far as she could without a surface to lay it on. Sure enough, the silver knives, the gold chain, and the other pouches peeked out at her. She smiled at Eloisa. "Thank you, Your Majesty. This is too kind."

Eloisa nodded at her and gestured to the empty seats at the table. Sophie tried not to sigh with relief. The first part of the night was done. Now she just had to pull off the Domina's spectacle and everything would be all right. But first there was dinner to get through.

⟨⟨⟩⟩

Dinner took a long time, but with Lord Airlight on one side and Cameron on her other, Sophie didn't have to speak directly to Eloisa.

The high table was set along the end of the ballroom, perpendicular to the two rows of tables that traversed the edges of the room, so they were all seated on one side, facing the rest of the guests. The position made Sophie feel like she was on display, but it also limited the conversations that could take place. Being out of Eloisa's direct gaze made things slightly less uncomfortable. So she managed to eat something of each of the myriad courses and make polite small talk with Lord Airlight when he and Cameron weren't discussing obscure points of military history without any disasters. She waved away the wine, though. She wanted a clear head for what came next. She could have wine later.

Eventually, Eloisa pushed away the last of the dishes— a ginger and honey sorbet—and rose from her chair. "It grows warm in here. We think a turn about the gardens before the dancing would be refreshing."

That was Sophie's cue. She rose to follow Eloisa as the queen moved toward one of the doors leading out to the gardens. The court, following along behind them, was chattering curiously, and Sophie wished Cameron were beside her. His solid presence would give her the confidence to actually pull this off.

The queen walked out into the darkened gardens— this part of the arrangements had nearly given the commander apoplexy—and Sophie was well aware just how many Red Guard were stationed out there in the darkness, guarding them all.

Once the court had reassembled behind them, the murmurs turning puzzled at the lack of the usual lighting in the garden, Eloisa turned to Sophie. "Lady Sophia, we thought there would be more light from the moon this evening. This will never do. Perhaps you could lend some assistance in this matter?"

"Of course, Your Majesty." She hoped her voice didn't reveal the extent of her nerves. She stepped forward and raised her hands. One long breath, then another as she focused. Then she sent her power out toward the first of the long double circle of torches ringing the gardens. It flared to life obediently, and as the court started to applaud, she kept her focus, feeling for the next torch, looking for the shimmer of magic that the blessed oil the torches were doused in gave off. To her relief, each one sprang to life in rapid succession until she came full circle and the last one, to the left of the queen, blazed to life.

Unless she was mistaken, she'd lit all of them in less than a minute. More than a hundred torches. She felt a surge of satisfaction, and she turned and curtsied to Eloisa. When the Domina had first told her what she was to do at the ball, Sophie had half suspected the Domina wished her to fail. "I hope you find that to your liking, my queen."

Eloisa nodded, smiling again. As Sophie rose from the curtsy, she spotted the Domina standing just behind the queen. Where had she come from?

Domina Skey's expression seemed half respectful, half annoyed. Had Sophie been correct? Had the Domina been hoping Sophie would fail and disgrace herself? Well, if she had, then she had miscalculated. It was done now, and the torches were lit. The court had had their spectacle, and now she was going to try to enjoy her birthday party.

Hours later, Sophie stepped off the dance floor with Cameron and fanned herself with her hands. "I think I need something to drink, my lord," she said, smiling up at him. "You dance very enthusiastically."

"That's the wild northerner in me," he replied, smiling at her. "Wine?"

"Yes, please." She had already had several glasses, but with no more public stunts to perform, she would allow herself one more. "I'll meet you at my parents' table."

Cameron bowed and turned on his heel to fetch the drink. Sophie headed in the opposite direction. She had spoken to her parents earlier but not for very long. As she passed by one of the doors that led out to the garden, she caught a hint of a breeze and changed her mind. First a minute to herself in the cool night air, away from the stifling ballroom. Then she would go to her parents.

The garden was definitely cooler than the ballroom. She apparently wasn't the only one who thought so. The gardens were alive with couples and small groups strolling through the torchlit grounds, laughing and talking quietly. Perhaps she should go back and fetch Cameron. Take a turn through the grounds with him. Stop for a minute or two in some dark spot and indulge herself in kissing her husband.

Smiling at the thought, she turned and went back inside. She wasn't more than a few feet through the doors when a man stepped into her path.

"Oh, look," he said, sounding a little worse for wear. "It's the little witch. Happy birthday, little witch."

She looked at him coolly. "Thank you, milord." He was tall, though not as tall as Cameron, solidly built in a way that suggested it was starting to run to fat rather than muscle, brown haired. A white scar slashed through the very tip of his left eyebrow. She tried to place his face, but couldn't bring a name to mind. In fact, she didn't think she had ever seen him before. He wore a burgundy jacket, though. Burgundy was one of the Farkeep colors. Maybe he had come to court with the new Lord Farkeep.

"Heard things about royal witches," he continued, smiling at her. There was a definite slur in the way he said "witches." Drunk, then.

Sophie straightened. Drunk she could deal with. "Have you, milord? How fascinating. Now, if you'll excuse me, my husband is waiting for me." She stepped forward and around him. He shot out a hand and grabbed her.

She froze, shocked. He definitely had to be new to court. No one with any experience of court protocol would lay a hand on a royal witch uninvited. "Let me go," she said fiercely. She kept her voice low, not wanting a scene if she could avoid it. Drunk was one thing. Stupid was another.

"That's not very friendly, little witch. Thought witches were meant to be hot little things. How about you show me?"

"I think not," she said. She jerked her arm, but he didn't let go. Instead his grip tightened, and she felt a sudden flicker of fear, followed by a flare of anger. She was a royal witch, goddess damn him, and she had put up with far too much lately to have any patience left for drunken imbeciles.

She put her free hand on his chest and shoved, jerking her arm at the same time. He knocked her hand away, and without thinking, she sent a flare of power toward him and shoved with that, feeling a blow to her torso as she did so. He rocked backward several steps, face registering shock as the hand around her wrist came free. Then, before she could even work out what had happened, he rocked back another few steps, hand flying to his jaw, and Cameron was at her side, his face like thunder.

"Do not," he said, his voice like ice, "make me hit you a third time. I won't be so restrained."

The man stared at him and then at Sophie. "She—"

"I don't know who you are," Cameron said. "But I don't tolerate anyone laying hands on my wife. As I said, don't make me hit you a third time. In fact, I think you should leave the ball before I am forced to explain to the queen that I found you harassing a royal witch. You'll find her tolerance for that behavior is quite low. Nonexistent, in fact."

The man's face went white, and he dropped his hand. There was a patch of rapidly reddening skin on his cheek, as though someone had actually hit him. But before Sophie could figure out why, the man turned and fled through the door out into the garden.

Cameron glanced around them. She did the same. No one seemed to have noticed anything amiss. No one was staring or whispering.

"I think we should go for a walk, milady," Cameron said. He took her hand and steered her rapidly through the crowd, not stopping until he reached another of the garden doors some distance away from the one her mystery assailant had exited. They went through the door and down the closest path at speed, not stopping until they were definitely alone in a part of the garden she wasn't familiar with. Though judging by the strong herb and manure scent in the air, it was likely the palace kitchen's garden.

"What in the name of the goddess?" she started to say when Cameron let go of her hand, but he interrupted her.

"How did you do that?" he demanded.

"Do what?"

He threw up his hands. "You used blood magic on him. You pushed him away with blood magic. I saw you."

"I did—wait, what? How? I don't know blood magic." Her skin went a little cold at the thought.

"I know," he said. "That's what is concerning me. What were you thinking?"

"I was thinking that he wouldn't let me go."

"All you had to do was yell. Any man in the court would have decked him for you. You're a bloody royal witch, Sophie."

"I know," she retorted. "Everybody keeps reminding me of that fact every few minutes."

"Perhaps you should start paying attention. Thank the goddess I saw you. And I hit him hard enough to rattle his brains."

"Hit him? You mean that was you? The second time. Using blood magic?"

"Yes," Cameron said, sounding exasperated. "Hopefully, I convinced him it was me both times. And I don't think anyone else saw."

"I don't understand," Sophie said, still rattled.

"I do," Cameron said. "Lord Sylvain was right. You can do blood magic as well as earth. Which means trouble if anyone else discovers it. Lots of trouble. Promise me you won't do that again unless someone is trying to kill you."

"I didn't mean to do it this time," she said. Her head was spinning. She'd done blood magic? Fear crept up her spine as she remembered what Lord Sylvain had said. That the Domina wouldn't tolerate an earth witch who broke the rules and used two magics. "Goddess. What are we going to do?"

Cameron shook his head. "Right now we're going to go back into that ballroom and pretend that nothing has happened. We'll discuss it later. Come up with a strategy. All right?"

"Yes," she agreed, though she wasn't all right at all.

"Good," he said. Then he pulled her to him and kissed her thoroughly.

"What was that for?" she asked when he finally let her go. Both of them were breathing heavily.

"Making you look like we've been out here doing

something other than talking about you being able to do things you shouldn't." He studied her a moment, then reached out and deliberately tugged a few of the curls piled up on her head loose at the back of the arrangement. "There. That should do."

⊷⊶

By the time Eloisa finally retired for the night, somewhere well after two in the morning, Sophie was ready to scream if she had to smile and act happy for one more minute. Her nerves were stretched thin from trying to work out if anyone was talking about her or had seen what she'd done. Several times she'd caught the Domina watching her, but her expression hadn't seemed any more disapproving than usual, and Sophie hadn't been escorted from the ballroom by a squad of Red Guard, so she had to believe that no news of her mistake had reached the Domina's ears. She didn't think the Domina would hesitate to disturb even the queen's party if she heard what Sophie had done. It seemed, for now, that she had gotten away with it.

The question was, could she stop herself from making such a blunder a second time?

"Can we go now?" she whispered to Cameron as they watched the queen and her party leave, the Domina at their heels.

Her heart fell when he shook his head ever so faintly. "We need to stay and say good night to everyone as they leave."

Fortunately, the court seemed to be as tired as Sophie, and soon enough after Eloisa's departure, they started coming up in drifts to wish her well for her birthday and make their excuses. She braced herself in case the man who'd grabbed her appeared, but apparently he had decided that discretion was the better part of valor and hadn't returned to the ball.

Still, it took close to another hour for everyone to make their good-byes. Sophie wanted nothing more than to sleep when they finally got back to their apartment, tempted to crawl onto the bed fully clothed.

But they needed a plan more than she needed sleep. "What are we going to do?" she asked as she removed the queen's pearls and put them back in the warded drawer at the top of her dresser along with the emerald bracelets.

Cameron came up behind her and started to unlace her dress. "We'll talk about it in the morning."

"It is the morning," she pointed out.

"Later in the morning," he said. "It's late. Or early. And I, for one, would prefer to wish you a happy birthday properly." His hands slid into the dress, coming around under the heavy satin to clasp her breasts over the corset. "What do you think?" he asked, stroking softly. "Want to forget all this nonsense for a time with me?"

Warmth spread over her with each touch, sliding through her body slowly, out along her arms, and down through her body to pool between her legs. "Yes, please," she said, and let him carry her to bed.

It went quickly. Hot and urgent as it had been the first time, both of them mindless with it. But as Sophie came back to herself, lying in his arms in the darkness, the fear and worry returned.

"What are we going to do?" she whispered again.

Cameron pulled her closer, rolling to curl around her, his big, warm body a shield against all the things that threatened her.

"Just you and me," he whispered. "We'll be fine. Go to sleep."

To her surprise, she did.

CHAPTER TWENTY

On first day, Sophie couldn't sleep. She lay in the dark, listening to Cameron breathe beside her and worrying. One more day. They had one more day of their marriage week, and then she had to return to the ladies-in-waiting and Cameron to his duties with the Red Guard.

He'd taken advantage of their current newlywed status to hide them away for most of seventh day after the temple services, patiently demonstrating battle magic for her, so she could see what it looked like, knocking a cushion off one of the chairs over and over again. Then he made Sophie try to do the same—until she was clear that she could feel the difference between earth and blood magic and know which one she was reaching for. And knew how to brace herself for the recoil from the blood magic. It took some time to get used to feeling the same pain she inflicted on anything alive returned to her. And Cameron only made her knock the pillow at him for that particular lesson. Even that was enough to convince her to try to avoid hurting someone with blood magic in the future.

"Good," Cameron said when she told him she thought she had absorbed his lessons. "Now we'll try illusions. I've never been very good at them, but you need to know. Can't have you conjuring a glamour out of midair in the middle of the queen's next audience or some-thing."

Despite his protests that he wasn't skilled at illusions, the small ones he produced—first a flight of butterflies dancing through the air, then a glamour to turn his dark hair pure black, then a ward that made him disappear in front of her eyes—seemed strong to her. Her first at-tempts to do any of the same had been complete failures, so he'd called a halt to the lessons and dragged her down onto the carpet to make love to her.

On first day, they emerged from their rooms, visiting her parents in the morning and going to the Inglewood suite for lunch, keeping up appearances of being happy newlyweds with nothing to trouble them. Cameron had taken her down to the stables to meet the mare carrying the foal that Liam had promised her for her birthday. The sheer number of presents she had received from the court had astounded her.

She had piles of silks and perfumes and small baubles and trinkets. Honoria had given her a small silver-chased dagger—suitable for a witch, yes, but Sophie had tested it and the edge was razor-sharp. So she'd put it in the purse she usually carried. And then there was the gun Cameron had presented her with. He'd shown her how to load it and promised that he'd take her somewhere to practice her marksmanship as soon as he could.

She'd gone to put it away when they'd been getting ready for bed but instead had slipped it into the drawer of her nightstand. Then she'd changed her mind again and put it under the pile of pillows she slept on.

Close at hand.

Maybe that was why she couldn't sleep. She was wor-ried that she'd accidentally shoot herself whilst fumbling with her pillows in the middle of the night. But that was ridiculous because she'd been sleeping like the dead since she'd been married. Well, for the hours of the night they'd actually spent sleeping.

The thought made her smile, and she contemplated sliding her hand down his body and waking him up to see if he could wear her out to the point where she could sleep.

But then she heard a soft scrape that made her freeze. It had sounded like leather on wood. A footstep, perhaps.

Someone is in the room. Her brain screamed the thought. But that was ridiculous. The room was warded— Eloisa herself had said she'd laid a layer of wards to the room—and there were guards patrolling all the residential parts of the palace at night.

She lay, ears straining, heart hammering, and she heard it again. The sound of air moving around someone who was doing an excellent job of being very quiet as they moved along Sophie's side of the bed.

She slipped her hand slowly, so slowly, scared that she'd make a sound, up under the pillow, and then slid the gun free. Another soft footfall, and she bolted upright, calling the nearest earth-light to light and aiming the gun at the man standing beside the bed with a drawn sword. Her finger tightened on the trigger, but Cameron suddenly surged up in bed. "Don't shoot," he yelled. In the same breath, there was a flare of the red light she associated with his magic, and the man collapsed, sword clattering to the floor.

Cameron gasped as though he'd been struck but didn't stop. He scrambled over her and out of the bed, to grab the sword. For a moment, he looked so impressive, naked and furious, standing over the unconscious assailant, that Sophie forgot to be terrified.

Then logic reasserted itself and her hand started to shake. She dropped the gun on the mattress beside her, unable to keep it steady.

"Who is that?" she asked, voice shaking as much as

her hands. She folded her hands over her stomach for a moment, willing the trembling to stop. She was safe. *They* were safe.

But someone just tried to kill you.

The thought was so ridiculous she almost laughed.

"I don't know," Cameron said. "But I'm going to find out. Hold this."

He passed her the sword. She had to wrap both hands around it and brace the hilt against the mattress to avoid dropping it. Once he was sure she had it, he lifted his shirt from the floor at the end of the bed where she'd tossed it earlier, donning it and his breeches swiftly before taking the weapon back.

The man lying on the carpet wore dark gray and dark brown. He had dark hair and the standard Anglion olive skin, but he was no one she knew.

Cameron bent down and studied the man's face, a steady, quiet stream of curses coming from his mouth. Then he yanked up the man's sleeve, to reveal an Anglion crest tattooed on his forearm.

"Do you know him?" Sophie asked again.

"Some of the lower ranks do that—get tattooed," Cameron said.

"He's Red Guard?"

Cameron shook his head. "No. I'd know his face. Former guard, most likely."

"Not Illvyan?"

"No. Someone earning some money as a sword for hire, I'd guess."

"But what was he—" She broke off. No point asking what he'd been doing in their rooms. That was clear. "He was going to kill me."

"You. Or us," Cameron agreed in a flat voice.

Sophie put her hand over her mouth, trying to remember how to breathe. Somehow hearing Cameron agree with her made the situation all too real.

"Sophie," Cameron said softly. "I need you to get out of bed and get dressed. Can you do that for me?"

She looked at him, shivering.

"Get dressed, love," he said.

She did as she was told, dragging a dress and petticoats and drawers out of the armoire and pulling them on automatically. The dress she'd taken was gray, one of her lady-in-waiting dresses that she could get in and out of herself. The clothes made her warmer, but she didn't stop shivering. She came back over to Cameron.

Cameron took her arm. "We need to find out who sent him."

"How?"

"Tie him up. Wake him up. Make him talk." Cameron's tone was grim. It was clear he'd done such things before.

"Tie him with what?" she asked.

"Get some of my cravats," he said. "They will serve."

She returned to the dresser and did as he asked. Cameron tied the man's hands and then dragged him into the bathroom.

Sophie followed, swallowing hard. "What are you going to do?"

Cameron, who was busy securing the man's ankles together, looked up at her. "I'll try cold water. That should wake him. I didn't hit him that hard." He proceeded to do just that, filling a pitcher with water from the basin and pouring it over the man's head. The man sputtered and coughed before opening his eyes. He froze when he saw Cameron holding the point of the sword near his throat.

"Who sent you?" Cameron demanded.

The man glared up at him, but he didn't speak.

"I gather from your tattoo that you used to be in the guard. Well, I'm a battle mage. I assume you know what that means. What I can do to you."

"Can't hurt me without hurting yourself," the man spat.

"Not directly. But there are many ways to indirectly hurt someone," Cameron said coolly. "For instance, I could make just the tip of this sword very hot. Heated steel does interesting things to skin." He pressed the point a little closer. A bead of blood welled on the man's neck. "Very painful, I'm told."

The man's eyes widened, but he shook his head. "Why should I tell you? You'll just kill me."

"No, he won't," Sophie said. "We're not interested in you, just who sent you."

"Though, if you don't tell us, then killing you would be simpler," Cameron added. "So it's best for you to be forthcoming and live to breathe another day. So. Who sent you?" He held the sword steady, not easing the pressure any. A bead of sweat ran down the man's temple.

"All right. I'll tell you what I know," he growled. "But it won't help you much."

"Why not?" Cameron asked.

"Because I don't know who she was."

"She?" Sophie said. She swallowed against the sudden sick feeling in her gut. A woman had arranged this? Who?

"Yes. Some girl found me at my lodgings. Offered gold. Plenty of gold."

"She didn't give a name?" Cameron demanded.

"No. Just directions to this room and that I was to take care of whoever was in here tonight."

"What did she look like?" Sophie asked.

"Like any other Anglion girl. Dark hair. Dark eyes. Taller than you. Older, too, I'd guess. Though she had smooth skin, and her hands didn't look like someone who did rough work."

An Anglion girl. One with either an indoor occupation or income enough not to have to work. Well, that wasn't particularly helpful.

"What was she wearing?"

"A dress. A brown dress."

Brown? As in the color the temple priors wore? Their robes were brown. And in her experience, they tended to favor brown even when they weren't dressed for temple duties.

"Anything else that you can remember?" Cameron said.

Their captive shook his head. Cameron turned the sword slightly. "Are you sure of that?" The prisoner winced, and another bead of blood rolled down his neck.

"All right! She smelled like that incense the priors use. Made my room smell like a bloody temple for hours."

Sophie went cold. Only the temples burned the incense used in their rituals. For the woman to have that smell embedded in her clothes, she would have to spend a lot of time in the temples. She had to be a prior or a devout.

Cameron stared down at him for a moment and then reversed the sword and neatly clipped the man on the temple. He slumped against the bathtub, unconscious.

"What did you do that for?" Sophie asked.

"He's not going to tell us anything else useful," Cameron said. "And we're wasting time. We should leave. Go to Liam. Or Lord Sylvain."

"No. Not them. They can't help us. We need to leave, Cameron. Not just the palace. But Kingswell."

"What?"

"Think about it. Whoever did this—tried to kill a royal witch—has to be powerful. Powerful enough to think they can avoid discovery. Or repercussions. That's a limited list. He said the woman who hired him wore brown. The temple priors wear brown. Which makes me wonder if the Domina found out about what I did at the ball." She shivered again as she looked at the man, and suddenly the familiarity of the sensation hit her. The same feeling she'd felt in the Salt Hall.

"If she did that, wouldn't she just accuse you?"

Sophie bent and started going through the man's pockets. "Not if she thinks she can kill two birds with one stone. Get rid of me and stir up the sentiment against Illvya." She slid her fingers into the inner pocket of his jacket, feeling them go colder as she touched a leather pouch. She pulled it out, opened it. Tipped a flat silver disk stamped with an unfamiliar symbol onto the bed. The chill she felt grew stronger. "How much do you care to wager that that's an Illvyan scriptii? I'm guessing he was supposed to leave it. Make it look like an Illvyan attack. There aren't many people in Anglion who would be able to lay their hands on such a thing or manufacture one. But I'd imagine the Domina is one of them."

"You really think the Domina wants you dead?"

"She seems the most likely candidate. She can't control me. Which makes me a threat. She's been working hard to have a position of influence with the queen. She's not the type to waste that. Besides, even if I'm wrong, I think I'd rather learn from Lord Sylvain's lessons and not take any chances. We can't stay here, Cameron. He came into our room. He got past the guards and the wards. Someone helped him do that. We can't trust anyone in the palace. If this was the Domina, then, yes, maybe she'll be desperate enough to accuse me in public. If that happens, then I'm doomed. Or maybe she'll just try again to get rid of me another way. I'm not going to sit here and wait for either of those things to happen."

Cameron's face had changed from surprised to angry. Anger was good. Anger would help them. "What are you proposing?"

"We need to get to Madame de Montesse," Sophie said. "The portals in the palace are guarded. We can use hers to get away from Kingswell. Find somewhere to hide whilst we work out what to do."

He blew out a breath. Then nodded, once. "All right. And this one?" He pushed at the man with his bare foot.

Sophie bit her lip. "You think we should kill him, don't you?" She didn't know if she could do that. Not in cold blood. Even if he had tried to kill her.

"It would be safest. We can't risk him waking him up when we're gone and alerting whoever sent him that he failed. No one's come to investigate yet, so I'm thinking perhaps that the plan was to leave us to be discovered in the morning rather than anything sooner. So we have a window of time. Not too long, though."

The maids usually woke them around seven. The hour bell had sounded midnight not long before the attack. She'd listened to each of the twelve long chimes when she'd been lying awake. "I have cylloroot powder that will knock him out for at least twelve hours," she said. It was one of the supplies in the kit that Eloisa had given her for her Ais-Seann. "If he's found here alive, then there's a chance he'll be interrogated. Have to tell someone else what he was sent here to do."

"Or else whoever sent him will just arrange for him to die, too," Cameron said, prodding the man with his toe. He didn't stir. Still unconscious, then. That would make things easier.

"Maybe, but we can take the chance. We have to leave him here, dead or alive. It will be hard enough for us to get out of the palace. We'll never manage it with a dead body. Though perhaps we should tie him more securely. Make sure he can't get away if by some chance he does wake." She was hardly an expert with herbs after all.

"All right. I'll find things to secure him with; you get the herbs," Cameron said.

She smiled at him gratefully and then whirled to get the cylloroot.

She mixed it carefully with some water, avoiding breathing any of it in, and carried the glass into the bathroom. Cameron had pulled the man closer to the basin, which was connected to several sturdy pipes, before he'd gone back into the bedroom to find more cravats to use. She could hear him rummaging through the drawers.

She watched the man for a moment, but he didn't stir. Still unconscious, then. Sophie bent over him, intending to pry his mouth open and pour the liquid down his throat. But before she could, he lunged upward, and his hands fastened around her throat.

She dropped the glass as her breath was cut off, heard it shatter as she fought for air, the room going dark around her. Then Cameron was there, and the grip at her throat loosened as something warm sprayed across her face. She fell backward, landing with a thud on the tiles, which made her teeth rattle.

When her vision cleared, she saw a severed hand lying on the tiles near her feet and Cameron standing over the bathtub, wiping the sword in his hand clean with one of their towels.

"Is he dead?" she managed. Cameron nodded, and she rolled to her knees and vomited onto the floor.

Cameron picked her up and carried her back into the bedroom, putting her down on the rug before the fire. Then he came back with a damp cloth and wiped her face. The cloth came away red, and she realized she and her dress were splattered with a shockingly bright spray of blood. Cameron put down the cloth and picked up the Iska decanter, pulled off the top, and passed it to her.

"Drink," he ordered. "Three good mouthfuls."

She obeyed, and the warmth of the liquor hitting her stomach burned away some of the panic. The earthy taste scoured the bile from her mouth as well. She wiped her lips with the back of her hand and put the decanter down. "He's really dead?"

"Yes." Cameron bared his teeth then in something that was probably meant to be a smile but was far more feral and terrifying. "There wasn't time to be subtle. He was strangling you." He rose then and tossed the cloth back through the bathroom door. His shirt was blood-spattered, too.

"Change your dress," he said. "Pick something dark. Do you have a bag that's easy to carry? Something with a strap maybe?"

She nodded. She had a leather satchel that held embroidery or painting supplies when Eloisa decided to take the ladies outdoors for the day. "It's not terribly large, but yes."

"Good. We need valuables. Money, your jewels. Whatever will fit, then whatever else you want to take that will fit and that's not heavy. Not clothes. We can buy those. Wear boots, not shoes. And a cloak. A dark one." He held out a hand and helped her to her feet. Kissed her. "We will be all right," he said, and then turned to start packing.

Madame de Montesse's shop was in darkness as they walked past it. Sophie's pulse was roaring in her ears, but she had to trust that the illusion—the cloaking ward—that Cameron had used to enable them to get out of the palace by walking inch by agonizing inch quietly through the hallways and out into the gardens still held. Cameron led her down the next street and then through three separate alleys before he stopped in front of a high wooden fence with no gate that Sophie could see.

"Where are we?" she whispered.

"Unless I've lost my sense of direction, this is the rear yard to Madame's building. As far as I know, she lives over the shop. Let's hope I'm right." He nodded at the fence, face just a pale blur. "We need to get over this. I'm going to have to let the illusion drop when I let go of your hand. Can you see any wards on the fence?"

"No." She didn't want to let go of his hand. The strong, sure warmth of it was the only thing that had stopped her from collapsing into hysterics at certain points of their flight from the palace. But she loosened her grip on his fingers as he stepped away from her. There would be no panicking. No giving in to the fear. They could do this. They would get away. Be safe. Even if she didn't know how just now. She stared at the fence but didn't see even the faintest hint of magic. "Can you see any?"

Cameron shook his head. "No. Good. You're stronger. I thought they might be too subtle for me. All right. I'll give you a boost. Drop down on the other side and stay there until I come over, too. I'll throw your bag over once I've helped you."

"Who's going to help you?" she said.

"I'm at least a foot taller than you," he said. "Plus I'm a Red Guard. I'd be a laughingstock if I couldn't get myself over a mere six-foot fence." He crouched down. "Here. Put your foot in my hands."

Sophie obeyed, trying not to think about what might be on the soles of her boots after the circuitous route they'd taken out of the palace and down to Portholme. So far it seemed that no one had found out they had left. There were no unusual lights or sounds coming from the palace, no squads of Red Guard charging through the city streets.

But still, her heart beat hard in her chest again as she let Cameron boost her over the fence and dropped down the other side. The soft thud of her bag landing beside her made her start and sent her pulse racing even faster.

If Madame de Montesse wasn't here, then she wasn't entirely sure what they were going to do. Go to her parents? Or try to steal horses and leave town? The only other portals she knew of were in the palace grounds and at the temple. Neither of those were options. Without Chloe de Montesse's assistance, she didn't have the faintest idea how they could even start to get out of the capital.

She turned toward the back of the building. It did look to be the simple three-story stone building that held Chloe's store. But her store was identical to the two that stood to either side of it. If Cameron had the wrong house, they would be in trouble. As Sophie stared at the building, trying to decide if it was the right one, she realized it was shimmering slightly. A ward. But not a ward that looked like any she had seen before. This was near black or maybe the color of water in moonlight, revealing glimpses of what lay beyond it, but only glimpses. Whoever had set that ward wasn't an Anglion, she thought, and relaxed. This must be Madame de Montesse's house.

Cameron landed beside her, making hardly any noise.

"Are you all right?" he said softly.

"Yes. But there's a ward on the house."

"Good," he said.

"Good?"

He led her forward to the rear door. "Yes. Good. Because if she's set them herself, she'll wake up when I do this." He put a hand through the ward, which didn't immediately react, then on the door handle itself. She saw a flare of red around his hand—his power, not the ward, as far as she could tell—and the door swung inward. Blood magic, she was learning, was far more practical than earth magic when it came to running away.

They walked into the house. Her skin tingled as she passed through the ward, and Cameron closed the door behind them. They were in a small back room, full of boxes with a neat metal trough set into one wall with a tap above it. That was about all she could see in the moonlight. The door on the other side of the room stood open. Cameron took her hand, and they walked out of the room.

They were barely three feet into the hallway beyond when Sophie heard a sound that she had become all too familiar with. The sound of a pistol being cocked.

"Whoever you are," Madame de Montesse's voice

said from somewhere above them, "I recommend that you stay exactly where you are."

"Madame de Montesse, it's me. Sophie Ken—Mackenzie."

"Lady Sophia?" Chloe sounded startled.

An earth-light came softly to light on the wall near Sophie. Nowhere near full strength but light enough that Sophie could see the stairway where Chloe stood. Presumably Madame de Montesse could see them, too. Still, Sophie didn't want to take any chance, and she stayed put.

"It's me," she said. "And Cameron."

Chloe came down the stairs in quick, silent steps. She wore a pale silk robe over a long nightgown, her hair caught back in a simple braid, much like Sophie's. The gun she was holding was quite a bit bigger than the gun Cameron had given Sophie, though.

She stared at Sophie and then at Cameron for a moment. Then she sighed and lowered the gun. "Well," she said, sounding resigned. "I imagine this cannot be good. Why don't you tell me what's going on?"

"We don't have time for the long version," Cameron said.

"Then perhaps the short version?"

"Short version is someone tried to kill Sophie in our room tonight. I need to get her out of the capital."

"What kind of someone?" Chloe said. Her accent seemed to have thickened as though surprise had loosened her hold on Anglion.

"If he's who I think he is, then once upon a time he was a Red Guard."

Chloe swung around to Sophie. "Someone in the palace tried to kill you?"

Sophie was starting to lose her grip on her hard-won sense of calm. "So it seems."

"Do you know who?"

Cameron shook his head. "We have our suspicions. Though it may be safer for you not to know. We just need to use your portal to get out of Kingswell."

Chloe tilted her head, the multicolored braid swinging gently. "Where are you planning on going?"

"We're not sure yet. We'll work that out once we're away from the city."

"Forgive me, but are you certain that anywhere in Anglion is safe? An attack on a royal witch in the palace itself. That is quite brazen. Whoever was behind it must be quite sure of themselves."

Sophie felt her stomach turn over. "What are you saying?"

Chloe shook her head. "I think before we discuss this further, you should come into the workroom. No one will see a light in there; there are no windows." She walked past them and opened the first door in the hallway.

"This isn't where the portal was," Cameron objected.

"No. As I said, there are things to discuss." She walked into the room, clearly expecting them to follow.

Sophie glanced at Cameron. He tipped his head as if leaving the decision up to her. She didn't really need to think about it. She followed Chloe into the room, heard Cameron behind her

"Close the door," Madame de Montesse said to Cameron.

He did so. Chloe waved a hand, and several earth-lights set on the walls came to life, illuminating the small room.

Cameron stood beside Sophie, his presence reassuring when nothing else was.

"Say what you have to say," he said.

Madame de Montesse nodded. "Very well. You say someone tried to kill Lady Sophia. If that is true, then your trouble is deep."

"That much we know," Cameron growled.

"It seems to me that there are two people who are threatened by your wife's recent ascent in both magic and the line direct," Chloe said. "The first is your Domina Skey. From what I can see of your wife's power, she is not bound like the other earth witches. I will not ask why, but I cannot imagine that it would sit well with your temple."

"It doesn't," Sophie agreed.

"So. You are a threat. A risk that the temple—at least under that woman's rule—is unlikely to tolerate for long, in my estimation. The second person threatened by you is the queen herself. You are strong, even if you are untrained. Stronger than Eloisa herself. And now very close in the line direct. A very attractive tool to those who may have been biding their time under King Stefan's rule."

"I am loyal to my queen," Sophie protested.

"That may not matter. So. A dilemma. If the Domina tried to kill you and you run, then she has all the resources of the temple behind her to search for you. If it was the queen, then she has both the temple and the Red Guard and the rest of the military. Do you truly believe you can remain hidden for long under these circumstances?"

"What other option do we have?" Sophie asked. She couldn't fault Chloe's logic, but she didn't see what else they could do besides run.

Madame de Montesse straightened her shoulders. "The route that brings Illvyan refugees to Anglion also runs in the opposite direction."

Sophie gaped at her. "You think we should go to Illvya? Illvyans hate Anglions."

Chloe shook her head, sending her long braid bouncing. "No. We do not. Not in the way that Anglions hate Illvyans."

"But—"

Chloe held up a hand. "Hear me out. It is true that my country has tried to conquer yours. But it is not out of any desire to kill all Anglions. I know that you are taught differently. Taught to fear us. But Illvya wants Anglion for its resources, mostly. We do not destroy the countries we add to our empire. That makes no sense. You would not be the first Anglions to take this road."

"I've never heard of such a thing," Cameron said.

"Nor I," Sophie added.

"It is hardly within the interests of those in power to let you find out, though, is it?" Chloe said. "They wish you to be afraid of us. Which is the other part of the reason Illvya would like to control Anglion. Just as you have objections to our beliefs and our practice of the fourth Art, so do my countrymen object to your suppression of it and the way your temple limits your knowledge and access to magic."

"Why should we believe you?" Sophie said. "After all, you fled Illvya. If it is such a perfect place—"

"It is not perfect," Chloe said. "And I have told you why I left."

Beside her, Cameron made a startled noise, and Sophie felt a twinge of guilt. She'd never told Cameron about her visit with Madame.

"Besides," Chloe said. "What reason do I have to lie? There is no benefit in it for me if you leave. I am merely offering you a choice. One that I think will give you a greater chance of survival than remaining in Anglion. And a far greater chance to explore your magic. To learn what you may truly be capable of with no restrictions. But it is your choice. You may use my portal to merely leave Kingswell, or you can listen to me and I will start you on your way to Illvya. From there you can make your way to another place in the empire if you prefer. Though I think you may be better served if you remain in Illvya itself."

Sophie turned to Cameron. "What do you want to do?"

His face was grim. "I think she's right. I think if we stay in Anglion, they'll find us. I want you to be safe."

He reached for her hand. "I don't want to lose you."

"Nor I you," Sophie said. Her head was pounding, too, now, the throbbing keeping time with her hammering heart. Leave Anglion. Leave her family. All that she had ever known. She'd never imagined such a thing. But then, she'd never imagined that someone would try to kill her.

And she wanted to live. Wanted Cameron to live. She tightened her fingers around Cameron's, fighting back fear and grief and confusion by holding on to that desire. "All right," she said. "Illvya, it is. How do we get there?"

"All the way to Illvya? No. If I were found with a portal link to Illvya, I'd be dead in short measure," Chloe said. "Not to mention if such things were simple to make, use, or maintain, Anglion would have been overrun by Illvya centuries ago. A portal trip of that distance . . . across an ocean. That would take more power than a thousand royal witches could produce."

Fear rose more strongly within her. She hadn't thought about that part. She'd just assumed that it would be a portal that would deliver them to where they needed to go.

"How, then?" she asked.

"This will be faster if you just listen and let me do the talking." Chloe went to a row of cupboards standing against one of the walls and pulled the middle one open, taking out paper and ink.

She carried it back to the table, and then she began to tell them what they needed to do. Use the portals to get to a tiny village that Sophie had never heard of somewhere on the west coast. Find a particular beach near that village. Then summon a ship using a lamp that would be hidden on the beach itself.

"Who will be in the ship?" Sophie asked, unable to help herself.

"Smugglers," Chloe said shortly. "Whoever sees the lamp first. The best of them is a man called Jensen. Did you bring money? Or jewels?"

Sophie nodded. "I have this." She pulled the queen's pearls out of the pouch at her waist, handed them to Chloe.

Chloe whistled softly. "Yes. Those will do." She went back to the cupboard, then returned with a silver knife. Several swift strokes slashed the pearl string into pieces. Of all the things that had happened that night, that was the first thing that was even vaguely pleasing. Chloe separated some of the pearls from the string, so they rolled free on the table. She gathered them in her hand. "Offer whoever comes six of these. Go up to eight if you must. If he asks for more, then he's trying to rob you. It might be better to wait and try again the next night if that happens, but that comes with its own risks."

"And if he agrees, he'll take us to Illvya?" Cameron asked.

"Not all the way. Not at this time of year, with the trade fleets out. Too risky," Chloe said. "There's a small island a few hundred feet off a cove on the southern peninsula. There's a portal there." Taking the pen, she scribbled a symbol on the paper. "This is the portal symbol for Lumia."

Lumia. The capital of Illvya. Right into the heart of the enemy. Or somewhere they would be safe. It was a gamble. But they had no choice. Sophie peered at the paper, memorizing the portal symbol.

"The island portal will take you only to the public portal in the nearest coastal town—Orlee di Mer—and no, that portal doesn't have the symbol to return you to the island. As I said, this is a one-way journey. But the Orlee portal should have a direct link to Lumia. Just look for the symbol. It's a long way to the capital. But I imagine the two of you can manage the power needed." She looked at them. "I'm not sure which Lumia portal it will take you to. They change every so often. But once you're in the capital, all the public portals have a crest on them." She sketched another symbol, which looked like a sun with a square imposed over it. "That's how you'll know you're in Lumia itself."

Cameron was studying the symbols. "Then what?" he asked.

"You speak decent Illvyan," Chloe said. "How about you, milady?"

"Some," Sophie said. "Not well enough to fool anyone, I'm afraid."

"Well, as I said, no one's going to hurt you simply for being Anglion there. They might try to rob you blind if you wind up in the wrong part of town, of course." She paused, thinking. "So perhaps a direct journey is safest." She drew a third symbol. "Once you're in Lumia, look for this symbol in the portal." This time the symbol she drew looked like a bird with open wings. Or maybe a flame. Sophie wasn't sure. "That will take you close to where I suggest you should go."

"Where exactly is that?" Cameron asked.

Chloe said something in Illvyan too fast to follow. Cameron's eyebrows shot up.

"Do you truly think that's a good idea?" he asked.

"I think it's the only logical place, given your wife's abilities."

"And they'll take us in?"

"I can't imagine they'd turn her away. And you two are kind of a two-for-one proposition, unless I'm mistaken."

"But if there's trouble?"

"Then ask to see the man in charge. Tell him I sent

you. Tell him I said . . ." She said something in rapid-fire Illvyan that once again Sophie couldn't quite decipher.

"That will make a difference?" Cameron, who apparently had no such trouble, said.

Chloe smiled. A little too brightly. "Yes."

"Why?"

"Well, for one thing, he's my father."

Cameron's mouth fell open. "Your father is—"

"Yes. You'll understand why I don't share that information here. So. That's where you need to go. Look for the portal symbol. There's only one portal in that sector of the city. When you leave the portal, turn right. Then follow this map."

She sketched quickly before handing the paper to Cameron. He folded it carefully and put it inside his jacket.

"I—" Sophie began.

"No, no more questions. You don't have time. The smugglers won't come if it's too light when you light the lamp to summon them. They need darkness to get back out to sea. Do you need anything else?"

Other than answers to about a thousand more questions? But she wasn't going to ask any of them. What mattered now was getting away.

"No," Sophie said. "We have money. And weapons." Cameron's sword and pistol were in their customary places at his hip. And her gun and Honoria's dagger were in the satchel she carried. She thought of the bundle of magic supplies she'd swept into her bag. Eloisa's gift. One that might also prove useful. "And other things."

"Food?"

"No."

"I will see what I have in the kitchen. Wait here." Chloe disappeared through the door and then reappeared before Sophie could think of anything to say to

Cameron. Her mind was whirling. Illvya. They were going to Illvya.

"Here." Chloe held out a small sack. "Bread. Cheese. Some apples. Enough if you have to wait until tomorrow. Though if you do that, I would suggest you go somewhere else via the portal and return when it's dark. Make you harder to follow."

"Thank you," Sophie said. "You don't know what this means."

"Luckily for you," Chloe said, "I'm one of the few people in Anglion who understands completely. Now, quickly. You must go."

∽✦∾

They stumbled down the rocky path that led to the beach, trying not to fall. The moon provided light. Too much light, even. Cameron tried to ignore the feeling that they had targets on their backs as he held Sophie's hand and led the way over the uneven ground. He'd kept up a punishing pace since they'd emerged from the portal. Sophie hadn't been sick when they'd arrived. Maybe her growing magic had cured her of that affliction. Whatever the reason, it meant that they had been able to get moving fast instead of having to wait for her to recover.

Still, no matter how quickly he wished to go, there was a limit to how fast they could travel at night over strange terrain. Chloe's warning that the smugglers wouldn't come to shore if it grew too light was replaying over and over in his head each time he slowed the pace to navigate an obstacle. But if one of them fell, that would slow them even more.

If they didn't get on a boat, he expected they wouldn't survive. Once the dead man in their room was discovered, people would be looking for them. If whoever had set this up was clever, as he suspected, they'd be waiting for a maid to find his and Sophie's bodies. Which should give them until breakfast before it was discovered they were gone.

But once that news was out, Eloisa wouldn't be slow to act. And she could draw the same conclusions that Madame de Montesse had, that the wisest thing for Cameron and Sophie to do would be to try to get to Illvya. She wouldn't want to let Sophie get away even if it wasn't her behind the attack. A royal witch fleeing the country? Going to the enemy? Eloisa would send soldiers to every portal in Anglion if she had to. If she wasn't the one behind the attempt on their lives, then her bringing them back to the capital would just give whoever it was a second shot. And if it was Eloisa, well, then they wouldn't make it back to the capital. Their bodies would merely be discovered somewhere in circumstances that would be explained away. There was nowhere to hide.

They had to leave tonight.

He registered sand rather than stones beneath the soles of his boots as they came around the last curve of the path.

"This is it," he said. He looked around. "Triple rock. Madame de Montesse said there was a triple rock."

"There," Sophie said, pointing. Her voice rasped through heaving breaths, but she followed when he started for the rock as fast as the sand allowed. He fell to his knees and started digging where they'd been told. When his hand touched leather, the relief was so overwhelming, he almost lost control. But his training and his need to save Sophie overruled his emotions.

He tugged the leather bundle free, sliced open the thongs that held it closed, and pulled out the lantern inside. He recognized the design. Shuttered on all four sides, it offered the ability to open just one panel so the light was limited and directed. They used such things in battles sometimes.

This one had a peculiar grid pattern in the lead separating the glass panes, which was how the smugglers would know this was their lantern, he supposed. He wondered if there was some sort of magic involved as well. Something that alerted the smugglers that the lantern had been lit in case they weren't looking for it.

Chloe hadn't mentioned it if there was. So they would just have to take their chances.

He reached into his pocket for the matches he usually carried when Sophie grabbed at his wrist.

"Wait," she said.

"There's no time."

Her grip tightened. "There is. I want you to listen to me. You don't have to come with me. You can go back. Tell them you found me gone and tried to look for me to bring me back but couldn't find me. You don't have to lose your family because of me."

He stared down at her, disbelieving. Did she really think he would abandon her? That he could let her walk away from him after everything they had shared? "You think I'm going to leave you? To let you do this on your own?"

Her eyes were wide in the moonlight, shining with what he was sure were unshed tears. "This is my fault. If you hadn't saved me in Portholme, none of this would be happening to you. You can still have a life here."

He laughed then, the sound wild and bitter. "If you think that, then the last few weeks haven't taught you much. Do you really think they'd believe I didn't help you? That the Domina wouldn't suspect? Wouldn't try to use me to find out where you are?"

"But your family." She was crying now. Shock, most likely, and the strain of it all overwhelming her.

"My family will be fine," he said fiercely. "So will yours. Once they figure out where we've gone, there's no point in doing anything to our families. It won't bring us back. At worse, Eloisa can banish them from Kingswell for a

time, and being out of the capital right now is probably
the best thing anybody can hope for. She can't take Liam's title away from him. It's too soon in her reign for her
to attempt anything so risky. It would likely backfire on
her and make the lords band against her. Same thing if
she tries to arrange any convenient accidents. The suspicion would fall straight on her. She needs to consolidate
power, not destabilize it." He held her tighter, hoping she
was listening, willing her to believe him. "Liam will protect your family. You're a Mackenzie now."

She made a noise that was half sob, half laugh, and
lifted her head.

"I won't leave you," he repeated. "Body and blood,
remember? Shield and shelter. Always."

She nodded and wiped her face with the back of her
hand. Then she straightened her shoulders and stepped
back, standing small and resolute on the sand, one hand
clasping the strap of the satchel draped over her shoulder. Her cloak fluttered gently in the wind from the water, and her hair, so hastily tied up back in the palace
lifted as well, shimmering in the moonlight.

She was beautiful, his wife. And he was going to keep
her alive if it killed him.

"All right. Good girl." He pressed a kiss on her forehead. "Now be a clever wildcat and light this damned
lamp for me because you made me drop the matches."

That made her laugh again, the sound genuine this
time, and the lamp sprang to life in his hand.

He put it on the top of the highest of the three rocks,
as Chloe had told them, wrapped Sophie up next to him
under their cloaks, and settled in to wait.

It took nearly an hour by his reckoning, and his nerves
stretched and tightened with each passing second as he
stared at the dark water and dark sky, trying to determine whether the latter was lightening or if it was just his
imagination playing tricks of him. He strained for any

sound of a boat, and then, when it finally came, he wasn't sure it wasn't just another wave. He leaned forward, which made Sophie, dozing against his shoulder, come awake.

"What?" she said sleepily.

"Ssh," he said softly, trying to hear. Then it came again. So faintly he still wasn't sure. A creak of wood, a splash that was out of time with the rhythm of the waves. The sound of a small boat being rowed to shore.

"Merciful goddess, thank you," he muttered, and ran down to the water to meet the boat.

CHAPTER TWENTY-ONE

"Captain Jensen?" Sophie made her way to the front of the small boat, where the man who'd introduced himself as Samuel Jensen stood looking out over the ocean. He'd agreed to take them where they needed to go for seven of Eloisa's pearls, his eyes lighting appreciatively when he saw the gems.

"Yes, lass?" He turned from the rail. He hadn't asked for their names, which made her rather suspect that his name was no more Samuel Jensen than hers was, but she didn't care. They were safely off Anglion soil. She'd stood at the rear of the boat once they'd come aboard, transferring from the small dinghy that had come to fetch them off the beach, watching as the Anglion shoreline disappeared into the darkness. She thought she'd feel sad at the sight when it finally faded from view entirely, but there was, at the moment, only relief.

"How long does it take?" she asked, gesturing in the direction they were headed.

He shrugged. "Depends a little on the winds. Most of a day, though. Should be there around dusk. Which will make getting wherever you're going a bit easier for you. Harder to be sneaky in daylight." He grinned at her, revealing teeth that gleamed very white in the moonlight. He hardly looked like her idea of a smuggler. No, he

looked more like a court gentleman. He wore a long dark-
gray jacket—velvet, she'd discovered when he'd helped
her into the dinghy and her hands had clutched his
arms—and a black shirt and breeches that were equally
well made.

"Is it safe to sail in daylight?"

"Safe enough. Don't worry, lass. My cloaking ward is
as good as any your man there could cast."

Her brows flew up. "You're an Illusioner?"

"Once upon a time," he said. "Best not to ask questions about that. No more than I'll ask why an earth
witch is taking herself off to Illvya in the middle of the
night. This business works better with a bit of ignorance
to help it along."

She smiled at that. "I imagine it does." She took another lungful of salty air, trying to believe she was safe
now. But goddess knew what was waiting for them in
Illvya. So maybe best not to believe in safety just yet.

"You should go below and sleep like your husband,"
Captain Jensen said. "Rest."

"I tried. I couldn't sleep."

"Ah. Yes. It takes some people like that."

"What does?"

"Fleeing for your life. Danger." He swept a hand out
over the water. "Freedom."

"Is that why you do what you do? For freedom?"

He shrugged. "Something like that. Now, if you'll excuse me, I've a ship to sail. You're welcome to stay up
here, but move if any of the crew asks you to. You needn't
worry about any of them. No paid passenger ever came
to harm at my crew's hands. Just mind you don't tip yourself overboard."

❦

In the end she did sleep, curled beside Cameron on a
straw pallet. Slept until one of the crew shook them both

awake an hour or so before dusk. They climbed back on deck and ate bread and apples and freshly caught fried fish with Samuel Jensen, washing it down with wine. Then Sophie took up her spot on the prow again, watching the small rocky island Chloe had told them about grow closer and closer. Cameron eventually joined her, and they sat in silence together.

Eventually the ship came to a stop, sails were drawn in, and the anchor thrown overboard. Evidently they would travel the rest of the distance on the dinghy.

Jensen came up to stand beside them as his crew bustled around them.

"Are you sure about this?" he asked as the dinghy was lowered onto the water. "Last chance to change your minds. We can take you safely home again. You wouldn't be the first."

Sophie looked at Cameron. Saw nothing but determination in his eyes. Felt his hand, strong and warm, tighten slightly in reassurance. She shook her head. "We're sure," she said, and climbed to her feet.

The captain left them on the tiny spit of beach on the rocky outcrop, pointing out the faint path that would—unless both he and Chloe had played them false—lead them up to the portal and wishing them good luck before he and the men manning the dinghy rowed rapidly back to the slight shimmering blur that was the warded ship.

Sophie brushed as much sand as she could off the damp hem of her skirt, then found a rock to sit on whilst she put her boots—removed for the wade through the shallows to the beach—back on. Cameron did much the same, tugging on his boots and checking his pistol for damp.

Then he stood. "Well, then. I suppose we should find this portal before it gets full dark."

She nodded and followed him. It was only a short

path, though steep in several places. It led up off the beach and then curved, climbing again before stopping abruptly in front of a cleft in the rock. A cave. The dark entrance didn't look inviting. But there was no other place to go.

"I don't suppose you brought a candle?" Cameron asked.

"No, but I can do this." She bent and picked up a stone. Then conjured earth-light around it. It wasn't the brightest light ever but better than stepping into a cave with nothing.

Cameron laughed. "I didn't know you could do that."

"Earth-lights are just stones," she pointed out. "Shaped to be pretty, and yes, the temple says they're blessed, but that's just show. It's the stone part that's important. Stone comes from the earth."

With the faint golden glow lighting their way, they moved cautiously into the cave. The air inside was damp and the footing slick but sure enough. The small earth-light revealed the symbol Chloe had drawn for them set, portal fashion, into the wall.

They both stared at it for a moment.

"No point waiting, I guess," Sophie said after a moment.

"No. Nothing much to see on this rock. And we're not going to suddenly look more like Illvyans if we keep standing here," Cameron agreed. He reached for her hand. "Let's go."

❧

Luckily, the portal at Orlee di Mer was empty when they arrived. Sophie watched as Cameron sucked the finger he cut to trigger the portal back on the island. She took a couple of breaths. Portals, it seemed, no longer made her physically ill, but her stomach still felt a little uncertain after the transit.

"We should keep going," Cameron said quietly. "This next one will be the hardest. Madame de Montesse said this was south. Lumia is almost halfway up the country."

Lumia was one of the few places in Illvya that Anglion children were taught the location of. "I know. But if we both power the portal, we can do it."

Cameron studied her. "You haven't triggered a portal before, have you?"

"No. But it's not difficult, is it? I mean, the magic is built into the portal itself, so I don't have to make it work, just trigger it, yes?"

"No, not difficult. But it feels different when you trigger the portal than when you're just being transported."

"Different."

"Less . . . pleasant."

"Now you tell me." She pulled a face. "Well, it's not like we have any choice." Honoria's dagger was plenty sharp, so at least the cutting her finger part wouldn't be too painful. "I'm ready when you are."

❧

The transfer to Lumia was, as Cameron had suggested, unpleasant, and Sophie stepped out of the portal dizzy and shaking. She almost collided with two women standing in the portal space before Cameron caught her arm, murmuring apologies in Illvyan. Something about his wife and illness.

The older of the two women looked sympathetic and clucked her tongue at Sophie, who managed a polite bob of acknowledgment but kept her mouth firmly shut. Chloe had said that being Anglion wouldn't cause trouble, that Anglions weren't hated here as Illvyans were at home, but she didn't want to put that to the test just yet.

The younger woman—whose hair was streaked red and black and piled up on her head in loose curls topped by a small red hat that echoed the stripes in her red-and-black cloak—said something to Cameron, something about tea and . . . a store perhaps? For which he thanked them and gestured toward the portal, stepping aside to let them get to their destination.

Sure enough, it was the younger of the two who removed her glove, produced a pin to prick her finger, then offered an arm to the older woman before she touched the portal stone and the two of them blurred and vanished.

"Do you think she was a free witch?" Sophie asked, fascinated. Her stomach had settled, curiosity chasing the last of the queasiness away.

"Perhaps we can worry about that once we get where we're going," Cameron said.

"Is this Lumia?"

Cameron pointed to the symbol over the wheel of portal symbols. "If Madame de Montesse told us the truth, then yes." He pulled Chloe's paper from his pocket, studied it and then the portal wheel. "That's the one we want." He pointed at the maybe-bird, maybe-flame symbol in the middle of the lower-right quadrant of the portal.

"Do you think we should go to where she suggested?" Sophie asked.

"I think her logic was sound," Cameron said. "And we've trusted her this far."

"Are you going to tell me?"

"We'll be there soon enough."

❧

This portal hop was just that, a hop. So brief it didn't even make her feel ill.

"Don't talk unless you have to," Cameron said as they walked toward the door in the portal chamber. "And if you do, try to stick to please and thank you and *queria ma hom mari*."

"What does that mean?"

"Ask my husband," he said with a grin, and opened the door.

It was dark outside, but that didn't mean the streets were quiet.

Quite the opposite, in fact.

There were people everywhere. Brightly dressed, the clothes more fitted and embellished than in Anglion. A carriage clattered past them, and it took Sophie a moment to register that it wasn't pulled by horses. Or at least not flesh-and-blood horses. Instead, the creatures looked like horses made out of clockwork or metal.

She clamped her teeth down over the question that sprang to her lips and held on to Cameron's arm as he led her into the streets.

They walked for nearly a quarter hour, or so she thought. She was so overwhelmed by the odd sights and crowds and sounds and the strange smell of the place—an odd oily scent that hung in the air over all the other city smells—that she wasn't sure of the time at all.

Eventually, they turned in to a street that seemed to be taken up by one huge building, built from dark stone, set back from the street a little way and guarded by a tall fence of wrought metal. A brass plate on the fence read L'ACADÉME DI SAGES. She was beginning to feel exhausted. So exhausted that her Illvyan failed her completely.

"What is this place?" she asked Cameron softly.

"They call it Maison Corbie," he said. "We'd say the Rookery. Come on. We should get off the street."

The gate in the fence opened to his hand—wherever they were, the occupants didn't see a need for locks, apparently—and they walked up the straight path to the front door. A knocker sat squarely in the middle of the door, fashioned in the likeness of a crow's head. Cameron reached out and used it.

The sound seemed to echo through the night. Sophie moved a little closer to Cameron.

"We'll be all right," he said softly as the door swung open.

The creature that stood in the doorway was nearly as tall as Cameron. Man shaped but not human. It wore black pants and a sleeveless black tunic. But the clothing did nothing to change the fact that it wasn't human. The skin bared by the tunic was mottled gray and black. Threads of something she would have sworn was silver moved over the skin. Its face was the same colors, the eyes deep pools of black in the bald head.

It opened its mouth and hissed something at them, the sound like rusted metal trying to speak softly.

Sophie had no idea if the language it was attempting was Illvyan or not. She was so astonished by the sight of it that she couldn't think at all.

The creature hissed again and then turned and roared over its shoulder before stalking off.

"Wh-what was that?" Sophie asked.

"Unless I'm very much mistaken, that was a demon." Cameron looked at her, shaking his head. She didn't know if he was as surprised as she was or warning her not to talk.

"'Familiaris sanctii' is the proper term," came an accented voice from the doorway. Sophie and Cameron both focused back on the doorway. A young man with near-white wildly curly hair stood framed in the light spilling out of the doorway. He, too, wore black, a robe over shirt and trousers. There was a young—judging by the size—crow perched on each of his shoulders. One of them cawed loudly and then launched itself into the air, circling Sophie.

"Tok," said the man. "No. Silly fam." He clicked his fingers sharply, and the bird came back to rest on his shoulder. "Forgive him. He is young. Almost ready to find his master. It makes him extra curious." He peered down at them. "Belarus said you are Anglion. What do you want?"

Belarus, Sophie assumed, was the demon. And if he knew they were Anglion, that explained why the man was speaking that language to them rather than Illvyan. She opened her mouth, trying to remember what Chloe had told them to say.

"We're here to see the master," Cameron said, beating her to it.

"What business do you have with Venable Matin?" the doorkeeper asked.

"Personal business," Cameron said shortly. "So unless you can tell me that he shares such things with you, I will keep it for him."

The man looked faintly chagrined and nodded vigorously, which made the crows caw again. Sophie rather thought the one called Tok was watching her. She'd never been so close to a crow before. Some of the ladies in the court kept tiny bright songbirds but nothing as large as a crow. Its gaze was unsettlingly intelligent.

"I will go and convey that you are here. You may come in and wait, but please do not leave the hallway. Our house is not ... safe ... for strangers."

Sophie had no desire to go into the house at all, let alone explore its depths, so she didn't think following his instructions would be a problem. She walked up the steps, Cameron right behind her, and stepped over the threshold.

The room they entered—more like a foyer really—wasn't overly large. There were doors in the wall to the right and left, whereas the rear wall was taken up by a large white marble staircase.

"Wait," the white-haired young man repeated. He turned and walked quickly up the stairs, then turned to take the next flight, the sound of his steps echoing over their heads.

"Can I ask again exactly where we are?" Sophie asked Cameron.

"The Rookery," he repeated. "It's where they train their wizards."

"Oh." There didn't seem to be much more to say. She'd grown up being taught that Illvyan wizards were monsters who would slay Anglions on sight with their demon sanctii. So far that hadn't happened. Apparently, Chloe had told them the truth. At least, so far it seemed to be true. So Sophie would try to stay calm.

Soon enough steps sounded on the stairs above them—fortunately, no more demons had appeared—and the young man appeared, a crow flying before him. This time it landed on Sophie's shoulder, making her jump. It was surprisingly heavy and the claws surprisingly sharp, digging into her shoulder through her cloak. She stifled the urge to shoo it away. For all she knew, it could be a demon, too.

"Tok," the young man said, sounding exasperated. The crow cawed at him. The man shook his head and turned his gaze to Sophie. "The master will see you." He looked somewhat surprised by his own announcement. "Follow me, if you please." He looked at the crow, opened his mouth, and then shrugged. "It may be easier to leave him there, madame. He's stubborn, that one."

Sophie nodded and reached for Cameron's hand. They ascended the stairs behind their odd escort, climbing four flights before being led down a short hallway to a double set of doors. The crow didn't leave her shoulder, just squawked in her ear and rustled its feathers when she stopped walking. The young man knocked and then opened the doors, ushering them in with a gesture. He clucked to the crow as Sophie passed him. It looked at the door and then at him, then left her shoulder to flutter to his.

Did that mean that whoever was inside was someone

even crows were afraid of? She tightened her grip around Cameron's hand as they walked through the doors.

A gray-haired man stood by a fireplace on the far side of the room, a book in one hand. He turned as they entered and put the book down on the mantel. He crossed the room, the black robes around his shoulders billowing behind him, glinting odd colors to Sophie's eyes. His close-trimmed beard was as gray as his hair.

As he got near to them, he stopped. Tilted his head. Studied them a moment with pale blue eyes. "Well," he said in fairly unaccented Anglion. "It's not every day a royal witch and a battle mage come to call. To whom do I owe the pleasure?"

"To your daughter," Sophie managed.

His brows rose, expression darkening, body stiffening. "Oh? What proof do you offer of that?"

Sophie looked at Cameron, who shrugged and reeled off the Illvyan phrase Chloe had taught him, speaking too fast for Sophie to follow.

The man relaxed slightly. "I see. And who do I have the pleasure of addressing?"

"My name is Sophia Mackenzie," Sophie said. "This is my husband, Cameron. We seek asylum, sir."

"Ah. Lord and Lady Scardale. How interesting." He smiled at her. "But I forget my manners, Madame Mackenzie." He paused, then swept her a grand bow. "My name is Henri Matin. I am master here at the Academe. Welcome to Illvya."

The wards sparked in front of me, faint violet against
the dark wooden door with its heavy brass locks,
proclaiming the house's protection. They wouldn't stop
me. No one has yet made the lock or ward to keep me
out. Magic cannot detect me, and brick and stone and
metal are no barrier.

It's why I'm good at what I do.

A grandfather clock in the hall chimed two as I stepped
into the shadow, entering the place only my kind can walk
and passing through the door as though it wasn't there.
Outside came the echoing toll of the cathedral bell, much
louder here in Greenglass than in the Night World bor-
oughs I usually frequent.

I'd been told that the one I was to visit lived alone.
But I prefer not to believe everything I'm told. After all,
I grew up among the Blood and the powers of the Night
World, where taking things on faith is a quick way to die.

Besides, bystanders only make things complicated.

But tonight, I sensed I *was* alone as I moved carefully
through the darkened rooms. The house had an elegant

simplicity. The floors were polished wood, softened by fine wool rugs, and paintings hung on the unpapered walls. Plants flourished on any spare flat surface, tingeing the air with the scent of growth and life. I hoped someone would save them after my task here was completed. The Fae might deny me the Veiled World, but the part of me that comes from them shares their affinity for green growing things.

Apart from the damp greenness of the plants, there was only one other dominant scent in the air. Human. Male. Warm and spicy.

Alive. Live around the Blood for long enough and you become very aware of the differences between living and dead. No other fresh smell mingled with his. No cats or dogs. Just fading hints of an older female gone for several hours. Likely a cook or housekeeper who didn't live in.

I paused at the top of the staircase, counting doors carefully. Third on the left. A few more strides. I cocked my head, listening.

There.

Ever so faint, the thump of a human heartbeat. Slow. Even.

Asleep.

Good. Asleep is easier.

I drifted through the bedroom door and paused again. The room was large, walled on one side with floor-to-ceiling windows unblocked by any blind. Expensive, that much glass. Moonlight streamed through the panes, making it easy to see the man lying in the big bed.

I didn't know what he'd done. I never ask. The blade doesn't question the direction of the cut. Particularly when the blade belongs to Lucius. Lucius doesn't like questions.

I let go of the shadow somewhat. I was not yet truly solid, but enough that, if he were to wake, he would see my shape by the bed like the reflection of a dream. Or a nightmare.

The moonlight washed over his face, silvering skin and fading hair to shades of gray, making it hard to tell what he might look like in daylight. Tall, yes. Well formed if the arm and chest bared by the sheet he'd pushed away in sleep matched the rest of him.

Not that it mattered. He'd be beyond caring about his looks in a few minutes. Beyond caring about anything.

The moon made things easier even though, in the shadow, I see well in very little light. Under the silvered glow I saw the details of the room as clearly as if the gas lamps on the walls were alight.

The windows posed little risk. The town house stood separated from its neighbors by narrow strips of garden on each side and a much larger garden at the rear. There was a small chance someone in a neighboring house might see something, but I'd be long gone before they could raise an alarm.

His breath continued to flow, soft and steady, and I moved around the bed, seeking a better angle for the strike as I let myself grow more solid still, so I could grasp the dagger at my hip.

Legend says we kill by reaching into a man's chest and tearing out his heart. It's true. We can. I've even done it. Once.

At Lucius' demand and fearing death if I disobeyed.

It wasn't an act I ever cared to repeat. Sometimes, on the edge of sleep, I still shake thinking about the sensation of living flesh torn from its roots beneath my fingers.

So I use a dagger. Just as effective. Dead is dead, after all.

I counted his heartbeats as I silently slid my blade free. He was pretty, this one. A face of interesting angles that looked strong even in sleep. Strong and somehow happy. Generous lips curved up slightly as if he were enjoying a perfect dream.

Not a bad way to die, all things considered.

I unshadowed completely and lifted the dagger, fingers steady on the hilt as he took one last breath.

But even as the blade descended, the room blazed to light around me and a hand snaked out like a lightning bolt and clamped around my wrist.

"Not so fast," the man said in a calm tone.

I tried to shadow and my heart leaped to my throat as nothing happened.

"Just to clarify," he said. "Those lamps. Not gas. Sunlight."

"Sunmage," I hissed, rearing back as my pulse went into overdrive. How had Lucius left out *that* little detail? Or maybe he hadn't. Maybe Ricco had left it out on purpose when he'd passed on my assignment. He hated me. I wouldn't put it past him to try to engineer my downfall.

Damn him to the seven bloody, night-scalded depths of hell.

The man smiled at me, though there was no amusement in the expression. "Precisely."

I twisted, desperate to get free. His hand tightened, and pain shot through my wrist and up my arm.

"Drop the dagger."

I set my teeth and tightened my grip. Never give up your weapon.

"I said, *drop it.*" The command snapped as he surged out of the bed, pushing me backward and my arm above my head at a nasty angle.

The pain intensified, like heated wires slicing into my nerves. "Sunmages are supposed to be healers," I managed to gasp as I struggled and the sunlight—hells-damned *sunlight*—filled the room, caging me as effectively as iron bars might hold a human.

I swung at him with my free arm, but he blocked the blow, taking its force on his forearm without a wince. He fought far too well for a healer. Who was this man?

"Ever consider that being a healer means being exposed to hundreds of ways to hurt people? Don't make me hurt you. Put the knife down."

I swore and flung myself forward, swinging my free hand at his face again. But he moved too, fast and sure, and somehow—damn, he was good—I missed, my hand smacking into the wall. I twisted desperately as the impact sent a shock wave up my arm, and the light dazzled me as I looked directly into one of the lamps.

A split second is all it takes to make a fatal mistake.

Before I could blink, he had pulled me forward and round and I sailed through the air to land facedown on the feather mattress, wind half knocked out of me. My free hand was bent up behind my back, and my other— still holding my dagger—was pinned by his to the pillow.

My heart raced in anger and humiliation and fear as I tried to breathe.

Sunmage.

I was an idiot. *Stupid. Stupid. Stupid.*

Stupid and careless.

His knee pushed me deeper into the mattress, making it harder still to breathe.

"Normally I don't get this forward when I haven't been introduced," he said, voice warm and low, close to my ear. He still sounded far too calm. A sunmage healer shouldn't have been so sanguine about finding an assassin in his house. Though perhaps he wasn't quite as calm as he seemed. His heart pounded. "But then again, normally, women I don't know don't try to stab me in my bed."

I snarled and he increased the pressure. There wasn't much I could do. I'm faster and stronger than a human woman, but there's a limit to what a female of five foot six can do against a man nearly a foot taller and quite a bit heavier. Particularly with my powers cut off by the light of the sun.

Damned hells-cursed sunlight.

"I'll take that." His knee shifted upward to pin both

my arm and my back, and his free hand wrenched the dagger from my grasp.

Then, to my surprise, his weight vanished. It took a few seconds for me to register my freedom. By the time I rolled to face him, he stood at the end of the bed and my dagger quivered in the wall far across the room. To make matters worse, the sunlight now flickered off the ornately engraved barrel of the pistol in his right hand.

It was aimed squarely at the center of my forehead. His hand was perfectly steady, as though holding someone at gunpoint was nothing greatly out of the ordinary for him. For a man wearing nothing but linen drawers, he looked convincingly threatening.

I froze. Would he shoot? If our places were reversed, he'd already be dead.

"Wise decision," he said, eyes still cold. "Now. Why don't you tell me what this is about?"

"Do you think that's likely?"

One corner of his mouth lifted and a dimple cracked to life in his cheek. My assessment had been right. He was pretty. Pretty and dangerous, it seemed. The arm that held the gun was, like the rest of him, sleek with muscle. The sort that took concerted effort to obtain. Maybe he was one of the rare sunmages who became warriors? But the house seemed far too luxurious for a Templar or a mercenary, and his hands and body were bare of Templar sigils.

Besides, I doubted Lucius would set me on a Templar. That would be madness.

So, who the hell was this man?

When I stayed silent, the pistol waved back and forth in a warning gesture. "I have this," he said. "Plus, I am, as you mentioned, a sunmage." As if to emphasize his point, the lamps flared a little brighter. "Start talking."

I considered him carefully. The sunlight revealed his skin as golden, his hair a gilded shade of light brown, and his eyes a bright, bright blue. A true creature of the day.

No wonder Lucius wanted him dead. I currently felt a considerable desire for that outcome myself. I scanned the rest of the room, seeking a means to escape.

A many-drawered wooden chest, a table covered with papers with a leather-upholstered chair tucked neatly against it, and a large wardrobe all made simply in the same dark reddish wood offered no inspiration. Some sort of ferny plant in a stand stood in one corner, and paintings—landscapes and studies of more plants—hung over the bed and the table. Nothing smaller than the furniture, nothing I could use as a weapon, lay in view. Nor was there anything to provide a clue as to who he might be.

"I can hear you plotting all the way over here," he said with another little motion of the gun. "Not a good idea. In fact . . ." The next jerk of the pistol was a little more emphatic, motioning me toward the chair as he hooked it out from the table with his foot. "Take a seat. Don't bother trying anything stupid like attempting the window. The glass is warded. You'll just hurt yourself."

Trapped in solid form, I couldn't argue with that. The lamps shone with a bright, unwavering light and his face showed no sign of strain. Even his heartbeat had slowed to a more steady rhythm now that we were no longer fighting. A sunmage calling sunlight at night. Strong. Dangerously strong.

Not to mention armed when I wasn't.

I climbed off the bed and stalked over to the chair.

He tied my arms and legs to their counterparts on the chair with neck cloths. Tight enough to be secure but carefully placed so as not to hurt. He had to have been a healer. A mercenary wouldn't have cared if he hurt me. A mercenary probably would've killed me outright.

When he was done he picked up a pair of buckskin trousers and a rumpled linen shirt from the floor and dressed quickly. Then he took a seat on the end of the bed, picked up the gun once again, and aimed directly at me.

Blue eyes stared at me for a long minute, something unreadable swimming in their depths. Then he nodded.

"Shall we try this again? Why are you here?"

There wasn't any point lying about it. "I was sent to kill you."

"I understand that much. The reason is what escapes me."

I lifted a shoulder. Let him make what he would of the gesture. I had no idea why Lucius had sent me after a sunmage.

"You didn't ask?"

"Why would I?" I said, surprised by the question.

He frowned. "You just kill whoever you're told to? It doesn't matter why?"

"I do as I'm ordered." Disobedience would only bring pain. Or worse.

His head tilted, suddenly intent. His gaze was uncomfortable, and it was hard to shake the feeling he saw more than I wanted. "You should seek another line of work."

As if I had a choice. I looked away from him, suddenly angry. Who was he to judge me?

"Back to silence, is it? Very well, let's try another tack. This isn't, by chance, about that Rousselline pup I stitched up a few weeks ago?"

Pierre Rousselline was alpha of one of the Beast Kind packs. He and Lucius didn't always exist in harmony. But I doubted Lucius would kill over the healing of a young Beast. A sunmage, one this strong—if his claim of being able to maintain the light until dawn were true——was an inherently risky target, even for a Blood lord. Even for *the* Blood Lord.

So, what had this man—who was, indeed, a healer if he spoke the truth—done?

His brows lifted when I didn't respond. "You really don't know, do you? Well. Damn."

The "damn" came out as a half laugh. There was nothing amusing in the situation that I could see. Either he was going to kill me or turn me over to the human authorities or I was going to have to tell Lucius I had failed. Whichever option came to pass, nothing good awaited me. I stayed silent.

"Some other topic of conversation, then?" He regarded me with cool consideration. "I presume, given that my sunlight seems to be holding you, that I'm right in assuming that you are Lucius' shadow?"

I nodded. There was little point denying it with his light holding me prisoner. There were no others of my kind in the City. Only a wraith is caged by the light of the sun.

A smile spread over his face, revealing he had two dimples, not one. Not just pretty, I decided. He was . . . Alluring wasn't the right word. The Blood and the Fae are alluring—an attraction born of icy beauty and danger. I am immune to that particular charm. No, he was . . . inviting somehow. A fire on a winter's night, promising warmth and life.

His eyes held genuine curiosity. "You're really a wraith?"

About the Author

M. J. Scott is an unrepentant bookworm. Luckily she grew up in a family that fed her a properly varied diet of books and these days is surrounded by people who are understanding of her story addiction. When not wrestling one of her own stories to the ground, she can generally be found reading someone else's. Her other distractions include yarn, cat butlering, dark chocolate, and fabric. She lives in Melbourne, Australia.